*Every Breath
You Take*

Also by Judith McNaught

SOMEONE TO WATCH OVER ME
NIGHT WHISPERS
PERFECT
PARADISE
ALMOST HEAVEN
DOUBLE STANDARDS
A KINGDOM OF DREAMS
ONCE AND ALWAYS
REMEMBER WHEN
SOMETHING WONDERFUL
TENDER TRIUMPH
UNTIL YOU
WHITNEY, MY LOVE

Books published by The Random House Publishing Group are available at quantity discounts on bulk purchases for premium, educational, fund-raising, and special sales use. For details, please call 1-800-733-3000.

Every Breath You Take

A NOVEL

Judith McNaught

BALLANTINE BOOKS • NEW YORK

Sale of this book without a front cover may be unauthorized. If this book is coverless, it may have been reported to the publisher as "unsold or destroyed" and neither the author nor the publisher may have received payment for it.

Every Breath You Take is a work of fiction. Names, characters, places, and incidents are the products of the author's imagination or are used fictitiously. Any resemblance to actual events, locales, or persons, living or dead, is entirely coincidental.

2006 Ballantine Books Mass Market Edition

Copyright © 2005, 2006 by Eagle Syndication, Inc.
Excerpt from *Can't Take My Eyes Off of You* copyright © 2006 by Eagle Syndication, Inc.

All rights reserved.

Published in the United States by Ballantine Books, an imprint of The Random House Publishing Group, a division of Random House, Inc., New York.

BALLANTINE and colophon are registered trademarks of Random House, Inc.

Originally published in hardcover in slightly different form in the United States by Ballantine Books, an imprint of The Random House Publishing Group, a division of Random House, Inc., in 2005.

This book contains an excerpt from the forthcoming hardcover edition of *Can't Take My Eyes Off of You* by Judith McNaught. This excerpt has been set for this edition only and may not reflect the final content of the forthcoming edition.

ISBN 0-345-47991-2

Cover design: Gene Mydlowski
Cover Illustration: Judy York, from photographs © First Light/Corbis (lake with dock) and Shirley Green (couple)

Printed in the United States of America

www.ballantinebooks.com

OPM 9 8 7 6 5 4 3 2 1

To Holly and Clay,
with all my love

Acknowledgments

To Michael Bublé, my favorite singer, with gratitude and affection; Dana and Richard LeConey, two beautiful people who make everyone else beautiful; Dick Smith, pilot and friend; James and Nicole Trussell III, whose wedding I missed in order to get this book out; Tamara Anderson, my legal consultant, fellow writer, and wonderful friend; Joe Grant, my other legal consultant and dear friend; the Genest family—Jordan, Michael, Genevieve, Alexandra, and Anastasia—who sacrificed Thanksgiving together and a lot more for the sake of this book; Dick Huber, Bob Smith, and Ed Willis, three trustworthy real-life heroes who came to my rescue when I needed them most . . . and, most especially, the production department at Ballantine, which will never fully recover from the effort required to get this book out on schedule.

Most of all, my heartfelt gratitude to three Ballantine employees, who accomplished the impossible by getting this book done on time: Charlotte Herscher, Daniel Mallory, and my editor of twenty years, Linda Marrow. And a very special thank-you to Linda's new twins, Callie Virginia and Matthew Clifton, whose feeding schedule was frequently disrupted because of me, and an equally huge thank-you to new daddy Jim Impoco, who is used to having his schedule disrupted by my deadlines.

Chapter One

*H*IGH ATOP A SNOW-COVERED HILL, THE WYATT MANSION perched like a regal crown, its Gothic stone spires pointing skyward, its stained-glass windows glowing like jewels.

A mile away, limousines and luxury cars paraded in a slow stream toward a uniformed security guard posted at the gated entrance to the estate. As each vehicle reached him, the security guard checked the occupants' names off the guest list; then he issued a politely worded edict to the driver: "I'm sorry, because of the snowfall, Mr. Wyatt does not want any vehicles parked inside the gates this evening."

If a chauffeur was at the wheel, the guard stepped aside, allowing the chauffeur to turn into the drive, proceed through the gates, and deliver his passengers to the house before returning to the main road to park and wait.

If the vehicle's owner was at the wheel, the guard motioned him toward a line of shiny black Range Rovers parked up the hill at a cross street, wisps of exhaust curling from their tailpipes. "Please pull forward and leave your car with an attendant," the guard instructed. "You'll be shuttled up to the house."

However, as each new arrival soon discovered, that process was neither as simple nor as convenient as it sounded. Although there were plenty of helpful attendants and available Range Rovers waiting within sight, large snowbanks and parked cars had encroached on the winding residential lane so that it was almost impassably narrow in places, and the steady procession of slow-moving vehicles had churned four inches of unplowed snow from earlier that day into thick slush.

The whole ordeal was unnerving and annoying to everyone. . . . Everyone except Detectives Childress and MacNeil, who were in an unmarked Chevrolet that was backed into a driveway one hundred and fifty yards up-hill from the entrance to the Wyatt estate. The two detectives were part of a handpicked team, formed earlier that day, assigned to keep Mitchell Wyatt under twenty-four-hour surveillance.

At eight PM, they had tailed him here, to Cecil Wyatt's estate, where he swerved around the security guard who was trying to wave him down, then turned into the private drive and disappeared from sight. Once Wyatt vanished, there was nothing for Childress and MacNeil to do but park and make a record of whom he was associating with. To facilitate that, Childress was observing the scene through a pair of night-vision binoculars, reporting license-plate numbers and miscellaneous information to MacNeil, who wrote it down in a notebook.

"We have a new contender approaching the starting line," Childress murmured as another pair of headlights reached the security guard at the gate. He read the vehicle's license plate aloud for MacNeil; then he described the vehicle and driver. "White Mercedes AMG, this year's model, or possibly last year's. Driver is a Caucasian male in his early sixties, passenger is a Caucasian female, early thirties, and she's snuggled up against her smiling sugar daddy."

When MacNeil didn't reply, Childress glanced at him and realized MacNeil's attention was focused on a pair of headlights slowly descending the hill from the right. "Must be someone who lives up here," Childress remarked. "And he's not only rich, he's curious," he added as the black Lincoln Town Car came to a full stop and cut off its headlights directly in front of the driveway where they were parked.

The back door opened, and a man in his late thirties wearing a dark overcoat got out. Childress rolled down his window, intending to make an excuse for their presence, but as the man paused and put his cell phone to his ear, Childress recognized him. "That's Gray Elliott. What's he doing out here?"

"He lives nearby. Maybe he's attending the party."

"Or maybe he wants to pitch in and do some surveillance with us," Childress joked, but there was admiration in his voice. After only one year in office as Cook County's state's attorney, Gray Elliott was a hero to the cops—a brilliant attorney who wasn't afraid to take on tough, risky cases. The fact that he was also a wealthy socialite who'd dedicated himself to public service rather than the pursuit of greater wealth added another facet to his heroic image.

MacNeil liked him for all of those reasons but MacNeil had always liked Gray—even when he had been a carefree, reckless teenager whom MacNeil had busted for several minor youthful offenses.

Elliott finished his phone call, walked over to the car, leaned down, and looked inside. "You must be Childress," he said by way of greeting; then he shifted his attention to MacNeil. "I'd like a word with you, Mac."

MacNeil got out and joined him at the back of the car. The wind had died down, and the engine was running, pumping warm exhaust at their feet. "I asked that you be assigned to this case," Gray told him, "because you headed the investigation into William Wyatt's disappearance, and you're familiar with all the players."

"Not all of them," Mac interrupted, unable to keep his curiosity in check. "I never heard of Mitchell Wyatt until today. Who the hell is he, and why are we watching him?"

"He's William Wyatt's half brother, and I believe he's responsible for William's disappearance."

"His half brother?" MacNeil repeated, his forehead furrowing into a doubtful frown. "When William disappeared, I interviewed all his family members and all his friends. No one ever mentioned a half brother. In fact, when I interviewed Cecil Wyatt, the old man repeatedly told me how important it was that we find his *only grandson,* and bring William home to his wife and kid."

"You were deliberately misled by an arrogant, devious old man who wasn't ready to admit he had a grandson he'd never acknowledged. I've known the Wyatts my whole life, and I never knew William had a half brother. For that matter, neither did William until this past June.

"According to the story I was just told, William's father, Edward, had an affair with his secretary when William was a couple years old and his mother was dying of cancer. The secretary got pregnant, and William's mother died a few months later, but when the secretary pressed Edward to marry her as he'd promised, he stalled, then denied the baby was his. She retaliated by threatening to take the whole sordid tale to the *Tribune.*"

Elliott's cell phone rang, and he paused to glance at the caller's name; then he ignored the call and continued. "At the time, Cecil had big political plans for Edward, which a scandal would have destroyed, but allowing 'a common little tart' to marry into the family was unthinkable. Cecil tried to buy her off, but she wouldn't budge about her child's right to be legitimate, to be named Wyatt, and to be raised as a Wyatt. She hired a lawyer, and eventually a deal was struck: Edward would marry her shortly before the baby was due, and then divorce her immediately after the birth. She relinquished all rights to the baby, granting full custody to Cecil. Cecil, in turn, was obliged to see that the baby was raised 'with all the benefits associated with Wyatt money and social connections,' including the finest education, travel abroad, and so forth. She received a substantial sum of money on the condition that she never divulge a word about anything that had happened and never again have contact with any of the parties involved, including the baby."

MacNeil turned the collar up on his jacket. The bottom half of his body was reasonably warm, but his ears were freezing. "Obviously, Cecil later changed his mind about the grandson," he said, rubbing his hands together before he stuck them in his pockets.

"No, he adhered to the letter of the agreement but not the spirit. He'd agreed that Mitchell would grow up 'with all the benefits associated with Wyatt money and social connections,' but Cecil never specifically agreed that the 'social connections' would be with the Wyatts themselves. A week after Mitchell was born, Cecil sent him to a family in Italy, along with a falsified birth certificate. When Mitchell was four or five, Cecil yanked him out of that family's home and had him sent to an exclusive boarding school in France. Later, Mitchell was sent to prep school in Switzerland, and then on to Oxford."

"Did the kid even know who he was, or who was paying for his fancy education?" MacNeil asked.

"The family he lived with in Italy told him what they'd been told, which was that he'd been abandoned as a newborn on a California doorstep and that his name was merely a combination of two names picked out of a phone book by a group of generous American benefactors who regularly put up the money to support and educate boys just like him. These supposed benefactors wished for nothing in return except the right to remain anonymous."

"Jeez." MacNeil shook his head.

"If that's pity I hear, save it for someone who deserves

it," Elliott said sarcastically. "From all accounts, young Mitchell enjoyed his life and made the most of his opportunities. He was a natural athlete who excelled at sports, he went to the finest schools, and he mixed easily with kids from Europe's leading families. After he graduated from college, he put his education, his good looks, and his acquired social contacts to excellent use, managing to make himself a load of money. He's thirty-four now, and he runs companies based mostly in Europe. He has apartments in Rome, London, Paris, and New York." Elliott paused to look at his watch, frowning as he tried to see its face in the dark. "Can you see the time on your watch?"

MacNeil pulled up his sleeve and glanced at the large glowing green numerals on his Timex. "Eight forty-five."

"I have to go. I need to put in an appearance at Cecil's party."

"How did Wyatt end up right here, right now, after all this time?" MacNeil said quickly, trying to make optimal use of the remaining time.

"Seven months ago, in early June, William came across the documents in an old safe, and he was outraged at the treatment his poor half brother had received from his father and grandfather. He hired detectives, and when they located Mitchell Wyatt in London, William took his wife and his son and flew to London to introduce them in person and explain what had happened."

"That was a nice thing to do."

Elliott tipped his head back and looked at the sky. "Yes, it was," he said in the carefully controlled voice of a man trying not to betray any emotion. "William was a thoroughly nice guy—the only male in his family for generations who wasn't an egotistical sociopath." Abruptly, he looked back at MacNeil and finished. "When William came back from London filled with glowing accounts of

Mitchell's amazing successes, Edward didn't want anything to do with his long-lost son, but old Cecil was evidently impressed enough to ask for a meeting. The meeting took place in August, when Mitchell was supposedly here on business. And then, after William disappeared in November, Cecil asked Mitchell to come back to Chicago so they could get to know each other better. Ironically, the old man is now quite taken with his prodigal grandson—so much so that he's asked him to be present tonight, for his eightieth birthday party. I have to get going," he said, already starting toward his car.

MacNeil walked beside him. "You haven't told me anything that explains why we're keeping Mitchell Wyatt under surveillance."

Elliott stopped abruptly, his expression tight, his voice cold and clipped. "Oh, did I leave that out?" he asked. "Here are just two of the reasons: In September, one month after that first reunion between Cecil and Mitchell, Edward—William and Mitchell's father—'fell' off his balcony and plunged thirty stories to his death. In November, William vanished. Coincidentally, according to U.S. passport and immigration records, Mitchell Wyatt entered the U.S. shortly before each event occurred and departed almost immediately afterward."

When MacNeil's eyes narrowed, Elliott said, "Now you're getting part of the picture. Here's more of it: Mitchell has been in Chicago for two weeks. He's staying at William's house, consoling William's beautiful wife, and befriending William's fourteen-year-old son." Unable to keep the loathing from his voice, Elliott said, "Mitchell Wyatt is systematically exterminating members of his own family and restructuring the family to suit himself."

"You think he's after the family fortune," MacNeil concluded.

"I think the Wyatt genes have produced another sociopath. The ultimate sociopath—a cold-blooded murderer."

When he walked away, MacNeil got back into the
Chevy with Childress, and they watched Elliott's town
car stop at the intersection and wait while a group of
party guests was transferred into Range Rovers. A gray-
haired woman slipped in the slush, and her husband
grabbed for her. A middle-aged couple shivered in the
cold while a nervous elderly couple struggled to step up
onto the Range Rover's elevated running boards with the
help of parking attendants.

"You know," Childress said, when the vehicles were finally on their way, "when we drove past the security
gates tonight, I got a look at the driveway leading to the
house, and I swear it looked perfectly clear—at least as
far as I could see."

"It was," MacNeil agreed.

"Then why in the hell is the security guard making
everyone leave their vehicles out here on the main road?"

MacNeil shrugged. "Who knows?"

Chapter Two

THE STREAM OF ARRIVING GUESTS HAD SLOWED TO A trickle when a new pair of headlights, moving slowly, approached the gates. Childress put down the cup of coffee he'd poured from his thermos and picked up the binoculars. MacNeil reached for the notebook and began jotting down the information Childress gave him.

"The vehicle's a vintage Rolls—probably 1950s—maroon in color, pristine condition," Childress said. "Chauffeur at the wheel. Female passenger in the back-seat. God, she's a *beauty*!"

"The Rolls or the passenger?" MacNeil asked.

Childress snorted with laughter. "The Rolls. The passenger is about ninety years old, and her face is wrinkling up like a prune over whatever the security guard is telling her chauffeur—who also happens to be about ninety. I'm guessing the old lady's unhappy about having her Rolls parked on the street."

Childress was wrong about that. Cecil Wyatt's sister, Olivia Hebert, was not unhappy over her brother's no-parking-on-the-drive edict: she was furious.

"That arrogant tyrant!" she exclaimed to her chauffeur as he drove through the gates behind three Range Rovers. "Look at this driveway, Granger. Do you see any snow on it?"

"No, madam."

"Cecil is herding his guests around like sheep, just to prove he can!"

"So it would appear, madam," her chauffeur of forty years replied, his voice quavering with age and indignation.

Satisfied that Granger understood and agreed, Olivia Hebert leaned back against the soft leather seat of her car, filled with impotent ire. Like everyone else who knew her brother, Olivia was all too familiar with Cecil's habit of developing sudden, rigid "eccentricities"—the ones he invented from time to time for no other purpose except to inflict his will upon his social equals, thus proving to himself, yet again, that he was still superior to one and all.

"I can't believe that people still put up with his arrogant behavior after eighty years," she said bitterly. "In fact, I'm amazed these people didn't turn around and go home the instant they realized this drive is perfectly clear!" Olivia added, but that part wasn't true. She understood exactly why Cecil's guests were willing to put up with tonight's pointless inconvenience. For one thing, Cecil was a generous benefactor who'd donated tens of millions of dollars to their favorite charities. For another, they'd come to join Cecil on his eightieth birthday not to help him celebrate but to help him get through an occasion that was marred by the disappearance of his beloved thirty-six-year-old grandson, William.

"On top of everything else, he's taking advantage of people's sympathy tonight, that's what he's doing," Olivia added as they pulled up in front of the house and she watched people climbing down from the Range Rovers.

Instead of replying, Granger conserved his strength for the arduous journey around the front of the Rolls to her back door. His shoulders were stooped with age, his back and knees were severely bent from arthritis, his hair was a thinning fringe of silver beneath his black chauffeur's cap, and his thin frame was swallowed up by a black overcoat that had lately gotten too large for him. He opened her door and held out his gnarled hand to help her out. Olivia put her gloved hand in his. "We shall have to see about getting your coat altered," she said as she eased herself out of her car and reached for her cane. "It's a little large for you."

"I'm sorry, madam."

Gripping her cane with her right hand and clutching his coat sleeve with her left, Olivia let him guide her slowly toward the house, where Cecil's butler was already waiting in the lighted doorway. "Do try to eat more, Granger. I used to buy a new car for what clothing costs these days."

"Yes, madam." As he helped her up the three flagstone steps that led to the front door, he said, "How will you let me know when you wish me to come for you?"

Olivia halted, stiffened, and glowered ferociously at him. "Do not even consider leaving this driveway!" she warned. "We, at least, shall not accede to the whims of a petty tyrant. Park over there under the porte cochere."

Cecil's butler heard that and coolly countermanded the order as he reached out to help her remove her coat. "Your car is to wait outside the gates, not under the porte cochere," he informed her imperiously as Granger turned and began making his slow way back to the flagstone steps. "Please instruct your driver—"

"I'll do nothing of the sort!" she interrupted scathingly, thrusting her cane at him and struggling out of her coat herself. "Granger," she called after him.

Granger turned on the second step and looked at her, his silver brows raised inquiringly.

"While you are parked under the porte cochere, if anyone approaches you, you are to run over them with my car!" Satisfied, she gave the butler a frosty stare. "There's a black foreign sports car parked under the porte cochere," she said. "To whom does it belong?"

"Mr. Mitchell Wyatt," the butler replied.

"I knew it would be his!" Olivia exclaimed gleefully, shoving her coat at the butler and snatching her cane out of his grasp. "He is not subject to the whims of a petty tyrant, either," she proudly informed him. Leaning heavily on her cane, she began making her awkward way across the foyer's uneven slate floor, toward the sound of voices in the living room. Behind her, the butler said, "Mr. Cecil said you are to await him in his study."

Despite her brief show of bravado, Olivia was uneasy about confronting her formidable brother in private. He had an uncanny way of anticipating defiance, even before an outward act took place. Rather than go directly to his study, she angled toward the living room on the left. Stopping beneath the arched entry, she craned her head, hoping to catch sight of an ally—an exceptionally tall, dark-haired man who'd also defied Cecil's order and parked his own car under the porte cochere.

The living room was crowded with guests, but there was no sign of Mitchell, nor in the dining room, where more guests were partaking of a lavish buffet. She was retracing her steps back through the living room when Cecil glanced up from the people talking to him and saw her. He stared at her with the cool, speculating expression of a long-standing opponent; then with a curt jerk of his head in the direction of his study, he ordered her to get herself there at once. Olivia put her chin up, but she complied.

Cecil's study was on the opposite side of the slate hallway from the living room, beyond the main staircase and toward the rear of the house. Normally, the heavy paneled study doors were closed during large parties to discourage guests from congregating in Cecil's private domain, but tonight a thin strip of mellow light glowed from between them. With one hand on the door handle, Olivia paused to give her legs and lungs a brief rest; then she straightened her back, lifted her head—and froze in surprise at the scene revealed to her in that narrow shaft of light.

Mitchell had his arms around William's wife, and Caroline's cheek was pressed against his chest, a handkerchief clutched in her hand. "I don't know how much longer I can go on like this," she said brokenly, lifting her face to his.

"We have no choice," he said flatly, but not unkindly.

Olivia's momentary shock gave way to sympathetic understanding. Poor Caroline looked as thin and pale as a waif. Naturally, she'd seek comfort and support from a male family member, but her profligate father was honeymooning somewhere in Europe with his fifth wife, and Cecil would offer her only more of his terse lectures on the need to show strength in times of travail. Caroline's fourteen-year-old son needed all the comfort his mother could give him, and Caroline put on a brave face for him, but she had no one to lean on herself—no one except Mitchell.

Olivia felt a rush of gratitude that Mitchell had come into the Wyatt family fold at exactly the right time to help Caroline and Cecil through their grief. Unfortunately, Olivia had the feeling Mitchell wouldn't "help" Cecil out of a burning house if he had a choice. He obviously had no desire to further a relationship with his family or meet any of their friends, and—worst of all— Olivia was quite certain he intended to leave Chicago very soon and without a word of warning to anyone except Caroline.

Olivia understood exactly why he felt as he did. The Wyatts had disposed of Mitchell as an infant as if he had been nothing but an offensive piece of litter cluttering up their perfect, tidy lives. She'd known a little about the fate of Edward's unwanted baby long ago, and Olivia had done nothing to change it; therefore, she accepted

Mitchell's contempt for her as her just deserts. What she could not accept was the thought of his leaving Chicago too soon. She wanted him to get to know her first and realize he could trust her. She wanted him to call her "Aunt Olivia" before he went away. Just one "Aunt Olivia" before he left, and she'd be satisfied. But there was something else Olivia wanted much more, something she had to have from him before it was too late: forgiveness.

At the moment, however, her most pressing concern was that Cecil might stalk up behind her, yank open the doors to his study, and put an entirely wrong interpretation on the scene inside. Rather than barging in on the couple and, in so doing, make Caroline feel guilty and force Mitchell to give unnecessary explanations, Olivia decided to alert them to her impending arrival. Accordingly, she banged her cane on the heavy door as she fumbled with the latch, and then for good measure, she held her cane out in front of her like a blind person's walking stick and entered the study, tapping and poking at the oak floor, her gaze fixed upon the old planks as if they weren't to be trusted with her weight.

"Do you need more light?" Mitchell asked.

Olivia raised her head as if surprised by his presence, but it was the irony in Mitchell's voice that startled her. He stood in front of the fireplace, exactly where he'd been before, but Caroline had dropped into a nearby chair. Olivia's heart ached at the sight of the dark smudges beneath her hazel eyes. "My poor child," she said, laying her hand on Caroline's golden hair.

Caroline tilted her head back and pressed Olivia's hand to her cheek instead. "Aunt Olivia," she said in a forlorn voice.

Olivia would have stayed at Caroline's side, but she realized Mitchell had stepped back from the fireplace and was idly surveying the study's many portraits. The large room was a veritable shrine to the Wyatts, with framed portraits of every size and description crowding the walls and covering the mantel. This was the first overt indication she'd seen him give that he had any interest whatsoever in any of the Wyatts—or at least Olivia wanted to think this was an indication of interest. "That is your great-grandfather," she told him, moving to his side and gesturing to the portrait above the fireplace. "Do you see the resemblance?"

"To what?" he said, deliberately mocking the notion.

"To you," Olivia persevered stubbornly, but he shot her a cold warning glance—one that looked exactly like those warning glances of his great-grandfather's; then he slid one hand into his pants pocket and strolled a few paces away. Olivia heeded his warning, but she watched him from the corner of her eye, hoping for another opportunity to chip away at his glacial defenses if he showed interest in a different portrait.

Cecil always kept people waiting; it proved his superiority over them. Normally it annoyed Olivia when he did it to her, but now she hoped he'd keep them waiting here for an hour. A few moments later, Mitchell paused to study another portrait, and Olivia hurried to join him; then she gaped at the picture he'd singled out. It was a portrait of a girl seated demurely on a garden swing, with pink rosebuds twined in her long hair and silk ones embroidered on the skirt of her white dress. Mitchell slanted Olivia a sidewise look. "You?" he asked.

"Good heavens!" she exclaimed. "How did you figure that out? I was barely fifteen at the time."

Instead of answering, he nodded toward another portrait. "And that's you as well?"

"Yes, I was twenty, and I'd just become engaged to Mr. Hebert. That's him, right there. Our portraits were made the same day."

"You don't look quite as happy about the engagement as he does."

"I wasn't," Olivia confided, forgetting that she had intended to draw Mitchell out and not the reverse. "I thought he and his family were a little . . . stuffy."

That brought a fascinated smile from him. "Why did you think they were 'stuffy'?" he asked, turning the full force of his undivided attention on her.

"It—it seems silly now, but one of his ancestors signed the Declaration of Independence, and another ancestor was a general in the Civil War, and I felt his family made too much of that—you know, boasted about it in an unseemly way."

"Appalling behavior," he agreed with amused gravity.

Basking in the glow of bantering with him, Olivia endeavored to do more of it. "Yes, it was. I mean, it wasn't as if they came over on the *Mayflower*!"

"I'm sure they tried," Mitchell joked, "but it was a small ship, and they probably couldn't get reservations."

"Well, if they couldn't," Olivia confided, leaning closer to him, "it's because *we* were already on it!"

He laughed, and Olivia lost her head and blurted out her thought: "The Wyatt men are a handsome lot, but in my day, *we* would have called *you* a dreamboat, young man."

His expression chilled the instant she implied that he was one of the Wyatt men, and Olivia was so desperate to recover the ground she'd lost that she pointed out a feature his forebears did not possess. "They all have brown eyes, too, but your eyes are blue."

"I wonder how that happened," he said in a bored drawl.

"Your moth—" Olivia cut the sentence off; then she changed her mind and decided he had a right to know. Might even want to know. "I remember that your mother had beautiful, deep blue eyes. I'd never seen eyes as blue as hers before or since—until now."

She waited for him to ask for more information about

his mother, but instead, he folded his arms across his chest and stared down at her, looking coldly impatient and very bored. Olivia pulled her gaze from his and pointed to a small portrait just beyond the one of George Hebert. "What do you think of him?" she asked, drawing Mitchell's attention to a portly gentleman wearing a starched shirt with a tie striped in shades of pink, blue, and yellow.

"I think he had appalling taste in neckties," Mitchell replied curtly, and walked away.

Olivia glanced at Caroline, who slowly shook her head, silently stating the obvious: Olivia had made a mistake by mentioning his mother and another mistake by trying to make Mitchell acknowledge his relationship to the men in the portraits.

Olivia watched him move from one painting to the next—a tall, broad-shouldered man who was looking at portraits of men who frequently resembled him so strongly that he had to feel as if he were looking in a mirror, a slightly blurry one at times, but a mirror nonetheless. Pride was causing him to deny the resemblance as well as his heritage, but as she studied him from across the room, she marveled at the futility of his effort. His forebears were tall, like he was, their bearing proud, their intellects extraordinary, their temperaments—uncertain. Just like his.

She thought of his criticism of the striped necktie her father-in-law had worn, and as she looked at Mitchell's profile, amusement lifted her spirits a little. From the toes of Mitchell's gleaming black Italian loafers to his custom-tailored charcoal suit and snowy white shirt to the impeccable cut of his thick black hair, Mitchell was—as all Wyatt men were—tastefully conservative and immaculately groomed.

However, three things she'd discovered about him while they looked at the portraits set him distinctly apart from his forebears: his dry sense of humor, his smooth urbane charm, and that smile of his. The combination was positively lethal—lethal enough to make even an old woman like her feel a little giddy. The Wyatt men were forceful and dynamic, but generally had little humor and even less charm. If they were Humphrey Bogarts, then Mitchell was Cary Grant, but with a hard jaw and chilly blue eyes.

"This will not take long," Cecil said in an abrupt voice as he stalked into the room.

Olivia stiffened inwardly and watched her brother walk to his desk. It irritated her that Cecil was two years older than she but arthritis hadn't bent his spine. "Sit down," he ordered.

Mitchell walked over to Olivia and pulled a chair out for her; then he walked over to the corner of Cecil's desk, shoved his hands into his pants pockets, and lifted his brows. "I said sit," Cecil warned him.

An expression of icy amusement flicked across Mitchell's face, and he looked around behind him.

"What are you looking for?" asked Cecil.

"Your dog," Mitchell replied.

Olivia stiffened and Caroline drew in a sharp breath. Cecil stared hard at him, his expression resentful . . . and then, almost respectful. "As you wish," he said; then he switched his gaze to Olivia and Caroline. "I wanted the two of you present because I feel that I owe it to Mitchell to say this in front of the entire family, and as fate would have it, we are the only adults left in this family."

Returning his gaze to Mitchell, he said, "Many years ago, pride and anger prompted me to do you a grave injustice, and I want to admit that now, in front of your aunt and your sister-in-law. My anger had nothing to do with you; it had to do with your father and the woman who was your mother. My son, Edward, was a womanizer, and I detested that in him. While his young wife was dying of cancer, he got another woman pregnant—your mother—and I could not forgive him for that. Nor could I overlook your mother's total lack of scruples. She consorted with my faithless son, knowing full well his wife was dying, and she was so utterly lacking in common decency that it was beyond her to understand the insult it would have been to Edward's dead wife had he married her and produced a child with her six months after his first wife's death."

Cecil stopped, and Olivia worriedly scrutinized Mitchell's face, wondering how he felt hearing these ugly truths about both his parents, but he looked detached— as if he were listening to a slightly distasteful story that had nothing whatsoever to do with him. If Olivia hadn't noticed the imperceptible tightening of his jaw, she'd have believed he was thoroughly bored.

Oblivious to such nuances of expression, Cecil said, "May I continue being blunt?"

"Please, by all means," Mitchell replied with mocking civility.

"I was disgusted—no—revolted by your parents' behavior, but when your mother hired a sleazy lawyer to try to extort money from me and compel me to raise her bastard child as a Wyatt, my revulsion for her became loathing, and I would have done anything within my power to thwart her. Anything. Can you understand my feeling in this regard?"

"Perfectly."

"If your mother had simply wanted money in order to raise her son and have a decent life, I could have understood that," Cecil added, and for the first time, Olivia thought she saw surprise or some other emotion flicker across Mitchell's enigmatic face. "But she hadn't a grain of maternal feeling in her body. Money and 'being around rich people' were all that counted to her, and she figured that should be enough for her child, too."

Cecil stood up. Olivia noticed he had to brace his hands on his desk, as if he felt weaker than he wanted to show. "You were the child of a spineless man without character or decency and a scheming, mercenary little slut. It never occurred to me that you could turn out well in view of all that, but I was wrong, Mitchell. Your Wyatt heritage came through strong and untainted. I loved your brother William, and he was a good father and husband, but he was soft and he had Edward's lack of ambition. You, Mitchell, are a throwback to your Wyatt ancestors. I tossed you out into the world with nothing except an opportunity to educate yourself and make social contacts. You turned that into an impressive little financial empire in a decade. You inherited your ability to do this from your Wyatt ancestors. You may not have been raised as a Wyatt, but you are one." Finished, Cecil looked at him expectantly.

Instead of sounding pleased, Mitchell sounded entertained. "Am I supposed to regard that as a compliment?"

Cecil's brows snapped together at the amusement in Mitchell's voice; then a satisfied smiled lifted his thin lips up at the corners. "Of course not. You're a Wyatt, and we Wyatts do not seek, nor do we need, the approval of others." As if he suddenly realized he had not softened the younger man up in the least, Cecil changed tactics. "Because you are a Wyatt, you will also understand how difficult it is for me to admit that my anger and pride caused me to make a disastrous error in judgment many years ago—an error for which you have paid your whole life. I don't expect you to forgive me, because Wyatts do not settle for mere apologies for what is unforgivable, and I am already eighty years old, so there aren't enough years left to me to atone. I, too, am a Wyatt, so I cannot ask for forgiveness I am not entitled to. I can only ask you for this—" The old man held out his hand, and it trembled slightly. "Will you shake my hand?"

Olivia was moved almost to tears, and Caroline's soft lower lip was quivering with an encouraging smile, but Mitchell ignored Cecil's gesture. "Not until I understand what we're shaking hands on."

"It is my eightieth birthday," Cecil said tiredly, letting his hand drop to his side. "I am responsible for Olivia, Caroline, and young Billy; but when I'm gone, there's no one left to look after them. I know that Olivia has developed an affection for you. No doubt she thinks of you as an ally, since you've both seen fit to ignore my request to park your cars on the street."

Mitchell flicked a surprised glance at Olivia, and she thought she saw a glint of amusement in his eyes before he returned his attention to Cecil.

"I know that William felt a bond with you from the moment he met you, and our William was an excellent judge of character. Caroline and young Billy tell me you've been spending time with them now that William is go—has disappeared, and I assume you share their affectionate familial regard." He paused, but Mitchell neither confirmed nor denied it, so Cecil put out his hand again and forged ahead. "Like it or not, you are my grandson. I need to know—and so do *they*—" he emphasized, "that you now accept that role, and that you agree to look after them should anything happen to me. Will you shake hands on that?"

Olivia marveled at how cleverly Cecil had rephrased his request, as if he were making it on behalf of Caroline and herself, and she was inordinately pleased that, this time, Mitchell hesitated only a second before reaching across the desk for his grandfather's handshake.

"That's settled then," Cecil said abruptly, casting off his mantle of helpless frailty as if it were an ill-fitting garment. "Olivia, Caroline, take Mitchell into the living room and make sure he meets the right people out there."

Olivia frowned. "Are you going to make some sort of announcement about who he is or where he's been all this time?"

"Certainly not! A formal announcement would open the door for additional questions that I have no desire to answer. I've already mentioned to a few people that Mitchell has been kind enough to ignore his business affairs in Europe so that he can spend a few weeks with us. When you bring Mitchell into the living room, I want you to behave as if you assume they already know who he is and, in fact, may already have met him here in the past." Satisfied that the matter was settled, Cecil started for the door.

"How in heaven's name am I going to do that?" Olivia asked.

He turned, and irritably demonstrated how to do it: "You walk up to a group of people, Olivia, and you say to them, 'You've all met Mitchell, haven't you?' And when they say they haven't, you act surprised. They'll spend the rest of the evening wondering how and when they offended me enough to be left out of the loop." He turned away again, took two steps, then turned back, a sly smile curving his mouth. "Better yet, now and then, when you take Mitchell up to someone, you should begin by saying, 'Mitchell, you remember so-and-so, don't you?' They won't remember meeting him, of course, but they'll be even more shocked that *he* doesn't remember meeting *them*. That will give Mitchell the upper hand." With that, he walked out.

Olivia looked at Mitchell to gauge his reaction to all this, but he was staring hard at Cecil's back; so she said, "Cecil is full of subtle but devious little tricks."

"Cecil is full of—" Mitchell jerked his gaze to Olivia's horrified face and bit back the rest of his sentence. Caroline's announcement diverted them both.

"I'm really not up to making small talk tonight or

being barraged with questions about William for which there are no new answers. I'd rather wait here."

"I'll take you home," Mitchell said quickly, but she shook her head and smiled up at him. "Cecil is right—it's best to present you to everyone tonight, when so many of Cecil's friends are already here."

"I am not a debutante," he pointed out sardonically.

"No one's going to mistake you for a debutante," Caroline said wryly, "but some of these women are going to look at you like you're a divinely dark and handsome bonbon."

He reached for her arm to draw her out of the chair. "Some other time."

Caroline pressed back farther into the chair and firmly shook her head. "This is the best time and the best way. Go with Olivia now. Please, do it for me—" she urged when he still looked unwilling. "After tonight, Billy and I will be able to go places with you without my having to worry that people will think I've already replaced William with a boyfriend."

"Fifteen minutes," Mitchell agreed impatiently, then he gave Olivia his arm, and she took it.

Chapter Three

AT THE ENTRY TO THE LIVING ROOM, OLIVIA PAUSED, AL-lowing him to take a good long look at the elegant socialites who were there, while she provided him with tidbits of information about their lofty pedigrees and important achievements. "The gentleman who Cecil just spoke to is the grandson of the founder of Universal Rubber. He's going to run for senator, and we all think he'll be president someday. The attractive brunette with him—the one who is looking in our direction right now—is his wife."

Mitchell let her go on, but he knew at a glance who these people were and *what* they were: self-important, pompous men who believed "good breeding" set them above all others; self-indulgent, vain women who were bored with their lives and their men, and who entertained themselves with charity work and torrid little affairs. The scene in this room wasn't new to Mitchell at all, except that it lacked the international flair and diversity he was accustomed to. Other than that, this was simply a miniature, and somewhat provincial, scene from his own life.

"The gentleman in the dark gray suit and maroon tie is Gray Elliott," Olivia confided. "Gray is from a fine old Chicago family, and he is the youngest person ever elected to the office of Cook County state's attorney. He's already proving his mettle and making a very big name for himself. In front of Gray is Evan Bartlett and his father, Henry. The Bartletts have handled legal affairs for the Wyatts for as far back as I can remember—longer than that, for generations."

Mitchell looked at the elder Bartlett and assumed Henry must have handled the messy details surrounding his birth—the falsified birth certificate, the terms of the divorce, the payoff to his mother.

". . . young Evan is a brilliant attorney," Olivia chattered enthusiastically, "who is already taking over the reins from Henry—"

Young Evan, Mitchell thought drily, *will be going through old files tomorrow after his father tells him what he remembers about Mitchell Wyatt.*

Olivia paused to scrutinize Mitchell's features and assess how he was reacting. "Are you bored already?" she asked, looking crestfallen.

Mitchell was worse than bored, but she was so transparently eager to impress him and make him want to be a part of all this that he found himself saying, "Not at all."

She looked doubtful. "Are you planning to leave us soon?" she asked bluntly.

"Yes, in two weeks."

She averted her face instantly, her hand clutching fiercely at his arm while a tremor seemed to shake her entire body. Mitchell automatically slid his arm around her back to brace her and looked for the closest chair. "You're ill—" he began, but the episode passed as swiftly as it had occurred.

"I am rarely ill," she replied stiffly, "and if I were going to be ill, I assure you, I would never let it happen in front of company!" To prove it, she lifted her face and looked at him with proud defiance and a sheen of tears in her faded amber eyes.

Mitchell's jaw tightened at the sight of those tears. He rejected her *right* to feel dismay over his leaving. He'd known in Cecil's study why she'd wanted him to look at those portraits of his relatives. He knew why she was so damned anxious to take him into the living room tonight and introduce him to everyone as her nephew. In the last thirty-four years, she hadn't so much as tried to send him a secret note telling him who he was or who she was to him, and now she intended to atone for that with a few empty gestures. Her woebegone face and clinging hand weren't manifestations of any real affection for him; they were manifestations of her guilt and fear.

She was a frightened old woman, facing death with a guilty conscience; she was an arrogant, manipulative old woman who wanted to make quick atonement; and she didn't want him to foil her by leaving too soon. In fact, she recovered from her bout of superficial distress almost immediately and inquired of him in a composed, impersonal tone, "Will you be going back to London, or will it be Paris?"

"Neither," Mitchell snapped, deciding to park her in the nearest chair and forgo the introductions in the living room. "It's getting late, and I want to take Caroline home."

"Do you plan to return to Chicago at some time in the future?"

"Two weeks after I leave," Mitchell replied, forcibly turning her toward an uncomfortable-looking antique chair right next to the entrance to the living room.

She stopped him from taking the first step toward it by angling her cane across the front of his knees. "You're coming back in a few weeks?"

Mitchell looked down at her ecstatic face and bright, tearful eyes, and a small boulder tore loose from the wall of indifference he'd erected and maintained against his unknown family members throughout his life. She was beaming at him and clutching his arm as if she couldn't bear to let it go.

She reminded him of a cute little spider, heedless of his

superior size and ready to brave the danger to those who venture near collapsing walls. He could have brushed her off his sleeve with a flick of his fingers, and even as he thought about doing exactly that, he heard himself say reassuringly, "I'm building a house in Anguilla. I need to spend a couple of weeks there, and then I'll be back."

"I'm so glad!" she said, and impulsively pressed her parchment cheek against his arm to prove it. "I've heard Anguilla is a beautiful island. There's a hotel there that everyone is always talking about. Henry Bartlett goes there often," she added, but her attention was returning to the delightful task she'd undertaken earlier and had yet to perform. "That's Matthew Farrell and his wife, Meredith Bancroft, over there. They've just returned from a trip to China. You've heard of them, I'm sure?"

"Yes," Mitchell said, amazed to discover that he already knew—and actually liked—two people in that room.

Craning her neck, Olivia prepared to lead him into the fray. "Now, who shall I introduce you to first?"

"Matthew Farrell," Mitchell promptly replied.

"Very well, but we have to walk right past Evan and Henry Bartlett, so let's start with them." She tucked her hand through the crook of his arm, smiled eagerly, and urged him forward. Left with no other choice, Mitchell pasted a polite expression on his face and let her take the lead.

Cecil had obviously put the word out that Mitchell was present, and the word had spread swiftly, because the moment Mitchell entered the living room with Olivia on his arm, fascinated faces turned in their direction, scrutinizing him from head to foot. The conversation level dropped off, then erupted into smiling whispers.

Olivia took careful note of the favorable impact he was having and began taking tiny, slow steps so she could show him off longer. "You are causing quite a stir among the ladies!" she confided delightedly. After another sly glance around the room, she added, "Even the married ones."

Especially the married ones, Mitchell thought drily. He was a new stud being led into the stable—and a thoroughbred, too, if he was a Wyatt. As a potential lover, being a thoroughbred made him so much more desirable than the usual tennis instructor, physical trainer, or penniless artist.

He'd been playing in the big leagues, with people like these, forever—he knew all the games that were played and how to play them. He also knew how to win them. He was neither proud nor ashamed of his past successes, nor interested in trying to repeat them. In fact, his only reaction to the roomful of women who were currently looking him over was a sense of relief that Olivia was too old-fashioned to imagine what some of them were thinking.

She squeezed his arm to get his attention, and Mitchell tipped his head toward her. "I know what the ladies are thinking," she informed him.

Startled, Mitchell said warily, "You do?"

She wagged her head in affirmation and dropped her voice to a happy whisper. "They're thinking you're a dreamboat!"

Henry Bartlett didn't think Mitchell was a dreamboat, Henry Bartlett knew *exactly* what Mitchell Wyatt was, and Henry Bartlett wanted Mitchell to know that. When Olivia said, "Henry, you've met Mitchell, haven't you?" just as Cecil had instructed her to do, Bartlett's frosty smile became a smirk.

"Yes," he replied, crudely putting his right hand in his pocket instead of extending it to Mitchell. "When we met, however, Mitchell was a lot smaller."

His unexpected answer threw Olivia into total confusion. "Henry," she said, "you must be thinking of someone else. You didn't know Mitchell when he was small—"

"I think Henry is right," Mitchell interrupted, directing his reply to Olivia while staring dispassionately at Bartlett. "In fact, I'll bet Henry took me for my first plane ride."

"I took you *to* it, not on it."

"Mitchell has a plane of his own now," Olivia put in smoothly, giving Mitchell the distinct impression that she didn't understand anything Henry had said, but that she was aware of the undertones, and she didn't like them. She turned to Bartlett's son and said, "Mitchell, this is Evan Bartlett, Henry's son." Then she realized her mistake and awkwardly added, "You remember Evan, don't you—"

"We've never met," Mitchell said bluntly, and her fingers flew nervously to the strand of pearls at her throat.

Evan Bartlett had better manners than his father. He shook hands with Mitchell, asked no probing questions, and adroitly used the topic of private planes to start a conversation. "We've been looking at a two-year-old Gulfstream G-3 for our firm. Flying on commercial airlines has become such a hassle and so time-consuming that we're at the point where it's becoming cost-effective for us to own our own jet."

Mitchell unjustly retaliated against Henry by letting his son flounder. Instead of replying, Mitchell lifted his brows and said nothing.

"The problem is," Evan said after an awkward pause, "it's hard to justify the price of the G-3 when a Lear would get us where we need to go just as well."

"But not as comfortably," Mitchell said finally.

"Right. Of course, if comfort and luxury were all that counted—and money was absolutely no issue—the G-5 is the only plane to own. God, that's a beautiful bird. I lust after that thing every time I see one on a runway. It's as exciting to look at as a beautiful woman. Have you ever been inside one?"

Mitchell presumed he was referring to the plane, not a woman. If Olivia hadn't been there, he'd have asked for clarification just to entertain himself with Evan's reaction. Since she was there, he said only, "Yes."

"So what kind of plane do you have?" Evan persisted.

"A G-5."

Olivia emitted a snort of mirth and then looked horrified. "Mitchell is going to Anguilla in two weeks," she burst out. "You go down there quite often, don't you, Henry?"

"Several times a year," Evan answered for his father, when Henry didn't reply. "I'm going down there for the first time myself in three weeks. I wanted to go in November, but I couldn't get reservations at the Island Club until the first of February. It's almost impossible to stay there if you aren't a regular guest. Are you staying at the Island Club while you're there?"

"No." To prevent Olivia from informing them that he was building his own home on Anguilla, which he sensed she was dying to do, Mitchell added quickly, "A friend of mine has a boat down there. I'm going to stay on board."

"I hope I don't end up canceling my trip," Evan said. "A client of ours died suddenly, and his daughter is understandably upset. She may not—" He paused, glanced at his watch, and frowned. "Speaking of our client's death, I have to go to his wake tonight, and I'm going to be very late." He said good-bye to his father and Mitchell, then he pressed a brief kiss on Olivia's cheek and began wending his way through the crowded room toward the front door.

Olivia took advantage of his departure and drew Mitchell away from Henry after a cool nod.

"Now let's see where Matthew Farrell is," she said,

craning her neck. "Oh, look, he's coming to us. I think he's very anxious to meet you."

"What makes you think that?" Mitchell replied, enjoying the puzzled grin on his friend's face.

"Look for yourself—he's smiling at you."

"He probably thinks I'm a dreamboat," Mitchell joked as anticipation drove off the irritation and boredom of the last few minutes.

Chapter Four

SURROUNDED BY A PRIVATE GARDEN FILLED WITH THE scent of blooming jasmine and frangipani, Kate Donovan stood on the terrace of the villa that Evan had reserved for them at the Island Club and gazed at a scene that looked very much like a slice of paradise.

Beneath a dazzling blue sky with puffy white clouds, graceful sailboats and gleaming yachts glided through the sparkling waters of Maundays Bay. Nearby, sunbathers relaxed on a crescent-shaped beach with sand as white as granulated sugar while attentive hotel employees hovered in the background in case someone raised a little flag, indicating they that wanted a chilled towel or a drink or something to eat.

A couple that was trying to paddle a kayak near the shore gave up and waded out of the water, laughing and dragging the kayak behind them. Kate smiled with vicarious enjoyment before a fresh wave of isolation swept over her and drowned it out.

The island of Anguilla was breathtakingly beautiful, and the hotel was a fairy-tale Moorish palace, with domes and turrets and fabulous gardens, but she was completely alone. Instead of distracting her from her grief over her father's death, being alone in this alien tropical paradise was compounding the unreality and isolation she'd felt since his funeral.

The telephone rang, and she rushed in from the terrace, hoping it would be Evan.

"Kate, it's Holly. Hold on a second—" Her best friend's cheerful voice was a balm to Kate's spirits, as was the familiar sound of barking dogs in the background. Holly was a vet who took in "rescued" dogs while she looked for homes for them. It was almost impossible to have a conversation with her that wasn't accompanied by a chorus of barking canines. "Sorry about the noise," Holly said a little breathlessly. "I just took in a rescued Doberman, and he's stirring up trouble. So, how's Anguilla?"

"It's a beautiful island, very pristine."

"How are you feeling? Have you had any more headaches?"

"Not since the one I had four days ago on the plane from Chicago. It was so bad that when we landed in St. Maarten, Evan made our cabdriver take us to a doctor. The driver took us to his own doctor, a nice old man whose office was in his house and who spoke only French. The cabdriver spoke some English, so he had to act as translator."

"Thank God you weren't having gynecological problems!"

Smiling at Holly's joking remark, Kate said, "Evidently, the cabdriver got the point across, because the doctor decided I was having migraines—that was the only word the doctor said that I completely understood. Anyway, he gave me a prescription for migraine pills that I'm supposed to take every day for the next two weeks. I've been taking them, but I think the headaches were probably from stress and they'd have gone away on their own when I got settled in down here."

"Keep taking them anyway," Holly ordered sternly; and when Kate promised she would, Holly changed to a lighter topic. "What about the Island Club—what's it like?"

Carefully keeping her tone upbeat for Holly's sake,

Kate described the hotel. "There are thirty private villas scattered along the beach, each with its own garden and terrace and a panoramic view of the water. Everything is white: the hotel, the villas, even the floors in the rooms. The bathroom is the size of my living room, and the tub is like a shallow sunken swimming pool. The main hotel where you check in is quite small, but the boutiques inside it are fabulous and the food here is superb."

"Have you seen anyone famous?"

"A bellboy told me Donald Trump stayed here last week and Julia Roberts was here a month ago. There's a family staying in one of the villas that has a bodyguard who follows their teenage sons around, but I don't know who the family is, and I don't think the staff would tell me if I asked. The staff is very, very discreet and extremely service oriented. In fact, there's a young waiter here I'd love to have working for us. For me, I mean," Kate corrected, trying to sound matter-of-fact instead of forlorn.

Holly wasn't fooled. "Do not think about the restaurant. Put Evan on the phone. I'm going to give him strict orders to make you laugh and make love to you so you can't think about anything else until you come home."

Kate hesitated and then reluctantly said, "Evan isn't here."

"Is he playing thirty-six holes of golf a day or only twenty-seven?"

"He isn't playing golf, he's in Chicago."

"What?" Holly said angrily.

"His father was supposed to get a continuance on an important case," Kate explained, "but the judge refused to grant it. Evan had to turn around and go straight back to Chicago to either try the case in court or persuade the judge to continue it."

"When is he planning to get back to Anguilla?" Holly asked bitterly.

"Tomorrow, possibly. Maybe."

"Evan is an arrogant, thoughtless jerk, and I don't care what his excuse is for not being there. He barely made it to your father's wake before it was over, because he had to attend some rich old man's birthday party. He knew you didn't want to go on this trip so soon after your father's funeral, but he made you feel so guilty that you went with him anyway. And now you're stuck there alone."

"There are worse places to be 'stuck,'" Kate teased, trying to calm Holly down. From the corner of her eye she saw a large dog sneaking out of the woods and trotting across her garden. She tucked the telephone receiver between her shoulder and ear so that she could unwrap the bacon she'd saved for him in a napkin. "Actually, there's a rather handsome male here that I've been seeing a lot of. Max and I have been having our meals together."

Holly was instantly intrigued. "What's he like?"

With the phone still cradled on her shoulder, Kate walked onto the terrace and described the dog as he wolfed down each piece of bacon she offered him, then waited patiently for the next one. "He's extremely tall with light brown hair and very intelligent brown eyes. He's surprisingly gentle, too, for such a big guy. I call him Max—short for Maximilian."

Holly heard the trace of wry amusement in Kate's voice. "What's wrong with him, Kate?" she said warily.

"He's much too thin, he needs a bath, and he's never seen a hairbrush."

"My God!"

"And he has four legs."

"Now, that's a problem you can't fix," Holly laughed. "Are we talking about a dog or a cat here?"

"A very big dog," Kate confirmed, grinning as she gave the dog the last of the bacon and wiped her fingers on the napkin. "He reminds me of a dog you rescued a long time ago—the one that took us forever to catch. He had short tan hair and a black muzzle. I think you said his breed was originally used to chase tigers and tire them out."

"Not tigers, lions," Holly said. "That dog was a Rhodesian ridgeback."

"Well, Max doesn't have a ridge on his back and he's definitely a stray. He has two scruffy girlfriends, much smaller than he is, and they always join us for meals, but Max has started dropping by without them, just to say hello. He's a bit of a flirt."

"While we're on the subject of flirting, will you do me one little favor while you're stuck there all by yourself, because Evan is 'too busy' to get down there?"

"What sort of favor?" Kate asked, instantly wary of Holly's change in tone.

"Are there any attractive unmarried *human* males staying at the hotel?"

"I don't think so."

"Okay, then have you seen a decent-looking doorman? A cute bellboy?"

"Why do you ask?"

"Because it would make me deliriously happy if I thought you'd had a fling with one of them while Evan was paying the damned hotel bill," Holly said spitefully.

Kate smothered a laugh. "Okay."

The anger in Holly's voice turned to surprise. "You'll do it?"

"No," Kate said with a wayward smile, "but I'll let you think I did, if that will make you 'deliriously happy.'"

Bantering with Holly had lifted Kate's spirits a little, and when she hung up, she tried to decide how best to keep herself occupied. She could go for a swim and then have a late lunch in the Sandbar, a cozy little restaurant with a covered patio and Moorish arches. It had a splendid view of the bay, and if she didn't feel like staring at the water, she could read the book she'd bought at O'Hare Airport called *Coping with Grief*.

If she didn't want to do that, she could start making a list of the tasks she needed to take care of as soon as she got back to Chicago. She had things she needed to handle at the restaurant, now that she was solely responsible for it, and she also had dozens of things to take care of relating to her father's death and his estate.

Normally, the simple act of writing things down in orderly lists made Kate feel much better and more able to cope. In fact, she made lists all the time when she was under pressure—lists of tasks to handle, in order of importance, and lists of pros and cons when she had a difficult decision to make. Holly teased her about being a compulsive list maker, but it worked for Kate.

Now that she had a plan for the afternoon, Kate felt better and more energized. Before another bout of sadness and helplessness could wear her down, she changed into a yellow bathing suit and wrapped a matching sarong-style cover-up around her waist; then she put her book and a tablet from the desk drawer into a green canvas tote bag she was using as a combination purse and beach bag, and she left for the beach. First an invigorating swim and then a delicious lunch.

A young waiter materialized the instant Kate's sandal touched the patio outside the Sandbar, but when he started to lead her to the only vacant table, she hesitated. For one thing, she needed to get away from the tropical sunlight before it scorched her fair skin right through her sunscreen. For another, the three teenage boys with the bodyguard were eating at the next table. They'd already tried their youthful, persistent best to flirt with her yesterday, and now they were eyeing her with renewed hope. "I think I'd rather eat inside," she told the waiter.

He was truly distressed. "But you would have to eat at the bar, unless you want to wait for a table to become available."

Kate paused beneath a Moorish arch and looked inside. No one was sitting at the small bar, and the high stools looked comfortable with nice backs to lean against. Eating at the bar would suit her fine. She chose a stool facing the patio so she could look out at the water; then she pulled her book, her notepad, and a pen out of her tote bag. Satisfied that she had everything she needed, she looped the canvas straps of the green bag over the back of her stool and ordered a salad and a glass of tomato juice for lunch.

Towels had been delivered to her on the beach when she walked out of the water, and now a balmy breeze blew through the little restaurant's open arches, softly drying her damp hair. It was nice to be away from the glaring sunlight, and the conversations at the tables inside were quiet enough not to intrude on her concentration. Kate gazed out at the water, thinking about what list to start on first, tapping the end of the pen on the tablet.

She decided to start with her relationship with Evan. The waiter brought her glass of tomato juice just as she drew a vertical line down the notebook page to make two columns. Above the left column she wrote, "Reasons to Continue"; above the right column she wrote, "Reasons to End."

She'd been drifting in her relationship with Evan, letting it flounder, because she was unsure whether she truly wanted it to go forward. Holly blamed Evan for many things, especially the fact that he hadn't put an engagement ring on Kate's finger after almost four years, but that was mostly Kate's doing. Whenever she sensed he was thinking about marriage, she did or said something guaranteed to make him hold off and rethink the issue. Her father had loved Evan, and he would have loved the idea of Kate marrying a Bartlett. He'd wanted Kate to have a beautiful life, with no worries about money, ever. . . .

"What's that?" she asked the waiter when he put a second glass of tomato juice next to the one she'd barely touched.

"Compliments of the young gentlemen on the patio," he replied with a smile. "They asked that you be given a glass of whatever you're drinking and that the charge for it be put on their parents' bill." Kate bit back a smile of her own and looked outside toward their table.

Three teenage faces grinned hopefully at her. The family at the table beside them obviously knew what the boys had done, because they were watching Kate—so was a couple seated near Kate who'd heard the waiter's announcement when he gave her the glass of tomato juice.

The boys looked as if they ranged in ages from thirteen to sixteen, and Kate debated a moment about the best way to handle the situation without crushing their egos. "Tell them I said thank you. And—tell them I'm working," she added. That was a little lame, Kate thought, but it would surely keep them from trying to join her at the bar.

By the time the waiter brought her salad, Kate had written several items on both sides of her list, but she realized she was too emotional right now to make objective judgments about Evan and their feelings for each other. She gave up on that list and turned the page to start a new one. At the top she wrote, "Things to Do at the Restaurant." She glanced up as her waiter put another glass of tomato juice in front of her.

"Compliments of the young gentlemen." This time he rolled his eyes and grinned.

When Kate looked around, several couples at tables inside were grinning and watching her, and when she glanced outside at the boys, everyone around them was watching her—except a man seated alone at the table she'd declined earlier. Embarrassed for the boys, not herself, Kate looked straight at them and shook her head slowly, but she smiled to take the sting of rejection out of her warning to stop.

She looked down at the title of her new list, and her hand trembled. Donovan's Restaurant would be forever linked in her mind to her father. Located downtown, Donovan's had begun as a little Irish pub founded by her father, and over the next thirty years it had repeatedly expanded and transformed until it was now one of Chicago's most elegant, and most popular, restaurants. Daniel Patrick Donovan had always been a fixture there—a witty, charismatic man who mingled with his special customers while keeping an eye on every minute detail involving food and service. He had been the spirit and life force behind Donovan's, and now it was up to Kate to try to carry on without him.

Struggling to keep her emotions under control, Kate went to work on her list. According to the maître d', the restaurant was booked solid with reservations for the next eleven days, and the waiting list was longer than the usual number of cancellations. Kate needed to learn every detail about the restaurant's operating budget, and she needed to set up safeguards to make sure she stayed within it. . . . She needed to have weekly meetings with the staff for a while, until they were confident she could actually take her father's place—and until she was sure of it. She also needed to see if the new menus her father had chosen were on order. He'd liked those padded maroon leather menus with the word *Donovan's* deeply embossed in gold.

He liked maroon leather chairs with shiny brass nail heads, she remembered achingly. . . .

And waiters in freshly pressed dinner jackets . . .

And sparkling cut-crystal glassware . . .

And gleaming brass foot rails in the bar . . .

Kate stopped writing and pressed her thumb and forefinger to the bridge of her nose to hold back the tears stinging her eyes. A chorus of laughter rang out from the patio and rippled through the interior of the restaurant. Kate blinked and lifted her head.

"Compliments of the young gentlemen," the waiter announced.

"Take it back to them and tell them I don't want it," Kate ordered, her voice ragged with emotion. She flicked an apologetic glance at her audience within the restaurant; then she bent her head and turned to a new page in her notebook. She began a list of things she had to do at her father's house.

On the patio outside, the boys let out a groan of dismay when the waiter walked out of the restaurant carrying an untouched glass of tomato juice on a tray.

At the table beside them, Mitchell Wyatt turned his head to hide his amusement and encountered laughing looks from several people on his left. By now, everyone seated on the patio was privy to the boys' repeated amorous attempts to make an impression on the woman inside.

Although Mitchell had a view of her sitting at the bar, she was in deep shadow, so he had no idea what she looked like. According to the boys, who'd repeatedly expressed their opinion to everyone within hearing, she was "Soooo hot" and "Such a fox."

The waiter put the glass of tomato juice on their table and sternly informed them, "The lady does not want another glass of tomato juice."

Trying to ignore the outburst of laughter and the youthful exclamations of disappointment that followed the waiter's announcement, Mitchell picked up the estimates his contractor had given him, but the youngest boy evidently decided to seek advice from an older, more experienced male. Leaning toward Mitchell, he held up his palms in a gesture of helplessness and demanded, "So, what would you do?"

Mildly annoyed at yet another distraction, Mitchell eyed the glass of unappetizing tomato juice and said, "I'd add a stalk of celery and a shot of vodka, if it was for me."

"Yes!" the kid exclaimed excitedly, looking at the waiter.

The waiter looked questioningly at the bodyguard, who was seated at the table with them and trying to read a newspaper. The boys looked hopefully at the bodyguard. "Give us a hand here, Dirk," one of them implored. The bodyguard sighed, hesitated, then nodded at the waiter and said, "Only one."

The boys cheered and exchanged high fives.

The man at the table on his left laughingly confided to Mitchell, "You can't blame them for trying. Hell, if I were single, I'd make a play for her. She looks just like Julianne Moore."

In disgust, Mitchell gave up trying to concentrate on the list of estimates and looked around for a waiter to bring him his check. The waiter wasn't in sight. He'd gone into the restaurant.

Oblivious of the commotion on the patio, Kate looked at the tasks she'd written down to do at her father's house, and the ache inside her grew and grew. *Donate clothes to the Salvation Army.* Her father's suits . . . His favorite green sweater that made his eyes look even greener. He had such wonderful eyes . . . warm, laughing, Irish eyes. She was never going to see those eyes again.

She was going to cry, Kate realized in horror! She had
to get out of there. She closed the notebook and got off
the barstool, just as the waiter put a Bloody Mary in
front of her and a man strolled in from the patio, heading in her direction. "Compliments of the young
gentlemen," the waiter explained.

"Tomato juice was cute," she told him. "A Bloody
Mary isn't cute. It's—inappropriate and offensive for
kids to do something like this."

"It wasn't their idea, miss," he said quickly.

"Then whose idea was it?" Kate demanded, not caring
that everyone in the restaurant—and probably on the
patio, too—was watching to see what she'd do about the
Bloody Mary.

"Mine," the newcomer said from right beside her.

Kate could tell from his deep voice that he was old
enough to know better, and she refused to give him the
courtesy of a glance. "It's reprehensible to help those
adolescents buy alcohol." With her left hand, she
grabbed her notebook and *Coping with Grief* from behind her plate; then she slid her right arm through the
long straps of the green canvas bag and picked up the
Bloody Mary, intending to give it back to him. "I don't
want this—" The straps of her canvas bag snagged on
the back of the chair, and she gave the straps an impatient jerk while she thrust the drink at him.

Red liquid erupted from the glass and drenched the
front of his white shirt.

"Oh, no—" Kate exclaimed, drowning out his startled
expletive and the gasps from onlookers. "I am *so sorry!*"
Dropping everything but the Bloody Mary, she put the
half-empty glass on the bar, swiftly exchanging it for her
glass of ice water and a cloth napkin. "The tomato juice
will stain if we don't get it out right away," she babbled,
unable to look him in the eye.

When she doused his silk shirt with freezing-cold

water, Mitchell's skin flinched, and when she began dabbing madly at the mess with her cloth napkin, and apologizing frantically, his annoyance switched to reluctant amusement, but when she told the hovering waiter to bring her some club soda, Mitchell drew the line: "Do not give her anything else to pour on me," he warned. "Bring us a towel instead." She'd spilled the drink on him before his eyes had adjusted to the shadows, and she hadn't lifted her gaze above his chest since then, so he had no idea what she actually looked like except that she was about five feet six inches tall, and she had long, dark red hair that was very thick, damp, and curly. Beyond that, all he could tell from his current vantage point was that her eyelashes and eyebrows were the same color as her hair. He tucked his chin down and addressed her eyelashes. "Didn't anyone ever teach you how to say, 'Thank you kindly, but no'?"

Kate finally realized he wasn't furious, but her relief was offset by shame. "I'm afraid your shirt is ruined," she said as she reached for the waiter's towel with her right hand and shoved the fingers of her left hand between the buttons of his shirt and his bare skin. "I'll try to blot as much of this off as I can."

"That sounds like a better plan than trying to drown it."

"I couldn't feel any worse about this," she said in a muffled voice.

"Yes, you could," Mitchell said, but his attention was on the title of the book she'd dropped, and he was trying to read it upside down.

"How could I?"

"I didn't intend for the boys to send you that Bloody Mary," he replied just before he realized the title of the book was *Coping with Grief*.

Stricken, she finally lifted her face to his, and in a flash of blinding clarity, Mitchell realized exactly why three teenage boys had been making fools of themselves over her. Framed by a mass of curling titian hair, and without a trace of makeup, her face was striking, with ivory skin, high cheekbones, and a small square chin with an intriguing cleft in the center. Her nose was straight, her mouth soft and generously wide, but it was her eyes that momentarily mesmerized him: Beneath gracefully winged dark red brows and a thick fringe of long russet lashes, she had large green eyes the startling color of wet leaves. Belatedly, Mitchell realized those eyes were shimmering with tears, and he felt a sharp, idiotic pang of regret for his part in causing them.

"Naturally, I want to pay for your shirt," she said, stepping back and turning away.

"I'd expect nothing less from someone with your lofty principles," Mitchell said lightly, watching her put the towel on the bar and reach for her canvas bag. She wasn't wearing a ring on her left hand, he noted.

Kate heard his joking tone and couldn't believe how nice he was being. Or how incredibly handsome he was. With her back to him, she took her checkbook out of her bag and groped in it for a pen. "How much shall I make my check out for?"

Mitchell hesitated, preoccupied with rapid observations and assessments: The Island Club was an extremely expensive, elitist little hotel, yet her wristwatch and the ring on her right hand were inexpensive, and her canvas bag had the name of a bookstore on it, not a designer logo. That meant she was probably here with someone who was paying all her expenses. With her striking good looks, she'd undoubtedly have wealthy men standing in line to take her to the best places and show her a good time . . . but the bathing suit top she was wearing was a little on the modest side for a "good-time girl." Besides that, there was something soft and vulnerable about her and even a little . . . prim?

When he didn't reply, Kate turned around and looked inquiringly at him.

"This is an extremely expensive shirt," he said gravely, but with the ghost of a smile at the corner of his mouth. "If I were you, I'd offer to take me to dinner instead."

Startled laughter welled up inside Kate, pushing past the aching misery she'd felt for nearly two weeks. "Your shirt is that expensive?"

He nodded with sham regret. "I'm afraid so. Taking me to dinner would be the wisest choice for you financially, believe me."

"After what I just did to you, you want to have dinner with me?" Kate said, finding that a little difficult to believe.

"Yes, but with only solid food around. No liquids within your reach."

Unable to keep a straight face, Kate bent her head, her shoulders shaking with mirth at his dire tone.

"I'll take that to mean you're prepared to discharge your debt—shall we say at eight o'clock tonight?" Mitchell said smoothly, wishing he could see her expression.

She hesitated a moment; then she nodded and finally lifted her face to his. Mitchell's gaze dropped from her eyes to her entrancing smile, and his heart missed a beat. When she smiled, she had the most inviting, romantic mouth he'd ever seen.

"I'm Kate Donovan," she said, her pretty mouth relaxing into a friendly smile as she held out her hand.

She had a nice handshake, Mitchell decided as her long fingers slid across his palm and grasped his hand. "Mitchell Wyatt," he replied.

Kate's mind switched to practicalities. Evan had made advance reservations for the two of them to dine that night at Voyages, the hotel's beautiful all-glass restaurant at the water's edge. "Let's meet at Voyages at eight o'clock," she said.

"Let's meet in front of the hotel, instead. I have another restaurant in mind."

Vague uneasiness crept over Kate, but she was preoccupied with his ruined shirt; his handsome, tanned face; and a sudden awareness that everyone inside the restaurant was either watching them or listening to them. "All right," she said, and gathered up her belongings. Rather than leave via the patio and walk past the teenagers' table, Kate turned toward the exit behind her, which also enabled her to cut diagonally across the sand to the villa where she was staying. Halfway there, she glanced over her shoulder, and when she didn't see a tall man behind her with a large red splotch on his shirt, she realized he'd left the restaurant via the front entrance. Guiltily she wondered what sort of hilarity he'd had to endure from the teenagers on the patio when he passed by them.

Chapter Five

STANDING IN FRONT OF THE BATHROOM MIRROR, wrapped in a white terry-cloth robe that the hotel provided, Kate finished taming her curly hair into soft waves, then switched off the blow-dryer and walked over to the closet to survey her choice of clothing. Most of the restaurants in Anguilla were casual, but a few were quite elegant, and she had no idea whether her dinner companion would be wearing jeans and a T-shirt, or a sport jacket and slacks.

Since he'd been wearing a white shirt, slacks, and loafers at lunch, it seemed likely he'd be dressed at least that well for dinner, and possibly more so. Based on that, Kate chose a pair of silk pants with a hazy version of Monet's *Water Lilies* on a pale blue background, a matching top with a wide off-the-shoulder neckline, and a pale blue satin sash; then she hesitated, hanger in hand.

Rather than try to second-guess him and end up making the wrong choice, she put the clothes back into the closet and walked over to the phone on the desk in the living room. A balmy breeze drifted in from the gardens through the open terrace doors as she pressed the button for the hotel operator and asked to be connected with Mitchell Wyatt's room.

"I'm sorry," the young man said after a pause, "but Mr. Wyatt isn't staying with us."

"You're certain he isn't registered here?" Kate asked.

"Yes, very certain."

The vague uneasiness Kate had experienced earlier when he said he had "another restaurant in mind" sharpened into alarm as she hung up the telephone. Gazing blindly at the *Hotel Services* notebook lying beside the desk phone, she reviewed the facts: She'd met a man in a hotel—a stranger about whom she knew absolutely nothing—and she'd agreed to get into a car and go somewhere with him. The man was extremely handsome, flawlessly charming, and very glib—the perfect combination for a gigolo who hung around expensive hotels, hoping to pick up wealthy women.

Or, he could be much worse than a gigolo. He could be a rapist. He could be a murderer—a serial murderer who moved from island to island, butchering his victims and burying their bodies in the sand.

Unnerved by her thoughts, Kate wandered outside onto the terrace; then she stifled a nervous gasp as a large canine head suddenly reared up from the bushes on the edge of the terrace. "You scared me, Max!" she said. The dog flinched at her accusatory tone, and Kate instantly switched to a soft, reassuring one. "You didn't really scare me. I was already scared, because I may have agreed to have dinner with Jeffrey Dahmer or Jack the Ripper."

The dog looked over his shoulder as if to be certain no one was watching; then he moved around the bushes and hesitantly put one paw onto the terrace. Just one paw, Kate noticed, not two. "I don't have any more food to give you," she told him, gesturing to the empty table beside her. "See, there's nothing here."

He put his second paw onto the terrace, still hesitant, but looking at her intently as if he wanted something from her. Stepping forward, she laid her hand on his head. "I don't have anything for you," she repeated, but his tail wagged as soon as she touched him. "Is this what you want?" she asked in surprise, and tentatively stroked her hand from the crown of his head down his neck. In response, he pressed the side of his head against her leg.

On her third stroke, he leaned the full weight of his body against her.

On her fourth stroke, he closed his eyes in quiet pleasure.

"I'm lonely, too, Max," Kate whispered. In the aftermath of her father's death her emotions were so raw that just the realization that this dog was also lonely brought tears of empathy to her eyes. Trying to concentrate on something else, she thought about the possible ramifications of her reckless decision to have dinner with a stranger that night, and stroked Max's head. When she finally glanced at her watch, it was fifteen minutes to eight. "I have to go now," she said, giving the canine's head a quick pat before moving away from him. "Tell you what," she added, trying to sound cheerful for his sake, "if I get back here alive and unharmed tonight, we'll have breakfast together in the morning, and I'll order you an entire, all-meat breakfast of your very own. How does that sound?"

Large brown eyes looked at her imploringly, and he wagged his tail. He wanted more petting, and that was as clear as if he'd spoken the words. Kate backed into the suite and put her hand on the sliding glass door to pull it closed. In an idiotic attempt to bribe the forlorn dog to feel better—and make herself feel less guilty—she made him promises as she slowly pulled the door closed. "I'll order you bacon and sausage. Better yet, I'll order you a steak with a bone that you can take with you and bury! You really have to go now," she urged, closing the door the last inch. On the other side of the glass, the dog stared at her intently; Kate reluctantly turned away.

Ten minutes later, wearing the outfit she'd originally chosen, Kate bent down to slip on a pair of light blue sandals with narrow straps, then picked up the little blue

clutch-style purse that matched the shoes. It was time to
find out if she'd made the most idiotic and possibly dangerous mistake of her life by agreeing to have dinner outside the hotel with a total stranger. If she didn't return
that night and ended up dead, no one would ever know
who murdered her.

Partway to the door, she had an idea and turned back.
From her green canvas tote bag, she dug out the pen and
tablet she'd used earlier and tore off a fresh sheet of
paper. On it, she wrote in large letters, "I've gone out to
dinner with a man who says his name is Mitchell Wyatt.
I met him this afternoon in the Sandbar when I spilled a
Bloody Mary on his shirt. The waiter can give you his description." Satisfied, she propped the note on the living
room telephone, where it would be easily spotted by the
police if they were investigating her disappearance. Once
they read her note, they'd surely check with the waiters
at the Sandbar, and one or more of them would be able
to give a good description of her abductor.

At the door to her suite, Kate paused again and
glanced over her shoulder at the terrace door. Max had
moved off the terrace into the grass, and was poised to
run. Evidently, he was too wily to hang around on her
terrace if she left, and Kate was glad of that. She assumed
he'd head for the safety of the trees and the company of
his canine friends, as he usually did, but when she was
only a few steps away from the white stucco villa that
housed her suite, the brown dog bounded around the
building and trotted straight to her side. Kate stopped
worriedly and he sat. "You're getting way too daring,"
she warned him sternly. "The groundskeepers are on the
lookout for you, and I can't protect you if I'm not here."
Pointing to the woods, she ordered, "Go!"

He glanced in the direction she pointed, then back at
her.

"I know you understand me," Kate told him firmly,

"because people are always chasing you off and telling you to go away, and then you do it. Now, I mean it." She patted his head because she couldn't help herself; then she pointed to the line of trees and ordered sharply, "Go away!"

He stood up slowly.

"Go on—go away!" Kate said sharply, and clapped her hands for emphasis; then she turned her back on him and walked purposefully down the path to the hotel's main entrance. From the corner of her eye she watched him running toward the trees, but angling in the same direction she was headed. He was so large and so agile that he covered an amazing amount of ground in an effortless, loping canter, she noted admiringly, but if he intended to try to meet her outside the front of the hotel, he'd get into trouble for being there. She thought of the way he'd leaned his body against her and closed his eyes a little while ago when she petted him, and she felt like a cruel witch for running him off just a few minutes later.

Chapter Six

"GOOD EVENING, MISS," THE DOORMAN SAID WHEN KATE walked past the lobby of the hotel's main building a few minutes before eight. Festive torches lit up the entrance and lined both sides of the long driveway. Couples were arriving and departing in a steady stream, some dressed for dinner at the hotel, others wearing shorts and heading for more casual island nightspots. "May I get you a taxi?"

"No, thank you." Kate looked down the line of waiting vehicles. Most were red or white compact rental cars, she noticed idly; then she remembered reading that Volkswagen bugs were the preferred choice of serial killers. If Wyatt was driving one of those, she would not get into it, she decided. Rather than going into the lobby and waiting there, she wandered slowly down a sidewalk bordered with giant bushes on her left and the hotel's main driveway on her right. As she neared the end of the bushes, she saw a black convertible with its top down turn into the drive, but a sudden outburst of angry male shouts from the other side of the bushes filled her with foreboding and made her quicken her pace in their direction.

Two bellboys trotted past her, apparently summoned by the shouting. Kate heard one of them say the word *dog,* and she broke into a run just as Mitchell Wyatt brought the convertible to an abrupt stop at the curb beside her. She saw the surprised look on his face as she raced past his car, but she didn't have time to stop and explain.

Reaching the end of the bushes, Kate came to a halt beside the bellmen, and her fear quickly turned to reluctant amusement. Two angry, shouting gardeners were chasing Max in circles and waving their rakes at him, but he was easily staying out of their reach.

Behind her, Mitchell Wyatt said drily, "For a moment back there I thought you were running toward my car because you were extremely eager to see me again."

Over her shoulder, Kate flashed him a distracted, laughing look. "Were you flattered or frightened?"

"You ran past me before I had time to react." A moment later, he added jokingly, "If you're interested in betting on the outcome between the dog and the gardeners, I'll give you the gardeners and ten-to-one odds."

"At twenty to one, that's still a sucker bet," Kate replied with a plucky smile. He grinned at her quip, and suddenly Kate's earlier fears that he could be a violent criminal seemed nonsensical. She waited a few more moments to assure herself that Max was in no danger of actually being caught; then she turned and walked with Mitchell toward his car. "I wish they wouldn't chase him," she said. "One of the maids told me that several of the local islands have problems with packs of dogs roaming around, but this dog isn't dangerous. He's just hungry. He isn't doing anyone any harm."

"If I understood what the bellmen were talking about just now, that dog is doing the gardens a whole lot of harm because he's so big," Mitchell said as he opened the car door for her. "And he also scares the hotel guests. Last week, he ran up to a little girl and she got hysterical."

"He's lonely," Kate said sadly, thinking of the way he'd leaned against her and blissfully closed his eyes when she petted him. As she slid onto the passenger seat, she said, "What language was the doorman speaking? A lot of the hotel staff speaks French, but that wasn't French."

"It was Dutch, and I may have gotten most of it wrong—" he said, but the screech of automobile brakes behind them made them both turn sharply, just in time to see the dog bounding across the drive between cars, followed closely by a golf cart with the two gardeners in it. The golf cart stopped safely at the curb and an arriving taxi stopped in time, but a departing taxi was accelerating on the other side of the median, and Kate screamed a warning to the dog. Max swerved at the sound of her voice and tried to run to her instead. The taxi hit him.

Kate was out of the car, running, before the taxi driver got out of his vehicle. Mitchell caught up with her and grasped her arm. "Let me take a look first," he insisted.

"I want to help," Kate cried frantically, trying to wrench free of his grasp. "Let go of my arm."

Stunned that she wanted to subject herself to what could be a gory scene, Mitchell let her go and quickened his pace to keep up with her.

When Kate rushed around the front of the taxi, her fear turned into anguish. Max's still body was lying on its side, his head against the curb, his eyes closed. Kneeling next to him, she felt frantically for a pulse at his throat. She found it and relief flooded through her. "He's alive," she said quickly, "but we need help." Lifting her head, she looked toward the bellmen and gardeners who'd gathered into a group next to the taxi driver and Mitchell. "Call a veterinarian right away," she told the hotel's employees.

One bellman looked blankly at the gardeners and then the other bellman. "A veterinarian?" he repeated as Kate began tentatively examining the bleeding cut on Max's • head.

"An animal doctor," Mitchell clarified impatiently in English, then again in Dutch.

The gardeners were aghast at the suggestion; the bell-men were obstinate. "No, miss, no doctor," one of them said. "We'll take care of the dog, you go now and enjoy your evening." He said something in Dutch to his companions and the group of men moved forward.

Their shadow fell across Kate just as she realized how they were likely to "take care of" a large, destructive, unconscious animal that was an annoying nuisance to adult hotel guests and a terrifying threat in the minds of some of their children. "What do you intend to do?" she asked stubbornly.

"We're going to drag him off the road now so the cars can get through, and then we'll take him away."

"No!" Kate said with an adamant shake of her head. "He shouldn't be moved. The cars can go around him. He may have spinal injuries or broken bones." They didn't care one bit about any of that, she realized, so she appealed urgently to the man she'd promised to take to dinner. "We have to help him!"

Mitchell gazed at her beautiful face and realized she expected him to agree that it was imperative to save the life of a mangy, homeless, mongrel dog. And, suddenly, he did agree—although it was her eyes and not the dog that caused him to come to that conclusion. Inwardly amused by the effect those beseeching green eyes were having on him, Mitchell said solemnly, "I'll see what I can do."

The doorman smiled politely as Mitchell approached. "Good evening, Mr. Wyatt."

Mitchell assumed the doorman would have witnessed the scene in the driveway, so he ignored the greeting, refrained from giving explanations, and tackled the problem: "The dog is badly injured. Where's the nearest animal doctor?"

"There's one here on Anguilla, but he will be closed by now." As proof that it was quite late, he glanced meaningfully at the setting sun.

Having already anticipated that that would be his answer, Mitchell strode past him into the lobby and headed for the front desk, where two couples were waiting to check in and another man was asking for directions. When he was halfway across the lobby, the manager emerged from a side door, saw Mitchell, and rushed forward to greet him. "Mr. Wyatt!" he exclaimed delightedly.

Mitchell reached into his pocket.

"I didn't realize you'd booked reservations with us," the manager said, holding out his hand for a handshake. "I've been busy with our new assistant manager because he'll be in charge for the next week. I have to make an emergency trip to the States tomorrow, and he's quite overwhelmed, I'm afraid."

Mitchell clasped the manager's outstretched hand and slipped a $100 bill into his palm. "I'm glad you're still here tonight, Maurice, because there's been an automobile accident in the hotel driveway that requires your special attention."

"Oh, no! Is anyone hurt?"

"Yes."

"One of our guests?"

"No, one of your stray dogs," Mitchell said, already striding toward the telephone on the front desk with Maurice rushing along beside him. "I need an ambulance and a physician here immediately."

"You . . . you want me to send for an ambulance and a physician because a stray dog has been injured out there?"

In reply, Mitchell picked up the telephone and held the receiver toward the flustered manager. "I want them to come as fast as they possibly can. I'm *extremely fond* of this particular dog."

The manager took the receiver, pressed one button on the telephone, and hesitated. "They'll refuse to treat a dog."

"Appeal to their humane instincts," Mitchell said drily as he withdrew cash from his pants pocket and began peeling off large bills to cover whatever inducement the ambulance driver and physician demanded before they'd make the trip.

The manager watched him a moment, then quickly dialed the rest of the ambulance's phone number.

Mitchell stayed until that call and the one to the physician were both successfully completed; then he left the "inducement money" with the manager to dole out to the recipients.

Kate Donovan was in clear view across the driveway when he emerged from the hotel. The taxi driver had left in his taxi, the bellmen and gardeners had dispersed, and she sat alone on the grass, in the median beside the curb next to the dog, with her legs curled beneath her. Captured in the glow of torchlight, with her red hair a silken mantle across her shoulders and her hand gently stroking the injured dog, she looked ethereal.

She looked up as Mitchell neared, searching his face for a clue as to what he'd accomplished.

"Help is on the way," he promised, crouching on his heels beside her. "How's the patient?"

She shifted her attention to the dog as she answered, her fingers gently stroking the animal's shoulder. "His breathing seems a little stronger and more regular. I can't feel any broken bones, and his cuts aren't deep, but he may be hemorrhaging internally. He started to come around a few minutes ago, or at least I thought he did." She fell silent, and Mitchell said nothing more because he was listening for a particular sound. He heard it very soon—a siren growing louder and louder.

Kate didn't notice the siren because she felt a slight

twitch of muscles beneath her fingertips and suddenly Max opened his eyes. "There you are!" she said joyously. "Stay quiet," she warned quickly, pressing him down with both hands when he made a feeble effort to roll onto his stomach. "Help is on the way," she promised him. Without looking up, she asked Mitchell, "What sort of help is coming?"

Her question was almost drowned out by a vehicle roaring up the driveway and screeching to a halt in front of the hotel.

"That sort of help," Mitchell replied, standing up.

Kate leaned forward and looked around his legs; then she looked up at him in laughing disbelief and unabashed admiration. "You called an *ambulance?*"

She would have said more, but Mitchell was already striding off toward the ambulance and the dazed dog was getting agitated, thrashing around in a feeble effort to roll to his feet. Soothing Max with her voice and hands, she watched two men jump out of the ambulance while a dark green car came racing up the driveway and lurched to a stop behind them. The car was still rocking when the driver flung open his door and got out, carrying a large black bag.

He was a physician, Kate knew at once, but her delight was doused by her fear that the doctor and ambulance drivers would all get back in their vehicles and leave as soon as Mitchell told them who their patient really was. Tensely, she watched Mitchell gesture toward the dog she was holding down.

Kate held her breath.

The doctor turned and started walking toward her. The ambulance drivers rushed to the back of their van and pulled out a stretcher.

Amazement and optimism soared through Kate, and she whispered to the dog, "I think we're in very good hands, Max." She was positive of it when the physician crouched down beside her, looked at the nervous, wary dog and opened his black bag. "Our local vet is on vacation, but I phoned a veterinarian friend of mine in St. Maarten before I left, and I brought along some things he recommended. Now then," he said calmly, "dogs usually like me. Let's hope this one does, too, because I don't want to sedate him just yet. Head injuries," he continued as he slowly reached out toward the dog, "can be—"

A low, throaty snarl began in the dog's throat and his lips curled back over white fangs.

The physician yanked his hand back. "Wounded animals often attack anyone who comes too close," he informed Kate; then he reached toward the dog again, this time cautiously, inches at a time. "But this fellow is willing to let you touch him, so he ought to let me do it. He's actually a little afraid of me . . . and all that snarling is really just . . . a bluff."

"No, I don't think it—" Kate's warning was drowned out by the physician's yelp of pain.

Chapter Seven

"*I* THINK THE DOG IS GOING TO BE FINE," THE PHYSICIAN told Kate and Mitchell as he looked around for his black bag.

The ambulance drivers had left earlier, after settling the dog on the floor near the coffee table in the main room. "He'll sleep through the night, assuming I gave him the right dosage. Tomorrow, you should take him over to St. Maarten and let a vet there have a look at him and take some X-rays of his skull and shoulder."

"I can't thank you enough," Kate said sincerely, "and I'm terribly sorry about your arm."

"The bite isn't extremely deep, but it is rather painful," he replied stiffly while collecting bandages and antiseptic from the table near the terrace doors. "And of course now there's the question of rabies to consider."

Kate stifled a smile that was part anxiety and part mortification. "You did say that whoever you spoke to at the hospital just now told you there hasn't been a case of rabies reported on the island in years?"

"Yes. However, it's imperative that you keep that animal with you until you leave. After that, I'll take care of him. I wish you would let me take him with me now."

"I want to look after him myself while I'm here," Kate said. She had a feeling the physician would prefer to euthanize Max to find out immediately if he had rabies, rather than wait out a ten-day quarantine period to see if Max developed symptoms.

"If he shows any symptoms of rabies while he's with you, I need to know about it immediately so that I can be treated. Agreed?"

"Absolutely," Kate said, and nodded for emphasis.

"And you understand clearly what those symptoms are?"

"I wrote them down right here," Kate said, holding up the tablet.

"If this dog were to disappear before ten days from now," the doctor lectured, "I would have to undergo treatment for rabies, whether he actually has rabies or not."

Mitchell had heard enough about this highly unlikely eventuality that didn't need to be addressed unless it became an unlikely reality. The dog had been so weak and disoriented that his bite had barely broken the physician's skin, but the man had howled in pain and bandaged his arm as if a major artery had been severed. "We understand perfectly," Mitchell said smoothly, and ushered the physician to the door. "We'll keep him on a leash when he goes outside," he added, and swept the door open.

In the doorway, the doctor hesitated, and turned back around. "Do you *have* a leash?"

"I'll get one in the morning."

The man still balked. "You'll do it *first thing* in the morning?"

"At the crack of dawn," Mitchell averred, and, putting his hand lightly on the other man's elbow, he turned him around and propelled him unceremoniously out the door.

Kate watched that maneuver from the other side of the room, amused and impressed by Mitchell's blasé sangfroid and his swift efficiency in times of stress. In the few hours she'd known him, she'd criticized him soundly—and unjustly—for the Bloody Mary; dumped a drink on his shirt; reneged on the nice dinner she owed him; and involved him instead in a dramatic canine-rescue effort. He'd handled all of that imperturbably—and very, very graciously. An hour ago she'd imagined he might be a murderer; now she regarded him as a friend and ally.

Kate's cordial feelings for him were evident in her warm smile as she said, "I still owe you dinner. I could call room service and we could eat out on the terrace, if you like." Since Evan planned to arrive the next evening, Kate suggested the only other alternative she could offer. "Or would you rather forget about dinner and let me pay for your shirt instead?" She wondered if Mitchell would notice that she'd limited him to only those two choices, but his reaction was so nonchalant that she decided he either didn't notice or didn't care.

"Dinner here will be fine," Mitchell replied. "You owe me a meal," he added mildly, "and I always collect on debts that are owed to me." She was obviously expecting a boyfriend to arrive the next day, he realized, or else she'd have offered an explanation for not being able to have dinner with him some other night.

Kate folded her arms loosely across her chest and regarded him with amusement. "Do you really?"

"Always," he replied, reaching for the *Hotel Services* folder on the desk.

"Then how much do I owe you for the physician and ambulance?"

"Nothing," Mitchell said, flipping to the Room Service section of the handbook.

"Didn't you offer them money so that they'd agree to come out here and treat a dog?"

"I appealed to their humane instincts."

"I see," Kate replied, pretending she believed his

story. "And is that why they got here so fast, too? I mean, they were here less than ten minutes after you walked into the lobby."

Mitchell glanced at her from the corner of his eye. She was watching him with a knowing little smile, and he had a sudden, impossibly premature impulse to wrap her in his arms and cover that tantalizing mouth with his. That thought made a smile tug at the corner of his own lips as he shrugged and said, "They got here quickly because it's a very small island."

"And also because you promised them a *very big* tip?"

Trying to ignore the impulse to laugh, Mitchell focused on the menu. "What would you like for dinner?"

Kate named the same delicious meal she'd ordered the night before. "I think I'll have the sea scallops and a prawn and avocado salad," she said, bending down to check on the sleeping dog.

"Would you like me to phone room service?" he asked.

"Yes, please," Kate said over her shoulder. "Order anything you like. Order *everything* you like," she joked, imagining the enormous tip he must have given to entice the ambulance drivers and a physician to race at top speed to the rescue of an injured stray dog.

Max's nose felt warm to her touch, and his breathing was shallow and a little fast, but the physician had told her to expect this. Behind her, she heard Mitchell pick up the telephone receiver, but a moment later he put it back in the cradle with a sharp clack. Puzzled, Kate glanced over her shoulder and saw him standing beside the phone, holding a piece of lined tablet paper in his hand, his dark brows drawn into a scowl.

A sheet of tablet paper . . . *her* tablet paper! *Her* tablet paper with the note she'd written to help the police identify him if she disappeared. "I can explain," she said, surging to her feet and walking over to him.

"I'm dying to hear it," he said coolly, and handed the note to her.

Kate reacted to the chill in his tone with an intensity that startled her. She didn't want to insult him or make him think badly of her—not now, not when she was so grateful to him and liked him so much. He hadn't sounded this curt and unfriendly when she blamed him for the Bloody Mary and dumped it on his shirt. Trying to think of the least offensive explanation she could give him, she reread what she'd written on the note.

"I've gone out to dinner with a man who says his name is Mitchell Wyatt. I met him this afternoon in the Sandbar when I spilled a Bloody Mary on his shirt. The waiter can give you his description."

Stalling for time, she laid the offensive note back on the desk. "Tonight," she began haltingly, "when I wasn't sure what I should wear to dinner, I decided to call you and ask where we were going." She paused, nervously rubbing her palms against the sides of her pants.

"Go on," he said brusquely.

"But when I phoned the hotel operator and asked him to ring your room, he said you weren't staying here. That made me . . . well . . . uneasy. Possibilities started to occur to me that I hadn't considered earlier, when I believed you were a guest here and agreed to have dinner with you."

"What possibilities?" he demanded.

Kate wanted to be evasive, but that was impossible with his rapier-blue gaze pinning hers. "There were certain things about you that made me think you might be a—" She almost choked on the word. "—gigolo."

His scowl deepened. "A *what*?"

"Please, just try to look at it from my perspective. You were hanging around a very expensive hotel that you're not staying at, you're outrageously handsome, you're incredibly smooth, you're totally charming, and you're a *very* fast worker—within two or three minutes of meeting me, you asked *me* to take *you* to dinner." His expression hadn't softened a bit, which told Kate two things: He wasn't flattered by her complimentary remarks about his looks and charm; and he was waiting for an explanation as to why she'd instructed whoever read the note to get a description of him from the waiter.

Raking her hair back off her forehead, she admitted the entire embarrassing truth. "I was upset at the possibility that I'd been tricked into having dinner with a gigolo, but then I realized you could be a lot worse than a gigolo."

"I can't think of anything more repulsive than being a gigolo."

"No, but you could have been worse than 'repulsive.' You could have been dangerous. You could have been a murderer who picks up single women in hotels in the islands, kills them, and buries their bodies in the sand . . . or . . . something like that. . . ." Kate trailed off, feeling like a colossal idiot.

"So you left a note for the authorities to find in case you disappeared?"

Kate nodded miserably.

"Because you wanted to be sure I wouldn't get away with *your* murder?"

Kate was so mortified and so annoyed with herself that she missed the thread of amusement in his deep voice. Unable to hold his gaze, she looked toward Max. "It didn't seem quite so idiotic then as it does now."

For the second time in a few minutes, Mitchell had to fight down the impulse to haul her into his arms. To distract himself, he turned away and picked up the telephone.

Startled by his abrupt move, Kate said, "Who are you calling?"

"Room service," he said mildly.

"In that case," Kate said contritely, "you may change my order to a large plate of humble pie."

Mitchell was still grinning when the room service operator answered his call.

Chapter Eight

*L*EAVING MITCHELL TO DEAL WITH ROOM SERVICE, KATE went into the suite's luxurious bathroom/dressing room to clean up. Twisting around in front of the full-length mirrors that lined one wall, she brushed at the bits of grass and dirt stuck to the back of her pants, but there was a damp stain on one side that was very noticeable.

Conscious of the passage of time, she walked over to the closet and considered her choices. Holly had helped her pack because the night before Kate was to leave for Anguilla, she'd gotten one of the fierce headaches that had been plaguing her since her father's death. Holly had chosen outfits that were suitable for a romantic holiday with Evan, and none of them seemed completely appropriate for this particular occasion.

Kate decided on a pair of cream silk lounging pants with a wide band of gold Moroccan embroidery at the hem and a delicate cream silk camisole with a straight neckline and narrow spaghetti straps that tied into bows on her shoulders. The outfit seemed a little too softly feminine to suit dining alone in a hotel room with a strange man, but it covered everything except her arms, and the neckline was perfectly modest, so it seemed like the best selection among the clothes she had with her.

She changed quickly and slipped on a pair of gold sandals. At the mirror above the hammered brass sink, she paused just long enough to run a brush through her hair and put on fresh lipstick. She was absolutely determined to atone for everything she'd put Mitchell through by making the rest of his evening as enjoyable as she possibly could, and that meant not keeping him waiting alone any longer than necessary.

The telephone began ringing while Kate was applying lipstick, and she reached automatically for the extension hanging on the wall beside the mirror; then she hesitated and let it continue ringing. Evan phoned every night at about this time, and this call was undoubtedly from him. If he was calling to explain that he couldn't make it to Anguilla the next afternoon, then he'd probably be relieved to leave that message on the hotel's voice mail for her. If he was calling to confirm that he was going to arrive as planned, she could listen to his message later. Right now, she had a rather urgent debt to repay to the man in the next room, and the only way she could repay it was by being the best hostess she could possibly be. That was one thing Kate knew how to do rather well, having grown up in the restaurant business.

She took a last glance at herself in the mirrored wall behind her; then she turned off the lights and left the room.

She expected to find Mitchell outside on the terrace enjoying the balmy, moonlit night, but instead he was standing beside the sleeping dog with his hands in his pockets and a bemused smile on his face. She stopped in the doorway, arrested by his expression, trying to guess what he was thinking, but then something else struck her: He looked as immaculately groomed as he had when he first arrived at the hotel that evening. His thick black hair was beautifully cut and styled—and completely unmussed; his snowy white shirt was as unwrinkled as his tan trousers, and his brown loafers were gleaming. He'd draped the navy blazer he'd been wearing earlier over a chair, and he'd folded his shirtsleeves back onto his forearms, but other than those two alterations in his appearance, he certainly didn't look as if he'd helped load and unload a large, unconscious dog on and off a stretcher.

Earlier that day, in the dim light of the restaurant, she'd been too mortified at having doused him with the Bloody Mary to do more than form an impression that he was handsome. Tonight, she'd been too busy with Max to actually study the man who'd gallantly responded to her appeal for help, but now she realized Mitchell Wyatt wasn't merely handsome, he was absolutely *gorgeous*. He was about six feet three inches tall, with extremely broad shoulders, a muscular chest, and narrow hips. His face was tanned, his jaw square, his brows thick and straight above dark-lashed eyes that she already knew were a deep indigo blue.

Normally Kate was unimpressed with exceptionally handsome men, because they were usually either vain and shallow or subtly effeminate, but this man was thoughtful and kind, and he was thoroughly male. Standing perfectly still in the living room, with his hands in his pockets, he positively emanated masculine vitality and sex appeal.

All of those attributes, combined with his wry sense of humor and blasé sophistication, made Kate decide that he was, in every respect, the most attractive man she'd ever encountered. Glamorous, sophisticated women undoubtedly dropped into his arms when he crooked his finger at them, Kate thought with an inner smile. She, however, was neither glamorous nor very worldly, and for once she was rather glad of those shortcomings, because he wouldn't be tempted to turn the full force of his charm and good looks on someone like her. The evening had already been nerve-racking enough without having to fend off halfhearted advances from a lethally attractive male. Belatedly realizing she'd been studying him for far too long, Kate stepped forward and announced her presence by saying the first thing that came to mind. "I'm sorry I took so long."

He turned at the sound of her voice; but instead of replying, he looked her over slowly from head to toe with a smile of frank masculine appreciation that was so flattering and unnerving to Kate that she had to concentrate on walking without tripping over her own feet. As his gaze traveled back up to her head, she braced for a suggestive compliment.

"Your curls are all tamed down tonight," he observed mildly. Kate's nervous misgivings evaporated in a relieved laugh.

"I tortured them into submission with a flat iron and blow dryer," she said, stopping beside him. "How's the patient doing?" she asked, bending down to lightly scratch behind Max's ears. Her fingertips encountered a light dusting of a powdery substance that hadn't been on him before, and she noticed more of it on the white carpet around where he lay. Kate glanced uncertainly over her shoulder and held up her powdery fingertips. "Do you know what this is?"

"Flea powder. I had housekeeping bring some in while you were changing clothes."

"Why do you think he has fleas?"

"Because they were dragging him toward the door while I watched," he said drily, as he grasped her arm, urging her up. "I'd stand back until that stuff does the job or you'll be awake all night scratching behind your own ears."

Surprised and touched to discover he'd gallantly taken care of yet another problem for her, Kate straightened and looked searchingly at his handsome, tanned face. She'd been uneasy about him simply because he was outrageously good-looking, and she had an impossible impulse to tell him that, and then to apologize for it. Instead, she said with soft sincerity, "You're very sweet."

Mitchell's reaction was sexual, not sweet; yet as he gazed into her luminous green eyes, he found himself wondering if there was actually some truth to the axiom that the eyes were a window into the soul. His attention shifted almost immediately to her full lips, but just as he started to act on his impulse to kiss them, the silence was shattered by musicians down at the beach launching into a rousing steel-drum rendition of "Jamaica Farewell."

Kate stepped back immediately, smiled, and tipped her head in the direction of the music coming in through the open terrace doors. "I love calypso music. Did you arrange for that, too, when you arranged for the flea powder?"

Her recovery was so smooth that Mitchell would have actually believed she hadn't realized what was about to happen between them a moment before, except that her skin was too fair to conceal the telltale pink tinge on her high cheekbones. Her pretense struck him as entertaining but humorously unnecessary. They were both adults, they were obviously attracted to each other; therefore, they were going to end up in that inviting king-size bed in the alcove later on. Mitchell saw no reason for either of them to pretend the situation was otherwise. "If I'd arranged for that music," he assured her drolly, "I'd have told them I prefer a much slower tempo—at first."

Kate's eyes widened at the double meaning she read into that remark. Earlier, she'd accused him of being a "fast worker," but even if he was, he surely couldn't intend to make flying leaps from a discussion of fleas to an aborted kiss to a blatant sexual innuendo, without pausing in between.

Or could he?

Kate decided her imagination was running wild and reminded herself that her goal tonight was to be a good hostess. "Let me fix you something to drink," she said with a quick smile as she turned toward the suite's well-stocked bar. "What would you like?"

"Vodka and tonic if you have ice. Otherwise, plain vodka."

"I'm sure we have ice," she said, and confirmed it when she lifted the top off the ice bucket. "The staff here looks after everything. They even give you chilled towels while you're at the beach." From the refrigerator, she removed a miniature bottle of vodka, some tonic, and a fresh lime.

"You had a phone call while you were changing clothes," he said.

Kate glanced at the red message light flashing accusingly on the desk phone and opened the bottle of vodka. "I know. I'll listen to the message later."

"When are you expecting him to arrive?"

His casual, conversational tone was as startling to Kate as his astute conclusion that she was expecting a man, but somehow she managed to glance over her shoulder, smile, and answer his question as casually as he'd asked it. "Tomorrow evening, probably." As she added ice to his glass, she waited for Mitchell to comment, and when he didn't, she felt compelled to fill the awkward silence with added information about a boyfriend she didn't really want to discuss with him in the first place. "He's trying an important case in court during the day and working to negotiate a settlement between the parties at night. He flew down here with me four days ago, but the judge decided not to continue the case again, and so he had to turn around and fly right back home. He thought the case would be over quickly, but it's been dragging on and on."

As Kate finished speaking, she realized the additional remarks about Evan were probably a good idea. She'd not only confirmed to Mitchell that she had a boyfriend, she'd provided enough additional facts about him to bring him into sharp focus right there in the room, where he would now be a barrier between Mitchell and her. If Mitchell's earlier comment about the "tempo" he preferred had actually been a sexual reference, Kate knew there would be no more of those to deal with now. He wouldn't try to kiss her again, either, and so she wouldn't be foolishly tempted to let him. No matter how likeable he seemed or how attractive he was, the fact remained that Mitchell was a total stranger and they were alone together in a hotel room. "We've been going together for years," she threw in for good measure, to further eliminate any lingering chances of overtures and temptations.

Kate poured the vodka over the ice in Mitchell's glass, serenely certain that everything she'd said about Evan would ensure that the lovely evening ahead would be completely free of any more unnerving sensual undercurrents.

Mitchell watched her, completely satisfied that the lawyer-boyfriend was no obstacle whatsoever to their going to bed together tonight. It was apparent to him that Kate didn't imagine she was in love with the lawyer; women who believed they were in love gave off unmistakable signals, particularly when they spoke of their lovers, and Kate Donovan wasn't giving off any of those signals.

The boyfriend wasn't even likely to be an annoying inconvenience if Kate and he also decided they wanted to enjoy each other for an additional day or two. In Mitchell's experience, lawyers who predicted that they could successfully conclude "an important case" in a few days were either deluding themselves or trying to delude someone else—in this instance, Kate.

In his mind, Mitchell envisioned a prosperous, middle-aged lawyer who'd managed to dazzle Kate years before, not long after she was out of college. He could have confirmed his suspicions with a few questions, but it was disadvantageous to the mood of the evening to further discuss another lover with her. Besides that, Mitchell felt it would be in bad taste for him to pry into the absent man's personal life at a time like this. Under Mitchell's personal code of European sexual ethics, sleeping with another man's lover was perfectly allowable if the lady was willing. However, discussing the absent man with her was a needless and tasteless invasion of the man's privacy. It was ungentlemanly. And Mitchell abhorred ungentlemanly behavior.

Unaware that her discussion of Evan had accomplished exactly the opposite of what she thought, Kate added a slice of fresh lime to the vodka and tonic, and took Mitchell the finished drink. When she held the glass out, he made a silent joke about the Bloody Mary she'd spilled on him earlier by stepping back and eyeing her warily before he cautiously took the glass from her outstretched hand. Of all his attractive qualities, Kate decided she liked his disarming sense of humor best—undoubtedly because it was easier to forget his good looks and relax when they were joking with each other. Smiling good-naturedly at his gibe about the Bloody Mary, she asked the first question that came to mind. "Where did you learn to speak Dutch?"

"In Holland," he replied, and took a sip of his drink.

"When were you there?"

"When I was eleven or twelve."

He seemed a little unforthcoming on the subject, but Kate stuck with it anyway, because it seemed like a good conversational starting place. "Why were you in Holland at that age?"

"I went to school with a boy whose family lived in Amsterdam, and he invited me to spend a couple of summers there with his family."

"I've never been to Europe," Kate said as she turned

away and headed back toward the liquor cabinet, "but Amsterdam is one of the places I'd especially love to see. Do you know what I think of whenever someone mentions Amsterdam?"

"No," Mitchell replied, studying the easy, unselfconscious grace of her walk and the way her dark red hair tumbled in a gleaming waterfall of waves and curls halfway down her back. "What do you think of when someone mentions Amsterdam?"

She shot him a rueful laughing look over her shoulder as she crouched down in front of the refrigerator. "The same two things you do, I'm sure."

"Marijuana and prostitutes?" Mitchell speculated with certainty.

She stood up with a bottle of Perrier in her hand, but instead of saying he was correct, she fumbled with the top on the bottle for several seconds, trying to get it off. Intending to offer to help her, Mitchell started forward; then he realized her shoulders were shaking with laughter and he stopped in surprise. "Whenever anyone thinks of Amsterdam," he stated with certainty, "the first two things that come to mind are restaurants with marijuana on the menus and prostitutes standing in storefront windows."

She laughed harder and she shook her head vigorously from side to side, causing her hair to shift across her ivory shoulders like a wavy crimson curtain. "That is *not* what most people think of," she managed unsteadily after she finally got the top off the Perrier and poured some of the sparkling liquid into her glass.

"What else is there to think of?" he asked.

She turned fully toward him then, her face alight with laughter. "Tulips!" she informed him, picking up her glass and crossing the room to him. "And canals. Everyone thinks of *tulips* and *canals* when they think of Amsterdam."

"Not *everyone*, obviously," Mitchell pointed out.

"Apparently not," she agreed, but she refused to concede the issue based solely on his opinion. "However, I would like to point out that when you see pictures of Amsterdam on calendars, you see fields of bright tulips and beautiful canals. You do *not* see photographs of menus with marijuana as an appetizer, nor prostitutes standing in store windows."

"The marijuana choices are listed on a separate menu," Mitchell corrected, deriving the almost-forgotten, boyish pleasure of an innocent, lively debate over meaningless trivialities with an impertinent girl who attracted, amused, and opposed him. "They aren't listed under *Appetizers*."

"They should be," Kate informed him, automatically thinking like a restaurant owner. "Marijuana is an appetite stimulant."

"Are you speaking from personal experience?" Mitchell inquired with a knowing grin.

"I have a college degree," she told him breezily, and *informatively*, he noted.

To stop him from pressing her further, Kate held up her hand and laughingly put an end to the subject. "Do not say another word about Amsterdam, or you'll spoil my entire image of the place before I get a chance to see it. You've already replaced my blissful thoughts of red and yellow tulip fields with images of restaurants reeking of pot, and my visions of lovely canals are now visions of sleazy alleys with prostitutes for sale. Besides," she added as someone knocked on the door, "our dinner is here."

Mitchell heard the relief in her voice and realized she'd been genuinely uneasy about a discussion of illicit sex and drugs with him. That puzzled and surprised him, but then virtually everything she did either confused or intrigued him. In the ensuing minutes, he watched her usher in the waiters and supervise the process of transferring the elaborate meals onto a table on the terrace as if she'd been presiding over the process in fine houses and hotels her entire life. Less than two hours ago, she'd knelt beside an injured stray dog and looked at Mitchell with tears of pleading in her eyes, and a few minutes after that, he'd found her sitting on a curb next to a busy driveway, serenely unconcerned with her comfort, or her clothes, or the reactions of the other hotel guests. A few moments later, when he told her help was on the way, she'd lifted her face to his and smiled at him with melting gratitude.

She genuinely liked him, and she wasn't trying to hide that . . . and yet, he had the feeling he made her nervous. She was vividly, almost exotically, lovely . . . but when he'd admired the way she looked in those flowing silk pants and a little white top held up by gossamer strings tied into bows at her shoulders, she'd seemed so self-conscious that he'd remarked on her hair, instead. A few minutes ago, they'd been on the verge of a kiss . . . but when the music interrupted, she backed away and tried to pretend nothing had happened.

In view of all that, Mitchell began to wonder if he'd been wrong about her feelings for the lawyer. Perhaps the reason she'd stayed with him for years was that she was emotionally committed to him—or at least determined not to stray. Mitchell fervently hoped neither was true, because she was attracted to him, and he was very attracted to her.

In fact, he was *extremely* attracted to her, he admitted to himself as he watched the waiters depart.

Behind him from the terrace, she said lightly, "Dinner is served."

Mitchell turned and saw her standing in candlelight beside the table, the island breeze ruffling her fiery mantle of red hair around her shoulders.

Wildly attracted.

As he neared the table, she reached up and brushed a wayward strand of hair off her soft cheek. He watched the unconsciously feminine gesture as if he'd never seen hundreds of other women do it.

"Please sit down," she said graciously when he started around the table to pull out her chair for her. "You've already had to wait too long for this meal."

Kate's earlier nervousness had vanished. She was on familiar territory now, standing beside an elegant, candlelit table and hovering near a special guest whom she wanted to make feel extremely important that evening. It was a role she could play to perfection. She'd studied under a master, and only he could do it better.

But she was never again going to see her father play this role.

Blinking back a sudden sheen of moisture in her eyes, Kate reached for the open wine bottle on a small table beside her. "May I pour you some wine?" she asked, smiling at his face through a blur of tears that blinded her to his sudden grin.

"That depends on where you're planning to pour it, and how good your aim is."

Kate's emotions veered abruptly from anguish to laughter. "I have excellent aim," she assured him, leaning toward his glass.

"All earlier evidence to the contrary," Mitchell pointed out. To Mitchell's dismay, she retaliated by smiling straight into his eyes while she poured just the right amount of red wine into his glass.

"Actually," she informed him, "I hit exactly what I was aiming for that time, too."

Before Mitchell could be sure whether she was serious, she turned away. He studied her closely as she slid into the chair across from his, her expression serenely blasé. "Are you implying that you intended to douse me with that Bloody Mary?" he asked.

"You know what they say about temperamental red-heads," Kate replied as she unfolded her napkin; then she leaned forward and looked at him as if a horrifying, but amusing, possibility had just occurred to her. "*Surely* you don't think I deliberately *dye* my hair this impossible color?"

Mitchell was dumbfounded to think she'd actually thrown a drink at him in a fit of childish, uncontrolled pique. He didn't want to believe he was wrong about her, and he didn't want to consider why it was becoming important to him that this one woman be all the things she seemed. With deceptive nonchalance, he said, "Did you really do it on purpose?"

"Do you promise not to be angry?"

He smiled good-naturedly. "No."

A startled giggle nearly escaped Kate at the vast contrast between his agreeable expression and his negative reply. "Then, will you promise never to bring the subject up again if I tell you the truth?"

Another lazy smile accompanied his answer. "No."

Kate bit her lip to keep from laughing. "At least you're honest and direct—in a misleading sort of way." Needing to avert her gaze from his, she picked up a basket of crusty rolls from the center of the table and offered it to him.

"Are *you* being honest and direct?" he inquired with amusement, taking a roll from the basket. Despite his affable attitude, Kate had a sudden, inexplicable sensation of an undercurrent. He was playing cat and mouse with her, she knew, and he was obviously a world-champion "cat," but she sensed that he wasn't actually enjoying the game. Since her goal was to repay his wonderful kindnesses by making the rest of the evening as pleasant for him as she could, she put an end to the whole charade.

Meeting his gaze, she said with quiet sincerity, "I didn't do it on purpose. I was only pretending I did in order to get even with you for teasing me twice about the Bloody Mary."

Mitchell heard her words, but the softness in her eyes and the expression on her lovely face were interfering with the pathways to his brain, and he decided it didn't matter if she'd done it on purpose. Then he realized she hadn't, and that mattered much more than he thought it should. What sort of family, he wondered, in what city, on what *planet,* had yielded up this jaunty, prim, unpredictable woman with a wayward sense of humor, a heart-stopping smile, and a fierce passion for wounded mongrel dogs?

Mitchell reached for his butter knife. "Where in the hell are you from?"

"Chicago," she said with a startled smile at his tone.

He looked up so sharply and with such narrowed disbelief that Kate felt compelled to reaffirm and amplify her answer. "Chicago," she repeated. "I was born and raised there. What about you?"

Chicago. Mitchell managed to smooth his distaste for her answer from his expression, but his guard was up. "I've never lived anywhere long enough to be 'from' there," he replied, giving her the same vague answer that had always satisfied anyone who asked. The question was perfunctory anyway, he knew. People asked because it was a convenient conversational item among strangers. People never really cared what the answer was. Unfortunately, Kate Donovan was not one of those people.

"What places did you live in when you were growing up—" she persevered, and teasingly added, "but not long enough to actually be 'from' any of them?"

"Various places in Europe," Mitchell replied, intending to immediately change the subject.

"Where do you live now?" she asked, before he could.

"Wherever my work takes me. I have apartments in

several cities in Europe and New York." His work occasionally took him to Chicago too, but he didn't want to mention that to Kate, because he wanted to avoid the inevitable discussion about whom they might know in common. There was little chance she actually knew anyone within the Wyatts' lofty social circle, but the Wyatt name was known to any Chicagoan who read a newspaper. Since Mitchell's last name was also Wyatt, there was a chance Kate would ask him if he was related to those Wyatts, and the last thing he wanted to do was admit to that relationship, let alone discuss what it actually was.

Kate waited for him to offer a clue as to what cities those apartments were in, or what his "work" was. When he didn't, she assumed he wanted to skip those specific topics. That struck her as odd. In her experience, men loved to talk about their work and achievements. She didn't want to pry into information Mitchell didn't want to offer, but she couldn't gracefully switch immediately to another topic, so she said instead, "No roots?"

"None at all." When she looked at him strangely, Mitchell said, "From the expression on your face, I gather you find that a little odd?"

"Not odd, just difficult to imagine." On the assumption that if she offered personal information freely, he might be inclined to follow suit, Kate said. "I grew up in the same Irish neighborhood I was born in. My father owned a little restaurant there, and for many years we lived in an apartment above it. At night, people in the neighborhood gathered there to eat and socialize. During the day, I went to St. Michael's grade school with kids from the same neighborhood. Later on, I went to Loyola University in the city. After I graduated, I went to work near the old neighborhood, although it had changed a lot by then."

With a feeling approaching amused disbelief, Mitchell realized that he was wildly attracted to a nice, redheaded,

Irish Catholic girl from a solid, middle-class American family. How totally atypical for him, and no wonder she seemed like such an enigma to him. "What sort of work did you go into after college?"

"I went to work for the Department of Children and Family Services as a social worker."

Mitchell bit back a bark of laughter. Actually, he was wildly attracted to a redheaded, middle-class, Irish Catholic girl with *a strong social conscience*.

"Why did you decide on social work instead of the restaurant business? I suppose you probably had enough of that business when you were growing up," he added, answering his own question.

"It wasn't exactly a restaurant. It was more of a cozy Irish pub that served a limited menu of tasty Irish dishes and sandwiches, and I loved everything about that place—especially the nights when someone played the piano and people sang Irish songs. Karaoke," she added with a smile, "has been a time-honored form of entertainment in Irish pubs for hundreds of years, only we never called it that."

Mitchell was familiar with the term *karaoke,* and intimately familiar with several pubs in Ireland, so he knew exactly what she meant. "Go on," he urged as he reached for his wineglass. "You loved the music . . . ?"

He was an attentive listener, Kate realized. Still harboring the belief that he might become a little more forthcoming about his own life if she chatted freely about hers, she did exactly that. "I loved the music, but I couldn't hear the music very well from my bedroom, and I wasn't allowed downstairs after five PM, so I used to sneak into the living room after my babysitter fell asleep, and listen to the music from there. By the time I was seven years old, I knew all the songs by heart—sad songs, revolutionary songs, bawdy songs. I didn't understand all the words, but I could pronounce them with the

Irish brogue of a native. The truth is," she confided after taking a bite of her salad, "I'd watched a lot of old musicals on television, and I wanted to become a nightclub singer and wear beautiful gowns like the women in those movies. I used to pretend our kitchen table was a grand piano, and I practiced draping myself across it while I sang into a pretend microphone— usually a broom handle."

Mitchell chuckled at the image she'd painted of herself. "Did you ever get to sing in front of an audience downstairs?"

"Oh, yes. I made my official singing debut there at seven."

"How did it go?"

The story was humorous, but it involved Kate's father, and she shifted her gaze to the garden, trying to decide if she could tell it without feeling sad. "Let's just say that— it didn't quite go the way I'd imagined," she said finally.

Mitchell was finding it difficult to pay any attention to his meal. She had been so candid before that now her winsome, hesitant expression when she thought back on her singing debut at the pub intrigued him and made him determined to pry out the details. Since courtesy demanded that he at least give her a chance to eat some of her meal, he stifled his curiosity, temporarily postponing his question.

The chef at the Island Club was world-renowned, and the prawn and avocado salad Mitchell had ordered for both of them was served with a wonderful Parmesan caper dressing. The red snapper he'd ordered for himself was sautéed to perfection and served with pine nuts and fresh asparagus, but the redhead sitting across from him was more to his liking, and he barely tasted what he ate. He waited until she'd eaten some of her salad and her main course; then he reached for his wine and said half seriously, "I have no intention of letting you ignore my question about your singing debut at the pub."

After the silence between them, the sudden sound of his rich baritone voice had an electrifying effect on Kate's senses, and her head jerked up. Trying to cover her reaction, she regarded him with what she hoped was an expression of amused hauteur. "I refuse to tell you that story until you've told *me* a story that makes *you* look ridiculous."

Instead of agreeing or giving up, he leaned back in his chair, toying with the stem of his wineglass, and eyed her in prolonged, thoughtful silence.

Kate tried to return his gaze unflinchingly, and ended up laughing and surrendering. "I give up—what *on earth* are you thinking?"

"I'm trying to decide whether to resort to bribery or coercion."

"Go for bribery," Kate advised him outrageously, because the stake was merely a story and she was positive he was going to offer a silly enticement.

"In that case, I will bring a collar and leash with me tomorrow—"

She rolled her eyes in mock horror. "Either you're a very sick man, or else you have absolutely no talent for accessorizing. Stick with neckties—"

"—And I'll help you get your Max to a vet over on St. Maarten," he continued, ignoring her gibe.

Understanding dawned and Kate's laughter faded. She looked at him, filled with gratitude and the strangest feeling that they were destined to become the best of friends—that it was somehow preordained. He returned her gaze, his blue eyes smiling warmly into hers . . . no, not warmly, Kate realized. Intimately! Hastily, she tried to divert him with humor. "That's a clever bribe. What were you going to say to coerce me?"

He quirked a thoughtful brow, a smile tugging at his lips. " 'You owe me'?" he suggested.

Kate felt like covering her face and ears to block out the sight and sound of him. Even relaxing in his chair, he exuded potent sexual vitality. When he laughed, he looked sexy. When he smiled, he looked dangerously inviting. And when he was silent and thoughtful, as he'd been just a moment before, he looked intriguing . . . and wonderful. He was so physically attractive, so witty and urbane, and so infuriatingly *likable* that she kept wanting to trust him and befriend him, even though he was probably the last man in the Caribbean who could be trusted or befriended in a hotel room, especially by someone like her. He was like a powerful, two-hundred-pound magnet, and she felt like a little paper clip, struggling against his pull but being tugged inexorably, inch by inch, across the table to him.

It was actually easier on her nervous system to distract and amuse him than it was to spend three silent seconds trying to resist him, she realized, and so she gave in and decided to tell the story.

He knew the instant she made the decision. "What did it?" he inquired with amused satisfaction. "The bribery or the coercion?"

"I'm completely impervious to bribery," Kate replied smugly, and was about to add that she was also impervious to coercion, but before she could do that, he said, "Good. I'll pick you up tomorrow morning at ten. Now, let's have the story of your singing debut at the pub."

With a sigh, Kate began the tale. "It was Saint Patrick's Day, so by seven PM the place was packed and the singing and drinking were in high gear. I knew my father was on an errand, because he'd come upstairs earlier to get his wallet, so I snuck downstairs even though the rule was that if my father wasn't on the premises, I was not allowed down there at *any* hour of the day. Our bartender knew the rule, too, but the place was so crowded, and I was so little, that nobody noticed me. At first, I just hovered on the bottom step, singing quietly to the music; but I couldn't see anything, so I moved a little farther into the room . . . and a little farther . . . and a little farther, until I ended up standing near the end of the bar. The piano was behind me and to my left, and on my right there was a middle-aged couple sitting at the bar. I didn't realize they'd been watching me doing my little sing-along, until the man leaned over and smiled and asked me what my favorite song was. I told him my favorite song was 'Danny Boy,' because my daddy's name was Daniel—" Kate reached for her wineglass to conceal her sharp, emotional reaction to the mention of the song she'd sung for her father for the last time, standing at his graveside with tears streaming down her face and mourners weeping into handkerchiefs.

"I'm not giving you much chance to eat," Mitchell apologized.

Kate ate a scallop and some rice to give herself time to compose herself, but Mitchell barely touched his food. For a tall, muscular man who should have been starving by now, he wasn't eating much, she realized.

"Any time you're ready to go on—" he prompted after a couple of minutes.

His grin was so uplifting that Kate smiled back at him and continued her story without the choking grief she'd felt moments before. "The man at the bar got up and apparently gave whoever was playing the piano some money, because the very next song was 'Danny Boy.' As soon as it started, he whisked me off the floor onto his chair and shouted to everyone to quiet down because *I* wanted to sing 'Danny Boy.' " Kate stopped again, but this time it was because she was trying not to giggle at the memory. "So there it was: my big moment. I was so nervous that I had to clasp my hands behind my back to keep my arms from shaking out of their sockets, and when I tried to sing, my voice came out a squeaky whisper."

"And that was the end of it?"

She laughed and shook her head. "Unfortunately, no."

Eager to know what happened, Mitchell tried to guess. "You finally managed to sing louder and you were bad at it?" His smile faded as he realized how cruel a room full of drunks might have been to a child in those circumstances, but Kate shook her head no, and said with mock affront, "I like *my* ending to the story better than yours."

"Then what's your ending?"

"Actually, once I finally found my voice, I was okay. Good enough, anyway, that everyone got quiet while I sang, and they stayed quiet for a few moments after I finished, and then the clapping started."

"A lot of clapping?"

"*Lots* of clapping. I naturally took that to be encouragement, so I sang another song for them—something more uplifting that I felt would also demonstrate my mastery of the Irish brogue. While I sang that one, someone gave me a green leprechaun's hat and a fake shillelagh. And that," she finished as she started to laugh helplessly, "is when my father walked in. Oh, my God . . ."

"He was upset," Mitchell speculated, thinking her father shouldn't have been all that upset, since she was obviously giving quite an excellent performance.

"He was a little upset," she confirmed, laughing harder. "You see, by the time he arrived, I was no longer standing on a chair, I was standing on the bar—so everyone could see me. I was wearing my green hat, strutting with my fake shillelagh, and singing a rousing rendition of 'Come All Ye Tramps and Hawkers' at the top of my lungs. In case you haven't guessed, a few of the lyrics are a little bawdy, and I was right in the middle of that part when my father's face appeared in front of mine."

"What happened?"

"My voice dried up in mid-word."

"What did your father do?"

"He whisked me off the bar, and the next day he asked my uncle to use his influence to get me into St. Michael's immediately so the nuns there could . . . um . . . have a hand in my upbringing. Until then I'd been going to the public school because it was much closer, and taking catechism classes at St. Mike's on Saturdays."

Lifting his wineglass to his lips, Mitchell said, "And that ended your singing career?"

"Pretty much. From then on, my singing was limited to the church choir."

At the word *choir,* Mitchell choked on his wine. "Thank God the nuns didn't lure you into their convent and turn you into one of them," he said aloud, without actually meaning to express the thought.

She chuckled. "*Lure* me into their convent? They wouldn't have *let* me in if I begged them to! There wasn't a rule that I didn't try to bend or twist, and I always, always got caught, just like I got caught singing on the bar by my father. I spent the next years staying after school for one offense or another, and I practically wore out the school's chalkboards writing things like 'I will obey the school rules' and 'I will not be disrespectful' one hundred times each. The nuns would have despaired of me completely if I hadn't sounded so 'angelic' when I sang in the choir."

Mitchell was still struggling to associate the image of an angelic choir girl with the alluring redhead sitting across from him when she added lightly, "Actually, it was probably my uncle's influence and not my singing ability that kept me from being expelled from the fourth grade."

"Your uncle contributed a lot of money to the church?"

"No, he contributed a lot of his time. My uncle was the parish priest."

Mitchell stared at her in comic horror.

Tipping her head to the side, Kate studied his expression. "You look dismayed about that."

"I'm less dismayed than I'd be if you told me you're a nun."

"Why would you be dismayed if I were a nun?"

The answer should have been obvious. Since it wasn't, Mitchell decided it needed to be. He let his gaze drift purposefully to her inviting full lips, her breasts, then back up to her eyes. "Why do you suppose, Kate?"

His meaning was inescapable, and Kate felt a sensual jolt that was centralized in the pit of her stomach, then streaked like hot lightning down her legs to the tips of her toes. Her body's reaction was so strong and so unexpected that she choked back a nervous laugh and stood up. Trying to look composed and amused, she said sternly, "Are you always so blunt?"

"I want to be sure we're on the same page."

"I'm not sure we're even in the same *library*," Kate said, nervously raking her hair back off her forehead. His gaze shifted from her face to her hand and then drifted admiringly over her hair in a way that was so flattering and so seductive that her hand stilled and she felt a flush heat her cheeks.

He noticed that, too, and smiled. "I think we are."

Trying to dodge the issue entirely, Kate gave him a look of tolerant amusement. "You're certainly sure of yourself."

"Not necessarily," he replied imperturbably. "I may simply have deluded myself into thinking you're almost as attracted to me as I am to you. If so, I'm guilty of wishful thinking, not overconfidence."

As if he hadn't already wreaked enough havoc on her, he lifted his brows and said, "Those are the possibilities. Take your choice."

You're on the wrong page . . . we're not even in the same library . . . you're deluding yourself. That's all she needed to say, Kate realized, but with his piercing blue eyes and his knowing smile leveled on her, she wasn't certain she could be convincing, not when she wasn't completely sure herself anymore. Trying to wriggle out of a perilous position, she ignored his instruction to make a choice and laughingly said, "I hate multiple-choice questions. They're so . . . limiting." Before he could say another word or lure her into another trap—or onto his lap—Kate said hastily, "I want to check on Max and get some more ice for us. Please go on with your meal." With that, she turned and fled into the suite.

Instead of stopping at the ice bucket, Kate walked straight into the bathroom, flipped on the lights, and closed the door. Bracing her palms on the vanity's intricate tiles, she let her head fall forward and drew a long, steadying breath, trying to recover her equilibrium. But what she thought about was how it would feel to be kissed by Mitchell and held in his arms.

Frustrated with the direction of her thoughts, Kate lifted her head and scowled at herself in the mirror. How could she even contemplate a brief, meaningless sexual liaison with a perfect stranger tonight when she'd never done anything like that before? The answer was obvious: The stranger waiting for her on the terrace was like a fantasy . . . he was witty, charming, urbane, thoughtful, kind, and—oh, yes—breathtakingly handsome and too sexy. Even the setting was idyllic—they were on a tropical island, dining in the moonlight, surrounded with the heady fragrance of frangipani blossoms and the stirring beat of steel drums playing calypso music on the beach.

The timing was flawless, too, Kate realized, because she was about to end her long relationship with Evan.

All those things were nudging her straight into Mitchell Wyatt's arms, tempting her to make what would probably be a bad decision she'd regret afterward. She'd never had a casual, one-night fling, not even in college with boys she knew. If she had one now, if she didn't get a tight rein on herself, her pride and self-respect would be in tatters tomorrow.

Straightening, Kate reconsidered. She was a grown woman, and she might not feel that way tomorrow. She did know that if she decided *not* to go to bed with him, she'd probably end up wondering for months what it would have been like.

Helplessly, Kate decided not to decide. She reached for the light switch on the wall beside the telephone. The red message light flashed imperatively, insistently, and whether from guilt or caution, she suddenly felt as if she needed to find out what Evan had called to tell her. She lifted the receiver and pressed the Message button on the phone.

"*You have one unheard voice mail message,*" the recording said, and a moment later, she heard Evan's familiar, cultured voice. "Kate, it's me. You're probably out to dinner." He sounded frustrated and harassed, so Kate knew what was coming next before she heard him say, "I'm so sorry, but I'm not going to make it down there tomorrow. I'm doing my best to wrap this case up, but I know you know that. There's no way this case can drag on beyond tomorrow, so I'll be there the day after. Count on it."

Kate had been "counting on it" for three days already. She hung up the phone.

Chapter Nine

*I*N THE LIVING ROOM, SHE PAUSED TO CHECK ON THE sleeping dog. Bending down, she touched Max's nose. It felt moist and cooler than earlier, and his breathing was even. Petting his head, she said softly, "How are you feeling, Max?"

To her delighted surprise, he opened his eyes a little and gave his tail a feeble, answering wag.

"You're going to be just fine," she whispered, scratching his ears. "If you happen to get your strength back in the next few minutes, and if you're a good watchdog, feel free to come outside on the terrace. I need some watching tonight, because I'm tempted to do something really stupid. Or maybe not so stupid."

She felt a strange prickling sensation on the back of her neck and looked over her shoulder. Mitchell was watching her.

"How is he?" he asked.

Kate's pulse edged up a notch. "He's better," she said, standing up. "I'll be right there as soon as I wash this flea powder off."

In the bathroom, Kate quickly washed her hands. As she passed through the living room, she saw the liquor cabinet, remembered the ice bucket she'd used as an excuse to get away for a couple of minutes, and she picked it up. For good measure, she swept up a bottle of brandy, too.

"I come bearing gifts," she joked, putting the ice

bucket and brandy on the small table with the wine. "Would you like more wine?"

"I poured some for both of us while I was waiting for you."

Kate glanced at his plate and realized he hadn't touched his food since she left and had let it grow cold rather than eat without her. On top of everything else, the man had impeccable manners. Trying to atone for being gone so long, she picked up her fork so that he would pick up his, and she let him choose the topics and conversational pace. To her relief—and just a tiny bit of disappointment—he kept everything impersonal after that, chatting easily with her about the hotel and the climate, and telling her an amusing story about two couples who rented a sailboat for three hours in St. Maarten and were lost for three days.

At the end of ten minutes, the only significant thing Kate had learned about him was that he excelled at the art of entertaining small talk.

The musicians had either finished playing for the night or taken a break, but an occasional burst of cheerful laughter from the beach meant hotel guests were still enjoying themselves. Kate gazed into the gardens on her right, listening to the surf tumbling rhythmically onto the shore, while she contemplated ways to get him to talk about himself without appearing to pry. She was more than just curious about him; she felt a compulsive need to know and understand him. Despite his veneer of relaxed charm and indulgent affability, Kate had the growing feeling that Mitchell Wyatt was a very complex man. There was something about his unwillingness to talk about himself that struck her as guarded and detached. He obviously had no qualms about sexual intimacy, but she was beginning to wonder if he was accessible on an emotional level to anyone—specifically, her. With an inner sigh, she chided herself for thinking—

and feeling—like an infatuated, overeager twelve-year-old who couldn't wait to find out everything she could about the object of her infatuation.

Mitchell picked up his wineglass and leaned back in his chair, content for the moment with a view of her pretty profile and a tantalizing glimpse of that romantic mouth of hers. A smile tugged at his lips as he imagined her as a seven-year-old with a riotous mop of long, curly red hair, draping herself across a kitchen table, pretending a broom handle was a microphone.

He tried to imagine her in a Catholic school uniform—probably a white blouse and plaid jumper with white socks and brown shoes, he decided. When he imagined her leaning up on her toes to write "I will not be disrespectful" one hundred times on the chalkboard, the corners of his eyes crinkled in amusement. The nuns thought she sounded like an angel when she sang in the choir, he remembered, and a new image of her instantly presented itself—that of a little girl in a long choir robe with her huge green eyes lifted heavenward as she held a songbook in her hands.

Mitchell was not a complete stranger to Catholic church choirs. In Italy, he'd lived with the Callioroso family until he was five and left to attend his first boarding school. Shortly before he was to leave, Sergio Callioroso and his wife realized Mitchell might never have been baptized, and since they were devout Catholics, they chose that religion for him. Mitchell actually remembered the July day he was baptized, because the little village church had been sweltering, and Rosalie Callioroso had starched and ironed his white shirt until it was as stiff as plasterboard. To add to his discomfort, the old priest had chosen the sacrament of baptism as the subject for an endless sermon, and as he droned on and on, all Mitchell could think about was how good it was going to feel to have a little cool water poured over his head, the way Rosalie explained it would happen. But when the time came, the water wasn't cool, it was lukewarm. So was the effect of the ceremony on him.

Being baptized as a Catholic didn't make him feel holy or pious; it didn't even instill the slightest partiality for Catholicism in him. At all of the boarding schools he attended afterward, church attendance was mandatory, so as soon as he ascertained which religious services were the shortest at that particular school, Mitchell immediately decided to "convert" himself to that religion. When he was fourteen and the only available rabbi became too ill to conduct services for the few Jewish boys at Mitchell's school, he promptly announced his devout desire to convert to Judaism, and thus avoided attending any religious services whatsoever for nearly half a year.

Somehow, Kate had flourished despite the stifling parochial atmosphere she was raised in. He took another swallow of his wine and marveled at how natural and unaffected she was despite having a face and figure that most women would envy. Mitchell had enjoyed the company of many glamorous, clever women, and he'd known a number of plainer women who were delightfully funny and intelligent, and he enjoyed their company, too. But Kate Donovan was the first woman he'd ever known who possessed an abundance of all their best traits, along with an amazingly soft heart and a trace of amusing primness. The package was damned near irresistible—so long as she didn't carry that parochial-school primness too far tonight.

She hadn't mentioned her mother or the existence of siblings, and Mitchell wondered about both those things, but he didn't intend to ask her. He knew if he questioned her further about her family, she'd expect to question him about his. And although he was prepared to indulge her with almost anything in order to get her into that king-size bed, he was not willing to gratify anyone's curiosity about his childhood or his family.

She was staring absently at the border of trees and shrubs at the edge of the garden—probably thinking up a list of questions for him, Mitchell presumed wryly—when she stiffened suddenly and leaned forward. "Did you see that?"

"See what?" Mitchell asked, already half out of his chair.

"Something moved in the trees, and I saw something shiny—a reflection in the moonlight, just for a second."

Shaking his head at the outlandish reaction of a born-and-bred city girl to the presence of a harmless nocturnal animal, Mitchell decided to stand up instead of sitting back down. "A cat or dog," he assured her, walking around to her side of the table. "Their eyes gleam when light touches them at night."

"Then this cat or dog was close to six feet tall."

"Because it's in a tree," Mitchell reasoned. When she continued to stare dubiously at the trees behind him, he added, "Don't expect me to start searching the woods. I've already exceeded my annual quota of heroic acts tonight."

Kate decided he was right about the animal being in a tree, and she fell into his joking mood. "Where's your sense of chivalry?" she chided.

His deep voice acquired a deliberately meaningful note. "My chivalry expires when dessert is finished."

He was standing so close that the legs of his tan trousers were touching her knees, and she had to tip her head way back to talk to him, but she did her best to appear amused and blasé despite her physical disadvantage. "We didn't have dessert," she pointed out.

"Let's have it now," he said with quiet implacability, and held out his hand.

Kate's heart slammed into her ribs. In slow motion,

her hand reached toward his, her fingers sliding into his warm handclasp. He held out his other hand, and when she took it she felt herself drawn upward. His right arm slid around her back, forcing her breasts into contact with a male chest like a wall of rock, and as he stepped farther away from the table, his left hand clasped her right, tucking it against his chest. Expecting a kiss, Kate started to tip her head back, but he stepped sideways and turned her slightly to the left. An instant before she lost her balance and tripped on his feet, Kate realized the band at the beach was playing "The Girl from Ipanema" and he wasn't trying to kiss her, he was trying to dance with her. The operative word was *trying,* she realized, stifling a paroxysm of embarrassed giggles, because she had to take two quick, awkward steps sideways in order to stay off his feet and two more forward steps to catch up with the rhythm.

"How's it going?" he joked.

Moments before, she'd been afraid to touch him for fear she'd go up in flames. Now she leaned her forehead against the same rock-solid male chest that had made her breasts tingle and she laughed helplessly. "You might have mentioned that you intended to dance with me, not try to ravish me."

"But I do intend to ravish you," he warned quietly, his lips so close to the top of her head that his breath stirred her hair.

Kate's laughter fled and her senses flared to life. With the sensuous samba melody pulsing in the night and his long legs shifting against hers, it was a full minute before Kate realized that he danced the way he did everything else—with effortless ease and competence. No doubt he would be just as expert in bed, she thought—just as demanding and tender and irresistibly male as he was out of bed.

Her traitorous body turned warm and pliant, and Kate

struggled against an overwhelming temptation to yield to the subtle pressure of his hand on her spine and move closer to him. What about *after* she went to bed with him, she asked herself sternly. He was so casual about sex that he undoubtedly forgot a woman as quickly and effortlessly as he seduced her. If so, then he'd find it doubly easy to forget about her. On the other hand, she was going to have a terribly difficult time forgetting him now, even if she didn't go to bed with him. If she did go to bed with him, she might not be able to forget him for months or even years.

Trying to focus on that dampening thought, Kate stared straight ahead, but that gave her a close-up view of his tanned throat and the vee of his open white shirt, where tiny dark hairs peeked out invitingly just above a button. Hastily, she shifted her glance to the right and found herself gazing at long, masculine fingers lightly entwined with hers. He had beautiful hands with short, well-manicured nails. Strong, knowledgeable hands that would unerringly seek out and explore her body's most intimate places if she let—

Kate surrendered to defeat. She was going to let him. Regardless of the consequences, she had to find out for herself what was waiting for her in his arms. She had to know. She had to understand why he could evoke this combustible combination of heady desire and warm friendship in her within a few hours of meeting him.

Laying her cheek against his chest, Kate closed her eyes and matched his movements as effortlessly as if they'd been dancing together forever.

Mitchell tipped his chin slightly, smiling at the sensation of her cheek resting against his chest and her body relaxing fully against his in silent anticipation of what was soon to come. Tilting his left wrist slightly, he looked at his watch and saw that it was 11:25. Within the next five minutes, the hotel's efficient room service staff should arrive to clear away the remains of their meal—assuming they arrived at the time Kate had specified earlier. She may have forgotten about their impending arrival, but Mitchell hadn't, and he didn't want another aborted kiss like the last one. Besides, he was in no great hurry now. As he'd learned from experience, anticipation of any intimate act—including a first kiss between soon-to-be lovers—was often as enjoyable as the act itself. Lately, the anticipation was frequently *more* enjoyable.

On the beach, the musicians finished playing and paused for a round of applause from their small audience. In his arms, Kate stopped moving and looked up at him with moonlight and surrender in her green eyes.

She expected to be kissed, Mitchell realized, and in an abrupt reversal of his last decision, he decided the time was right for a light, short kiss—a brief little kiss to seal what was to come.

As soon as he bent his head, Kate braced herself for some sort of demanding sensual onslaught, but his kiss was surprisingly light—merely a friendly, tentative stroke of his mouth on hers—his smiling mouth, Kate realized, and she smiled a little, too, as she curved her hands over his shoulders and returned the "get-acquainted" kiss.

And then the kiss started to change as he began smoothing his lips back and forth over hers, subtly increasing the pressure of each sliding stroke until her lips parted beneath his. When they did, his fingers shoved deep into the hair at her nape, holding her mouth locked tightly to his, and his free arm angled across her hips, clamping her against his rigid length.

Kate was so lost in the hot demanding kiss that the knocking sound she heard seemed to be coming from inside of her, until Mitchell finally pulled his mouth from hers and scowled at something over her shoulder. "Room service," he said in a strained voice. He dropped his arms. "You told room service to come back at eleven-thirty to clear away the remains of dinner."

Kate finally registered what he was telling her and quickly turned away from him, heading for the door to let the waiters in.

Mitchell watched her walk away and swore under his breath, trying to get his rampaging lust under control. When the physical evidence of it wouldn't diminish even slightly, he turned on his heel and left the terrace, forced to retreat into the darkness of the garden to conceal a rigid arousal that shouldn't have resulted from just one relatively chaste kiss. Or six of them.

Chapter Ten

KATE OPENED THE DOOR TO TWO SMILING WAITERS, ONE of them in his late twenties, the other in his late forties. "How was your dinner, miss?" the younger waiter asked as he wheeled in a cart.

"Wonderful." She couldn't remember what she'd eaten for dinner and she sounded a little breathless.

"The wine was satisfactory?" the older waiter inquired, stepping carefully around the sleeping dog.

"Yes," Kate said. "Very," she added with a quick smile, trying to recover her equilibrium. She checked to be sure Max was all right; then she smoothed her hair down and stepped back outside onto the terrace. Mitchell was standing in the garden with his hands shoved in his pockets, staring out across the moonlit water as if lost in thought.

The music had begun again, and as Kate moved around the table, the younger waiter paused in his struggle to force the cork back into the unfinished bottle of red wine. "There's a private party down there," he said. "I hope the music has not disturbed you and your husband."

"We—I've enjoyed it very much," Kate said, but the word *husband* made her falter momentarily, not because Mitchell wasn't her husband, but because she realized how awkward this situation would feel tomorrow night, or the night after, if these same waiters served Evan and her a meal. It hit her then that the same possibility might have occurred to Mitchell and that was why he'd moved off into the darkness at the far end of the garden.

Kate forced her worries about the future aside and stepped off the terrace onto the grass. Soon enough, she would have to cope with the ramifications of her decision to be with Mitchell tonight, but for now, that decision was made. She couldn't turn back. She didn't want to turn back. Not after their kiss. There had never been a kiss like that—not for her—and she had the thrilling feeling that Mitchell had been almost as surprised and carried away by it as she'd been.

He turned toward her, and Kate searched his features for some sign that the kiss had affected him as much as she thought it had. She wanted to believe it had been no ordinary kiss to him. She needed to believe it, and yet in the pale moonlight, he almost seemed to be frowning at her. However, he was too far away for her to gauge his expression accurately, so Kate smiled tentatively at him and tried to decide what to say to him when she was close enough. He didn't smile back at her, and she wondered why.

Mitchell wasn't smiling because he was studying the woman who had just managed to drive him to the brink of uncontrollable, possessive lust with one kiss, and he wasn't entirely happy with what he saw. With her hands clasped behind her back and the breeze teasing her long hair and ruffling the hem of her long pants, she reminded him of an Irish choir girl, and the beguiling outfit she was wearing—which he'd mentally stripped off her during dinner—now struck him as being virginal white.

Kate Donovan was not at all in his normal style, and neither was his profound physical reaction to a single kiss. Earlier, when she dumped that Bloody Mary on him, his desire to see her again had been an ordinary response to a captivating face framed by a beguiling mass of red hair. Tonight, however, his attraction to her had intensified so fiercely with everything she did and said that a simple kiss—which he'd intended to be nothing more than an expression of languid desire soon to be gratified—became something much different: a kiss of wild urgency.

He watched her as she stopped to pluck a white flower from a bush covered with white blooms. She held the bloom to her nose, inhaling its fragrance as she looked out across the water. Suddenly, Mitchell was catapulted ten years back in time to a party he'd attended at the home of a Greek businessman. Bored with the party, Mitchell had taken his drink outside, where he eventually wandered down a path that ended at the entrance to a small, torchlit garden at the edge of a cliff. In the center of the garden stood a life-size statue of a young woman with flowing hair holding a flower in her hand. Based on the garments she was wearing, the statue was fairly recent, but something about her had captivated him. "Do you mind if I join you?" he'd asked the statue as he studied her features.

That question had been as idiotic, Mitchell realized, as the fact that he was now comparing a redheaded Chicago girl to a Greek statue carved in alabaster. His response to Kate Donovan was not only fanciful, it was unpredictable, and although Mitchell had no idea why she affected him that way—or exactly where all this was heading—he was suddenly a little wary of the general direction it had taken him. He resolved to chart the remainder of the course more carefully and on his terms.

Kate stopped in front of him and glanced over his shoulder toward the beach, where the musicians were starting to play another samba. "We have music again," she remarked lightly, trying not to feel uneasy about the fact that he was looking at her with a rather cool smile and keeping his hands in his pockets. "The waiter told me there's a private party down there," she added.

Mitchell shifted his gaze in the direction she indicated and named the song the musicians were playing. "Corcovado," he said, but he didn't make a move to dance with her, and Kate decided the continued presence of the waiters on the terrace was the explanation for his hesitant behavior.

Since she couldn't restore the mood to what it had been just before the waiters arrived, she decided to try for the friendly banter she'd shared with him at dinner and, hopefully, an opportunity to learn a little more about the man she was about to go to bed with. "I know you like music," she said lightly. "I can tell that from the way you dance. What's your favorite kind of music?"

"Jazz."

Kate sighed in exaggerated despair. "Men prefer jazz because you don't bother listening to lyrics. With jazz, you don't even have to pretend you're listening to them. What's your second favorite kind of music?"

"Classical," Mitchell replied.

"Which has *no* lyrics to listen to," she said so smugly that Mitchell grinned in spite of himself. "What's your third favorite?" she asked.

"Opera," Mitchell replied.

"Which has lyrics *you don't understand,*" Kate pointed out drily, lifting her palms as if his answers had completely proven her point, but a hesitant flicker in his expression made her drop her hands and study him more closely. "Do you understand Italian?"

Italian was Mitchell's first language, not English, but rather than tell her that and provoke more questions, he nodded and said a dismissive, "Yes."

"Do you *speak* it as well? I mean, are you fluent in Italian as well as English and Dutch?"

"I'm not fluent in Dutch," he reminded her.

From that reply, Kate deduced that he was, however,

fluent in Italian, and she looked as impressed and fascinated as she felt. "How many languages do you speak?"

"I've never counted them."

"Let's do it now," Kate joked, and started to hold up her fingers.

"Let's not," Mitchell replied curtly, dousing her smile and her enthusiasm with a swift efficiency that made him dislike himself so thoroughly that he made a quick, clumsy effort to atone for his rudeness and ended up giving her an ill-advised explanation that confused her and required clarification. "Most Europeans are multilingual," he said.

"You sound so much like an American that I never imagined you're a European."

"I'm not."

"Then what are you?" she asked, her green eyes searching his.

"I'm neither," Mitchell replied bluntly. "I'm a hybrid," he added, because that's exactly how he thought of himself, but when he realized that he'd just been lulled by a soft voice and shining eyes into saying something he'd never admitted aloud, he didn't like the feeling it gave him. Impatiently, he glanced toward the terrace, and then he put his hand under Kate's elbow, turning her in that direction. "The waiters have left. Let's go inside," he said, intending to take her to bed without further conversation.

When she nodded and walked obediently beside him, Mitchell assumed she was willing to go along with that plan, but when they stepped onto the terrace, she foiled him either purposely or inadvertently by backing up and sitting on the stone balustrade. "Mitchell—" She said his name for the first time in a low, sweet voice; then she glanced down and paused as if saying his name had given her the same twinge of surprised pleasure that he'd felt hearing it.

Mitchell perched his hip on the opposite balustrade

and folded his arms over his chest. "Yes?" he said, resigned to naming a few foreign languages he spoke before he could get her to go inside with him.

She lifted her face to his, her smile quizzical. "Why did you call yourself a 'hybrid'?"

"Because I'm an American by birth and a European by upbringing."

She nodded as if satisfied. "Do you have brothers or sisters?"

Startled and annoyed by her unexpected line of questioning, Mitchell said shortly, "No, not really."

"Not really," she repeated, and then half jokingly she said, "What about a mother or a father?"

"No."

"You have no family anywhere, is that it?"

"What the hell difference does it make?"

"None, really, I suppose," she said, but a hint of sadness and resignation had crept into her voice, giving Mitchell the distinct impression that for some reason, any further refusal to answer her questions was going to weigh heavily against him in whatever decision she was struggling with.

"I have a sister-in-law, a nephew, and a great-aunt," he conceded in a clipped voice, refusing to acknowledge the existence of his grandfather.

"How can you have a sister-in-law or a nephew if you have no brothers and no sisters?"

"Where is this conversation going?" he said shortly.

"Are you in the CIA or MIA or something?"

If he hadn't been so annoyed, he would have laughed. "Neither one."

"No, of course not," she said lightly, standing up. "If you were, you'd have a much better cover story, wouldn't you?"

Mitchell stood up and answered with a curt, impatient question of his own. "Are you always so inquisitive?"

It was a thinly veiled reprimand and a warning to back off. And Kate backed off—literally as well as figuratively. Turning away from him, she faced the cold reality of the situation and not the dreamy idyll she'd cherished a short while ago. The only thing he wanted to share was an hour or so in bed, and his only interest in her was as a convenient sex partner. For a moment she actually considered settling for that, but she already had all the sorrow and uncertainty she could shoulder waiting for her when she returned to Chicago. She didn't need to add humiliation and guilt to her burdens.

Her body language was unmistakable, and Mitchell suddenly decided the evening was better off ending exactly this way. Much better off. In fact, he was relieved it was ending like this. Tomorrow, when they were in St. Maarten, he could enjoy her at arm's length—mentally and physically. "It's getting late," he said in a calm, matter-of-fact tone. "I'll pick you up at ten tomorrow."

Instead of agreeing to that as he expected, she shook her head; then she cleared her throat and said, "No. I'll manage on my own tomorrow, but thank you."

She was sulking, Mitchell decided, and because he couldn't stand women who sulked, he was perversely pleased to discover she was one of them. Except that when she turned around and looked at him, he realized she wasn't sulking at all. Smiling softly, she said, "Good-bye, Mitchell. Thank you for a lovely, memorable evening. I wouldn't have missed it for anything in the world."

Mitchell was so disarmed by her expression and what she said that he reversed his earlier decision about the best way to end the evening. "It doesn't necessarily have to end now," he pointed out.

"Yes, it does."

Although Mitchell was willing to change his mind, he was not willing to be backed into a corner or forced into a compromise. "Because I don't want to tell you the story of my life?" he speculated impassively.

"No, because you pried the story of my life out of me, but you're offering nothing in return."

"Nothing?" he mocked, lifting his brows.

He was reminding her that he'd offered her his body in bed, in lieu of his biography, and as Kate fought down a fresh surge of temptation, she suddenly rediscovered that strange feeling of preordained friendship that had come over her earlier. Without realizing what she was doing, she laid her hand against his hard cheek and smiled winsomely into his shuttered eyes. "What you're offering would be enough for any woman, I know," she teased, "but the problem is that I have a feeling you're a whole lot more than just another pretty face—"

At that remark, reluctant laughter flickered in his eyes and a muscle twitched at the corner of his mouth, and the warm connection Kate felt with him grew stronger, along with her aching sense of loss. "The truth is, I think you have a lot of layers, and if we were together again tomorrow, I would keep trying to peel off one layer at a time to peek beneath it and see what's hiding there." When he didn't reply, she did it for him: "But you won't let me, and you won't like it if I try, will you?"

Caught between shock at her candor and admiration for her courage, Mitchell gave her the tribute of an honest answer. "No."

"I knew that," she whispered with another smile, and pulled her hand slowly from his cheek, sliding it down over his shoulder until she finally forced herself to lift it away from him entirely. "Now go away before I change my mind."

Mitchell noticed the way her hand lingered, he heard the slight shake in her voice, and he knew beyond any doubt that he could pull her into his arms and change her mind. He even sensed that on some level, she wanted him to do precisely that almost as much as he was tempted to do it. Instead he decided to do exactly what she *said* she wanted him to do, partly because he knew that was probably the wisest course. However, rather than end their brief acquaintance on a grim note, he deliberately joked with her about her decision as he prepared to leave. "You'll regret it," he predicted with sham gravity.

She nodded in complete agreement and matched his tone perfectly. "Without a doubt," she assured him, but her eyes were suspiciously bright.

Attuned to each nuance of her expression now, Mitchell assumed tears were responsible for that sheen in her eyes. "If you change your mind about tomorrow—"

"I won't," she interrupted quietly. "Good-bye," she added, and held out her hand to shake his, just as she'd done twelve hours before when she introduced herself after spilling a drink on him.

He looked down at her hand, and without warning or reason, he felt a sharp compulsion to change her mind for her and spend the night with her after all. Ignoring her outstretched hand, he took her chin between his thumb and forefinger, tilted her face up to his, and smiled into her eyes. "In Europe, when a man and woman have spent an evening together, they kiss each other good-bye."

If she'd looked away or tried to free her chin from his grasp, Mitchell would have forced her to kiss him and subdued the rest of her objections with his mouth and hands. Instead she gave him a confused, innocent look. "What part of Europe would that be? Would it be France? Or Sweden? Or Belgium?"

Mitchell's brows snapped into a scowl. "You're stubborn as hell, aren't you?"

"Or Spain? Or Transylvania?" she persisted. Mitchell dropped his hand in irritation. She stepped back. "I'll show you out," she said politely, and turned to walk into the suite with him.

He declined her offer in a bored, impatient voice. "Don't bother; I'll take the path around the building instead."

Fighting back tears, Kate watched him walk off the terrace and turn left, striding along the back of her villa, but as he reached into his pants pocket and withdrew his keys, he stopped for a moment, his dark head bent in thought, then he turned toward her. Kate's hope soared at the sight of his brief smile, but the words he spoke yanked her back to painful reality. "You made the right choice."

Inwardly, Kate flinched at the additional damage he inflicted on her with his perfunctory smile and indifferent words, but she forced her aching facial muscles into an answering smile. "I know," she lied.

He nodded, as if completely satisfied with matters between them now; then he strode down the path and disappeared around the corner of the villa. And out of her life.

In the trees at the border of the garden behind her, something made a rustling noise, but this time Kate didn't feel any alarm or bother to look around. Since she knew it wasn't Mitchell, she didn't care what else was back there. Squeezing her eyes closed, she dropped her head in a losing battle with doubt and shame.

The reasons she'd given Mitchell for putting an abrupt end to their time together were nothing but half-truths. When she originally decided to go to bed with him, she hadn't needed to know how many languages he spoke or how many siblings he had before she could make that decision. The reasons she'd given herself for backing away were logical, but lame and dishonest. She'd realized all along that she might feel guilty or mortified later if she slept with him tonight, and she'd been prepared to risk that, and accept it if it happened. What she had *not* been prepared to do was go back to Chicago and torture herself with more unanswerable questions. The reason for her father's death was a mystery; the future of the restaurant he'd devoted his life to was an uncertain mystery with Kate in charge. When Mitchell refused to talk about himself, she'd panicked at the realization that yet another frustrating mystery was presenting itself to her—standing right in front of her, in fact, looking at her with sexy, heavy-lidded eyes and a deceptively lazy smile while he practically dared her to try to unravel what was going on inside him.

And what made Kate so furious with herself now, and so ashamed, was that she could have *done* it, at least partway. She had a master's degree in psychology and several years of experience dealing almost exclusively with the living results of dysfunctional families. At dinner tonight, she'd realized within minutes that there were carefully erected emotional barricades around Mitchell, and she'd presumed that they'd been there a very, very long time—probably since childhood.

Instead of granting him the right to have boundaries and admiring the amazing amount of warmth and strength he obviously possessed—instead of letting him put all that irresistible, confident sexuality of his to use, which he'd intended to do with her, Kate had focused on the probable foundation of his barricades and started digging there with probing questions about his family members.

Finally, he'd asked her the one-million-dollar question: *"What the hell difference does it make?"*

And the answer to that question was, Kate admitted miserably—no difference. Every adult male had some sort of useful emotional barricades. Sometimes, they let them down for a woman they cared deeply for, but never did they let them down simply because a woman they scarcely knew wanted to *make* them do it—and do it immediately!

Swallowing back tears, Kate stepped off the terrace where she'd laughed and joked and danced with him . . . and been melted by one unforgettable kiss. Lifting her hand, she rubbed the aching muscles at her nape, then dropped her hand to her side. Less than half an hour ago, she remembered poignantly, his long fingers had been at her nape, shoved into her hair, his mouth hungrily on hers.

The music had ended when he left, she realized as she wandered aimlessly toward the beach. The night had died when he left.

She thought about the way he'd turned back when he was walking away, as if the act of taking his keys out of his pocket had suddenly reminded him of another act he needed to perform . . . *"You made the right choice,"* he'd told her with a brief smile; and for the first time, Kate finally understood his seemingly odd behavior: He was politely assuming all the blame for the failure of the evening—like a perfect gentleman. His manners weren't merely excellent, Kate realized, they were impeccable. Whether he was being doused with an ice-cold drink or sent away with unfulfilled sexual expectations, he lost neither his temper nor his composure.

She paused, trying to link that vaguely familiar behavior with something she knew, and then she remembered what it was: Supposedly, the British upper class behaved as if they were impervious to chaos. Any outward display of temperamental frustration was regarded as a sign of bad breeding. Evidently, Mitchell had somehow acquired the manners of the British upper class.

She would never be sure if she was right about that.

Because of her own cowardice and her infatuated eagerness to know everything about him, she'd spoiled her chance to discover anything about him at all.

Knowing that made her feel so miserable that it was almost a consolation to think he hadn't really given a damn about her. At least she couldn't blame herself for spoiling chances she'd never have had with him.

Chapter Eleven

LISTLESSLY, KATE WANDERED TO THE EDGE OF THE GARden. IMmersed in regret and helpless yearning, she watched the shimmering surf spill onto the sand and then chase itself back into the moonlit sea.

She was so wrapped up in her thoughts that she didn't notice soft footsteps in the grass behind her until a shadow moved directly across her line of vision. She froze, afraid that if she glanced around, she'd discover that it was only a hotel guest going for a late stroll on the beach. A breathless moment later, her dread exploded into a burst of elation when Mitchell put his hands on her waist and moved so close behind her that his shirt brushed her back and arms. For several moments, all Kate heard was the pounding of her heart and the restless rustling of palm fronds overhead. And then he said solemnly, "My brother's name was William."

His use of the past tense told Kate that his brother was dead, and she dropped her head in shamed remorse for forcing him to talk about it.

As if to reassure her, he said, "We barely knew each other. We had the same father but different mothers. I grew up in Europe and Bill grew up in the States with his father's family."

"I'm so sorry for asking," Kate whispered, "but thank you for telling me."

He slid his hands soothingly up and down her arms, and when he spoke again, he hesitated between each sentence as if he found it difficult to articulate what he was trying to tell her. "Neither of us knew the other one existed until a few months ago when he discovered by accident that he had a brother. He traced me to my address in London and sent me a letter explaining who he was. The next week, he telephoned several times. The week after that, he packed up his wife and teenage son, and the three of them arrived, unannounced, on my doorstep."

Warning flags went up in Kate's mind about his father's apparent lack of any role in this reunion, but the last thing she wanted to do was pry further. Instead, she seized on the most uplifting part of his story and smiled as she turned around to face him and made her comment: "Your brother was a good strategist."

"Why do you say that?"

"Because, by bringing his wife and son, he demonstrated that his family was in complete accord with his desire to know you."

"Actually, he brought his wife and son in order to make it more difficult for me to throw him out."

"Why would he have expected that you might do something like that?"

"Probably because I hadn't answered his letter or accepted his phone calls," he said drily.

"You hadn't?"

"No," he said, but his expression had softened enough to make Kate hazard a guess: "When you got to know him, you liked him, didn't you?"

He looked away from her before he answered and stared over her head at the sea. "Yes," he said, and after several seconds, he added in a low voice, "I liked him very much."

Tears stung the back of Kate's eyes at the wealth of concealed emotion in that last sentence.

He tipped his chin down and looked at her. "What else would you like to know?"

The only thing Kate wanted to know now was how to extricate them both from this painfully serious topic. Despite her earlier belief that she was utterly insignificant to him, the truth was that he'd come back here to tell her whatever she wanted to know. He'd actually come back. That was all that mattered. After a moment's thought, she came up with a playful way to answer his last question and hopefully transform their mood. Trying to look extremely solemn, she said, "There is only one more question I really need an answer to—it's very personal, but it's extremely important to me to know the answer." His brows lifted inquiringly, but his expression was so wary and unenthusiastic that Kate laughed and asked the "extremely important" question: "How many languages *do* you speak?"

His startled chuckle transformed into a lazy, sensual smile as he pretended to seriously contemplate his answer. "I'm not certain," he said, shifting his hand down her spine and drawing her closer. "I'll name them for you and you can count them." His gaze fixed on her mouth, and he bent his head. "I'm fluent in Italian—" His warm mouth touched hers and slid languorously from corner to corner and back again in a long, slow exploration of the shape and texture of her lips that twisted Kate into knots.

"And Spanish—" He deepened the kiss, his mouth stroking hers insistently, his arms tightening. His tongue slid across the seam between her lips, and Kate's pulse rate soared.

"And French—" His hand curved around her nape, his mouth slowly opening on hers. His tongue made a brief foray into her mouth, probing lightly, and Kate returned the intimate kiss, wrapping her arms fiercely around his neck and molding her body to the hardening contours of his. To Kate's surprise, her response made him abruptly end that kiss. Instead, he brushed a light kiss on her forehead and whispered, "I also speak some German and some Greek . . ." Touching his lips to her temple, he added, "and a little Russian, and a little Japanese." He slid his mouth across her cheekbone to her ear, and his warm breath made her shiver and lean into him as he finished playfully, "and almost *no* Dutch."

Despite Mitchell's lighthearted tone, her shivering response made him yearn to make her shiver again, only harder, and longer, and he had to force himself to lift his head. He could not fathom why kissing her had such a powerful physical effect on him, and he was genuinely relieved that he'd managed to name all the languages he spoke while keeping things from getting out of hand.

Kate stirred in his arms and tipped her chin up. "You forgot to mention English," she said with a smile.

In the interest of conformity, Mitchell suddenly felt that the English language needed to be mentioned in the context of a kiss, just as the others had been. "Did I?" he asked, slowly rubbing his thumb over her soft bottom lip; then he looked at what his thumb was doing. His restraint snapped. He pressed his thumb down hard, forcing her lips apart, and abruptly seized her mouth in a hungry, devouring kiss. His tongue plunged into her mouth, and the kiss went wild. She kissed him back, her fingers flexing against the muscles in his back, clasping him to her while his hands slid restlessly over the sides of her breasts, then swept behind her, cupping her hips and pulling her tightly against his rigid erection.

When Mitchell finally pulled his mouth from hers, lust was raging through his entire nerve stream, and the idea of walking toward her villa in the condition his body was in struck him as being too humorous to consider. Instead, he held her in his arms, her face pressed to his chest, her titian hair spilling over his arm in a rumpled cascade. Lifting his gaze from the top of her head, he looked out at the shifting sea, his emotions caught somewhere between excitement, amusement, and disbelief. She was leaning against him for support, her hand splayed over his pounding heart, her fingers moving slightly in a feathery caress. He liked the way she was touching him. He knew she was in much the same emotional and physical state he was in, and he liked that, too.

In fact, he liked *everything* about her.

He liked her humor, her warmth, and her sensuality. He liked her courage and her candor and her pride. He liked her smile and the musical sound of her laughter. He liked her face, and her hair, and the way she'd laid her hand on his jaw earlier, when she said, *"I have a feeling you're a whole lot more than just another pretty face."*

He liked the way her body fit itself to his, and the way her breasts felt in his hands. Mitchell checked the direction of his thoughts and tipped his chin down, ready to relinquish his hold on her and walk back to the suite. "How many languages was that?" he asked with a grin.

She lifted her head from his chest, leaned back in his arms, and looked at him blankly for a moment; then she gave him a smile filled with charming chagrin. "I don't know. I lost count after you said French."

"Then we'll have to start over."

"Oh, God—" she said on a choked laugh, and dropped her forehead weakly against his chest.

"But not here," Mitchell said, amused and flattered by her reaction; then he curved his arm around her waist and directed her toward the villa. As they walked across the grass, he tried to remember the last time a woman had made him experience such strong, frequent, and repeated transitions from laughter to lust, and frustration to fascination. He couldn't remember that ever happening to him before. The experience was surprising, challenging, and exhilarating. He didn't want to do anything to diminish it, or the woman who affected him that way, and as he glanced at the open terrace doors, he wondered if it was a mistake to take her to bed in her boyfriend's hotel room. Then he wondered exactly who he thought that would bother—her? Or him? Or both of them?

The possibility that *he* might not like the idea of going to bed with her in another man's hotel room seemed ludicrous, since he'd done similar things in the past and without the slightest qualm. In view of that, Mitchell decided that his concern was strictly for her sake—until they walked into the suite and they both saw his navy sport jacket hanging on the back of a chair in the living room.

Kate reacted with a surprised statement of the obvious. "When you left earlier, you forgot your jacket."

"That might have been difficult to explain to the lawyer," Mitchell replied without intending to say any such thing. The lawyer was an off-limits subject under the circumstances, and he couldn't believe he'd just been foolish enough—or crass enough—to bring him up at such a time as this.

"I would have noticed it and . . ."

"And what?" Mitchell inquired, even though that completely compounded his last transgression and made him even more annoyed with himself.

Kate shot him an uneasy smile and bent down to check on the sleeping dog. Max's nose was cool and moist, and he opened his eyes when she touched him; then he gave his tail a feeble wag and drifted back to sleep. Satisfied, she stood up and rubbed her palms on the sides of her pants. She was trying to think what she would have done with Mitchell's jacket, and she wished the subject hadn't come up, because it was making her feel sneaky and guilty about going to bed with him here in Evan's suite, when moments before she'd been happy and excited. "I guess I could have left it at the front desk in a bag with your name on it."

Mitchell knew that was a perfectly logical solution, but for some reason he suddenly found the notion extremely distasteful—almost as if it were he, rather than merely his jacket, that she would be pulling a bag over and hustling out to the front desk.

"Or I guess I could have put it in the closet and waited for you to phone and tell me what to do with it."

Mitchell restrained the idiotic urge to ask her if she thought the lawyer and he wore the same size jacket; then he glanced at the telephone and imagined the lawyer standing there, answering Mitchell's phone call about the jacket or playing back Mitchell's voice mail about it. As he looked at the telephone, it occurred to him that the red message light was no longer flashing, as it had been earlier. That meant Kate had already retrieved her voice mail message sometime during the evening.

He glanced at her, half expecting her to be looking at the telephone, too, but she was looking at the bed with a decidedly guilty expression, rather than the soft, yielding expression she'd had a few minutes ago. Although the lawyer wasn't present in the room, he'd become a pronounced obstacle to their unrestrained enjoyment of each other, Mitchell realized with disgust. "Is he still planning to arrive tomorrow?"

Kate shook her head. "The day after tomorrow," she said, but their conversation about Evan had made her feel so uneasy that she couldn't look at the bed in the alcove without feeling despicable about being there with Mitchell. Ethically speaking, this wasn't her hotel room or her bed. Evan was paying for them. *Decide now,* her brain prompted. *Decide. Decide.* Engaged in her personal struggle with ethics and logistics, Kate turned in shock when, from the corner of her eye, she saw Mitchell shrugging into his jacket. "Are you leaving?" she asked, sounding as stricken as she felt.

He nodded; then he partially dispelled her fears over his reasons by capturing her wrist and pulling her firmly into his arms.

He looked amused, not annoyed, she noted. "But, why?"

"Because," he said drily, "something tells me that nice Irish choir girls think it's naughty to sleep with a man in another man's room."

Kate's eyes widened at his acuity, but the term *choir girl* seemed so inappropriate under the circumstances that she couldn't hide behind the falsity of it. "I am hardly behaving like a choir girl."

"Did I guess wrong about the room?" he countered with a knowing smile.

"Not exactly, but—"

"And I also think that if we sleep together 'on the first date,' one of us will decide tomorrow that our behavior tonight reeked of tacky, indiscriminate sex."

"Do you mean you?" Kate said dazedly, and he gave a short bark of laughter.

"Not me. You."

Kate thought about what he was saying, and she made no effort to hide the yearning or confusion she felt. "I never realized what a prude I must be."

In reply, he slid his fingers through the sides of her hair and turned her face up to his for a demanding kiss that ended on a gruff command. "Get over it by tomorrow."

Kate tried to think of a clever rejoinder and instead said softly, "I will." Satisfied that the matter was settled, he dropped his hands and turned toward the terrace doors, apparently intending to walk outside and around the building. "There's a front door in here, you know," Kate pointed out.

"If I walk past that bed with you, I'll have you in it in thirty seconds."

"You're awfully sure of yourself," she teased.

He tipped his head back, closed his eyes, and said, "Please, just dare me to prove it. Just give me one excuse. That's all I need right now—just one infinitesimal excuse and my fragile new scruples won't matter."

Kate wisely decided not to do that, and he opened his eyes. "I'll pick you and Max up at ten o'clock. We'll take him to a vet in St. Maarten and spend the day on the island. And the night," he added meaningfully. When she didn't object to that, he said, "Do you like to gamble?"

Kate looked at the man she'd agreed to spend the night with after knowing him only a few hours and said with a winsome smile, "Obviously."

He caught her meaning and grinned. "Then bring a change of clothes for the evening—something nice."

He turned and disappeared through the doorway.

Chapter Twelve

SEATED ON THE AFT DECK OF ZACK BENEDICT'S YACHT with a cup of coffee, a plate of toast, and a newspaper on the table in front of him, Mitchell looked toward the railing as the yacht's captain swore under his breath and glared at an approaching boat.

Clad entirely in white, from the starched collar of his short-sleeved shirt to the toes of his spotless deck shoes, Captain Nathaniel Prescott was tall and gray-haired with a ramrod posture and an aura of exacting competence. "Brace yourself," he warned Mitchell. "Here comes another one." As he spoke, a ferryboat, bound for one of the neighboring islands and loaded with tourists, slid by the yacht less than fifty feet away, and the ferry captain's voice blared an announcement over the boat's loudspeaker to his passengers. *"Ladies and gentlemen, lying off to our starboard side—that's 'right' to you—is the 125-foot yacht owned by movie star Zack Benedict, which is named the* Julie, *after his wife. Get your cameras ready, and I'll take us in a little closer. I see a man aboard who could be Benedict."*

Mitchell swore under his breath and raised the newspaper, concealing his face. "I don't know how Zack puts up with this. I'd start waving a shotgun at them."

Until yesterday, the *Julie* had been peacefully docked at a pier in one of St. Maarten's beautiful marinas, but some avid fans of Zack's had seen the yacht and realized to whom it belonged. The word had spread like wildfire across the island. Within hours, their pier became a tourist attraction of its own, with Zack's fans milling around the boat, hoping for autographs, taking photographs, and making a damned nuisance of themselves. Some of them were still hanging around last night when Mitchell returned from his evening with Kate, and to give Mitchell some peace, Zack's captain had moved the boat away from the pier as soon as Mitchell was aboard. Now the yacht was anchored just outside the marina, which isolated them from annoying pedestrians, but gave them no protection from tourists on the ferries and tour boats.

"I'm checking with the other marinas to see if they have a slip available that's large enough to accommodate us," Prescott said in the resigned tone of a man who'd been through this drill many times in the past. "Unfortunately, for now, we'll have to use the launch to get you back and forth to shore."

"That's fine," Mitchell said. "I have some errands to do in St. Maarten this morning."

"I'll tell Yardley to have the launch ready to leave in—?" He paused, waiting for Mitchell's answer.

Mitchell glanced at his watch. It was 8:15. "In half an hour."

"I'll call you on your cell phone, and let you know where we're docked so you can find us this evening," Prescott volunteered.

"I won't be back tonight. I'm staying in a hotel."

"You'll probably get more peace and quiet that way," Prescott said with an apologetic sigh. He started to leave; then he turned and said with a slight smile, "Mr. Benedict phoned from Rome earlier. I told him we'd been forced to move out of the marina last night. He said to tell you everything is delightfully quiet and pleasant where *he* is."

Mitchell acknowledged Zack's joke with a brief smile.

Zack was staying at Mitchell's apartment in Rome while he finished shooting scenes for his new movie there; then he and Julie were flying to St. Maarten to join Mitchell.

When Prescott left, Mitchell leaned back in his chair and watched a flock of seagulls wheeling in circles overhead, his thoughts drifting to his extraordinary behavior with Kate Donovan the night before.

This morning, in the bright light of day, he was amused and a little embarrassed by the lengths he'd gone to to please her. When she'd asked him to help a stray mongrel, he'd promptly summoned an ambulance and physician and then volunteered to help take the dog to a vet. Later, when she refused to sleep with him or see him again unless he told her about himself, she'd been giving him an ultimatum, and he'd known it at the time. He'd known it, he'd refused to be manipulated, and he'd left—exactly as he should have done. But then, driven by the severest case of brain-numbing lust in his recollection, he gave in and went back to answer her questions. And if that weren't strange enough, he'd then suffered an unprecedented attack of comical chivalry and decided *not* to take her to bed in her boyfriend's hotel room, but to wait until today and take her to a hotel in St. Maarten instead.

That particular decision to wait was doubly bizarre in view of the fact that he'd been needlessly and outrageously blunt with her all evening about his intentions to sleep with her. In hindsight, most of his behavior the night before was baffling and yet, not entirely. Minutes after he'd arrived at her hotel last night, everything about her began to resonate with him.

At least, that's how he'd felt yesterday. But this was today, and without the moonlight and music—without the combination of circumstances that had made the night before seem somehow momentous—it was possible the "magic" would be gone. Right now, Mitchell wasn't completely certain which way he wanted it to be. Ever since his brother and his family had arrived in London, Mitchell had felt at times that he was getting "soft" inside, and it was an alien and rather disturbing sensation. First William had gotten to him; then he'd let his aunt Olivia get under his skin, and he'd even shaken his grandfather's hand. Now, a redheaded Irish girl was getting to him.

In the midst of that thought, Mitchell noticed another ferryboat headed straight toward the yacht. Instead of reaching for his newspaper, he reached for a slice of toast, tore off a piece, and tossed it overboard. Seagulls screeched and dove. He tossed four more pieces overboard, and white gulls came from everywhere.

"*Ladies and gentlemen,*" the ferry captain's voice blasted out. "*If you're fans of the movie actor Zack Benedict . . .*"

Mitchell flipped two more pieces of toast overboard, and seagulls rained down out of the sky, screeching and diving.

"*. . . Get your cameras ready . . .*"

Mitchell picked up the rest of the toast and slowly flipped the slices overboard one at a time. Seagulls by the hundreds descended in a thick curtain of gray and white.

"*. . . Look out for the gulls . . .*"

Mitchell glanced at his watch and pushed his chair back. He still had to pack an overnight case.

Shielded from the ferry's view by flocks of frenzied gulls, he strolled across the deck.

Kate's dark blue suitcase lay at the foot of the bed, packed and ready.

From the white sofa in the sitting room, she idly petted Max's head while she stared at that piece of luggage and nervously tried to recapture the emotions she'd had last night—emotions that had made it seem completely appropriate and perfectly right for her to agree to spend the night with him. This morning, what she was planning to do seemed a little insane.

She thought about how overjoyed she'd felt last night when Mitchell walked up behind her in the garden and told her, "*My brother's name was William.*" In retrospect, she'd apparently become totally besotted with a man merely because he'd been reluctantly willing to mention a few facts about his brother and to reveal the languages he spoke. That made no sense at all.

Obviously she'd been absurdly affected by the setting they were in—the setting, combined with his fantastic good looks and his urbane charm, had evidently seduced her—which was exactly what he'd intended to happen. From early in the evening, he'd made it abundantly clear that seduction was on his mind: *I'm less dismayed than I'd be if you told me you're a nun. . . . I want to be sure we're on the same page. . . . But I do intend to ravish you.*

Even the way he kissed was deliberately seductive. Those slow, stirring kisses that turned hot and demanding—the suggestive way he'd held her hips clamped against his rigid thighs while he kissed her. That was kissing with a single-minded, unmistakable goal, she realized. However, she was not foolish enough to feel honor-bound to sleep with him just because she'd agreed to do it last night.

After Mitchell left, she'd been too nervous and excited to sleep, so she'd sorted through the clothes she'd brought with her, trying to put together outfits that would be exactly right, no matter what Mitchell decided they should do while they were together. By the time she was finished, it was nearly three AM, and several outfits were neatly laid out beside her suitcase, including shoes, handbags, bracelets, and earrings. The only thing she hadn't decided on was what she should be wearing when he arrived to pick her up and how to wear her hair.

This morning, she'd been too preoccupied to worry about her appearance. Instead of fussing with her hair, she'd pulled it up into a ponytail, and she'd chosen the first articles of clothing she noticed when she opened her closet door—a pair of jeans, a white, short-sleeved T-shirt, and leather sandals.

With a nervous sigh, Kate leaned down and ruffled the short hair on Max's head. "This is all your fault," she joked. "Just because he helped me rescue you and then arranged for some flea powder, I felt obliged to sleep with him—"

She broke off as three short, solid knocks sounded on the villa's front door. Max rolled to his feet and walked beside her, trailing the makeshift "leash" she'd created by tying two belts together from the white terry-cloth robes the hotel provided to its guests.

She glanced at her watch. It was exactly ten o'clock.

Chapter Thirteen

WITH HER HAND ON THE DOORKNOB, KATE HESITATED, nervously bracing herself to confront the virtual stranger she'd agreed, in a moment of obvious insanity, to spend the night with. She fixed a bright smile on her face, and on the chance that he intended to kiss her hello, she purposely took three steps backward while pulling the door open.

Mitchell's tall, wide-shouldered frame loomed in the doorway. Clad in casual black slacks and an expensive-looking black knit T-shirt that deepened his tan and turned his eyes the color of blue steel, he looked lethally handsome and incredibly sexy.

Kate took another cautious step backward. "You're right on time," she said brightly.

He paused momentarily, measuring the distance she'd carefully put between them; then he lifted knowing eyes to hers and slowly walked inside. "Punctuality is one of my very few virtues," he replied with a shrug, glancing casually around the room. Kate watched him register her blue suitcase lying on the bed; then he transferred his attention to the dog, who was directly in front of him. "How is Max?"

"He seems to be feeling fine," Kate replied, looking at the bag in Mitchell's hand. "I hope you have a leash and collar in there. I had to tie together two belts from bathrobes to take him outside this morning."

"I noticed. He looks like he's escaped from a spa for canines," he quipped, handing the bag to her.

Memories of the laughter they'd shared last night came flooding back, drowning out some of the uneasy unfamiliarity Kate had felt all morning. "I'll lock the doors," Mitchell volunteered, starting toward the terrace.

"There's lots of food left over from breakfast on the table out there. Help yourself," Kate said to his back as she unrolled the top of the flat, almost weightless paper bag.

"I couldn't find a store that sold leashes and I ran out of time, so I bought those instead," he said, walking outside to inspect the covered plates on the table.

From the bag, Kate extracted two of the gaudiest neckties she'd ever seen, one with palm trees on it, the other with the words *St. Maarten* emblazed in neon yellow on a background of electric blue. With an inner smile, she crouched in front of Max, blocking him from Mitchell's view, while she swiftly removed the makeshift terry-cloth leash. Kate had learned to tie a Windsor knot in a man's necktie when she worked at Donovan's during college, and her fingers worked rapidly as she wrapped the palm-tree necktie over Max's neck and duplicated the procedure. She glanced over her shoulder as Mitchell lifted the lid off one of the breakfast dishes. "Call me overly fastidious," he remarked, "but I refuse to be the second one to chew on a steak bone."

Moments later, she heard him close and lock the terrace doors, and she straightened the ends of the necktie with an expert tug; then she pulled her sunglasses off the top of her head and perched them on top of Max's head, giving him a reassuring pat so that he wouldn't shake them off.

"I'm not sure your 'tourist look' is an improvement

over my 'spa look,'" Kate said as Mitchell came to a
stop directly behind her. Swiveling on her heels, she gave
him an unobstructed view of Max.

"At least the ties are lightweight—" he began; then he
gave a shout of laughter and looked down at Kate, his
eyes warm, his grin lazy and appreciative. "Very clever."

Kate stood up slowly, smiling back at him, her eyes
locked with his, and she felt the spell of the night before
begin to wrap itself around them. He obviously felt it,
too, because he slipped his hands around her waist in a
light caress, and his deep voice acquired a husky, intimate note. "Hi," he said, smiling into her eyes.

"Hi," Kate whispered back. The telephone rang, and
she jumped; then she looked guiltily at it. Mitchell
glanced at the ringing phone, mentally grimacing at the
lawyer's irritating sense of timing. Instead of kissing her
as he'd intended to do, he dropped his hands and said,
"Let's get out of here."

Kate nodded and bent down to remove Max's necktie;
then she knotted it together with the other necktie in the
bag, creating a long, makeshift leash.

"He was a little uneasy about being on a leash when I
took him outside in the garden this morning," she told
Mitchell as they walked down the path from the villas toward the hotel's main entrance, "but he didn't try to get
away from me."

"Which proves he knows a good steak when he eats
one," Mitchell replied, but he noticed that the big dog
seemed content to walk close by her side, rather than
trying to test the length of his makeshift tether, and he
thought it surprising that a wild stray would come so
willingly to her heel. Evidently, he decided wryly, Kate
Donovan had that same effect on male "strays,"
whether they were canine or human. "Let's hope he's
just as docile about getting into a car and riding on a
boat," he added.

Mitchell had already put the convertible top up so the dog couldn't jump out of the car, but no amount of urging or shoving from Kate could get the animal to climb into it. After tossing her suitcase into the trunk, Mitchell went around to the passenger side of the car to help Kate, and ended up standing back, enjoying the view instead. She was bending over the dog, trying to plant his front feet onto the floor of the backseat, and for the first time, Mitchell realized that, from the rear, Kate Donovan looked adorable in snug jeans. "If you get in first," he suggested finally, "Max may be willing to follow you." The ploy worked, and Mitchell closed the passenger door behind the dog; then he walked around the car and opened the driver's door so Kate could climb out of the backseat and get into the front.

In the parking lot on the other side of the driveway, Detective Childress watched Wyatt's vehicle pulling away from the curb and glanced at his watch. Reaching for the surveillance notebook lying on the seat of the little white rental car, Childress jotted down the exact time of Wyatt's departure while Detective MacNeil emerged from the hotel lobby and jogged across the driveway. "Did you find out who the redhead is?" Childress asked, shoving the car into gear the instant MacNeil's door closed.

"Not yet. The doorman gave me the same answer I got last night from the manager and the other doorman—that it's against hotel policy to divulge the names of hotel guests to anyone."

Wyatt's convertible was already making a right turn onto the main road, and Childress accelerated sharply. "Did you slip the doorman five bucks before you asked?"

MacNeil snickered. "I slipped him ten bucks, not five, and that's the answer I bought. However, the assistant manager, Mr. Orly, is in charge today, and Orly looks very flustered. While I was in the lobby, a couple named 'Wainwright' checked in, and Orly couldn't find their reservations. After he got that ironed out, he sent for a bellman to show them to their villa and referred to them as 'Mr. and Mrs. Rainright.' I didn't ask Orly about the redhead while I was in there because he wouldn't have told me, but maybe 'Mr. Wainwright' can get it out of him."

As he spoke, MacNeil pulled his cell phone out of his shirt pocket and called the Island Club. "I'd like to speak to Mr. Orly," he told the hotel operator.

After a significant delay, Orly answered MacNeil's call, sounding so harassed that his sentences ran together. "This is Mr. Orly I'm sorry to have kept you waiting How may I be of service?"

"This is Philip Wainwright," MacNeil lied, trying to sound authoritative and, at the same time, willing to overlook Orly's earlier screwups during the check-in procedure if he cooperated now. "When my wife and I were on our way to breakfast, we met a young woman who remembered us from when we were here before. My wife and I both recall spending an enjoyable evening with her last spring, and we'd like to invite her to have cocktails on the beach with us later, but we cannot—for the life of us—recall her name. She has red hair and she mentioned she's staying in villa number six. What the devil is her name, anyway?"

"I'm very sorry, Mr. Wainwright, but it's strictly against hotel policy to reveal the identity of a guest to anyone."

"I am not just 'anyone,' I'm another guest!" MacNeil exclaimed indignantly.

"The hotel's policy applies to other guests, as well as to outsiders."

"Let me speak to Maurice," MacNeil demanded, knowing the manager was absent. "I've known him for years, and he won't hesitate to tell me who she is!"

The assistant manager hesitated. "Maurice is away ... however, if you're certain he wouldn't hesitate to tell you ..."

MacNeil smiled to himself as he heard the sound of pages being flipped back and forth, but Orly's next words were frustrating, rather than informative. "Villa number six is registered to a gentleman, and there is no indication of the lady's name. I'm sorry, but I have another phone call—"

"What's the gentleman's name in villa six?" MacNeil said quickly. "That might jog our memory."

"His name is Bartlett, and I don't mean to be rude, but I really must answer another call now."

"Well?" Childress asked expectantly.

MacNeil turned off his cell phone and slipped it back into his pocket. "Villa number six is registered to a gentleman named 'Bartlett,'" MacNeil replied, repeating Orly's words. "There is no indication of the lady's name."

Traffic on the island moved at a lazy pace, and the black convertible was mired in it, less than a quarter mile ahead. "I'll bet you Wyatt is heading for Blowing Point," Childress predicted, referring to the wharf where ferries and charter boats picked up passengers and returned them to the island. A minute later, the black convertible's right turn signal began to flash. "Shit, I was right—Wyatt is heading for Blowing Point and we're in for another damned boat ride. I'm already getting nauseated."

"Take a pill."

"I can't take them, they make me groggy."

"Then you should have taken one last night, instead of hanging over the edge of the boat, barfing your brains out."

"When you report in to the state's attorney today, you

tell Elliott that if I have to sleep on a boat tonight because the yacht Wyatt is on is out in the middle of a harbor, then we need a bigger boat—one that doesn't bob like a cork every time there's a ripple in the water. I don't mind being seasick for half an hour when we chase him from island to island, but I can't do my job when I've been up all damned night blowing chunks."

That last remark doused most of MacNeil's amusement, because Childress was truly superb at vehicular surveillance. Behind a steering wheel, Childress could maneuver through any kind of traffic, darting and ducking in and out of it, without attracting any notice. He also had an almost uncanny knack of knowing when he needed to close the distance between Wyatt's vehicle in order to see where Wyatt was about to go, and when it was safe to drop far back and stay completely out of Wyatt's rearview mirror.

Because of that, Childress did most of the driving on land, while MacNeil handled piloting their boat. As a precaution, they rented different cars and different boats each day, but MacNeil was far more confident of Childress's ability to handle his job than he was of his own ability to pilot a boat larger than the twenty-four-foot outboard fishing craft they were using today.

"How big is the boat Wyatt is using today?" Childress asked as he flipped on his right turn indicator.

"I don't know—thirty-six feet, maybe thirty-eight feet."

"If I have to sleep on a boat again, I want one that size." He waited until Mac finally looked directly at him and said, "I'm not kidding, Mac."

MacNeil opened his mouth to make a joke but bit it back. Beads of sweat were already popping out on Childress's forehead at the mere anticipation of another boat ride, and beneath his newly acquired tan, Childress's skin was turning a grayish-green. Rather than admit that he didn't think he could handle a larger boat, MacNeil said, "Wyatt left his luggage at the hotel in St. Maarten this morning. I don't think he plans to sleep on Benedict's yacht tonight."

Chapter Fourteen

THE WHARF AT BLOWING POINT WAS BUSTLING WITH activity. Two catamarans flying brightly colored flags and loaded with tourists were pulling away from the dock, and more tourists were lined up to board the regular ferry that ran back and forth between Anguilla and St. Maarten at half-hour intervals.

Mitchell found a parking space near the far end of the wharf where the boat he had chartered was tied up, its captain standing on the bow, smoking a cigarette. "I hope Max is as willing to follow you onto a boat as he was to follow you into a car," he said, opening Kate's door and helping her out. Leaning into the backseat, he picked up the end of the dog's makeshift leash. "He's shaking all over."

"He's nervous," Kate said sympathetically. Patting the side of her leg, she called, "Come here, Max, let's—"

The big dog erupted from the backseat in a frenzied leap that nearly knocked her over. Laughing, she staggered backward, recovered her balance, and reached for his leash.

"Let me hold on to that until we get him on the boat," Mitchell said. Wrapping the end of the necktie-leash around his hand for better control, he tightened his grip; but he needn't have worried, because once the dog's feet were firmly on the ground, Max sidled up next to Kate and trotted happily beside her. "Have you always been able to tame wild beasts, or is Max an exception?" Mitchell asked half seriously.

"Max isn't completely wild," Kate said, scratching Max behind his ears. "He may have been running loose his whole life, but he likes humans, which means that he was around someone who played with him and handled him when he was a little puppy. If that weren't true—if he hadn't been 'socialized' back then—he wouldn't want anything to do with us now." She shot Mitchell an apologetic look and explained, "My best friend and former roommate is a vet."

They reached Mitchell's chartered boat, and Kate's attention turned to the task of getting Max aboard. "Let me get on first," she said. Taking the captain's outstretched hand, she stepped off the dock into the boat's stern; then she turned and patted the side of her leg as she had before. "Come on, Max," she called.

Max backed up, body trembling with fright, but just as Kate decided they would have to lift him aboard, he gave a giant leap forward and landed against her legs, knocking her into the captain, who grabbed her arms to steady her.

"So far, this has been easier than I expected," Mitchell remarked, stepping down into the boat.

"Easier on *you,* not me," Kate laughed, dusting dog hair off her jeans.

Mitchell chuckled at her quip and walked over to the railing to stand beside her, trapping the dog between them. The captain started the engine and Mitchell angled sideways, idly watching her long ponytail shifting in the breeze as the pier slid away and the boat picked up speed.

"Why are you staring at me?" she asked.

Mitchell was staring at her because she had the greenest eyes, the smoothest skin, and the most beautiful mouth of any woman he'd ever known. And, if her tender devotion to a stray mongrel was any indication, she also had the softest heart. He was thoroughly enchanted with all her attributes except the last one. For some reason, that one made him feel vaguely, inexplicably uneasy. "I was thinking that you have a beautiful smile," he replied, then he turned toward the railing and leaned his forearms on it, watching the boat's churning wake spread into a wide V.

The unexpected compliment filled Kate with pleasure, but since he hadn't sounded entirely pleased—or convincing—when he answered her question, she decided not to reply.

Ten minutes later, as they neared St. Maarten, the captain finally broke the silence. "Are either of you folks fans of Zack Benedict, the movie actor?" he called.

When Mitchell said nothing, Kate looked over her shoulder at the captain. "I'm a huge fan of his."

"That's Benedict's boat over there," the captain told her, pointing off to the left at a gleaming white motor yacht riding at anchor inside the harbor. "It's called the *Julie*."

"Then it's named after his wife," Kate explained to Mitchell as she admired the graceful lines of her favorite movie star's boat.

"Some tourists told me they saw Benedict aboard this morning, reading a newspaper," the captain provided. "Do you want me to take you over there? I can get you in real close, and you could get a look at him if he's on deck."

"No," Mitchell said emphatically at the same time Kate said politely, "No thank you."

Startled by his forceful reply, Kate looked curiously at him. "You aren't a Zack Benedict fan?"

His brow furrowed and an inexplicable smile edged his mouth while he appeared to give her question grave consideration. "I can't, in good conscience, describe myself to you as Zack Benedict's fan," he said finally. "However," he added, "I'd be interested in hearing why you're such a 'huge fan' of his."

Kate thought he was being condescending, but she refused to back down from her statement. "I admire him even more as a person than as a movie star," she explained very firmly. "Men thought he was ultramacho when he escaped from prison a few years ago and took Julie Mathison hostage, but women all over the world fell madly in love with him when he forgave her for leading him into a trap and getting him recaptured. When he went back to the small town she lived in and asked her to marry him, half the women in America were in tears when they saw the newsclips of how he did it."

"Were you in tears?" Mitchell asked, turning fully toward her.

"Of course."

"You sound like a hopeless romantic."

"I probably am," she admitted.

"She betrayed him," Mitchell reminded her. "If the real murderer hadn't been found, Zack Benedict would still be rotting in prison because he trusted her when he escaped and she betrayed him."

"You aren't very forgiving, are you?"

"Let's just say I'm not a romantic."

Although he sounded very sure of that, as Kate looked at his handsome face, she considered some of his actions the night before and arrived at her own conclusion. Smiling a little, she turned away from him and gazed at Zack Benedict's yacht instead.

"What was that all about?" he asked with amused curiosity.

"I was deciding for myself whether you're a romantic."

"What did you decide?"

"I think you are."

"And you think you can tell things about me by look-ing into my eyes?"

Kate nodded in the affirmative, but her answer was a little shaky. "I really, really hope so."

Mitchell suppressed a grin at her uneasy tone and toyed with the idea of surprising her tomorrow by taking her aboard Zack's boat and explaining that he knew both Zack and Julie well, and that he liked Julie. At the moment, however, he wasn't inclined to say anything that would lead to a prolonged discussion of her favorite romantic hero, and he didn't want to commit himself to any plan other than going to bed with her.

Chapter Fifteen

"THE VET'S OFFICE IS A FEW BLOCKS FROM HERE," Mitchell said as he helped her off the boat at Captain Hodges Wharf in Philipsburg, a bustling, picturesque little town on the Dutch side of St. Maarten. "We could walk there easily, but with your suitcase and the dog, we'll be better off with a taxi."

"You're probably right—" Kate began, but her cell phone rang and she paused to take it out of her purse and look at the caller's name. "I need to take this phone call. I left a message for a business associate to call me at this number."

"I'll take the dog and your suitcase and find a taxi," Mitchell said, already walking toward the street.

Kate put the phone to her ear and covered her other ear with her hand, but there was so much background noise from street traffic and boat motors that she finally took the phone away from her ear and turned the volume all the way up. "I couldn't hear you before, Louis, but I can hear you now. Did anything happen yesterday that I should know about?"

Following slowly behind Mitchell, Kate listened to Louis Kellard go over one day's events at the restaurant: The vegetable supplier had delivered only half their order, and the featured evening entrée had to be changed partway through the night; the bartender had refused to serve any more liquor to an inebriated customer who made a scene and had to be escorted out; this morning his attorney had called, threatening to sue the restaurant for causing embarrassment to his client; the wine cellar needed to be replenished before Kate returned . . .

Kate slid into the backseat of the taxi and Max jumped in behind her, so she scooted to the middle of the seat while she gave instructions to Louis: "If the attorney calls back, do not say anything to him, just refer him to our attorney. Which bartender was involved?" When Louis told her it was Jimmy, she said, "Tell Jimmy to exercise more tact from now on. My father told me Jimmy was becoming a prima donna, and he was thinking of letting him go. Did you talk to our vegetable supplier and find out why we got only half our order?"

While the taxi made its slow way along Front Street, which was lined with shops and crowded with tourists, Kate listened to the rest of Louis's litany of problems, and she did her best to help solve them, but most of the time she could only answer Louis's questions with a question of her own: "What would my father have done?"

By the time Louis was finished, Kate felt panicked and helpless. "Call me back this morning, as soon as you find out what happened to our vegetable order and why our linen inventory is suddenly so low," she reminded him before he hung up. She ended the call and slipped the cell phone into her purse; then she glanced at Mitchell and found him watching her, his dark brows drawn together in puzzlement. "I imagine you're wondering about that phone call," she said.

"I couldn't help overhearing it. I was under the impression that you're a social worker and that your father owned a restaurant. Just now, it sounded as if you're running it for him."

Kate drew a shaky breath but managed to keep her voice steady. "My father is dead. He was killed on his way home from the restaurant three weeks ago. It was late at night, and the police think it was a random, drive-by shooting, because there had been another one in the same neighborhood a few days before."

"And you're going to try to run the restaurant in his place, is that it?"

Kate nodded. "I quit my job at DCFS so that I could give it my best effort. I worked at the restaurant part-time during high school and college, but I'm not at all sure I know how to run it the way my father did. I'm—" She broke off and looked down at her lap, belatedly realizing that Max's head was resting on her knee, his eyes fixed worriedly on her face.

Mitchell quietly finished the sentence she'd been unable to complete. "You're afraid you're going to fail."

"I'm *terrified*," Kate admitted.

"Have you considered trying to sell it?"

"That's not as easy to consider doing as it seems. My father loved that restaurant, and he invested his whole life in it. He loved me, too, and because he spent most of his time there, most of my happy memories of being with him are centered right there. The restaurant was a part of both of us. Now, it's all I have left of him—and it's also all that's left of 'us.' It's difficult to explain . . ."

Surprised by a sudden desire to tell Mitchell about her life with her father, she reached out and stroked Max's head, trying to resist the impulse. After several moments of indecision, she stole a look at Mitchell, half expecting him to look preoccupied or bored.

Instead, he was watching her intently. "Go on," he said.

Kate tried to think of a good example of why the restaurant held such cherished memories of her life with her father and settled for the first one that came to mind. "Normally, the restaurant was closed in the afternoons between three o'clock and five o'clock, so when I was young, I used to do my homework sitting beside my father at the bar while he did whatever work he had to do. He sat next to me so he could help me with my homework anytime I needed it. Actually, he sat next to me because that was the only way he could be sure I *did* my homework. Anyway, he enjoyed math and history and science, but I knew he hated English grammar and he hated drilling me on spelling." With a rueful smile, Kate finished, "I hated homework, period, so I used to make him help me with English grammar and drill me on spelling, day after day after day, just to get even with him."

Instead of commenting, Mitchell lifted his brows, silently inviting her to say more. A little surprised that he seemed genuinely interested, Kate tried to think of another example to give him. "When I was in fourth grade," she said after a moment, "I decided I wanted to take roller-skating lessons at the rink. My father disapproved of the sort of kids who hung around there, so he enrolled me in ballet classes twice a week instead, even though I didn't really want to take ballet lessons. The ballet school burned down the day after I started my lessons—I had nothing to do with that, in case you're wondering."

"The possibility never crossed my mind," Mitchell said.

Kate realized he was completely serious and bit back a laugh at his apparent belief that she was a little angel, rather than the little brat she had actually been. "When the ballet school burned down, the nearest one was a bus ride away, and I knew he'd never let me take the bus to it, so I went on and on about how bad I felt for the ballet teacher and how disappointed I was *not* to be able to take ballet lessons any more . . ."

"And?" Mitchell prompted when Kate drew a laughing breath.

"And so my father invited the ballet teacher to conduct

her classes at the restaurant instead. God, it was so funny to see him trying not to grimace while thirty ballerinas in little tutus pirouetted around his dining room twice a week and a three-hundred-pound woman pounded away on his antique piano."

Kate fell silent, smiling . . . thinking of the birthday parties her father gave for her at Donovan's. When Mitchell seemed to be waiting for her to say more, she told him what she was remembering: "Every year on my birthday, he threw a big 'surprise' party for me at the restaurant and invited all my classmates from school. He had balloons all over the place and a beautiful cake—always a chocolate cake decorated with pink frosting, because I was a girl. For weeks beforehand, he'd try to fool me into thinking he wasn't going to have the party. He'd tell me he'd booked the dining room for someone else because we needed the money, or he'd tell me he had to be somewhere else that day. He wanted me to be surprised when I walked into the restaurant after school and saw everyone there."

"And were you surprised?"

Kate shook her head. "Never. How could he possibly have expected me not to notice a big vat of pink frosting in the kitchen the day before my birthday, or all the extra containers of chocolate ice cream in the freezer, or two hundred balloons and a helium machine in the back room? Besides that, he always asked one or two of my friends to be sure all my classmates were invited, so of course I heard about it from one of them."

"I see why you were never fooled," Mitchell said with a grin.

Kate started to return his smile, then she sobered and said, "Actually, I did get fooled once—on my fourteenth birthday."

"How did he fool you that time?"

"By deciding not to have a party for me at all." To divert him from asking about that one miserable birthday, Kate ended her reminiscences completely and returned to his original question about whether she'd considered selling the restaurant. "Even if I decide I should sell the place, I'd still have to keep it open in order to do that, so I really have no choice right now except to run it—if I can."

Rather than offering her empty words of encouragement about her ability to do that, which was what Kate expected him to do, he put his arm around her shoulders and curved his hand around her arm, sliding it slowly up and down in a gesture of comfort. Kate leaned against him, letting the movement of his hand soothe away her qualms about the future, at least for now.

"I'm sorry about your father's death," he said after a minute. "I wondered why you had a book about coping with grief with you in the restaurant yesterday."

Kate shot him a startled look. "You don't miss anything, do you?"

"Not when I'm concentrating on something. Or *someone*," he added, and shifted his gaze meaningfully to her lips.

Kate knew he was deliberately flirting with her in an effort to distract her and cheer her up, and she smiled and went along with his plan. "You were concentrating on your shirt yesterday, not on me."

"I have a rare gift—I can concentrate on two things at the same time."

"So can I," she teased, "which is why *I'm* aware that the taxi has stopped and the driver is waiting for us to get out."

Chapter Sixteen

THE VETERINARIAN'S OFFICE WAS IN A NARROW PINK
clapboard house, and the waiting room area was obviously the vet's living room. Mitchell had found the vet's name in a phone book earlier that morning and phoned for an appointment, but even so, they had to wait nearly forty-five minutes, during which time Kate filled out the vet's information sheet and Max sniffed every inch of the cramped room, including an indignant cat, a shy poodle, and a terrified yellow canary in a birdcage, all of whom were already there with their owners when Mitchell and Kate arrived.

When the vet finally came out and asked for "Mary Donovan," Kate left her purse on the chair next to Mitchell so that she'd have both hands free to deal with Max while the vet looked him over.

Mitchell watched her disappear through a doorway; then he picked up a tourist guide written in Dutch because there was nothing else in the waiting room to read. Kate's cell phone rang shortly afterward, and he let the call go through to her phone's voice mail system, rather than trying to answer it for her.

A few minutes later, it rang again, and her voice mail picked up that call, too.

Ten minutes later, she received another call. Mitchell frowned at her purse, wondering if the lawyer-boyfriend was trying to reach her. If so, he was either very persistent, Mitchell decided, or else some sixth sense was warning him that his girlfriend was ignoring his calls because she was straying with another man. Gazing at her purse, Mitchell envisioned a prosperous, middle-aged attorney who'd probably been physically attractive when Kate first met him years before, but who was now getting fat and out of shape—and becoming desperate to maintain his hold on a much younger woman—one who, he feared, might be tiring of her role as his "plaything."

Mitchell had witnessed that scenario often enough in the past to be certain he was right, but this time he reminded himself to feel a little gentlemanly compassion for the lawyer. After all, the poor son of a bitch had spent a small fortune to take her on a vacation at a premier spot in the Caribbean, and while he was stuck in Chicago, Mitchell was about to take her to bed.

He looked up as Kate emerged with the vet, who was repeatedly patting her arm in a way that struck Mitchell as being rather inappropriate. "I'll take some X-rays of Max's head and shoulder just to be on the safe side," the vet promised. "I'll dip him for fleas and give him all his shots. If you want me to board him again tomorrow night, just give me a call. In the meantime," he added as Mitchell rose to his feet, "I'll get all the papers ready so you can take him back to the States."

Mitchell stared at her in amused disbelief; then he picked up her suitcase from beside his chair and handed her purse to her. "Instead of calling an ambulance for Max last night," he joked as he held the front door open for her, "I should have bought him a plane ticket."

Kate accepted the gibe with a quick smile and explained her decision. "I have to take him home with me, or he'll end up being euthanized."

"Is that what the vet told you?" Mitchell asked as he stepped off the cracked sidewalk in front of the vet's house and flagged down a cab turning the corner.

Kate nodded. "He said there's virtually no chance of

finding a good home for him here or on Anguilla. Max is a stray, and because he's large, he's expensive to feed."

A battered gray Chevrolet with the word *taxi* on the door stopped in the street in front of them, and when they were both inside, Kate elaborated and Mitchell gave the driver instructions. "I phoned my friend, Holly—the vet in Chicago—this morning," she clarified. "Holly told me the treatment for rabies isn't a big deal anymore, but on rare occasions, the rabies injection has serious, even fatal side effects for some people. That physician last night was already in a panic even though rabies isn't a problem on the island. Instead of quarantining Max for the rest of the ten days, the physician can euthanize him and find out immediately if Max had rabies. And I think he'd decide to do exactly that."

She was probably right, Mitchell knew, so he changed the subject. "You had several phone calls while you were with the vet."

"Probably from Louis at the restaurant and Holly," Kate said, already reaching for her purse. Forgetting that she'd turned the volume on her phone up to its maximum, Kate pressed the button to retrieve her voice mail messages while Mitchell politely pulled a tourist booklet from the pocket on the back of the driver's seat and glanced through it.

The first message wasn't from Louis; it was from Evan, and he sounded so concerned that Kate felt a stab of guilt. *"Kate, why didn't you return my phone call last night, honey? I called you again at the hotel this morning and left a message, and I still haven't heard from you. I'm getting worried. Are you feeling ill? Are the headaches back?"*

Evan's second message made Kate feel even worse. *"Honey, I just called Holly and she said she talked to you yesterday and this morning, and you're feeling fine. Evidently you're so angry with me for not being there that you won't even take my calls anymore. I miss you terribly, Kate, and I'm tired of having to go away with you so that we can spend all our days and nights together. We should be able to do that right here in Chicago. We've been together for years, and we know we make each other happy. We both want the same things—a home, children, and each other. What else matters? I—"*

Unable to bear another word, Kate snapped her cell phone closed without listening to the next message. She stole a sidelong glance at Mitchell, relieved that he seemed to be engrossed in reading the tourist pamphlet he was holding, but he was frowning and his jaw looked tense. After a moment of uneasy silence, Kate said brightly, "Everything is fine."

In response to that he stuffed the pamphlet back into the seat pocket and directed a challenging brow at her. "Your boyfriend seems to think otherwise."

"You heard?"

"I couldn't help hearing it. Is he married?"

"No, of course not! Why would you think such a thing?"

"For one thing, you said you've been together for years, but from what I heard him say just now, you apparently don't live together. How old is he?"

"He's thirty-three. Why do you—" A realization hit Kate and she twisted toward him in the seat. "Are you under the impression I'm some sort of"—she hesitated and then settled for the least awful of the descriptions that came to mind—"a kept woman?"

"I haven't dwelled on the possibilities, but that was the most likely one, based on what I know of similar situations."

"Do you have a lot of experience with 'similar' situations?"

He leaned back, stretched his legs out, and hesitated; then he looked at her and said bluntly, "Yes."

Before Kate could recover from that statement, he changed the subject: "Why did the vet call you 'Mary'?"

"Because I filled out his questionnaire with my legal name, which is Mary Katherine. Until I was a teenager and could make them stop, everyone called me Mary Kate. My father never stopped calling me that."

"Mary Kate," he repeated a little grimly. "Very cute. Perfect, in fact, for an Irish choir girl."

Startled by his tone, Kate said, "I was never a choir girl in the way I think you mean. In fact, I was a wild child."

"Good," he said tightly.

Kate turned her head and gazed at the foothills of the mountains on her right while she tried to come up with an explanation for his attitude. Something he'd heard in the last few minutes was bothering him, but she couldn't figure out exactly what it was.

Chapter Seventeen

AFTER SEVERAL MINUTES, KATE GLANCED SIDEWAYS AND caught him looking at her, his forehead furrowed into a thoughtful frown. Suppressing a self-conscious impulse to smooth her hair, she broke the silence with the first inane subject that came to mind. "The weather here is certainly beautiful this time of year."

"Yes, it is."

"I thought it might rain today, but there isn't a cloud in the sky."

"If it rained without a cloud in the sky, it would be surprising," he agreed solemnly, but he was on the verge of smiling, and Kate was so relieved that she gave him a rueful grin.

Mitchell's gaze dropped from her bright green eyes to her soft lips, and the impulse to kiss her was so strong that he had to turn his head and look in a different direction. His conscience had suddenly developed a voice after decades of silence on the subject of sexual ethics, and it was in an uproar over the true picture he'd just formed of Mary Kate Donovan. In the taxi, on the way to the veterinarian, she'd told him about her father and their lives together. As she spoke, it had been obvious even to Mitchell—who had little personal knowledge of loving family relationships—that Kate had loved her father deeply and she was grieving over his death. She was also, by her own admission, terrified of the responsibility she now had of trying to run his restaurant in Chicago.

The absentee boyfriend, who Mitchell had originally assumed was a wealthy, aging playboy using Kate for a toy, was actually a year younger than Mitchell, and he not only cared about Kate, he wanted to marry her. He'd taken her to a wonderful hotel on a lush, tropical island, undoubtedly to help her recuperate. When he needed to return to Chicago, he'd left behind in that seductive setting a beautiful, grieving, worried Kate who had probably never cheated on him before, but who was so weakened by loneliness and sorrow that she was ready to fall into Mitchell's arms.

Next week, or next month, she'd start regretting going to bed with him, and then she'd have guilt to deal with on top of all her other burdens. She was so tenderhearted that in the midst of her own misery over her father's death, she was determined to take a stray dog home with her to keep him safe. She'd end up torturing herself for doing anything as "cruel" as betraying her boyfriend.

Mitchell's conscience pointed out that if he truly liked Kate as much as he felt he did, he'd spare her the ramifications of sleeping with him by telling the cabdriver to turn around and take them back to Philipsburg. He himself wasn't boyfriend material. Among other things, he had no intention of staying in Chicago longer than a week after he returned. His appearance at Cecil's birthday party had been noted by the *Tribune*'s social columnist, and if he continued to be seen in Chicago, someone was going to start digging around, and sooner or later his personal history would become tantalizing gossip among people he wouldn't voluntarily share an evening with, let alone the sordid story of his life. Furthermore, he felt an inexplicable, intense aversion to acknowledging his relationship to the illustrious Wyatts, but in the city where Kate Donovan lived, he no longer had a choice.

Mitchell's logic went to battle with his conscience and

argued that Kate was old enough to decide for herself what she wanted to do and what was best for her. Moreover, prolonged passionate lovemaking would provide her with an excellent, temporary diversion from her woes. That last part wasn't logic, it was lust, Mitchell's irate conscience pointed out.

The cabdriver chose that moment to look over his shoulder and ask Mitchell for instructions. "How much farther ahead is the turn?"

Lost in his thoughts, Mitchell hesitated, and then said, flatly, "Several miles." Lust and logic had fewer arguments, but louder voices, than his conscience.

Kate expected him to turn to her now and explain where they were going, but he looked out his own window again and said nothing. Baffled by his silence, she reached across him for the tourist pamphlet he'd been looking at earlier. She'd already gotten a similar pamphlet in the lobby of the Island Club, and this pamphlet reiterated much of the same information: St. Maarten was a small island occupying only thirty-seven square miles; it was divided between two governments—the northern section being French, the southern section Dutch.

A map of the island was attached to the back of the pamphlet, and Kate unfolded it, hoping to gauge where she was. They'd been traveling on a main highway, and according to the map, there was only one of those, and it made a full circle of the island. She remembered passing exit signs to Simpson Bay and Princess Juliana Airport soon after they left Philipsburg, which meant they'd been going east. Based on the landmarks she'd seen since then, they were now traveling north along the coastline of the French section, with the Caribbean Sea on the left and the foothills of the mountains on the right.

Their destination was obviously in the French section, so Kate started reading about the French section's exciting nightlife, fabulous shops, open-air markets, and glorious beaches, some of which were nude. Concentrating on all that was easier than wondering what was bothering the man beside her. It also prevented her from thinking about Evan's phone messages.

She was reading her third pamphlet when the taxi rounded a curve, slowed, and then turned right into a winding landscaped lane bordered by ornamental stone walls. For several minutes the lane wound upward around a hill covered in dense tropical foliage; then the cab rounded a sharp bend and stopped at a stone gatehouse, where a uniformed guard stood next to a pair of tall black iron gates with "The Enclave" in brass lettering across them.

Mitchell leaned forward and gave the guard his name; the gates swung open, the cab drove inside and rounded another bend, and Kate gasped with pleasure at her first glimpse of their destination: An elaborate, four-story, Mediterranean-style hotel was snuggled back against a hillside overlooking the Caribbean Sea, with several sets of balconied stone steps leading down to a long, secluded crescent of pristine white sand. Waiters were trotting up and down the steps carrying trays of food and drinks to sunbathers on the beach, who were concealed from view by large aqua beach umbrellas attached to chaise longues. "What a beautiful setting!" Kate exclaimed.

A doorman opened her door and Kate slid out of the cab, tipping her head back to look up at the hotel. The roof was made of aqua tiles, and the structure was of white stucco with gracefully rounded open balconies dotting its facade and much larger, enclosed balconies on each side.

Inside, the lobby was cool and elegant, with polished stone floors and French doors opening out onto a hillside dining balcony. Kate walked with Mitchell past the concierge's desk, where a couple was arranging for scuba gear and a sailboat, but when Mitchell continued past the elevators toward a desk with a sign on it that said Guest Registration, she glanced uncertainly at him.

"I haven't registered yet," he explained.

"Aren't you staying here?"

He shook his head. "I'm staying on a friend's boat, but I thought this would be more comfortable for the two of us."

Rather than go with him to the registration desk, Kate gestured toward a group of chairs near the elevators with a table between them that held a stack of hotel brochures. "I'll wait over there."

As Mitchell strode toward the registration desk, two very attractive women emerged from one of the shops in the lobby. Both women glanced at him, stopped laughing, and then turned partway around to stare after him. They held their comments until they neared the elevators, where Kate was seated.

"Is he not the best-looking man you've ever seen in your life?" one of them said to the other.

"He is what you call a *god*!" her friend agreed in an awed French-accented voice; then she turned clear around for another look at him.

Kate automatically followed her gaze. Mitchell was standing at the registration desk signing the usual forms. From behind, his shoulders looked a yard wide, Kate realized—but then another realization hit her that banished all thoughts of his manly physique: The "god" hadn't brought a suitcase with him!

The only explanation she could think of for this was that Mitchell had decided to remain naked with her until they checked out tomorrow, and that conclusion made Kate's stomach lurch. Last night he'd specifically told her to bring something nice to wear because he wanted to take her out gambling, but he hadn't brought a single change of clothes, not even a bathing suit—

Because the beach and swimming pool here were probably nude!

According to the pamphlet she'd read in the taxi, some beaches in the French section were nude beaches, and this hotel was definitely in the French section. The prospect of being on a nude beach—let alone being nude herself on one—sent a shiver of horror dancing up and down Kate's spine, and she sank back in her chair. She couldn't possibly walk around naked or even topless in front of strangers. She just could *not*.

The hotel manager waylaid Mitchell when he finished registering and was on his way toward her. "I'm so glad I was able to accommodate you with the suite of your choice, Mr. Wyatt," the manager said, reaching out to shake Mitchell's hand. "It required some delicacy, but the other party was very satisfied with your offer. Actually, they were greatly relieved."

Kate watched Mitchell casually reach into his pocket before he shook the manager's hand, and she wondered idly how much money changed hands during that handshake. Then she wondered what "offer" had been extended and who the "other party" was.

"Diederik is upstairs, waiting for you," the manager continued. "He's already taken care of all your needs."

Kate hoped those needs included some clothing and a bathing suit for Mitchell. That notion was so unlikely it was absurd, and she looked down to hide her nervous urge to giggle. Mitchell's shoes appeared directly in front of her a moment later.

"Ready?" he said.

Kate's gaze slid upward along his legs, past his narrow waist, over the black shirt covering his muscular chest and broad shoulders, and finally encountered his tanned face and piercing blue eyes. "What needs of yours has Diederik taken care of?" Kate asked as she rose, a laugh in her voice.

His expression softened at the sight of her smile. "I hope it's lunch."

Chapter Eighteen

THE SUITE OF MITCHELL'S "CHOICE" TURNED OUT TO BE on the top floor of the hotel at the end of a hall. One of its double doors was slightly ajar, and a discreet plaque on the wall beside it proclaimed it to be the Presidential Suite.

Mitchell opened the door all the way for her, and Kate walked past him, stepping into a spacious foyer, then turned left and caught her breath. The exterior walls of the palatial suite were made entirely of glass, providing an uninterrupted, panoramic view of the Caribbean, both to the west and to the north. The carpeting was the same shade of aqua as the sea, the furnishings predominantly white, with huge vases of lush tropical flowers providing splashes of color.

Near the foyer was a formal dining table with six chairs. Directly in the center of the suite, facing the windows, was an enormous bed covered in a fluffy white duvet and a mountain of pillows. It was situated so that the occupants could lie in bed and view the Caribbean. In the ceiling, muted cove lighting mirrored the outline of the bed, bathing it in a pale glow. The lighting was positioned so that the occupants of the bed could see what they were doing to each other . . . Kate yanked her gaze from the bed and moved a few steps forward.

Beyond the bed, on the other side of the room in front of the windows, was a grouping of white sofas and chairs covered with plump pillows and arranged in a U so that they all looked out across the Caribbean.

"This is absolutely breathtaking," Kate said.

"I'm glad you're pleased," Mitchell replied, starting toward the large, enclosed balcony that opened off the western side of the suite. A man who Kate assumed was Diederik was standing out there at a table beneath an aqua umbrella, pouring wine into glasses. "Take a few minutes to look around while I see if Diederik has done anything about food out there."

"You sound like you're starving," Kate teased.

He turned and Kate felt the full seductive force of his slow white smile and direct gaze. "I have a very hearty appetite, Kate."

His meaning was unmistakable, and Kate's entire body tensed, partly from nervousness and partly from anticipation. He'd been so preoccupied and distant in the taxi that she'd wondered if he was having second thoughts about going to bed with her. After his last remark, she wondered now if he planned to have lunch with her in it, in order to save time. Belatedly realizing that she was standing there as if she'd taken root in the carpet, Kate wandered slowly along in his wake.

A large wet bar with four stools was positioned near the open balcony doors. In the wall to the right of the bar was an arched entrance into another room, which turned out to be a bathroom/dressing room with a beautiful wall mosaic depicting an island scene. In the center of the room, beneath a domed skylight, four steps descended into a huge sunken tub lined with mosaic tiles and surrounded by pillars. A shower large enough for four or five people was enclosed in glass on three sides with shower heads at various heights and an array of faucets on the remaining wall.

Kate put her purse down on one of the vanities that ran

most of the length of the room on two sides; then she used the bathroom. She was drying her hands when she looked down at her purse and Evan's phone messages came back to haunt her.

She'd always known he cared very much for her, but she never imagined he could be driven by worry and fear for her into actually proposing marriage on the telephone—no, in a voice mail message! What a touching, uncharacteristically impulsive thing for him to do. Until now, he'd let her evade the subject of marriage, and Kate had always assumed that was because he was secretly satisfied with the status quo—a life that was filled with work he enjoyed, a woman he enjoyed, and all the golf games he could sandwich in between those two things.

But maybe that wasn't true at all. Maybe he cared so deeply for her that he'd been willing to postpone a marriage he wanted very badly because he didn't want to pressure her into making a commitment until she was completely ready.

What a generous, selfless, tender way for him to behave . . .

Kate shook her head, trying to clear away the guilt she was feeling; then she picked up her purse and carried it with her into the main room. She put it on the barstool at the end of the bar, started toward the balcony doors, stopped, and turned back around. Earlier, when she'd checked her voice mail, she'd had three unheard messages, but she'd listened to only two of them. The third message was probably from Louis at the restaurant. If so, she really ought to listen to it. With her back to the balcony, she reached into her purse, grasped the phone, and then let it go.

If the message was from Evan, she couldn't bear to hear it. Not now. Not when she'd just checked into a hotel with a stranger to whom she was drawn so deeply, and on so many confusing levels, that she couldn't begin to understand what was happening. All she knew for certain was that she'd felt something profound and magical last night, and she wanted to experience it again, all of it: the desperate longing that came from being kissed by Mitchell; the exquisite joy of being crushed in his arms with his body straining against hers; and the unexplainable sense of profound closeness she felt at times just looking at him or listening to him speak.

But there was no denying that she'd known him only one day, which made everything she was thinking and planning to do seem terribly rash. Totally reckless. A little insane.

Tension and indecision tightened the muscles at the back of her neck into a knot. Thinking she might be on the verge of getting another headache despite the pills she was taking, Kate reached up to rub her nape; then she pulled the elastic band out of her hair and shook it loose.

Standing on the balcony, Mitchell watched Kate's thick hair tumble down over her shoulders in a wavy dark red waterfall, and he lost track of what the suite's butler was telling him. She was wrestling with some sort of decision, he sensed, and then she gave her head a toss, turned on her heel, and started toward him. Lifting his wineglass to his lips to hide his appreciative smile, he watched her walk out onto the balcony—a wholesome, unaffected, all-American girl who looked artlessly feminine in a white T-shirt and jeans . . . a churchgoing Irish girl with lofty principles, an amazingly soft heart, and a prosperous, well-educated would-be fiancé who lived in the same city she did.

Mitchell had no right to take her to bed and jeopardize any of that for her.

She stepped out onto the balcony and walked up to

him—a smiling, sexy, desirable woman with a provocative mouth that was made to be kissed, heavily lashed green eyes that melted him, and a slender body he was dying to caress and join with his own.

Mitchell decided he had *every* right to take her to bed, as long as he was honest with her in advance and made sure she had no false illusions or unrealistic expectations.

He picked up a glass of white wine and handed it to her. "Diederik was telling me about the former occupants of this suite." His expression told Kate he didn't give a damn about that topic but was making polite small talk while Diederik was there.

Diederik was in his early forties, with a bald head and neat mustache, and he'd definitely anticipated Mitchell's desire for food. The table was already laden with trays of fruit and cheese, a huge fresh salad, a plate of finger sandwiches, a tureen of soup, and two hot covered bowls, and he was in the process of arranging sliced lemons and parsley around a platter of prawns. He'd been speaking to Mitchell in Dutch, but he switched automatically to English because that was the language Mitchell had used to speak to her. "The former occupants were young newlyweds, inexperienced at foreign travel, who arrived three days ago for a four-day stay with us," Diederik explained. "On their first day, they visited some markets on the other side of the island, and they ate some food that was not fresh. The next morning, they were so ill that the hotel doctor had to start them on medication for food poisoning, and they haven't been able to get out of bed, except for necessities, since then."

Kate remembered the hotel manager's brief discussion with Mitchell in the lobby, and she aimed an accusing look straight at Mitchell while directing her question to Diederik. "Where are the young newlyweds now?"

"I had them dragged out of here and thrown off a cliff," Mitchell replied.

"They are in another suite," Diederik provided simultaneously, "which Mr. Wyatt very kindly offered to pay for. The young bridegroom was greatly distressed over the cost of this suite, which they were unable to enjoy." Satisfied with his garnishment of the prawns, he looked at Kate and said, "I will unpack for you before I leave. Do you have anything with you that you would like me to press for you?"

"No, thank you," Kate replied as she picked up half a watercress sandwich and walked over to the chest-high balcony wall for a better look at the view below.

Behind her, Diederik said, "I've pressed your clothes, Mr. Wyatt, and hung them in your closet."

Unaware that Mitchell had followed her, Kate whirled around and almost smashed her sandwich against his chest. "You have clothes to wear?" she exclaimed in delight.

Bracing his hands on the wall on either side of her, he trapped her and studied her with amused fascination. "You look ready to cheer with relief."

Before Kate could respond, Diederik said politely, "When I finish unpacking, may I be of any further service?"

With his smiling gaze still fixed on Kate, Mitchell replied, "Please turn down the bed before you leave, and see that we are not disturbed."

Kate gaped at him in horror. "Could you possibly be more obvious?"

"This is a hotel," he pointed out reasonably.

"I know it is. But in the last five days I've checked into two of them with different men. I'm feeling like a complete floozy."

He chuckled at her description of herself and ran his

knuckles up her arm in a lazy caress. "So you thought I didn't bring any clothes with me?"

"You didn't have a suitcase with you in the taxi," Kate pointed out, trying to sound less affected than she was by the touch of his skin against hers.

"I dropped it off this morning when I came out here to try to arrange for this suite or at least a better one than what the reservations clerk was offering me." His knuckles slid across her shoulder and followed the curve of her jaw, which allowed his fingertips to slip beneath the neckline of her shirt and glide over her bare collarbone. "Just out of curiosity, what did you think I was going to do about clothes while we were here?"

"I thought you'd decided you weren't going to need any clothes," Kate said shakily, trying to concentrate on his words and not his fingers. "According to the tourist pamphlets, some beaches in St. Maarten are nude."

"The casinos aren't."

"No, of course not. I thought maybe you intended to skip the casino tonight."

"And do what instead?"

"I don't know."

"Yes, you do."

Swallowing a laugh, Kate glanced toward the doorway. "Shhh. Diederik is in there. He'll hear you."

"Who cares?"

"I do. This may sound hopelessly unsophisticated to you, but I've never actually checked into a hotel for the sole purpose of going to bed with someone, and I'm a little self-conscious about it. I suppose you've done it lots of times, haven't you?"

"Now *I'm* feeling self-conscious."

"I shouldn't have asked that question," Kate said ruefully.

"Probably not," he whispered.

Kate stiffened at the implied reprimand, but before she could think of a suitable response, he twined his left hand through her hair and tipped her head back. His warm lips came down on hers in a long, slow, searching kiss filled with lazy hunger. Finally, he lifted his mouth from hers. "Let's go inside."

Kate nodded agreement. By then, she would have nodded agreement if he'd suggested they jump off the balcony headfirst, but once they were in the suite, his tone and his words startled her out of her sensual haze.

"We need to talk, Kate; sit down."

Surprised by his businesslike tone, Kate perched her hip on the arm of a sofa and watched curiously as he walked over to the windows, shoved his hands into his pockets, and looked down for several seconds as if composing his thoughts. When he turned, his expression was friendly but resolute. "Before you get into that bed with me, I want to be sure you don't have any false illusions about what's going on between us. I'm telling you this because I never want you to look back on our time together with any kind of regret."

"Go on," Kate urged when he paused to let his words sink in.

"By your own admission, you're a 'romantic,' and last night, we were caught up in a situation that might have seemed more . . . meaningful . . . than it actually was. What I'm trying to say is that there's an amazing amount of physical chemistry between us, but last night, on the beach in the moonlight, those few kisses of ours may have seemed . . . What's the word I'm looking for?"

"Magical?" Kate suggested, using the word that best fit her own impression of last night. The instant she said it, she regretted betraying that much of her own feelings about the night before, but Mitchell seemed to agree with her assessment.

"'Magical' is close enough. You weren't the only one who was influenced by the setting and the moment. I was influenced enough by it that I actually came back to you to answer your questions, which is something I never would have done under ordinary circumstances. However, that was last night and last night was an . . . aberration."

Struggling desperately not to leap to any conclusions and to appear serene, Kate tipped her head to the side and asked with a slight smile, "Are you trying to warn me off?"

"Not at all. I've been dying to get you into bed since we sat down to dinner last night."

"Are you trying to establish some sort of ground rules, then?"

"I don't think so."

"Then what are you doing?"

"I'm having an attack of scruples," he said with disgust, "and I'm trying to deal with it."

"Is this an unfamiliar occurrence for you?"

"In these circumstances, it's *unprecedented*," he said bluntly.

"In that case, I'm flattered," Kate replied, but she wasn't flattered; she was confused and uneasy and becoming more so by the moment.

"I'm trying to explain that I need to be sure you're here with me now for the right reasons, not the wrong ones. Until this morning, I didn't know your father had just died. The two of you were obviously very close, and you're feeling a little lost and alone. On top of that, you're faced with the burden of trying to run his business. You're worried and you're scared. All those emotions may be clouding your judgment about what

you and I are doing." He paused for some response
from her.

Wary of saying anything, Kate simply nodded that
she understood, even though she didn't. Not completely. Not yet.

"Until an hour ago," he continued, "I thought your
boyfriend in Chicago was some middle-aged jerk who
likes showing you off and traveling with you. Are you
following me so far?"

Kate nodded slowly.

"Good. Then here's the reality: In Chicago, there's an
eligible man who wants to marry you. Here, in this
room, there's a man who wants to take you to bed and
make love to you until neither of us has the strength to
move anymore. But it can't go any further than that. It
would get much too complicated."

"And you don't like complications?"

"No," Mitchell said. "Especially not the kind we'd
have."

"I appreciate the warning," Kate said, struggling to
view her predicament unemotionally, without feeling
mortified that she'd let herself land in this predicament
in the first place. Viewed from the right perspective, she
knew she was better off finding out now, rather than
later, that Mitchell's only interest in her was as a brief,
convenient partner for a little recreational sex. Now
that she understood, she also knew she'd end up feeling
guilty and disgusted with herself for betraying Evan for
something as tawdry and meaningless as what Mitchell
was blatantly suggesting.

Furthermore, Mitchell's summation of her state of
mind was probably right: she was an emotional mess
over her father and she wasn't thinking rationally.
Thankfully, Mitchell was thinking very rationally and
behaving very honorably by letting her know how he

felt. And to give him even more credit, he wasn't pressuring her to settle for what he was offering her, either. Quite the opposite, in fact.

Having arrived at these conclusions, Kate felt truly relieved and blessedly clearheaded—and, somewhere deep inside of her, painfully disappointed and thoroughly wretched. For the moment, however, there was nothing she could do except try to be philosophical and good-natured, and then deal with the mental turmoil later, when she was alone.

"You were undoubtedly right when you said I'm overly emotional these days because of my father's death, and my judgment is probably impaired, as well." Even as she said that, Kate's instincts and her heart insisted that although she may have been wrong about everything else, there *was* something special about the "connection" she felt with him and that he damned well felt it, too! She decided to take a small risk and lay that all out for him. There was nothing he could do but make fun of her, and she didn't think he would do that. Raising her eyes to his, she said softly, "I think fate may have intended for us to meet the way we did and to become friends—that it was predestined."

The instant she said "predestined," he gave her a skeptical look, leaned his shoulder against the window, and folded his arms over his chest.

His body language was an eloquent rejection of any supernatural influences being involved, but Kate refused to let him mock her theory before he understood it. "I like you very much," she persevered quietly, "and I think you like me, too—"

"I do. Very much," he admitted with a sudden smile that was warm and genuine.

"That's what I meant when I referred to fate and predestination. I'm usually slow and cautious about really liking someone, and I was totally *predisposed* to *dis*like you—"

"Why?"

She chuckled. "Have you ever taken a good look at your face?"

"I shave it every morning."

"Well, it's too good-looking to be owned by a man who also possesses kindness and character and—and a lot of layers." Out of words and explanations, Kate gave him the only actual example she could think of. "The best way I can illustrate what I've been trying to say is this—" Holding her hands out palms up, she smiled wryly and said, "Look at us now. We're in a hotel room, the topic is sex, and we're discussing it as if we've been friends forever. Without any anger or pretense, we've been deciding we shouldn't go to bed together." Finished, Kate waited for him to agree.

With eyes narrowed in thought, he nodded slowly as if he was arriving at a conclusion that surprised and somewhat displeased him. "*That's* what we've been deciding?"

Since he seemed to be asking himself that question, Kate saw no reason to answer it. Furthermore, it was an odd question under the circumstances, and she was running low on clever, rational answers. Instead of replying, she stood up and strolled over to the balcony doors. "Now, since I haven't cheated on my boyfriend," she said lightly, "and neither of us has done anything we'll regret later, why don't we do what two new friends should do on such a gorgeous island—let's go sightseeing. When I'm back in Chicago and you're— wherever you are—we can exchange postcards from other places we go, and write things like—'Remember that charming little café in St. Maarten?' After we're done sightseeing, you could drop me off at the vet's office, if you wouldn't mind. I'll pick up Max and take him back to Anguilla."

When Mitchell didn't reply after several moments, Kate glanced over her shoulder and saw that he hadn't moved. He was still standing with his shoulder propped against the window and his arms folded over his chest, only now he was looking at her with his brows drawn together. She studied his handsome, inscrutable features and could not make out even a hint of what he was thinking. "Can I ask you something?" she said hesitantly.

He nodded.

Unable to meet his gaze while she asked her question, Kate turned back toward the balcony, absently rubbing her arms. "Are you disappointed that there was no real magic between us last night? That it was just the setting and the moment?"

When he didn't immediately answer, she flicked a glance over her shoulder. No longer looking at her, he'd tipped his head slightly down and to his right, as if he were studying the carpet. "No," he said curtly; then he lifted his head and looked straight at her. "No," he repeated.

A realization hit Kate like a physical shock from an electrical outlet. As clearly as if he'd said it to her, she knew it was true, and surprise made her turn fully toward him. "You're not disappointed that the magic is missing, because you didn't *want* it to be there in the first place, did you?"

"You used the term 'magic' to describe last night, I didn't," he said as he straightened from his lounging position. Strolling toward her, he gave her an impatient lecture on his reality: "I do not believe in 'magic' or 'magical' events in the human experience. I also do not believe in fairy tales, miracles, spells, witchcraft, fairies, or leprechauns."

"Watch your tongue," Kate tried to joke.

Some of the tension went out of his face at her joke. "You don't really believe in that garbage, do you?"

The disappointment Kate felt earlier was turning to hurt, because now she realized he was pleased with their situation today and even purposely causing it to some extent. Struggling to keep her tone neutral, she said, "At this point it no longer matters what I believe."

"Pretend it does."

"All right, I do not believe in Santa Claus or the Easter Bunny. But I know magic when I feel it, and I felt it last night. I'm willing to agree that you weren't the cause of it, but—"

He cut her off with a mocking challenge: "I suppose you're going to try to convince me you have 'magic' with your lawyer boyfriend?"

Kate sobered. "First of all, I'm not trying to convince you of anything. Second, if the answer to your question was yes, I wouldn't have been with you last night and I wouldn't be here now. Third, and most important of all, do not mention him again," she warned implacably. "You have no right to discuss him, and neither do I."

It was this first-time defense of the boyfriend that warned Mitchell he had now run out of rope with her and he was standing precariously close to the edge of a dangerous precipice. She had too much pride and self-respect to settle for what little he was willing to offer. She wanted magic, and without it, she was staying faithful to her boyfriend. In fact, her mind was already made up to stay with him.

"What matters," she continued in a sweet, apologetic voice as she unknowingly shoved him clear off the precipice, "is that you refuse to believe in magic, and I refuse not to believe in it. And therein lies the gap we can't bridge. Not in this room or anywhere else."

Mitchell felt himself plunging through thin air, sent over the edge by a beautiful young redhead with the face of an angel and the stubborn pride of an Irish rebel. Even so, he made a manful attempt to gain a foothold and stop his fall by suggesting, "Why don't we go to bed and see what happens there?"

She shook her head and smiled that Mona Lisa smile of hers. "Why? So I could try to make you feel magic while you try to prove there is none? One person can't make that kind of magic. It takes two. It's inevitable that you'd succeed and I'd end up being disappointed. If I'm going to be disappointed," she admitted with gentle candor, "I don't want it to happen with you. I don't know why, but that's very important to me." She turned away and stepped through the balcony doorway, looking out at the water. "Let's go sightseeing now and try to get to know each other a little bit before I pick up Max and take him back to Anguilla with me. I'll wait out here if you'd like to change clothes."

Mitchell experienced the full force of his renewed free fall, complete with sensations of his stomach twisting into knots and wind howling in his ears. Drawing a long, steadying breath, he gazed at the slender back of the woman he'd allowed to do this to him. His balance returned, he felt the floor beneath his feet. On the balcony was an exquisite Irish girl who touched his heart, overheated his blood, and made him laugh. She was passionate and sweet, honest and intelligent, proud and unpredictable. She sang in a choir, smiled like an angel, and adopted ugly, stray dogs with fleas. She was a fairy tale. And he was . . .

Completely enchanted.

Walking up behind her, he slid his arms around her and drew her back against his chest. "Let's get complicated, Kate," he said with a smile in his voice.

"Thank you for the offer," she said politely, "but it's better to leave things just as they are."

Ignoring that, Mitchell pressed his lips to the top of

her head and whispered, "Chant your incantations and get out your amulets, lovely witch. Weave your magic spell."

"Please stop this, or we won't end up being friends, after all," she warned.

"We're already friends," he murmured, trailing his mouth to her ear. "We're about to become lovers."

She shivered at the touch of his breath on her ear, but refused to relent. "I told you, I don't want to."

"Yes, you do, and so do I," he said, and kissed her temple. "Put your arms around me and wrap us up in magic. I can't do it without you."

"Oh, for heaven's sake!" she burst out. "What do you think you're—"

Mitchell switched from tender persuasion to assertive action and clamped his hand over her mouth before she could finish. "Kate," he warned in a low, implacable voice, "for the next hour, the only sounds I want to hear from you are moans of delight and the words 'yes,' 'more,' and 'please.' "

He lifted his hand a fraction of an inch, and she said, "Stop it!"

"Wrong words," Mitchell said, and twisted her around. "Look at me, Kate."

Green eyes, wary and annoyed, glared at him from beneath graceful russet brows drawn into a dark, warning frown.

Mitchell heeded her expression and carefully softened his tone. "I am trying to concede. The truth is that I felt all the same things you did last night, and you *know* I did."

Looking into his cobalt eyes, listening to the slightly husky timbre of his baritone voice, Kate sensed that he was telling her the truth as well as allowing her a glimpse beneath another of his "layers," and she felt a sharp tug on her heart. His next explanation was equally revealing:

"The discouraging things I said to you a few minutes ago were mostly the result of my halfhearted desire to protect you from me—" He stopped, cocked his head to the side, and after a moment's thought, he admitted with amused irony, "Actually, it may have been the reverse."

Trying desperately not to laugh, Kate bit down on her lip and swiftly shifted her gaze to his shoulder, but looking away didn't help. She was so hopelessly drawn to him in every way that there was no refuge. Marveling at her own helplessness, she shook her head a little. Mitchell evidently mistook that shake of her head as an indication that she was about to reject what he'd said, and he gave her a stern warning: " 'No' is not on the list I gave you of acceptable words."

Caught between mirth and tenderness, Kate succumbed to defeat. Smiling into his eyes, she laid her palms on his chest and softly sighed a word that was not on his list. "Mitchell . . ."

She saw pleasure flicker in his eyes when she said his name that way. "You may add that word to your list."

Leaning up on her toes, eyes shining with laughter, voice shaky with awakening desire, Kate twined her arms around his neck. "Please," she whispered, her lips almost touching his.

"An excellent choice," Mitchell decreed, and brushed his lips back and forth over hers in a light, teasing kiss.

"More," Kate murmured when he lifted his mouth.

"An even better choice," Mitchell said with a grin, and gathered her tightly into his arms, preparing to leisurely savor and explore that mouth of hers. She took him from relaxed humor to raw hunger in minutes.

He maneuvered her—without resistance—to the side of the bed, and let go of her while he pulled his shirt off.

When he dropped it to the floor and reached out to help take her T-shirt off, she smiled up at him and shook her head slightly as if she wanted to do it herself for him. She tugged her T-shirt out of her waistband, caught it by the hem, and drew it up and over her head. When she finished, she stood in front of him in a white lacy bra, and Mitchell found himself smiling back at her—a warm, playful smile tinged with a challenge.

He dropped his gaze from her green eyes, and his hands went to his belt.

Kate had to take off her sandals before she could step out of her jeans, so she bent to deal with them. In front of her lowered eyes, his pants and briefs hit the floor. With shaky fingers, Kate concentrated on unfastening one sandal, then the other. She stepped out of them and started to straighten. Part way up, her gaze slid up a rigid male member, and she hastily jerked her eyes away. Looking at that magnificent chest of his was less nerve-racking than seeing him naked at the hips for the first time. His hands went to her shoulders, his thumbs pulling her bra straps down, leaving them loose on her arms, before he slid his hands around her back and unhooked her bra with the ease of man who had unhooked many.

Thinking that, she raised her gaze to his and saw a knowing expression sweep across his face, before he lowered his eyelids and pulled her bra away from her breasts and down her arms. Kate stepped out of her jeans, and his slow, languorous gaze drifted boldly over her, examining her breasts and waist and belly, then down to the curly hair at her thighs. In the way that she often sensed what he was thinking, she knew he expected her to put him through the same appraisal, but although she was ready to touch and be touched, she wasn't quite ready to take a deliberate look at what she'd seen unintentionally moments before.

His voice was deep and sure as his hand finally reached toward her, but not for any of the places she expected him to want to touch. His hand settled under her chin, tipping it up. "Are you feeling shy?" he asked.

She met his gaze unflinchingly and said, "No, just a little . . . uncertain."

He mistook her meaning. "Don't even consider uncertainty now."

Kate bit her lip to hide her smile, laid her palms against the muscles of his chest, and, while his hands settled on her waist, she exerted pressure. She slid her hands slowly up over his nipples, and then spread her fingers and slid them slowly back down while she watched the banked fires in his eyes begin to smolder. "Not that kind of uncertain," she whispered back.

They stood naked, face to face. She had beautiful breasts, not large, but full, and as he trailed his hand up from her waist, his eyelids closed with pleasure at the sensation of her skin. At her nipple, he opened his fingers and captured it. He increased the pressure until he wrung the first gasp of pleasure out of her.

Her hands glided over his shoulders, while she covered his mouth with her soft lips and brought her body into full contact with his.

The lazy pleasure of moments ago exploded in a deluge of pure lust, and Mitchell wrapped his arms around her and twisted his body, sending them back onto the bed. His hips landed unerringly against the seductive curly hair between her thighs, and his hands shifted back to her breasts. She gazed at him, sultry and playful, eyes smiling warmly into his. He couldn't believe how much intimate pleasure he felt just watching her face and knowing she was watching his.

Her hands smoothed slowly over his back and down his buttocks, holding him tight to her. She opened her legs, and he reminded himself that this was too soon, the preliminaries having barely begun. But he let his body touch the entrance to hers, experiencing the delight of finding her already wet. He edged inside of her just an inch, smiling a little at her hazy expression. He moved his hands to her hair. He shoved his fingers into it and, lowering his mouth to hers, slowly, deliberately forced her lips to part, opening them wide, while his hips lifted and forced her to open wide. He intended to ease just a little deeper into that tight, enclosing warmth, except that just then, she tightened her hands on his buttocks, arched her hips as much as his heavy weight would allow, and whispered an aching, imperative "Please."

He drew back, deliberately resisting the invitation.

"Please . . ."

He rammed himself into her, burying himself full length into her arching body, and his own body began to move without his volition, capturing her and forcing her to move with him. With the last ounce of willpower he possessed, he rolled onto his back, putting her astride his hips to slow them both down. Pressing her palms against him for support, she forced herself into a sitting position, her rumpled hair falling down her sides. She began to move on him with a rhythm that became a part of his breathing, of the coursing of blood through his veins. He could have continued pleasuring her by forcing his body higher into hers, except that she lifted her head and gazed straight into his eyes, looking as aroused as he was but a little baffled.

"Take your time," he whispered—an act of almost suicidal unselfishness given the urgent state of his body.

Her answer explained the bafflement in her green eyes. "I can't," she whispered, and with a groan of anticipation and defeat, Mitchell tossed her onto her back and began driving into her with long, deep, slow strokes. She clasped him to her and buried her face in the curve of his neck, her fingers biting into his back, her body straining and moving with his. She cried out and clung to him tighter while spasms rocked her, and Mitchell slammed forward, climaxing with her.

Afterward, she lay in his arms, looking into his eyes, her fingers idly smoothing the hair at his temple. "More?" she said hopefully.

Mitchell burst out laughing and tightened his arms around her. "That is my *favorite* word."

Chapter Nineteen

DETECTIVE CHILDRESS TOSSED HIS SUITCASE ONTO ONE of the beds in room 102 at the Enclave. "Did you see that damned bellboy trying to arm-wrestle me for my suitcase?"

"He was hoping for a ten-dollar tip," MacNeil replied as he pulled a lightweight laptop computer out of his own suitcase.

"You know what pisses me off about being here?" When MacNeil didn't reply, Childress explained, "We're surrounded by gorgeous women who are prancing around in string bikinis, and we look like we're a pair of fags."

MacNeil glanced up at his partner, whose desire to look like an ordinary tourist had translated into a pair of Bermuda shorts, a T-shirt with the words *St. Maarten* intertwined among palm trees, a baseball cap, sunglasses, and a camera slung around his neck. "It's your Bermuda shorts," MacNeil said.

Childress's thoughts had already skipped on to other issues. "I don't like being this 'up close and personal' when I'm working surveillance. It triples the probabilities of Wyatt spotting us." As he spoke, he wandered over to the door and studied the room rates posted there. "One night in this place costs more than the down payment on my last car. The DA is going to have a coronary when the bill for this place comes in."

"I'll tell him the truth: There was no place to park on

the main road or on the private road into this place where we could spend day and night waiting for Wyatt to leave. The guard at the gatehouse would only give us a one-hour pass, and when that expired, a hotel employee appeared and tried to run us off. We had to register here."

"Yeah, I know all that, but I'm glad you're the one who has to explain it to Elliott."

MacNeil glanced at his watch and reached for his cell phone. It was time for his daily check-in call.

"Mr. Elliott?"

Gray Elliott looked up from the photographs spread out across the credenza in his Chicago office, a frown on his face. "Yes?"

"Detective MacNeil is on the phone."

"Close my door, will you?" Gray said. Swiveling in his chair, he waited until the door closed behind his secretary before he picked up his telephone. "Hi, Mac," he said.

"Did you get the report and pictures we e-mailed to you last night?" MacNeil began.

Too restless to stay seated, Gray stood up and turned to the credenza. "I got them," he said shortly.

"Wyatt picked up the redhead at her hotel this morning, and they've just checked into a hotel in St. Maarten. We still don't know who she is, but her hotel room in Anguilla was registered in the name of a guy named Bartlett. Sooner or later, she'll use a credit card here or produce a driver's license, and we'll get a make on her—"

"Don't bother," Gray interrupted tightly, staring at a close-up of a man and woman locked in a passionate embrace near a beach. The photo was taken at night using an infrared camera. It was a little grainy, but the subjects were easily identifiable. "Her name is Kate Donovan."

"Should that name mean something to me?" Mac asked. "It seems familiar."

"Her father was Daniel Donovan."

"The restaurant owner—that Daniel Donovan?"

"That's the one," Gray said sarcastically. "The Daniel Donovan who died a few weeks ago in what was presumed to be a random drive-by shooting."

MacNeil sank down on the edge of his bed, already putting together the pieces and arriving at the same conclusion Gray had drawn. "That's three people who Wyatt is connected with who've met untimely deaths in the last few months."

"Right."

"How does this guy Bartlett fit into the picture?"

"Kate Donovan is Evan Bartlett's girlfriend," Gray spit out. "Or at least I thought she was. Evan and I have known each other since we were kids. He's a lawyer from a long line of lawyers, all of whom have spotless reputations. I'm quite sure Evan Bartlett knows nothing about whatever she's involved in."

Rather than debate that, MacNeil said calmly, "We didn't see any sign of Bartlett last night, but he's registered at the hotel in Anguilla that she's staying in."

"She's using his name then, but Evan isn't there. I saw him at the courthouse yesterday; he's trying a case." Rather than let MacNeil think he was letting his personal feelings interfere with his objectivity—which he was— Gray said curtly, "Don't let Wyatt or Donovan out of your sight. I have to go into a meeting now. One more thing—" he added, "if Benedict's yacht moves into international waters, I want you to let me know immediately. The same is true if there's any indication that Wyatt's plane is being made ready to take off from St. Maarten."

"We've got a couple of mechanics at Princess Juliana Airport watching the plane for us. We tailed Wyatt to the hotel in St. Maarten this morning, and he left his luggage there. I don't think he plans to go back to Benedict's yacht tonight, but if he and the Donovan woman split up, we can't keep an eye on both of them and the yacht, too."

"My budget won't stretch any further than it's already stretched now on this case. Ignore the yacht, if you have to. If it moves into international waters, there's nothing we can do to yank Wyatt off it, but we can exert a whole lot of unpleasant pressure on Zack Benedict to hand Wyatt over to us."

"Are you expecting Wyatt to lead us to the body down here, or meet up with an accomplice or something?"

"I don't know about an accomplice, but you can bet your pension that William's body is somewhere up at the family farm. There are five hundred acres of woods up there, and we've been helping the locals comb through them. The ground is frozen, and there's still some snow on it, but the body is going to turn up any day now. When it does, I want to know exactly where to find Wyatt. Don't ask me how I know Wyatt's our murderer or that the body's at the farm. Once the body is found, the witness will come forward and give testimony. Until then, I've promised absolute anonymity."

Chapter Twenty

STANDING ON THE BALCONY WITH HIS ELBOWS PROPPED on the wall, Mitchell watched the lights of a distant cruise ship gliding slowly northward as he waited for Kate to finish dressing so they could leave for the casino.

After their first bout of lovemaking, they'd gotten up to eat; then they'd gone back to bed, made love again, and fallen into a deep, exhausted slumber. The sun had already set when he woke up with Kate in his arms. He'd felt utterly contented and totally relaxed lying there, and he still felt the same way.

"I'm sorry I took so long," she said behind him.

Mitchell straightened and turned, his relaxed smile widening into an appreciative grin. Dressed in a short black strapless sheath with a scalloped bodice edged in lace and sassy high-heeled sandals with slender scalloped straps, Kate Donovan was a vision of lush curves, luminous skin, luxuriant hair, and long, long legs. His gaze riveted on her legs again, and Mitchell tipped his head back, grinning at his astonished reaction to what was, very possibly, the most beautiful pair of legs he'd ever seen.

"Are you smiling because I look surprisingly nice, or because there's something wrong with my dress?" she teased, but she sounded a little anxious.

"I'm smiling because I just realized you have gorgeous legs," Mitchell replied wryly, "and I never saw them before."

"I was wearing both of them earlier," she said flippantly. "In fact, I distinctly remember that they were attached to me when we were in bed."

"I was too close to get a full-length look when we were in bed."

She walked up to him and turned her back. "Would you pull my zipper up the last inch?" she asked, lifting her hair out of the way for him. "I can't reach it."

Mitchell had performed that same service for other women countless times in the past, but as he looked down at Kate's exposed nape, there was an intimacy and pleasure associated with the simple act that surprised him. As he located the tab of the zipper and slid it up, she joked with him about his reaction to her legs. "Let me guess," she said, "you're a leg man, aren't you?"

Normally, Mitchell would have answered "yes" without hesitation or thought, but for some obscure reason, the question seemed all wrong, especially coming from her. Curving his hands over her shoulders, he bent his head and kissed her cheek. "Let's not have that conversation," he whispered.

Kate turned slowly around and looked at him. He hadn't answered the question for the same reason she'd instantly regretted asking it—she didn't want to know what female body parts he was partial to. In fact, right now, she wanted to think he was partial to her as a whole being. "Nice answer," she said, smiling into his eyes.

"I thought so, too."

The casino he took her to was in the Dutch section, and it was a large private club where the members spoke an amazing variety of foreign languages and the table limits were very high. On the way there, Mitchell had described the casino as having a "European flavor," which Kate now realized translated into an atmosphere that was elegant, sophisticated, and subdued. It was an atmosphere that suited him perfectly, Kate thought. Wearing an impeccably tailored gray suit, dark gray shirt, and pale gray tie, he personified elegant sophistication and calm self-assurance.

The only resemblance between the casinos she'd been to in the States and this one was that gambling was legal in both. In fact, the only times she'd ever seen casinos like this were in movies that were filmed in locales like Monaco.

Trying not to look as if she'd never been inside a place like this, or been around people like this, Kate glanced past baccarat and roulette tables populated by wealthy men with large stacks of chips in front of them and well-kept women with glittering jewels at their wrists and throats.

"Are you looking for something in particular?" Mitchell asked.

"Yes," Kate replied, flashing him a laughing look, "James Bond."

"You'll have to settle for me tonight."

"I can do that," she replied unhesitatingly, and he grinned.

"My original question referred to what game you prefer," Mitchell explained, suppressing the sophomoric impulse to put his arm around her as they walked.

"I prefer whatever game I can win money playing."

"In that case, we need to leave now," he joked.

"I'm actually very lucky at cards," Kate said truthfully. "Slot machines like me, too. And craps tables are often very friendly to me."

"How is your luck at blackjack?"

"It varies."

They found two seats together at a blackjack table, and although Kate inwardly shuddered at the $100 minimum, she opened her purse and resolutely withdrew five $100 traveler's checks before she sat down. "I need to cash these first."

"I intended to back you or I wouldn't have brought you here."

"I can't gamble with your money. One of the things my father taught me was that a lady *always* gambles with her own money, or she doesn't gamble at all."

"Your father had some very novel notions," Mitchell replied drily as she turned and walked away, heading toward the cashier's window nearby. With an unconscious smile, he watched her walk, admiring her natural grace and the way her flame-colored hair changed from waves into thick curls below her shoulders.

"Belle femme," the man on Mitchell's right remarked, his gaze also following Kate.

"Yes, she is," Mitchell replied. He signaled to the dealer and signed the usual table form to draw money against his line of credit. "See that the young lady doesn't run out of chips when she gets low," Mitchell instructed the dealer as he began sliding Mitchell's chips toward him.

"Certainly, Mr. Wyatt."

An hour later, she was $2,400 ahead, and Mitchell had stopped playing so that he could lean over and watch Kate play her hand. It had been obvious from the first that she knew when to ask for another card, when to stay with the hand she had, and when to doubledown. When she followed the usual procedure, she won an inordinate amount of times, but what fascinated him was that, on a whim, she would do the opposite of what she should—and she still won. Unfortunately those intuitive whims of hers made it difficult for the other players to anticipate her actions, and they were screwing up their own hands as a result. He was wondering if she realized that, when she slid her chips toward the dealer and said, "I'd like to cash these in, please"; then she looked at the four men seated at the table with her and said graciously, "I apologize for disrupting your hands. It's difficult for me to ignore my hunches when I have them."

The Frenchman who'd spoken to Mitchell earlier grinned broadly at her, lifted her hand, and kissed it in sheer gratitude. *"Elle est une* très *belle femme!"* he said to Mitchell. Caught between amusement and shock, Kate gathered up her winnings while the man spoke animatedly in French to Mitchell, who replied to him in the same language.

"What was that all about?" Kate asked as they walked away.

"He noticed that you're not only very beautiful, but you are also very lucky at blackjack."

"He said more than that. He asked you a question, too, because you shook your head and answered him in a rather chilly voice."

Mitchell grinned at her. "Did I sound 'chilly'? That was rude of me, and I'm rarely rude."

"What did he ask you?" Kate persevered.

"He asked if I would be willing to let you stand beside his chair so that he would have not only the benefit of your beauty but also, perhaps, your good fortune at cards."

Kate gave an indelicate snort and shook her head. "He's an old letch, and that was a total crock." Mitchell's shoulders shook with laughter at her phrasing, and he suppressed another sophomoric urge—the urge to snatch her up into his arms and indulge in a public display of affection.

"What did you say to him?"

"It's difficult to translate it accurately."

"Give it a try."

"Loosely translated, I told him that he's an old letch, and what he said was a total crock."

Kate laughed, but she wasn't buying it. "That's not what you said."

Mitchell bent his head and whispered against her cheek, "I told him to get his own girl because I wasn't going to share mine with him"; then he straightened, and continued walking as if having his lips on her cheek had been the farthest thing from his mind.

Kate's heart did a somersault at hearing Mitchell refer to her as his "girl," but she knew it was just a figure of speech, and she tried not to think it meant anything else. She had a wonderful time for the rest of the evening, even though she lost half her winnings.

Mitchell gambled with the same effortless competence with which he did everything else, but what particularly fascinated Kate was his reaction to several women who made frank visual overtures to him during the evening: He had no reaction; he simply acted as if the women were invisible. Either he was so accustomed to it that he didn't notice, or else he didn't enjoy being looked at like a delicious sexual feast. Kate preferred to think the latter was true.

Shortly after midnight, when they'd finished gambling, they stopped in an intimate little lounge on the first floor of the casino, where a small band was accompanying a male singer. They found an empty table, and while the singer launched into the familiar lyrics of "The Way You Look Tonight," Kate watched Mitchell sit down, unbutton his jacket, lean back in his chair, and casually stretch his long legs out. That picture of him—relaxed, handsome, and utterly at ease in an exclusive private casino—imprinted itself on Kate's heart while the words to the song entwined around his image, framing it. Trying to hide her admiring smile, she put her elbows on the table and leaned her chin downward on her folded hands, watching him from beneath her lashes.

A moment later, he evidently felt that a waiter should have already arrived, so he lifted his head an inch and glanced to his right with the merest trace of a frown. Two waiters materialized from opposite directions, almost colliding with each other in their haste to answer his summons, and Kate swallowed a laugh. In her father's restaurant she'd observed all the known signals used by male customers to attract the attention of waiters—from the most boorish signals to the most timid—and she silently gave Mitchell the highest score possible, both for "style employed" and "effectiveness of style."

"How does cognac sound?" he asked while the waiter stood beside him.

"Fine, thank you," Kate said, knowing she'd have only a sip. Still amused by her observations, she turned her head, watching the singer, a smile hovering at her lips.

Mitchell ordered their drinks and then mistook the reason for her smile. "Are you especially fond of that song?"

Kate nodded.

"Any particular reason?"

Since she couldn't explain her current reason, Kate lowered her eyes and gave him a different one that was equally true. "When I was thirteen, Michael Bublé and his grandfather were visiting Chicago and, purely by chance, they had dinner in our restaurant. Michael's grandfather happened to mention to my father—very proudly—that Michael was about to launch his singing career in Canada, so my father offered to let Michael make his 'United States debut' in our bar. Michael was only sixteen at the time, but he was so amazing that my father brought me downstairs from the apartment to listen to him."

"And?" Mitchell prompted when she looked slightly embarrassed.

"And Michael sang the song we're listening to now. Actually, he sang it to me."

"Should I be jealous?"

"Of course," Kate joked with a winsome smile. "I fell madly in love with him right then and there. The next time I saw him sing," Kate finished, "he was at Carnegie Hall."

Feeling a little foolish because she'd told him yet another story about her life when she still knew virtually nothing about his, Kate glanced down at the table and realized Mitchell's hand was resting beside hers, less than an inch away. The sight of his long fingers lying so close to hers enthralled her. Telling herself that she was being naïve and foolish, she finally pulled her gaze away.

Mitchell's head was bent, his gaze fixed intently on their hands, just as hers had been. Slowly, he lifted his hand, and then he laid it over hers.

Kate felt a thrill run through her entire body. Swallowing, she watched to see if he had any noticeable reaction at all. He tightened his grip on her hand.

Chapter Twenty-one

SCANNING THE SURFACE OF THE WATER FOR A SIGN OF Mitchell, Kate absently brushed sand off her legs and reached for one of the robes they'd brought from their room. The night was balmy, but she was beginning to shiver in her wet bathing suit, more from alarm than cold.

When they left the casino, Mitchell had offered to take her to Maho Bay so she could spend her winnings in one of the high-fashion boutiques that stayed open to cater to the nightclub and casino crowd. Kate had suggested they go back to the hotel and go swimming instead. In her mind she'd envisioned lazily floating in four feet of buoyant salt water for a half hour. They'd done that, but when Kate was ready to get out, Mitchell said he was going to swim a little longer for some exercise.

As she discovered as soon as he kicked off, when Mitchell swam for exercise he did it with ferocious force, driving his body through the water at maximum speed, as if demons were closing in on him. At first, Kate watched him in admiration, but a few minutes after she lost sight of him completely, she began to worry about his safety.

Trying not to let her concern escalate to panic, Kate continued to search the moonlit water as she shoved her arms into the sleeves of her robe and tied the belt. Finally, she made out a speck on the surface and sank onto a lounge chair, weak with relief.

Freed at last of her worry about Mitchell, she drew her knees up to her chest and wrapped her arms around them. Tipping her head back, she gazed at a black satin sky encrusted with shimmering stars while a profound sense of her father's presence slowly swept over her. It wrapped around her, warm and strong, enfolding her in sweetness, as if it were a hug—a fierce celestial hug. Kate reveled in the sensation, clinging to it while tears stung her eyes and slid down her cheeks.

Finally she reached up to brush them away and glanced at the water to check on Mitchell. He was swimming in a straight line directly toward her, his shoulders and arms visible above the surface.

And in that moment, she suddenly understood. She understood it all, just as surely as if her father were sitting next to her on the chaise longue watching Mitchell, too, and smiling.

This was meant to be; *they* were meant to be. That's why she'd felt such an inexplicable sense of magical closeness with him from the very first. Mitchell's poignant admission came back to her: *I felt all the same things you did last night.* They had been destined to meet and fall in love, but capricious fate wasn't pulling the strings.

Wiping away another tear, Kate looked up at the sky and whispered, "Thank you, Daddy. I miss you."

The sensation of his nearness had lessened but was still there a few minutes later when Mitchell stood up in the water. Raking his hands through the sides of his hair, he waded out of the sea with water streaming from his powerful shoulders and long legs, his dark swimming trunks clinging to his muscular thighs. He was so outrageously beautiful that Kate shook her head. Smiling, she glanced back up at the stars and silently said, *What on earth were you thinking when you decided I deserve someone this good-looking?*

Mitchell reached for the towel she held out to him and suppressed the urge to rumple the springy wet curls framing her face and tumbling over her shoulders. With her hair like that, she looked delectable; in fact, she looked exactly the way she had when he first met her in the restaurant. "Hi," he said with a smile.

She smiled back at him. "How was Jamaica? Did you pass any sharks on the way?"

Grinning at her quip, Mitchell started toweling off his chest and arms. "I've been lying around down here for a week," he explained. "I needed the exercise."

"Do you normally swim for exercise?"

He shook his head. "A man who works for me is a martial arts specialist. I get most of my exercise working out with him."

"What sort of work does he do for you?"

"He's my driver."

"Your driver," Kate repeated, thinking that over. "As well as your bodyguard?"

"He thinks he is," Mitchell replied, bending over to dry his legs.

Kate waited until he tossed his towel aside and picked up a robe before she asked the question that was bothering her a little: "What sort of business are you in that you need a bodyguard?"

"In Europe, it's fairly common for drivers to be body-guards."

Either by accident or intent, he hadn't told her what sort of business he was in, Kate realized, and he hadn't mentioned a word on that subject last night either. They were sleeping together and she was falling more in love with him every passing minute. She was dying to know more about him and to understand him better. As they strolled down the beach toward the terraced steps leading up to the hotel, she repeated, "What sort of business are you in?"

"I'm in the business of making money," Mitchell replied, automatically giving her the same pat answer he gave to most people who asked him that question; then he felt bad for treating her as if she were a prying stranger.

"I don't run a business," he clarified. "Even if I had the inclination to run one, I doubt I'd have any talent for it. I invest money in the ideas and genius of other people who do have a talent for running businesses."

Kate shoved her hands into the pockets of her robe and considered her next question.

"How do you decide which ideas and people you should invest in?"

"I rely partly on information and partly on instinct, which amounts to making an educated guess."

He intended that to end the conversation, Kate realized from his tone. Careful to sound as if she was making a wry observation, rather than trying to keep him talking, she said, "When someone has an instinctive knack for doing something, I think it's called talent."

"In my case, it's more of an acquired skill than an actual talent."

"How did you acquire your skill?"

He stopped walking, turned, and studied her with a mildly impatient frown. "I had a mentor—Stavros Konstantatos."

Kate's eyes widened at the mention of the reclusive, self-made Greek tycoon who was reportedly one of the richest men in the world. "Are we talking about the man who lives on an island with armed guards posted everywhere and who had his yacht equipped with torpedoes?"

Mitchell's resistance dissolved into amusement. "Not

torpedoes, antiaircraft guns," he said, lacing his fingers through hers and holding her hand as they started walking again. "His son, Alex, was my roommate at boarding school. One year, Alex begged me to spend the winter holiday with him on their island so that he wouldn't 'die of boredom alone' while he listened to Stavros talk about business at every meal. Like most wealthy kids, Alex wasn't interested in making money, he was interested in spending it."

Kate noticed that Mitchell seemed to have excluded himself from the category of "wealthy kid," but she didn't attempt to pursue that observation. Instead she said conversationally, "Did Alex's father really talk about business at every meal?"

"Stavros talked about business incessantly," Mitchell said with a chuckle, "but I wasn't bored, I was mesmerized. He realized it, of course, and I think he hoped my attitude would rub off on Alex. The next holiday, he insisted that Alex bring me back to the island. I saw a lot of Stavros after that. Over the years, he took me under his wing and coached and prodded me until I grasped his concepts. When I finished college, he gave me a job working directly under him, so that he could 'complete my education.' Eventually he started letting me make my own deals and share in the profits—or losses."

"What a wonderful man and what a lucky experience for you."

Mitchell nodded in agreement. He didn't mention that Stavros's wife had repeatedly tried to seduce him from the time he was seventeen. Nor did he mention any of his earlier, less "wonderful" experiences with some of his classmates' wealthy families—the pleasant, well-bred parents he met when their sons invited Mitchell home to spend a holiday with them. They asked him the same dreaded questions parents always asked—questions about where he was from and who his relatives were. Once they realized he was a total outsider without family or connections, they frequently treated him like an opportunist who was trying to insinuate himself into their sons' lives for reasons they regarded as highly suspicious and undesirable.

Some of them went so far as to call the administrators of the boarding schools and complain about the questionable caliber of the boy their sons were associating with. In reply they were told that Mitchell was a "scholarship student" and a "gifted athlete" who was of special interest to a very influential American foundation. Mitchell learned about that from the sons of the complaining parents.

Walking beside Kate, he tried to recall how many times during his boarding school years he'd been asked by a classmate's family if he was any relation to the "Chicago Wyatts." How ironic that he'd answered no all those times. Which suddenly explained why he could barely force himself now to acknowledge that the answer was actually yes.

Chapter Twenty-two

ROPPED UP IN BED WITH MITCHELL'S ARM AROUND HER, Kate watched the night sky giving way to dawn. When they'd returned from swimming, they'd showered and then discovered they were famished. The remnants of their shared feast of strawberry crepes and eggs Benedict were on the coffee table.

Afterward, they went to bed, but sleep was not what Mitchell had in mind. The fierce, demanding urgency and relaxed playfulness of his earlier lovemaking were gone. This time, he made love to her with slow, torrid sensuality, driving her steadily toward a final climactic destination, while detouring on previously unexplored erotic routes to get her there, whispering directions and encouragements that were as arousing to Kate as the things he was doing with her. By the time he finally let her finish, Kate was writhing wildly in his arms, frantically whispering "Please," over and over and over.

When the last spasm had shaken her, he changed the tempo of his strokes and Kate's limp body suddenly arched up like a tightly strung bow, straining toward him of its own volition while he poured himself into her. Kate heard herself moan, and she clung to him, caught up in a moment that was not only tumultuously sexual but almost fiercely spiritual.

Later on, when she looked back on it all, she might have seen herself as a naïve student who'd just been tutored by a consummate, perhaps less-involved master—

except that afterward, he'd gathered her against his full length and kept their bodies clamped tightly together with his face buried in the curve of her neck for a very long time, as if he'd been profoundly affected by their lovemaking, too.

Even now, as they watched the sunrise, his hand was curved around her arm, his thumb caressing her skin. They were both drowsy, the periods of silence between them growing longer, but as the sky continued to lighten, the dawn of a new day was banishing Kate's quiet euphoria and filling her with worry and fresh guilt about Evan.

She'd waited to return his phone call yesterday until she was getting dressed for the casino, because she knew Evan would be playing tennis at his club by then. She'd left him a voice mail message assuring him that she wasn't at all angry with him, that she was having a lovely time visiting neighboring islands, and that there was absolutely no need for him to worry or feel guilty about anything. Everything she told him was true, but the things she did not tell him made her message a tawdry, unforgivable deception. On the other hand, she couldn't possibly break up with him by phone, not after the years they'd been together, and especially not after he'd just brought up marriage. There were only four days left of their planned ten-day trip. If his case dragged on another day or two, he'd surely decide there was no point in flying back down to Anguilla.

Sensing her change in mood, Mitchell glanced at the woman who was responsible for the most exhilarating, fulfilling sexual experience of his life. Her red curls were in wild disarray, tumbling over her shoulders and the tops of her breasts, and her porcelain cheeks were still slightly flushed from their lovemaking, but her expression had turned very pensive. Mitchell assumed she was probably thinking about her boyfriend and wondering whether he was going to arrive that day. He'd been thinking about the same thing.

"Troubling thoughts?"

She turned her head on the pillow. "Not really. Not about you, anyway," she amended. After a moment, she smiled and said, "Have you ever been married?"

Ordinarily, that question in this particular location would have evoked a wary reaction in Mitchell, but they'd been lying there asking each other desultory questions off and on since they finished making love. They were, after all, two people who had intimate carnal knowledge of each other, and they had feelings for each other, but they had no facts. And since they'd already traded information about favorite pastimes, favorite foods, least favorite politicians, and so forth, her question seemed perfectly reasonable to Mitchell. "Yes, have you?"

"No," she said.

This, unlike all their previous questions and answers, she clearly thought required some amplification, because she lifted her brows and looked at him expectantly.

"I was married to Stavros's daughter, Anastasia, for three years," Mitchell added to satisfy her. It didn't satisfy her. Rolling onto her side facing him, she reached up and pressed her finger across his sealed lips. "If I die of curiosity in this bed," she warned, "you will have a lot of explaining to do to the hotel management."

Mitchell tried to scowl, but a lock of her soft hair was brushing his cheek, her finger was brushing his mouth, and her smile was irresistible. "Anastasia was Stavros's youngest child and only daughter," he explained in defeat. "He kept her under his thumb and in his sight by preventing her from having any money of her own to spend."

"I thought Greek heiresses ran wild."

"So did Stavros," Mitchell replied drily. "By the time she was twenty-one, she was so desperate to have some freedom and to 'experience life' that it was almost pitiful. Marriage was her only ticket out of bondage, but Stavros wouldn't let men near her—except for a couple of them who suited him but not Anastasia.

"We'd known each other since we were kids and we understood each other. We also liked each other. So we made a deal. We got married and I allowed her to accumulate all the life experiences she wanted."

"What went wrong?" Kate asked, searching his features.

"Anastasia decided she wanted one life experience that I refused to allow, one that she'd expressly agreed to forgo before we ever got married."

"What was it?"

"Motherhood."

"You divorced her because she wanted to have your children?"

"No, I let her divorce me."

Warned by his tone that the topic was now closed, Kate dropped her gaze, wondering whether she ought to try to get more information. She decided she wasn't likely to succeed right now, and she didn't want their mood spoiled any more than it had been already.

She sought for an innocuous question to ask and after a moment decided to ask about the tiny scar on his right arm. "Where did you get this scar?" she asked, touching it with her fingers.

He looked down to see what she was talking about, and his tone lost its edge. "When I was fifteen, I bumped into a rapier."

"That would have been my first guess."

His blue eyes warmed with laughter and a grin tugged at the corner of his mouth. Lifting his hand to her face, he brushed his thumb over what he thought was a cleft in her chin and teasingly asked, "Where did you get this cute little dent in your chin?"

"When I was thirteen, I bumped into a U.S. mail-box."

Mitchell laughed at the joke and started to kiss her chin, but she shook her head and said, "I'm serious."

He pulled back in amused surprise. "How in the hell did that happen?"

"Just before my fourteenth birthday, I decided to make an unauthorized trip to Cleveland to visit some-one I hadn't seen in a long time. I persuaded a fifteen-year-old boy I knew to give me a ride, so Travis borrowed his brother's car in the morning, and we cut school at lunchtime and took off. Three miles away, Travis lost control of the car, ran over a curb, and hit a U.S. mailbox. I banged my chin on the dash-board."

"Are fifteen-year-olds allowed to drive?"

"Not legally. Which was one of the reasons we got busted when the police arrived on the scene."

"What were the other reasons?"

"Possession of a stolen vehicle, truancy, possession of marijuana, and destruction of government property."

Mitchell's guffaw lifted his shoulders clear off the pil-lows.

"It was a bum rap," Kate protested, rearing up on her elbows, and he guffawed again. "Well, it was. Travis simply 'forgot' to tell his brother he was taking his car, so his brother reported it stolen. And the marijuana wasn't ours; it was his."

"My choir-girl image of you is undergoing a radical change."

"Those were my wild-child days. Anyway, they came to an end that same day."

"Why?"

"I had to be taken to the hospital for stitches in my chin, and naturally, the hospital called my father. He was so scared and so furious that he ranted at me all the way back to the restaurant. When we got there, he sent me upstairs and told me I was grounded for two months. He said he was going to cancel my surprise party for my fourteenth birthday that week, and that there would be more punishment to come when he was calm enough to think straight. Then he walked into his office and slammed the door so hard that it popped back open."

"Poor little wild child," Mitchell teased, his thumb touching the dent in her chin. "Grounded for two whole months."

"I didn't intend to be grounded for two whole hours. I was just as furious with him for grounding me and yelling at me when I'd just had stitches. I hung around upstairs for a few minutes, and then I snuck downstairs, intending to go to a girlfriend's house for a little while. As I tiptoed around the stairwell toward the back door, I heard a sound coming from his office, a sound that froze me in my tracks."

"What was it?"

"Sobbing," she said. "I could see his reflection in a wall mirror outside his office. He was sitting at his desk with his hands over his face, crying his heart out. He was such a strong, indomitable man that it never occurred to me that anything could make him cry. It was the most wrenching moment of my life."

"What did you do?"

"I went back upstairs and grounded myself for two months. I never cut school again, and I stayed out of trouble—at least big trouble—from that day forward."

Mitchell fell silent, assimilating what she'd told him,

trying to get a three-dimensional picture of her life, but he'd never known anyone from a background even remotely like hers.

"You never mention your mother," he said finally.

Lifting her brows, Kate said, "You never mention your mother either."

"Is she alive?" Mitchell persisted.

"I refuse to tell you, unless you tell me about yours first."

"I think you'll tell me anyway."

"You couldn't pry it out of me with a crowbar."

"I can pry it out of you with two fingers," he promised with absolute certainty, sliding his hand under the sheet.

"Don't you dare—" Kate warned, clamping her legs together. Suddenly it was important that he not be able to keep his secrets while manipulating her so easily into divulging hers.

His fingers slid through the triangle at her thighs. "Open your legs, Kate."

"No." It hit her then that her logic was totally wrong and that she was silly to resist. She relaxed the tension in her legs, gasping when he slid one finger deep inside of her and rubbed his thumb against the curly hair above it; then she relaxed and let him spread pleasure and warmth through her.

"Is there something you want to tell me?" he asked, slowly increasing the pressure and altering the movements of his fingers.

"Not yet," Kate whispered faintly, putting her arms around his shoulders and closing her eyes. He was getting her so close she could barely stop herself from moving with him.

"Isn't there something you want to tell me now?"

She was clinging to him, her heart racing, her nails digging into his back.

"No," she gasped, but her body was on the verge of convulsing.

He stopped. "How about now?"

She was hanging on a cliff, desperate, and he knew it; he'd intended to deprive her of a climax just when she was on the verge and withhold it from her until she yielded. Somehow she'd mistakenly thought he believed he could get an answer out of her by giving her pleasure, while he intended to do it by depriving her of pleasure.

Her body was begging her to give in; her heart wouldn't let her. She let go of his shoulders and dropped back onto the pillows, looking up at him with wounded eyes, silent and disappointed.

He stared back at her, his blue eyes heavy-lidded, his expression unreadable. Suddenly, he scooped her into his arms, his fingers seeking the same places he'd touched and left, driving her all the way to the climax he'd deprived her of before.

Kate clung to him while shudders shook through her, and when they passed, she lay back on the pillows and lifted her hand, sliding it across his hard jaw, tenderly smoothing back his thick black hair. "My mother lives in Cleveland," she whispered, conceding victory to him—but a victory that was won on her terms, not his.

Unfamiliar emotions swelled in Mitchell's chest, unfolding and unfurling. She was meant for him; they were meant for each other. But later today, or tomorrow, another man was going to come for her; a man who had more right to her than Mitchell did. . . .

In his mind, Mitchell heard the trumpets blast and the heralds calling out his name, summoning him to appear in the Coliseum of Commitments and present himself before the roaring crowd—a gladiator, without sword or shield, armed with only his secrets and fragile hopes. The horns were already blaring, and he was already striding toward his fate, defenseless but fearless.

Kate's hand was lying against his cheek, her fingers caressing his jaw while her green eyes beckoned him. Smiling, Mitchell turned his face into her hand, kissed her palm, and whispered, "We who are about to die salute you."

Chapter Twenty-three

SEATED ON A CHAIR IN FRONT OF THE WINDOWS IN ROOM 102, with his feet propped up on the windowsill and a pair of binoculars in his lap, MacNeil yawned and stretched and watched in weary boredom as rosy pink streaks appeared in the sky above the sparkling waters of the Caribbean. He and Childress were sleeping in shifts, and Mac's shift had just begun.

Hotel employees were already moving around at the beach, setting up for breakfast and wiping down chaise longues, and several taxis were in line at the front entrance, ready to take early risers to destinations of their choice. If Wyatt decided to leave the hotel, he had to pass by MacNeil's window to get a taxi. From this same vantage point, Mac had been able to use the binoculars to watch Wyatt and the Donovan woman last night until they finally went up to their room.

At eleven, Childress and he switched places at the window, and Childress poured himself a cup of coffee from the carafe that room service had delivered while MacNeil was on watch. "I've been here too long," Childress remarked, spooning sugar into his cup. "Last night I read the hotel brochure, and I started thinking that my toenails really need attention, and I can't go another day without aromatherapy." He put his coffee cup on the table beside his chair and picked up the binoculars Mac had laid aside. Lifting them to his eyes, he slowly scanned the beach, looking for a particular blonde. "There she is, lying on her favorite lounge chair. I'm falling in love. Look at that . . . she's got a little tattoo on her butt on the left cheek. How did I miss that yesterday? He paused to zoom in closer and adjust the focus. "It's a ladybug—is that cute, or what?"

"I'm going to take a shower," Mac replied, then quoting from the same brochure as he started toward the bathroom, "and drown myself in the luxury of frangipani shampoo."

Childress looked sharply over his shoulder and called, "Leave some for me."

MacNeil chuckled, stopped at the closet to take out a fresh shirt and pair of pants, and then laid them on the bed, because his cell phone began vibrating on the dresser.

Gray Elliott's voice was grim and brisk. "We just found William Wyatt's body, with a shotgun hole in the chest, in an old well on a neighboring farm that was owned by the Udall family. Actually," he corrected, "*we* didn't find it; the developer who bought the farm a few months ago found it when he tripped over a rusty well cover underneath an inch of snow. While he was picking himself up, he noticed something wedged under the cover that struck him as odd. He knew William had disappeared when he was supposed to be at the farm next door, so he dragged the cover aside to have a look. The local cops responded to his call, and they've handed the whole thing over to us. William's body and the shotgun that undoubtedly killed him arrived by helicopter a little while ago. Ballistics is going over the gun now."

"Any prints left on it?"

"Not a one," Gray replied, sounding surprisingly unconcerned.

MacNeil immediately guessed at the reason: "What was wedged under the cover?"

"A black leather button, about the size of a button from a man's overcoat, with the thread still attached."

"A button?" MacNeil repeated, frowning, and sat down on the edge of his bed.

"A very distinctive, handmade leather button," Gray amplified, "with an interesting design stamped on the front and a symbol on the back, identifying its creator."

"I take it you think you can trace it back to whoever made it?"

"We should be able to do better than that. It turns out that buttons like these are ordered exclusively by European tailors who keep careful records so that matching buttons can be obtained for their clients as needed."

"Europe is a big place. How long do you think it will take to track down the tailor or the button maker?"

"Forensics says the leather and dye used on the button are British, so we're focusing first on London tailors. Right now, my problem is time. It's only a matter of hours before the media gets wind that we've recovered William's body, and if Wyatt hears about it, that jet of his will take off from St. Maarten, heading as far away from U.S. jurisdiction as it can take him.

"If I can lure him back to Chicago, I have enough grounds to detain him for questioning and force him to surrender his passport. That will give us time to locate the tailor who made the overcoat for him, or better yet, the overcoat itself. Once we have either one, I can get a warrant signed for his arrest. I've already arranged with NYPD to search his New York apartment later today when I give them the go-ahead. He also has apartments in Rome, London, and Paris, and I'm trying to arrange for a simultaneous search of them, but the authorities in Europe won't play ball with me yet. I'm going to start pulling some personal strings after we hang up."

"You're going to need a hell of a big lure to tear him away from the Donovan woman."

"I have a plan," Gray said. "I'll get back to you in a little while. In the meantime, just don't lose him, and don't worry about tailing Kate Donovan if they split up. I'll deal with her myself as soon as I get Wyatt into our jurisdiction."

"We'll stay on him," MacNeil said.

"Mac?"

"Yeah?"

"I also have a witness who has seen Wyatt wearing an overcoat with a button just like the one found at the well."

Chapter Twenty-four

KATE'S CELL PHONE BEGAN RINGING ON THE BAR JUST AS Mitchell picked up a can of shaving cream in the bathroom. Absently shaking the can, he watched from the corner of his eye as she walked in from the balcony and picked up the phone to look at the caller's number. She hesitated, biting her lip; then she raised the phone to her ear and answered the call.

With the hot water running in the sink, he couldn't hear what she was saying, but her shoulders were stiff, her head was bent, and she was rubbing the back of her neck with her free hand. Her body language spoke of tension and apprehension. From that, Mitchell deduced that the lawyer was either telling her he was planning to leave for St. Maarten, or else giving her hell for not taking his other calls. A few moments after the call began, it ended, and she put the phone down.

The call hadn't lasted long enough for any sort of temperamental outburst—not from a lawyer. Lawyers made a career out of haranguing, and that phone call wasn't long enough for a lawyer to even start getting wound up. The only remaining logical conclusion was that Kate's lawyer boyfriend had simply told her he was coming to Anguilla and, also based on the brevity of the call, Kate hadn't attempted to discourage him. That was not the behavior Mitchell had expected from her.

When Kate walked into the bathroom, Mitchell was standing at the sink with a towel around his hips, shaving. Surprised by the sweet intimacy of the moment, she leaned against the vanity and watched in the mirror as he finished shaving his throat. His face was covered in lather, with nothing visible except black eyebrows, long-lashed deep blue eyes, and a finely sculpted, sensual mouth.

He rinsed the razor under running water and glanced at her in the mirror, his mouth quirking in a half smile at her fascinated interest; then he resumed his task. Stroke by deft stroke of the razor, his tanned face, with its chiseled jawline and strongly molded cheekbones, began to emerge from beneath the lather.

Kate watched, but thoughts of the phone call she'd just received from Evan's secretary soon furrowed her forehead into an apprehensive frown. According to Patricia, she and Evan had worked late into Sunday night, and Evan had finally hammered out a satisfactory out-of-court settlement with the opposing counsel. He'd tried to call Kate from his office to tell her he was catching a 2:30 AM flight, arriving at 12:35 PM, St. Maarten time, but all he'd gotten was a voice mail message at the villa and on her cell phone. Refusing to leave a voice mail message, he'd slammed his phone down and instructed Patricia to start calling Kate on Monday morning and to keep trying until Patricia actually heard Kate's voice. "If I were you," Patricia had laughingly warned, "I'd meet him at the door with a soothing smile and a martini this afternoon. He's pissed off over not being able to get through to you for two days." Evan was going to be feeling a lot worse, Kate knew, when she met him at the door with her luggage packed.

Mitchell noted her expression in the mirror. "You look like a woman with a problem," he observed conversationally.

"He's on his way to Anguilla."

"You definitely have a problem."

"I'll have to meet him at the villa and try to explain things there. I don't know what I should do or say—"

"That's a much bigger problem."

Surprised and a little hurt by his glib responses and seemingly cavalier attitude toward a situation that was going to be very difficult for her, Kate said quietly, "You seem to have all the answers. Do you have any guidance to offer in a situation like this?"

"Since he's already on his way here, the scenario is set and it's too late to alter it," he replied, rinsing off the razor again. "Assuming he and I are both gentlemen, our roles are now fixed and there are prescribed rules to follow. Assuming you plan to be with me from now on, rather than staying with him, the same is true for you."

Vaguely surprised by his use of an indefinite phrase like "assuming you plan," Kate watched him shave his upper lip, and then she said, "Exactly what is your 'gentlemanly' role?"

"I am obliged to express a willingness to bow out temporarily so that he can have whatever is left of his vacation with you, along with the opportunity to fight for you during that time."

"What's his role?"

Passing the razor from jaw to cheekbone on the left side of his face, he said, "As soon as he understands that you're serious about wanting to be with someone else, he is obliged to accept defeat gracefully and wish you well—thus impressing you with what a prince you're losing while drowning you in guilt and doubt— and then to get the hell out of my way."

"And my role is?"

"To convince him that you're serious in the shortest possible time—measured in hours, not days—and to avoid letting him get you near that nice big bed while you're doing your explaining and convincing."

The reason for his curt tone and his reference to the bed hit her, and Kate stared at him. "Are you *jealous*?"

"Not yet, but I'm heading in that direction," he said, making short, quick razor strokes beneath his left ear.

"But why?" Kate said, trying to hide how shamefully pleased she was by his admission. "I can't just break up with him on the telephone or meet him at the airport and tell him there. I need to be at the villa so I can talk to him and let him down easily."

Instead of responding to that, Mitchell rinsed off his face and asked a question of his own: "How long does it take to fly here from Chicago?"

"Around eight hours, since there aren't any direct flights."

"It seems to me that encouraging him to fly eight hours to get here, thinking he's going to be with you for the rest of his vacation, is a curious way to 'let him down easily.' "

It finally dawned on Kate that he was under a mistaken impression, and she quickly clarified the situation for him. "That phone call wasn't from him; it was from his *secretary*. He had her call me to tell me his flight left at two-thirty this morning, and lands at twelve thirty-five. I didn't think he'd try to come down here at all when there are only four days left of our vacation. If I'd had a chance to talk to him before he left, I would never have let him come here thinking everything was going to be the same between us."

"I'm sorry. I should have known that."

Kate dismissed his worry with a smile, but she was intrigued by the flattering discovery of her feminine power over him, and fascinated by the rules of conduct that he'd recited with such absolute certainty. Deciding to put both of them to a harmless test, just for fun, she folded her arms over her chest, tipped her head to the side, and pretended to inspect her manicure. "About those rules you talked about— What would you, as a gentleman, be required to do if I were to vacillate a little about breaking up with my boyfriend?"

The studied nonchalance in her voice instantly alerted Mitchell to what she was up to, and he suppressed a smile as he reached for a towel. A stranger to the games that tipped the delicate balance of power between male and female he was not. "Under those circumstances," he said mildly, "the rules are very clear, and very simple: You would be required to telephone me to tell me that you're having doubts, and then I would simply switch roles with him."

"You would just accept defeat gracefully, wish me well, and then get out of his way?" Kate asked, disappointed.

Behind the towel, Mitchell's smile widened to a grin. "Are you sure you want to play this particular game with me, sweetheart?"

"I don't think so," she said warily, and he laughed.

Suffused with pleasure at his endearment, Kate added sternly, "Just don't let my Orphan Annie curls and guileless choir-girl image fool you; I can hold my own with you."

"You have a police record; your choir-girl image is shot."

Kate laughed and shook her head at him in feigned disgust. He lifted his brows, waiting for a verbal comeback, and when she had none, he gave her a boyish grin of satisfied superiority and turned back to the sink to comb his hair.

Kate glanced at her watch. "I don't want him to have to watch me packing, so I need to be finished before one, which is about when he'll arrive at the villa. It's a little after eleven now, so I should leave in fifteen minutes." She glanced down at the bright blue silk shirt she'd knotted at the midriff above a pair of white shorts, and decided to wear pants instead for what lay ahead of her. "I think I'll change clothes," she said aloud as she walked over to the closet. She took out a pair of white pants and noticed that the black dress and shoes she'd worn the night before were missing. "Do you know what happened to the black dress I wore last night?"

Mitchell paused, comb in hand, and frowned in disbelief as she walked behind him. "If that's what you're planning to wear while you're doing your explaining and letting him down easily, I don't think you've completely grasped the concept behind the rules we discussed."

Kate reacted with horror, then hilarity, at his imagining she had any such intention; then she quickly lowered her eyes and slid serenely onto the chair at the dressing table opposite the sink to brush her hair. "There's that tone again," she mused as if thinking to herself. "Was that—yes, I think it was—the sound of a slightly jealous man who claims he would give me up without so much as a protest if I were to change my mind today at the villa."

Briefly closing his eyes in amused resignation, Mitchell silently conceded the last verbal round to her and resumed combing his hair. "I'm beginning to understand why your father wept." The truth was the opposite—as he watched her brush her glossy red hair, he couldn't remember ever feeling as utterly lighthearted and content as he felt at that moment. "Diederik took our clothes from last night away while you were in the shower. He'll return everything nicely pressed and brushed in a little while."

She joined him on the balcony ten minutes later, where he was standing at the wall, looking out at the water. "I have to leave."

Mitchell turned, noticed the suitcase she was carrying, and the sight of it gave him a moment's pause before he realized she'd need it to pack her things at the villa.

The cheerful mood of a few minutes earlier turned somber as she put the garment bag on the table and walked over to him to say good-bye. "Are you sure you don't want me to go with you and wait in Philipsburg?" he asked, slipping his hands around her waist.

Kate rested her hands against his chest and shook her head. Beneath his white knit polo shirt, she could feel his heart beating in a slow, steady rhythm, and she drew strength from that. "I need some time alone before I see him, time to separate mentally and emotionally from us and focus on him instead. I'll meet you at Captain Hodges Wharf, right where we got off the boat yesterday, at four o'clock."

"Depending on how he reacts, you may end up there in a lot less than three hours after you break the news."

"Then I'll use the time to separate myself from him and begin to focus on us."

Mitchell smiled down into her green eyes, admiring her ethics and sense of fairness.

She smiled back, the breeze teasing her hair, her fingers splaying across his heart in a tender touch he was already associating with her.

She was absolutely right, Mitchell knew, about the wisdom of forgetting about "them" for the next few hours. "Kiss me good-bye," he said, prepared to give her a brief, chaste kiss, but she wrapped her arms around him, molded her parted lips to his, and gave him a long, scorching kiss that made his hands flex and his fingers dig into her back.

On the beach below, Detective Childress lifted his camera and aimed it casually at the façade of the hotel; then he shifted it to the left and up, and casually snapped yet another picture of the couple on the fourth-floor balcony.

Mitchell stayed where he was, rather than walking her to the door of the suite, but his view from the balcony included the main entrance of the hotel, so he saw her a few minutes later when the doorman signaled a taxi for her and put her suitcase into the backseat. As the taxi passed below their balcony, she smiled and waved at him through the open window.

"Hurry back," he called to her, and she nodded.

The taxi made a U-turn and drove off down the private drive toward the main road, and Mitchell watched it vanish; then he turned his head toward the beach and leaned his forearms on the balcony wall, watching a cruise ship gliding slowly across the horizon. Tomorrow, he decided, he'd take Kate for a cruise aboard Zack's boat. In a few days, Zack and Julie would arrive from Italy, and he could introduce Kate to them. He wanted to show her the house he was building on Anguilla, too—his first house, one that was being built amid a grove of palm trees on a gorgeous stretch of pristine beach with a breathtaking view of the water.

Of all the places in the world where he could have built a home, he'd chosen on a whim a tiny island in the Caribbean where a redhead with shining green eyes and a heart-stopping smile was going to douse him with a drink, delight all his senses, warm his heart, and then steal it. All of that—in less than forty-eight hours.

Chapter Twenty-five

THE DOOR TO THE STATE'S ATTORNEY'S OFFICE IN THE Richard J. Daley Center on Washington Street was closed. Outside the office, the atmosphere was unusually hushed, and Paula Moscato, Gray Elliott's secretary, was keeping it that way by frowning at anyone who approached her desk and then pressing her finger to her lips.

Inside the office, two assistant state's attorneys were standing at the far wall, watching Gray Elliott prepare their prize witness in the investigation of the murder of William Wyatt. The witness was seated behind Gray's desk in his comfortable swivel chair; in front of him was a pencil and a pad of paper containing a few phrases to prompt him during the phone call he was about to make, a call that was intended to lure Mitchell Wyatt back into Cook County's jurisdiction.

The witness's mother was seated in front of Gray's desk, twisting a handkerchief in her lap, her beautiful face stricken with grief over the discovery of her husband's body, her expression dazed as she watched her son lay a trap for her husband's killer. Lily Reardon, one of the ASA's observing the procedure, nodded her head toward Caroline Wyatt and whispered to her colleague, "Can you imagine what it must be like to realize that your husband's killer has been your houseguest since his death?"

Jeff Cervantes shook his head. "If Gray doesn't get

this over with pretty quick, she looks like she's either going to pass out or be sick."

Gray perched his hip on a corner of his desk. "Are you feeling all right, Billy?"

The handsome fourteen-year-old looked at him, swallowed, and nodded. He was tall, slim, and well-built for his age, and he wore his dark suit, white shirt, and patterned tie with the relaxed aura of a privileged, preppy kid who was as accustomed to wearing suits as jeans. In that respect, he was no different from what Gray had been at his age.

"Take another drink of water while I go over this one more time, okay?"

"Okay, Mr. Elliott."

"Please, call me Gray. Do you think you're up for this call?"

Despite the boy's visible anxiety, he nodded; then he nodded again with more conviction. "He killed my father. I will do whatever it takes to get him here."

"I know you will," Gray remarked, smiling a little because at that moment, sitting behind Gray's polished desk, in Gray's executive chair, Billy exhibited both his father's likability and Cecil's steely resolve. "Okay, let's run through it one more time. All you have to do is tell Mitchell that your father's body has been discovered and his killer has confessed—"

"Got it."

"Then you'll tell him your grandfather and your mother have taken the news very badly, and you need him to come back here because you're really, really scared."

"Okay," Billy said; then he added, with a twinge of touching ingenuousness, "I know I can do the last part, Gray, because I am—really, really scared."

"Try to be as convincing as you can about all of it."

"I will."

Satisfied, Gray leaned across the desk to his telephone and pressed the intercom button. "Make the call, Paula." Trying not to do anything to unnerve the fourteen-year-old more than he already was, Gray reached slowly behind him and flipped the switch on the tape recorder; then he glanced at his watch. It was one-thirty in St. Maarten, and according to Childress, Mitchell Wyatt was in his suite at the hotel.

In an effort to make time pass more quickly and to distract himself from thoughts of the ordeal Kate was facing, Mitchell had phoned his New York office and asked his assistant to fax some documents that Stavros had asked him to go over.

When his cell phone rang, Mitchell continued reading the documents in his right hand and reached absently toward his cell phone on the coffee table with his left.

"Uncle Mitchell, it's me. It's Billy," the boy clarified needlessly in a voice so shaken he was nearly stuttering.

"What's wrong?" Mitchell asked, rising slowly to his feet in anticipation of very bad news.

"It's my dad—"

Closing his eyes, Mitchell waited for what he'd known he would hear someday.

"They've f-found my dad's body in a well out near the farm."

"I'm so sorry," Mitchell said hoarsely; then he opened his eyes and shook his head to clear it. "A well? He fell into a well?"

"No, he didn't fall; he was murdered. He was shot in the chest."

Afraid to say the wrong thing, Mitchell waited helplessly for the boy to say more. "Go on, Billy, I'm right here. I'm listening."

"The Udalls' caretaker shot him. He—he's confessed.

He's a filthy old drunk, and he admitted everything to the police when they finally came down hard on him. That worthless old bastard—he shot my father! Please, Uncle Mitchell, can you come home? My mom is locked in her room, and I don't know if she's okay, and Grandpa Cecil—they're taking him to the hospital with angina."

"I'll come home," Mitchell promised.

"Tonight? Please say you'll come tonight. I'm trying to be brave and be the man of the family, like Grandpa Cecil said I should do, until you get here to take care of things." His voice broke, and Mitchell's heart squeezed in sympathy. "Uncle Mitchell, I'm really scared for my mom. She has sleeping pills up there and she isn't answering me."

"I'll be there."

"Will you leave right away?"

Mitchell glanced at his watch. "I'll leave here around five, that's three your time. I should be there by eight."

"Okay," he said meekly. "Uncle Mitchell?"

"What, son?" Mitchell said.

"My dad really loved you. He said—said—that *you* made *him* proud to be a Wyatt."

Mitchell swallowed over an unfamiliar constriction in his throat and stared out the windows. "Thank you for telling me that."

In Chicago, Billy leaned back in Gray's chair and grinned broadly at his mesmerized audience. "How did I do?" he asked, tapping his pencil on the yellow pad like a drumstick on a drum. "It was a bunch of bullshit, but I think it did the job, don't you? I thought the way I improvised about the 'old drunk' had a nice touch."

On the other side of the office, Lily Reardon suppressed a shiver and avoided meeting her colleague's eyes.

"You're amazing, Billy," Gray said proudly, and stood up. "You are absolutely amazing."

Chapter Twenty-six

FOR SEVERAL MINUTES AFTER BILLY HUNG UP, MITCHELL stood beside the coffee table, immobilized, his head bent, his forehead furrowed, trying to cope with the flood of grief he felt at the loss of a half brother he scarcely knew, and whose death he'd only just accepted.

Until eight months ago, he couldn't even have conceived of how it felt to have a relative, let alone how it felt to lose one. Now he understood a little of both, and the emotions running through him were poignant and painful.

In his mind, he saw William standing in his London living room with Caroline and Billy in tow. "I understand why you haven't returned my phone calls and letters, Mitchell," William had said with a smile when Mitchell stalked angrily into the living room, intending to throw them out once and for all, "but you cannot choose your relatives, so I'm afraid you're stuck with us."

Despite the fact that he'd been determined to reject this long-overdue overture from his family when he strode into the living room that day, Mitchell experienced a shock at coming face-to-face with a man who bore an indefinable but definite resemblance to him. "I'm not interested in acquiring a brother," Mitchell snapped.

"I am," William replied with that combination of warmth, friendliness, and surprisingly strong will that was uniquely his. "May we sit down?"

The word *no* was on Mitchell's tongue, but Billy was

there watching him closely, and Caroline was smiling at him as if to say, "We know how you must feel; this is awkward for us, too."

Before he knew it, he'd agreed to see them the next day, and the next, and the next.

William was eager to get to know Mitchell personally, even though he already knew more about Mitchell than Mitchell knew about himself. Besides possessing all the facts surrounding Mitchell's conception and birth, he'd also gone through all the old files he'd discovered in Cecil's safe, including letters and reports from Mitchell's schools—none of which had been opened, William had frankly admitted.

What William couldn't find out from those files, he'd discovered by researching Mitchell on the Internet. He knew about Mitchell's degrees from Oxford and Cambridge, and about Stavros Konstantatos and about Mitchell's marriage to Anastasia. He even teased Mitchell about several of his highly publicized flings over the years.

Mitchell hadn't wanted to hear anything about his father or grandfather, who had not made a similar overture, and William seemed to accept that at first, but as Mitchell soon discovered, his older brother was like a silent locomotive that couldn't be derailed and whose arrival at any given point couldn't be anticipated.

One night when Mitchell was in Chicago, meeting with Matt Farrell, he'd had dinner with William and his family, and William had played what he hoped would be a trump card to interest Mitchell in exploring his relationship with Cecil. "There's a great deal of money to be considered—"

"His or mine?" Mitchell sarcastically replied, even though he already knew Cecil Wyatt was an extremely wealthy man. Caroline had looked down quickly to hide her smile. William had laughed out loud and then sobered. "Half of my inheritance is rightfully yours."

"I don't want it."

"I'm not asking you if you want it; I'm telling you that I won't accept it. As your older—albeit perhaps not wiser—brother, I reserve the right to look out for your best interests." He grinned with embarrassment, and added, "I've been thinking about how it would have been if we'd grown up together, and in my imagination, I see you tagging around after me, and me protecting you from bullies, and you, well, you know—"

"No, I don't know," Mitchell said honestly.

Caroline finished the sentence for him, smiling softly at Mitchell, "—and, *you* would have looked up to your big brother and asked him for advice, and all that."

Mitchell gazed at the "big brother" who was seated at the head of an elegant table in a Chicago mansion. He was several inches shorter, several years older, and many pounds heavier than Mitchell. He was also the most decent, generous man Mitchell had ever met. *I look up to you now,* he thought, and with amusement, he added, *but if you're going to walk around giving away half your fortune, I'm the one who should be giving the advice.*

Not long afterward, Caroline brought up William and Mitchell's father, when she and Mitchell were alone, and what she said explained more than merely why Edward still wanted nothing to do with Mitchell. "William's father—your father—is the most self-absorbed human being I've ever met. He strolls through life hiding the truth about who he is from himself and everyone else, and he drinks to make sure he never has to face it. He never paid the slightest attention to William when he was growing up, and that's why William has been so determined to build a relationship with you," Caroline finished. "William's angry that the two of you grew up feeling as if you had no one who cared, when you could have had each other, and he is determined to make up for lost time." She stood up then because dinner was being served, and tucked her hand into Mitchell's arm as they strolled to the dining room. "By the way," she confided, "in case you aren't aware of it, he loves you, he thinks you're brilliant and he's outrageously proud of you."

Instead of telling her how he felt about William, which was what Mitchell knew she hoped he would do, he smiled and said, "He's very lucky to have you."

"I'm lucky to have him," she said simply.

Now, as Mitchell stood in the suite at the Enclave, he was filled with remorse that he hadn't at least told Caroline how much he liked and admired William, so she could have relayed that back to her husband, just as she'd done with William's feelings about him. Why hadn't he been able to say the words? Why hadn't he just said them, so that William would have known how he felt before he died?

With a harsh sigh, Mitchell dragged his thoughts back to the present and focused on what he needed to do. Billy's fear that his mother would overdose on sleeping pills was groundless, Mitchell knew. Caroline had known all along that William hadn't vanished of his own volition, no matter what the police thought. She'd also known that nothing would have kept William away from his family except his death. They'd talked about all that often since William's disappearance. Furthermore, the last thing on earth that Caroline wanted was for Billy to be left alone in the world, so there was no chance she'd ever consider taking her own life.

On the other hand, there was no question that Mitchell needed to leave for Chicago immediately and lend what moral support he could to Caroline and Billy for the next few days. That much he needed to do for the brother he had . . . loved.

Once he explained to Kate why he needed to be in Chicago, she would understand and forgive him, he knew that without a doubt. She was so kind and soft-hearted that she couldn't bear to abandon an injured stray dog, so she would instantly realize that he couldn't abandon Caroline and Billy.

He could fly back and forth between Chicago and St. Maarten for the next few days. It was only four hours each way, and he could get what sleep he needed on the plane. However, the idea of leaving her behind in another hotel, just as her boyfriend had done, was untenable.

She'd mentioned that she liked boats, he remembered, and the best possible solution suddenly occurred to him—he could arrange for her to cruise the islands on Zack's boat during the day while he was gone. She'd enjoy that. In a few days, Zack and Julie, and Matt and Meredith, were flying down for a longer cruise, and she'd enjoy meeting them, too, Mitchell decided, already reaching for his telephone.

His first call was to his pilots, instructing them to be ready to leave for O'Hare at five o'clock.

His second phone call was to the hotel's front desk, notifying them that he would be checking out immediately.

His next phone call was to Zack in Rome.

Chapter Twenty-seven

STANDING AT THE WINDOW OF MITCHELL'S APART-ment in Rome's Piazza Navona, Julie Mathison Benedict gazed down at Bernini's spectacular Fountain of Four Rivers. It was evening, and the fountain was bathed in light, the little cafés lining the piazza were serving dinner, and lovers and tourists were strolling by in a steady stream. In the living room behind her, her husband was seated in a seventeenth-century baroque armchair going over his notes on the day's filming of his new picture. They'd been there two weeks, filming on location, and they were finished in Rome, but Zack wanted to stay a few extra days to shoot some extra exterior footage.

"I'm going to miss this place," Julie said, glancing over her shoulder. "I'm even going to miss Giovanni."

Zack looked up and grinned. "Really? When did you decide he wasn't a thug masquerading as a chauffeur?"

"Yesterday," Julie admitted, "when he practically threw me into the car and ran after a thief who'd stolen an old lady's purse."

Zack looked up sharply. "When were you going to tell me about that?"

"Right about now," she admitted serenely, "when we're ready to leave Rome and you won't worry that it might happen again. Did you realize Giovanni has known Mitchell since he was a little boy, when he lived in Italy?"

"I didn't even know Giovanni could speak more than a few words of English," Zack began, but the telephone rang and he paused to answer it.

When he hung up a few minutes later, he had an odd, thoughtful expression on his face.

"What's up?" Julie asked.

"That was Mitchell. Evidently, he's met someone in the islands, and he has to leave her there and go back to Chicago. He asked me to call Prescott and arrange for her to go aboard and cruise the islands while he's gone."

Julie studied his amused expression. "What's the part you haven't told me?"

"The best part. Mitchell intends to fly back and forth every day to join her on board."

"Are you serious?"

"Very serious. And so, I think, is he."

Zack sobered and added, "The reason he has to go back to Chicago is because they've discovered his brother's body." He glanced at his watch and reached for the telephone to call Prescott. "It's one-thirty in St. Maarten," he said, "and Mitchell said he'd be bringing her aboard at five."

"Do we have a name?" Julie teased.

"Kate Donovan."

Chapter Twenty-eight

KATE ZIPPED HER SUITCASE CLOSED, CARRIED IT INTO THE living room, and put it down next to her garment bag. She'd gone over what she wanted to say to Evan so many times that she was afraid it was going to sound like a well-rehearsed speech, even though she felt anything but unemotional about the hurt she was about to cause him.

With nothing else left to do, she stepped outside onto the patio, and a sense of nostalgia and well-being began to bloom inside her. Only three days ago she'd stood in this spot, talking to Holly on the phone and feeding Max strips of bacon. The future had seemed so bleak that morning, and now it was dazzlingly bright and filled with poignant promise. Everything had changed in three short days. She'd fallen in love.

Smiling, she walked forward and ran her hand along the patio's stone balustrade while sweet memories drifted through her mind. At the edge of the garden near the beach was the clump of palms she'd been standing under when Mitchell relented and came back to answer some of her questions . . . *My brother's name was William.*

On the patio, exactly where she was standing right now, they'd danced together for the first time. She'd mistakenly thought he intended to kiss her and ended up laughing and chiding him: *"You might have mentioned that you intended to dance with me, not try to ravish me."*

"*But I do intend to ravish you,*" he'd whispered.

He'd really been outrageously frank about his intentions that night, but he'd wanted her badly enough to change his mind and come back to her in the garden. He'd been just as frank the next day in the suite at the Enclave, Kate remembered with a smile . . .

In Chicago, there's an eligible man who wants to marry you. Here, in this room, there's a man who wants to take you to bed and make love to you until neither of us has the strength to move anymore. But it can't go any further than that. It would get much too complicated.

A few moments later—a compromise. And when Mitchell compromised, he was utterly irresistible.

"*Let's get complicated, Kate . . . The truth is that I felt all the same things you did last night, and you know I did.*"

"Kate?" Evan's voice made her whirl around in time to see him closing the door—a tall, fit, attractive man with brown hair and gray eyes who'd been part of her life for four years. A good man she was going to hurt. "I didn't think you'd have a key to get in," she said, as another surge of nostalgia, this one painful, hit her.

"Since you're never here," he said, striding toward her, "I stopped at the front desk and—" His gaze riveted on her suitcases and ricocheted back to her face. "What's going on?"

Nervously rubbing her hands on the sides of her pants, Kate tried to smile as she nodded toward the sofa and said, "Come over here, and let's sit down. We need to talk."

"Let's go straight to the summation instead," he said coolly. "You're angry because I left you down here, and I'm just as angry because you paid me back by ignoring my calls and putting me through long periods of daily hell, worrying that your headaches were incapacitating you and thinking about things like brain tumors. Does that about sum it up?" he demanded. Without waiting for an answer, he turned on his heel and walked over to the bar.

And in that bizarre moment, when Kate knew it was over between them, she watched him and understood the reasons he'd appealed to her from the beginning—his intelligence and self-assurance, his ability to go right to the heart of the matter and see it from both sides, and his ability to keep his head when everyone else was losing theirs. These talents made him a superb lawyer and a terrific companion.

She watched him take a swallow of his drink, and when he lowered the glass and scowled at her, she smiled a little and made a fervent wish that he'd find someone wonderful right away.

"Why are you smiling?"

"I'm hoping you get exactly the woman you deserve."

"You don't do sarcasm well," he observed flatly. "It comes off as sincerity and loses its edge."

Torn between laughter and tears, Kate bit her lip and looked down. He'd been more than her lover; he'd been her friend. She was losing a friend and about to hurt him, too. Lifting her head, she drew a long breath and said softly, "I wasn't being sarcastic, Evan. I meant that with all my heart."

His hand stilled in the act of raising the glass to his mouth. With his gaze riveted on her, he reached out and put the glass back on the bar. "What are you talking about?"

"I met someone here, and there's something special between us. I have to give it a chance."

He was so still it was unnerving. "When did all this happen?"

"Two days ago. Two and a half days ago," Kate corrected, trying to make what she was doing seem less insanely impulsive.

"Who is he?"

"No one you know. He lives in Europe and New York."

"Where did you meet him?"

"Evan, please—"

"Help me understand how a man you've known for two days can make you throw away a four-year relationship. Give me some details!"

"I met him in a restaurant here."

"What does he do?"

"I—I don't know exactly."

"What's his name?"

"It doesn't matter what his name is."

"It damn well matters to me. I want a name to curse in private. That's what men do, Kate. We pretend we're taking things very well, and that our hearts aren't being broken, and then we get roaring drunk and we curse the bastard who stole the woman we loved."

Tears stung Kate's eyes.

"You've already slept with him, haven't you?" he concluded bitterly. "It took me two months to get you into bed, and he accomplished it in two days."

"I'd better leave," Kate said, and reached down for her suitcase.

"Let's have a name before you go."

"Mitchell Wyatt."

An expression of utter disbelief froze his face. "Mitchell Wyatt?" he repeated. "You've gotten involved with *Mitchell Wyatt* down here?"

"You know him?"

"I know him," he clipped. "He's Cecil Wyatt's bastard grandson."

Other than being taken aback that Evan had apparently met Mitchell at some social function somewhere,

Kate attached no particular significance to Evan's statement. As she knew from boring experience, people in Evan's lofty social class had widespread connections in many cities, they all kept close tabs on each other, and they gossiped incessantly about all that. Long ago, she'd stopped accompanying Evan to nearly all their gatherings. She was just a social worker and a restaurant owner's daughter, and since her relationship with Evan remained undefined, they didn't know what to do with her, other than to treat her courteously for Evan's sake. Kate did the same thing for the same reason. Occasionally, Evan tried to relate a tale from one of these functions, but as soon as he started talking about who was there and how they were related to so-and-so, Kate's brain automatically changed to another channel before he ever got to the point. She wasn't completely sure who Cecil Wyatt was, so the revelation that Mitchell could be his "bastard grandson" had no effect.

"This is one *hell* of a big coincidence," he said, sounding as if it might not be a coincidence at all.

"What is?" Kate asked, relieved that something was distracting him from his hurt feelings.

"When I met him at Cecil Wyatt's birthday party, I specifically told him that you and I were going to be down here now, staying at the Island Club. He said he was going to be down here at the same time, staying on a friend's boat. Forgive me for sounding paranoid, but I find it just a little strange that he supposedly ignored all the women at that party who were flinging themselves at him . . . and he hasn't been able to find a single woman to suit him anywhere on any of these islands . . . until he 'happened' to bump into you—in a hotel that he isn't staying at—and while I'm away. This whole thing doesn't look like coincidence to me; it looks like payback."

"He has no idea I know you," Kate interjected. "I've never told him your name."

"The villa you're staying in is in my name," Evan retorted.

Kate saw no reason to argue that inconsequential point, but she was stunned that her desertion was driving him to such incomprehensible leaps of fanciful logic. "Payback for what?" she said calmly.

"Did Wyatt tell you anything about his background?"

"I'm not interested in his pedigree or his legitimacy."

"Then *get* interested in it, Kate," he ordered sharply. "It's an ugly little story, and it involves my father as well as me."

"Okay," she sighed, "I'm listening."

"Until a few months ago Mitchell Wyatt believed he'd been abandoned at birth and that his name had been picked out of a phone book by someone. He attended the best boarding schools in Europe with some of the richest kids in the world, but he was led to believe he was a charity case."

Inwardly Kate was appalled, but anxious to get this over with. "What does that have to do with you?"

"My father created and maintained the entire deception, and Wyatt discovered the truth eight months ago. Now Cecil has suddenly brought him out of obscurity to Chicago, and he's parading him around like the heir apparent. My father and I are the only ones who know the truth about his pathetic past, and he's bitter as hell that we do, as well as about the fact that my father actually orchestrated it for Cecil. At Cecil's party, Wyatt came up to us, and you could have cut through the hostility with a knife. I stepped in and tried to smooth things over with a discussion about our vacation in Anguilla. I told him about you and that your father had just died and that I was on my way to his wake."

"Are you saying you told him my name?" Kate said uneasily.

"Yes. At the time I did it, I was completely clueless about what was eating him. I had no idea until the next morning what Cecil and my father had done to Wyatt as a kid.

"Now," he said with a solemn smile, "before you go, will you answer a question for me?"

Kate realized he was bringing the ordeal to an end without forcing her to acknowledge that he could be right about Mitchell, and she loved him for that. He believed he was right, she knew, but he didn't know Mitchell the way she did. Furthermore, no matter how straightforward he was trying to be, he was being jilted for another man, and that was understandably coloring his view of his adversary. She didn't want to hurt him by siding with Mitchell, singing his praises, or playing devil's advocate on his behalf. She wanted to get through this as soon as possible, doing as little damage to Evan's pride as she could, and then she wanted to go to Mitchell and never let on that she knew the heartbreaking story of his childhood. He'd confide in her in his own time. He already had, a little bit. In answer to Evan's question, Kate nodded and smiled. "What question is that?"

"I've known you for a long time, and you're not easy to dazzle, Kate. Or maybe I just didn't try the right methods. You never seemed to give a damn about social status, or money, or anything else like that that I had to offer. So my question is this: How in the hell did he accomplish in two days what I couldn't accomplish in four years?"

"Evan, please don't do this—" Kate said, her eyes filling with sudden tears because she'd never imagined he loved her so much that he would humble himself this way.

"Tell me. I need to know. Wyatt's aunt, Olivia Hebert, told people at the party that he's building a house here on Anguilla. Have you secretly dreamed of a house on an island? Did he show you around it and make you envision yourself living in it?"

Kate managed to keep her expression noncommittal. It didn't matter that Mitchell hadn't mentioned building a house here. They'd been too busy making love and getting to know each other. "No," she said calmly.

"On the ferry coming over here, I heard that Zack Benedict's yacht is down here, and according to what I read on the Internet, Wyatt is a bosom buddy of Benedict's—and a big investor in his films. Benedict's yacht is undoubtedly the friend's boat that Wyatt said he was going to stay on down here. Did he take you for a cruise and promise you a life of leisurely cruising with movie stars? Is that what you've always wanted?"

"No," Kate said, trying to sound offhand. But the realization that Mitchell had let her go on and on about Zack Benedict after their boat captain pointed out the *Julie* made Kate feel a little ill. Still, he hadn't really lied when he said he wasn't "a fan" of Benedict's. Mitchell was apparently Zack Benedict's friend. And to give Mitchell credit, he was certainly no braggart, either.

Evan wasn't fooled by her replies. Her complexion was too fair and her eyes too expressive to hide shock or dismay. "You didn't know about the house or the yacht, did you?"

"I think this conversation is pointless and needs to end," Kate said firmly.

"Right after you answer one more little question for yourself, not for me: How in the hell does it happen that you know Wyatt lives in Europe and New York, but you don't know that he also has a *Chicago* address?"

"He doesn't know anything about Chicago," Kate

said before she could stop herself. "I talked a lot about Chicago—he would have told me if he knew anyone there. In fact, he had to ask me how long it takes to get down here from there! Evan, we aren't talking about the same man."

"I hope you're right, honey, because the man I'm talking about has been living in Chicago with Caroline Wyatt."

"Who?" Kate said in frustration.

"Caroline Wyatt. Late last year, a man named William Wyatt disappeared. Remember?"

"Vaguely."

"The beautiful Caroline was, and still is, William's wife. Your Mitchell is shacked up with his half brother's wife, and he moved in just as soon as her husband disappeared!"

"He told me about his brother," Kate said quickly, glad for once that she knew something. "He liked William very much, and if Caroline's home is typical of most of your friends' and relatives' houses, then it's the size of a hotel."

Lifting his hand, Evan smoothed her hair back off her forehead, then he dropped his arm. "Don't let that son of a bitch hurt you too badly. And when he does," Evan added tenderly, "you remember that it was me, not you, he wanted to hurt. Maybe that will make it easier." He picked up his drink and glanced at her luggage. "I should carry those for you, but I can't make myself help you go to him. I'm sorry, Kate." It was a gruff apology, not a parting taunt.

Shaking inside, Kate watched him walk out onto the patio and into the garden.

Questions and doubts were raging through her as she walked into the bathroom to make sure she wasn't leaving anything behind. Instead of doing that, she stood in front of the sink, trying to rid herself of Evan's slant on everything Mitchell did, and to think things through for herself. In her mind, she heard Mitchell whispering, *I felt all the same things you did last night, and you know I did,* and her spirits lifted. That was real. That was the real Mitchell, not Evan's version of him.

Evan's description of Mitchell's childhood explained exactly why he'd evaded Kate's questions that first night. The story of his life wasn't the sort of story a man would want to share with a stranger. Furthermore, the fact that Mitchell hadn't simply invented a more impressive past for himself, one that he could dispense freely and impress strangers with, was even more to his credit. It showed tremendous strength of character.

As far as everything else Evan had brought up, Kate could think of valid reasons and explanations for all of it, including gossip. There was just one thing she couldn't justify, no matter how hard she tried: If Evan was right about Mitchell living, even temporarily, in Chicago, there was only one possible reason for Mitchell's having concealed that from her—he had no intention of seeing her after they left St. Maarten.

She needed an answer to that right now, not later when they were face-to-face and he could disarm her or distract her. A simple, straightforward answer. After all, Mitchell had sent her here expecting her to break up with Evan "in the shortest possible time," and then to "hurry back." She had every right to expect a straightforward answer to her question.

Closing the bathroom door, she dug in her purse for her cell phone and the brochure from the Enclave. Her fingers trembled as she pressed the buttons on her cell phone, and her pulse edged up with each ring. By the time the Enclave's operator answered the phone, Kate was leaning back against the vanity for support, and her voice actually wavered with nervousness when she asked to be connected to Mr. Wyatt in the Presidential Suite.

"I'm sorry, ma'am," the operator said a moment later, "Mr. Wyatt has checked out."

"Checked out? Did—did he leave a message for me, for Kate Donovan, I mean?"

"One moment please." Kate's knees began to knock while she waited. "No, ma'am. No message," the operator stated with certainty.

Kate twisted around and made a grab for the vanity, trying to hold her quaking body upright while Mitchell's mocking voice whispered in her ringing ears. *"I want to be sure you don't have any false illusions about what's going on between us. . . . It can't go any further than that. It would get much too complicated. . . . But I do intend to ravish you."*

The sound of her own sobbing drowned out his voice, and Kate groped blindly for a towel, holding it tightly to her face, trying to muffle her cries before Evan heard them. Desperate to get herself under control and to get out of there before Evan walked in from the garden, she threw the towel down and splashed cold water onto her face; then she opened the door a crack and saw that the living room was empty. With tears pouring from her eyes and blurring her vision, she grabbed her suitcase and garment bag, made an awkward dash for the door, and struggled with the knob.

Her shoulders shaking with silent sobs, she nudged the door open with her knee and was halfway outside when Evan walked in from the patio. "Kate, wait, let me help you with—"

"I'm fine, stay there," she called, keeping her face averted, but she couldn't stop her shoulders from jerking.

"What the hell—?" His hands locked on her arms,

turning her around. He took one look at her tormented face and pulled her against his chest. "What's wrong, honey?"

"Please d-don't be n-nice to me; I was l-leaving you for him, and he's gone."

"Don't worry," he said drily. "I don't feel like being very nice to you right now. Why don't I take you home?"

Kate nodded, too choked up to speak. "I have to pick up Max."

Max bounded onto the floor of the taxi's backseat and Kate scooted over into the center. Evan went around to the passenger side and opened the back door. "This is going to be a tight fit," he said, wedging himself in beside her. Once he was inside, his left thigh and leg were pressed against hers, and there was no room for his left arm, so he put it across the back of the seat behind her.

They'd sat this way hundreds of times before, but now their proximity felt awkward, and having his arm casually resting there seemed all wrong. He felt it, too; Kate could sense his tension. He was wounded and angry at her betrayal. She didn't deserve his kindness or his compassion, and the fact that he was offering both right now, when she needed them most and deserved them least, made her feel so ashamed that she bent her head and tears gathered in her eyes. Max laid his big head on her knee, his unblinking, adoring gaze on her face, and she reached out to scratch his head while two tears ran down her cheeks. It belatedly dawned on Kate that she hadn't even given Evan the courtesy of an apology, and she swallowed twice, trying to drag her voice through the knot of emotion in her throat. "I'm sorry," she whispered.

"I know you are."

Wishing desperately that she had a tissue, Kate felt in her purse, but there were none in there. His duffel was on the seat beside her, and she reached for the zipper on it while tears began streaking in earnest from her eyes. "Do you have tissues or a handkerchief or something I could use in here?"

"I think so," Evan replied. "Pass it over to me and I'll look."

"Don't bother," she said, already tugging on the zipper. "I'll do it—"

"Don't open—" Evan said, but it was too late.

Lying atop all the neatly packed masculine apparel in Evan's duffel was a thick, square, robin's-egg-blue Tiffany box tied with a cream ribbon. It was a ring box.

Kate stared at it through a fresh haze of tears, and for the second time in less than an hour, she covered her face and wept.

He hesitated, and then he lowered his arm around her shaking shoulders and curved his hand around her arm, drawing her close so she could weep against his chest. "I should be the one comforting you," Kate whispered brokenly.

"I'm beyond comforting," he whispered.

"I hate myself," she said fiercely.

He thought about that for a moment. "I hate you, too," he said, but there was a smile in his voice.

Kate closed her eyes. She couldn't let herself think about Mitchell yet or she would shatter. Exhausted from the turmoil, and the struggle to keep thoughts of him at bay, she dozed as the old taxi jolted and bumped along the short distance to the airport.

When she opened her eyes, she found that Evan had taken her hand in his and he was holding it. "Wake up, we're here," he said, and took his hand away. While she was sleeping, he'd slid the dazzling diamond solitaire from Tiffany's onto her ring finger. Kate stared at it and started to shake her head. "I can't—"

"Here is what I'm 'proposing.' " Evan clarified, "I need some time to get past what's happened, and so do you. In the meantime, I suggest we announce our engagement in the newspaper."

"Why?"

He leaned close and whispered, "Well, for one thing, that ring will look very nice with whatever gown you wear to the Children's Hospital benefit Saturday night. We're one of the sponsors."

Kate looked at him in stupefaction as he took his arm away and reached into his pocket to pay the cab fare. "What's the *other* thing?"

"The Wyatt family will be there. Now," he continued conversationally as he counted out money, "I don't know about you, but if I were in your place, I'd like it if Mitchell Wyatt was forced to realize that *he'd* been used—"

"Used as what?" Kate asked bitterly.

He slanted her a sideways smile tinged with just a little regret. "*Your* last fling."

Chapter Twenty-nine

BY FIVE-THIRTY, THE TIDE OF TOURISTS ON THE STREETS around Captain Hodges Wharf was receding rapidly. Cruise ship passengers, carrying bags of duty-free bounty, were heading back to departing ships, and tourists staying on the island were returning to their hotels to nap before a long night of dining, gambling, and nightclubbing.

In a parked car, MacNeil phoned Gray Elliott to report again on Wyatt's whereabouts. "Wyatt's still hanging around the wharf," MacNeil said. "That's the bad news. The good news is, I just checked with our contact at the airport. He said Wyatt's plane is on the ramp at the hangar, fueled up and ready to fly. His pilots are waiting in the lounge, drinking coffee. So he's planning to leave soon."

"All right, stay in touch," Gray replied. "Interpol is on standby, prepared to conduct simultaneous searches of his apartments in Europe, but I can't give them the go-ahead until Wyatt's plane is in the air. Otherwise, I run the risk that some doorman or housekeeper will phone him, and he'll figure out that *he's* the subject of our investigation. He has a telephone in the plane, but I don't think he'd give that number to underlings and domestics."

"I'll call you as soon as he's on the move," MacNeil said.

As MacNeil lowered his phone, Childress raised the

camera and focused on Wyatt for another quick shot. "The guy is a chick magnet," Childress remarked a little wistfully, watching through the camera's eye as a pretty blonde strolled into the frame.

"Excuse me," a female voice said. "Could you tell me what time it is?"

"It's five-thirty," Mitchell replied without looking at his watch or the woman. He'd just checked the time, and his attention was now fastened on a new boat appearing on the horizon.

As the boat grew larger, it appeared to be about the right size and moving at about the right speed for a tourist boat. St. Maarten's coastline was dotted with marinas and wharfs, however, and most boats coming over the horizon appeared to be headed in his general direction at first, so Mitchell kept a tight rein on his expectations. A few minutes later, the boat was still angled toward Captain Hodges Wharf, and Mitchell's pulse began edging up, notch by notch, while his gaze fastened on the boat's bow, willing it not to change direction.

The boat came nearer, grew larger, and Mitchell began searching for a glimpse of shining red hair among the blur of passengers on deck. A few minutes later, the *Island Sun* had docked and the last passenger had filed past him. Mitchell returned to his vantage point on the other side of the wharf and scanned the horizon for signs of another inbound tourist boat. Obviously the boyfriend's flight had been delayed, and he'd arrived an hour or two late, which was delaying Kate.

Smiling a little, he marveled, yet again, that neither he nor Kate had thought to exchange cell phone numbers. In the hours before she left this morning, they'd shared a sunrise, laughter, several stories, long kisses, and the most exciting, profoundly satisfying lovemaking of his life. They had not, however, shared their phone numbers—which wasn't all that surprising on his part, Mitchell thought wryly, because he'd lost the ability and the desire to concentrate on anything else when she was near.

After twenty minutes and another boat arrival, Mitchell was no longer smiling. The sun was beginning to set, and as darkness loomed, his mind began conjuring unbearable images of Kate cowering in a corner from her enraged boyfriend or lying alone in the villa, injured or worse.

Once those possibilities had occurred to him, he was powerless to ignore them. He pulled his cell phone out of his pocket, and after being transferred to two operators, he was finally able to get through to the Island Club. At the last moment, he remembered Maurice was away, and he asked to speak to whoever was in charge instead. A male answered, identified himself as "Mr. Orly," and asked how he could be of service.

"This is Mitchell Wyatt," Mitchell replied, trying to sound less frightened than he felt. "Miss Donovan, in villa six, was feeling ill earlier, and she isn't answering her phone. Please send someone down to check on her while I hold on."

"Miss Donovan?" Mr. Orly repeated. "Villa six? Are you certain?"

"Very certain," Mitchell snapped. "Send someone down there immediately."

"I'm happy to be able to allay your fears, Mr. Wyatt," Orly said cheerfully after a moment. "The phone in villa six isn't being answered because the villa is unoccupied."

"What do you mean it's unoccupied?"

"I mean that the party occupying villa six checked out at three o'clock today. Is there anything—"

Mitchell closed the cover on his cell phone, disconnecting Orly in midsentence, but his brain refused to process the obvious implications of what he'd heard. Paralyzed with disbelief, he stood where he was, gazing blindly at the horizon, his phone hanging loosely from his hand.

Not once since Kate had waved good-bye to him this morning had he ever considered that she'd leave him standing there at the wharf. She was in love with him, and he was in love with her. Their feelings for each other were deepening with every hour they spent together. They were meant to be, and Kate had realized that even before he had. Kate wanted magic, and they had it in unbelievable abundance. She didn't have that with her boyfriend. She would never have checked out of the Island Club and gone home with him.

The obvious answer was that the boyfriend had checked out and gone home alone. Kate was probably on her way to Mitchell right now, as eager to kiss him hello as he was to return her kiss. There was a way to find out.... Slowly, Mitchell pulled his wallet out of his pocket and removed the slip of paper he'd put there yesterday with the veterinary's address and phone number on it. Looking at it, he flipped his cell phone open again with his thumb, his heart beginning to beat with dread.

"This is Mitchell Wyatt," he told the vet when he answered the phone. "I was wondering if Miss Donovan came by to pick up Max yet."

"Yes, she did. She picked him up several hours ago, and he was very happy to see her. I had all the documents ready that she needed to get him into the States."

"That's good . . ." Mitchell said, his chest constricting in pained disbelief. "Did she bring someone along to help with him?"

"Yes, a nice gentleman."

* * *

Standing beside their car, Childress and MacNeil watched Wyatt's jet taxiing away from its hangar. Minutes later, it roared down the runway; then it lifted off and vanished swiftly into the darkness, its presence in the sky marked only by tiny flashes of light.

Chapter Thirty

UNLIKE HIS TRADITIONALLY FURNISHED APARTMENTS in Europe, the interior of Mitchell's plane resembled a luxurious Art Deco living room, and the color scheme of silver, black, and chrome was enlivened with splashes of color from the period art pieces he'd carefully collected. A stylish oyster-gray leather sofa, long enough for him to stretch out on, was positioned between a pair of round end tables with black granite tops and polished chrome lamps in the stepped profile of the Art Deco period.

Two oversize gray leather swivel recliners were across from the sofa. Beyond that was a Macassar ebony desk and credenza where he frequently worked, another row of seats, and a doorway opening into a compact but elegant bedroom-and-bathroom suite.

Normally, when Mitchell boarded for a flight of several hours, he went either to his desk or to the bedroom, depending on the time of day. Tonight, he went straight to the curved ebony bar near the front of the cabin and poured brandy into a crystal tumbler instead of a snifter.

From the sofa, he watched the twinkling lights of St. Maarten vanish; then he stretched his legs out in front of him and lifted the glass of brandy to his lips, eager for the fiery liquid to start dulling the ache in his chest.

He'd turned off the cabin's lights and switched on a table lamp.

Slowly and methodically, he began reviewing the last

three days, searching for some clue that should have alerted him to the fact that he was overestimating the depth of her feelings for him.

An hour later, all he'd come up with were haunting memories of an irresistible redhead with a heartwarming smile who'd kissed him and set him on fire—memories that all led him to the same unanswerable question: How could she have left with her boyfriend, without at least meeting Mitchell at the wharf to tell him good-bye?

How could she have done that when she'd been so candid and brave about her feelings:

I think fate may have intended for us to meet the way we did and to become friends—that it was predestined. . . . I like you very much, and I think you like me, too. . . . If I'm going to be disappointed, I don't want it to happen with you.

Swallowing over the unfamiliar constriction in his throat, he drew a long breath and leaned his head back, willing himself into a state of pleasant numbness where he could think about her without this gnawing sense of bewildered loss. Instead, he remembered the quiet joy of sitting up in bed, drowsy and contented, watching the sunrise together, and the inexplicable pleasure of seeing her hand resting next to his on the table in the casino.

She'd made her decision to stay with her boyfriend, and thanks to his glib description of their "roles" that morning, he was stuck with that decision and bound by the very role he'd described and intended for her boyfriend to play:

As soon as he understands that you're serious about wanting to be with someone else, he is obliged to accept defeat gracefully and wish you well and then to get the hell out of my way.

About those rules—she'd asked—*What would you do if I were to vacillate a little about breaking up with my boyfriend?*

Under those circumstances, you would be required to telephone me to tell me that you're having doubts, and then I would simply switch roles with him.

On his way to the airport tonight, he'd phoned the Enclave to see if she'd left a message for him there, but she hadn't.

Briefly, Mitchell considered the possibility that her disappearance was a sophomoric attempt to prove she could make him jealous enough to come after her. If so, she wasn't the woman he thought she was.

He knew how to find her—she wasn't lost to him. If she wasn't listed in the phone book, he could trace her through her father's newspaper obituary.

Several times he considered the possibility that something dire had happened that made her leave without a word.

Each time, he squelched that thought, along with the temptation to use it as an excuse to find her. She'd had the time, and the presence of mind, to pick up a stray dog at the vet. She'd intentionally left him to wait at the wharf.

The telephone on the table beside him began ringing and he ignored it.

"Why isn't he answering the damned phone?" Matt Farrell asked his wife. Shoving his hands into his pockets, he turned and gazed out the living room windows of their penthouse apartment overlooking Lake Shore Drive. "I know he's on the plane."

Meredith laid aside the agenda she was supposed to be preparing for the next board of directors meeting of Bancroft & Company, a chain of luxury department stores founded by a Bancroft ancestor, and which she now headed. "He's probably in bed," she said, but Matt heard the apprehension in her voice, and he remembered something that made Mitchell's situation seem less grim.

"Speaking of that . . ." he said, and raised his brows, letting the sentence hang unfinished.

Meredith studied his expression but couldn't connect it with anything other than possibly a hint that they should go to bed, which seemed unlikely given his urgent need to contact Mitchell and warn him that police on two continents were searching his apartments. "Speaking of what?" she prompted finally.

"Speaking of Mitchell being in bed," Matt provided unhelpfully.

"Yes?" she said in smiling exasperation when he merely lifted his brows and left her hanging again, without any information.

Satisfied that she was fully engrossed in this new topic, he said, "When Zack called tonight to tell me Mitchell's apartment in Rome was being searched, he also mentioned that Mitchell had phoned him earlier today from St. Maarten with a very interesting request— It seems that Mitchell has met someone down in the islands, and since he needed to come back here to be with Caroline and Billy for a few days, he wanted to be sure the lady would have a *very* pleasant time cruising the islands on the *Julie* while he was in Chicago."

Tipping her head to the side, Meredith looked at him, puzzled. "That doesn't sound particularly significant."

"That's not the significant part. The significant part is that *Mitchell* intended to fly back to the islands every night to be with her on the yacht. Hence," he finished, with satisfaction at his wife's look of surprised interest, "the connection between Mitchell being in bed on the plane and this discussion. I'm thinking maybe she's with him and that's why he hasn't answered my calls. Her name is Kate, by the way."

Meredith's smile faded and so did Matt's, for the same reason. "I hope she's on the yacht and not on the plane," Meredith said, putting both their thoughts into words.

"It would be awful for him if she's there and the police are waiting to talk to him when the plane lands, like Zack thinks is going to happen."

"Zack may be leaping to conclusions," Matt replied, walking toward the telephone.

"But you don't think he's leaping to conclusions, do you?"

"No." He hesitated, reluctant to worry her, but unwilling to lie to her.

Meredith wasn't certain what to expect. Years before, Matt had watched his friend Zack Benedict get wrongly convicted of murdering his actress wife, and the bitter experience had left both men intensely mistrustful of the criminal justice system. As a result, Matt had already arranged for his chauffeur to be ready to head for the hangar at O'Hare with two attorneys from the law firm that handled both Matt's and Mitchell's corporate affairs in Chicago.

The telephone next to the sofa began ringing again, and Mitchell ignored it, but very few people had the plane's phone number, and all of them were important to him for one reason or another. Since the brandy he'd been drinking had only made him sink deeper into a state of confused longing for Kate, he finally reached for the telephone to give himself a distraction. "Whoever you are," he said aloud when he answered, "you're persistent as hell."

"It's Matt," his friend said after a startled pause. "Zack called an hour ago to say the police were swarming all over your apartment, searching for something. He also said your assistant in New York called because NYPD was searching your New York apartment."

Mitchell straightened slowly to an upright position. "What are they searching for?"

"Your assistant said the search warrant was for a

man's outdoor coat or jacket, black in color, and any item of apparel with buttons bearing a particular symbol on the back. The cops had a picture of the symbol. I have no idea what the Italian warrant was for, but Zack faxed me a copy of it."

"Read it to me," Mitchell said, as anger began to replace some of the desolation he was feeling. He listened to Matt struggle through the Italian words, mispronouncing most of them. "That's what they're looking for," Mitchell said, halting Matt's recitation.

"What is it?"

"A man's black outdoor coat or jacket, and anything with buttons bearing a particular symbol." Standing up, Mitchell ran his hand around the back of his neck. "I have no idea what this is about."

"Zack and I both think it's related to the discovery of your brother's body."

Mitchell shook his head in denial. "My nephew said the police already have a confession from an old drunk on a neighboring farm."

"That's what the police told your nephew, because that's what they want *you* to think," Matt argued. "Listen to me very carefully, because I've been through this before, and I know how the police operate. The searches of your apartments are occurring immediately after the discovery of your brother's murdered body, which undoubtedly means you've become a suspect in his death. If so, the police want you back in Chicago, where they can either question you or arrest you. I think they'll be waiting for you when your plane lands, and so does Zack."

He paused, waiting for that to sink in, before he continued, "I've phoned Levinson and Pearson and put them on standby to meet you at your plane. Joe O'Hara is ready to leave with the car and pick them up as soon as you give me the go-ahead. Zack disagrees with this plan. He doesn't think you should land in Chicago at all.

He thinks you should land somewhere else, out of U.S. jurisdiction tonight; hire criminal defense attorneys tomorrow; and then let them arrange with Cook County for you to voluntarily return. Zack is probably right."

Mitchell stood up, walked over to the bar, and put his glass down on a tray. "I'm not going to run for cover. I'll call Levinson and tell him to find out who is in charge of this fiasco. Levinson can then let this person know that I'm aware of what's going on and that I'm still going to land at O'Hare. That may not convince the police that I'm innocent, but it will at least give me the enormous satisfaction of embarrassing them."

Despite the grimness of the situation, Matt Farrell chuckled. "And then what?"

"Then the police can either rush out to grab me at the airport, or they can let Levinson arrange for both of us to stop by in the morning for a civilized discussion. Personally, I hope they choose the second option."

Mitchell phoned Dave Levinson at home and told the attorney what he wanted him to do. He hung up, glanced at his watch, and realized it was still set for St. Maarten time. With his thumb and forefinger, he pulled out the stem to set the time back two hours, and reality struck him with painful force: less than sixteen hours ago he'd been lying in bed watching the sunrise over the Caribbean with Kate snuggled up beside him, telling him a funny story about how she got the "dent" in her chin. Before he'd finally fallen asleep, he'd decided they would dine aboard the yacht tonight and go for a starlight cruise.

Instead of that, she was in Chicago with a man she preferred to Mitchell, and he was trying to avoid being arrested for the murder of a brother he had loved.

Forcing Kate out of his mind, Mitchell got up and headed to the bedroom to shave and change clothes. From now on, he needed to concentrate solely on dealing with the police and helping Caroline and Billy through the ordeal to come. Kate was gone. It was over. Finished. She and their brief affair had to be put away now. Mentally, Mitchell forced her out of his consciousness and shoved her into a dark cubbyhole from which she couldn't escape or come back to haunt him. Compartmentalizing was one of his greatest talents; it was a survival technique he'd developed as a boy, and it had served him extremely well.

In the bedroom, he pulled off his shirt; then he went into the bathroom, opened a cabinet, and took out a razor and shaving cream. He smeared lather on his face, picked up his razor, and started shaving beneath his chin.

His traitorous mind conjured up an image of Kate from this morning. She was looking at him in the mirror, hiding a smile, trying not to look as if she was deriving pleasure from the casual intimacy of watching her lover shave. Beneath the lather, he'd been hiding a smile of his own, because he was experiencing a similar pleasure from having her watch him.

The razor slipped, and he swore as he grabbed for a tissue.

Levinson called back just as Mitchell finished buttoning a fresh shirt and tucking it into his trousers. "I couldn't find anyone who knows anything about the search warrants or who's in charge of the investigation into William's death," he said. "The investigation used to be headed up by a Detective MacNeil, but he's away on special assignment. Since nobody seemed to know anything, I decided to go straight to the top and phoned Gray Elliott, the state's attorney, at home.

"Gray and I had an interesting chat in which I did all the talking and he did all the listening. In fact, I wasn't sure whether he knew anything about the investigation until the end of our conversation. I'm now convinced he's handling it personally."

"Why is that?" Mitchell asked, irritated by the lack of solid information.

"Because at the end of our conversation, he said to tell you, 'Welcome back,' and to have a pleasant evening and that he's looking forward to getting to know you better at eleven-thirty tomorrow morning."

"I gather that means I'm not going to be met by the cops when I land?"

"Coming from Gray, that could just as easily mean, 'Please continue to cherish your false sense of security, and land that damned plane at O'Hare, where I can impound it.' Either way, you can count on being interviewed by the police at eleven-thirty tomorrow morning, with or without spending the night in jail first."

"In that case, you and Pearson should meet me at the airport when we land," Mitchell said curtly.

To Mitchell's surprise there was only one vehicle waiting for his plane when it taxied to the hangar, and it was a limousine with Pearson and Levinson in the backseat and Matt's chauffeur at the wheel.

"My chat with Gray obviously convinced him that you're not going to try to evade being questioned," Levinson said as they pulled onto the expressway ramp.

In the front seat, Joe O'Hara was watching the rearview mirror. "We're being tailed," he said. "Two cars. Do you want me to try to lose them?"

"Absolutely not!" Pearson said.

Chapter Thirty-one

"BE NICE TO HIM, LUCY," KATE MURMURED SLEEPILY. "Max doesn't know the bed is for cats only." Reaching out, she pulled the hissing cat away from Max, who'd unknowingly violated Lucy's territory by resting his head on the comforter. She settled the gray cat on the pillow next to hers and turned her face toward the nightstand. The clock stared back at her. It was eight-thirty.

Kate closed her eyes, trying to return to the peaceful amnesia of sleep, but a few minutes later she gave up, shoved back the covers, and climbed wearily out of bed. "How did you sleep?" she asked Max. He wagged his tail in response, and she smiled, ruffling his fur. "You have to learn to get along with Lucy and Ethel," she said as she paused to scoop Ethel off her dresser and give the tabby a hug.

Max followed her into the kitchen, and she let him out into the fenced yard of the little house she rented in an old, partially restored Chicago neighborhood near where she used to work. He trotted outside onto the frozen ground and sniffed the snow; then the unfamiliar cold penetrated his fur and he beat a hasty retreat back to the house.

Kate pretended to ignore him as she made coffee. "Please let him be easy to housebreak," she prayed to no one in particular. Her belief in the power of prayer, which had undergone fairly wide swings throughout her life, was at a record low after her night on the beach with Mitchell Wyatt.

Watching him swimming toward her under a blanket of bright stars and sensing her father's presence so close to her had been the most moving, mystical experience of Kate's life—proof at last that there really was a Divine Presence, a Grand Plan, just as her uncle, the priest, had always insisted. Maybe he was right, Kate decided as she listlessly spooned coffee into a filter. If so, then based on her own recent experience, the Divine Presence had a cruelly perverse sense of humor and His Grand Plan needed drastic revision.

While she contemplated those weighty matters, coffee brewed and Max went out into the yard again, where he made use of all three catalpa trees. Kate let him back inside and congratulated him on a job well done with as much enthusiasm as she could muster; then she poured herself a cup of coffee.

A very early riser as a rule, she usually took her coffee into her tiny living room, opened the drapes, and curled up in a chair beside the front window to watch the neighborhood slowly come to life. This morning, however, she was three hours too late to watch the "show" and she was in no mood to do anything except go back to bed, crawl under the covers, and try to get warm.

After stopping in the hallway to turn up the thermostat, she carried her coffee into the bedroom, put it on the nightstand, and got back into bed. Trying to encase herself in a safe cocoon of sheets and down-filled comforter, she propped pillows against her headboard, drew her knees up to her chest, and wrapped her arms around them. Ethel hopped off the dresser and curled up at her feet; Lucy settled deeper into the pillow near her hip.

By nine o'clock, she'd already drunk the hot coffee, but she was still shivering inside from the aftermath of everything that had happened in Anguilla and St. Maarten. She decided to call Holly and tell her she was back, and engaged to Evan, and maybe ease into the story about Mitchell after that. Holly's hours on Tuesdays and Thursdays were from noon to nine PM, and since Holly lived only twenty minutes away, they might even be able to get together.

She was already reaching for the phone when it began to ring.

"Kate," a cordial, but unfamiliar, male voice said, "this is Gray Elliott. You probably don't remember me, but we've met a few times when you've been with Evan."

"Yes, of course I remember you," Kate said, wondering if "Chicago's most eligible bachelor" was actually that unassuming, or just pretending to be.

"I phoned Evan this morning, and he told me how to reach you and that you're engaged now. I hope you'll both be very happy."

"Thank you."

"I know this is short notice, but I was wondering if you could drop by my office at ten-thirty this morning."

Kate sat up abruptly and swung her legs over the side of the bed, dislodging Ethel in the process. Apparently, being engaged to a successful young attorney with the right social connections had some definite perks. Before this, she could barely get the detectives handling her father's case to call her back. Now, the state's attorney himself was calling her voluntarily. "Is this about my father's case?"

"Indirectly."

"What does that mean?"

"I'd rather explain that in person."

There was something about his voice that unsettled her. At first his tone had been affable, but the invitation to his office sounded businesslike. "Should I bring a lawyer along?" she asked, trying to joke.

"You may bring anyone you wish," he said warmly, and just as Kate began to chide herself for being edgy about his call, he added, "However, I don't think you'll want Evan to be present."

Kate hung up the phone and immediately dialed Holly. "Hi," she said when Holly answered. "I got back late last night. Gray Elliott—the state's attorney—just called me and asked me to come to his office at ten-thirty. It has something to do with my father's case. I could use a little moral support if you have the time."

"I'll make the time," Holly said. "I'll pick you up in forty-five minutes, and you can tell me about your trip on the way there."

Exactly forty-five minutes later, Holly stopped in front of the house in her sporty SUV. She smiled as Kate got inside, then she sobered. "You look awful. What happened down there?" she asked as she pulled away from the curb.

Kate was so glad to see her that she immediately fell into their time-honored habit of turning even bad events into material for lighthearted banter. "Let's see, what happened down there? I fell in love with a new guy and got engaged."

"To Evan, or the new guy?"

"I got engaged to Evan. Max is my new love."

"Then everything is perfect, right?"

"Right."

"Then why do you look so . . . unhappy?"

"Because I also took your advice and went to bed with someone."

Holly shot her a long, amazed glance and had to slam on the brakes to avoid running a stop sign. "How did that go?"

Kate leaned her head back and closed her eyes, trying to force her lips into a smile. "Not very well," she whispered.

"It couldn't have lasted more than a couple of days. How bad could a thing like that go in a couple of days?"

"It could go really bad. Really, really, *really* bad."

"Let's hear the details," Holly persisted.

"Later—on the way back. Evan was wonderful about it, though."

"You *told* him about it?"

"He'd brought a ring with him," Kate said, opening her eyes and smiling more naturally. "Look—"

Holly reached out and took Kate's outstretched fingers. Holly was wearing faded jeans, scuffed boots, a white turtleneck, and a bulky navy peacoat that had seen better days. Her long blond hair was scrunched into a big tortoiseshell claw clip at the crown to keep it from falling into her face, and she was wearing no makeup. "Very impressive," she said sincerely. "A little over four carats, E in color, nice proportions." Holly was the errant daughter of wealthy New York socialites. She knew her jewels. She had a trust fund, which she refused to touch, and which she said was obscenely large. She also had the knack of looking delicate and feminine when she was dressed like a lumberjack and the extraordinary ability to morph herself into a haughty former debutante on a moment's notice and hold her own in any social situation.

She rarely talked about her family in New York except to say laughingly that she and her sister both felt honor bound to atone for their robber-baron ancestors by serving the less fortunate. Holly took care of animals; her sister, Laurel, was a lawyer who worked pro bono on cases involving women and children.

Chapter Thirty-two

"THANK YOU FOR COMING BY ON SUCH SHORT NOTICE, Kate," Gray Elliott said after she'd introduced him to Holly. "Let's sit over there," he added, gesturing to a sofa with a coffee table in front of it and a pair of chairs facing each other at opposite ends.

Kate sat down on the sofa and Holly sat next to her. Curious and tense, Kate watched Elliott pick up some folders from his desk; then he carried them over to the coffee table and sat down on the chair nearest Kate.

He smiled sociably and leaned his forearms on the tops of his legs. "How well do you know Mitchell Wyatt?"

Kate stiffened in shock, her heart thundering all the way up into her throat. "I thought you said this was related to my father."

"It may be. That's what I want to find out. How well do you know Mitchell Wyatt?" he repeated calmly.

"Did Evan tell you I know him?"

"No, he did not, and he won't hear it from me, which is why I suggested you not bring Evan along." That was definitely a kindness on his part, Kate realized, trying to reassess her opinion of him. "Let me ask a different question," he said patiently. "How *long* have you known him?"

"A couple of days. We bumped into each other in Anguilla."

"And you'd never met him before then?"

"No."

"How well do you know him?" he asked, returning to that question.

"Not well at all," Kate said half truthfully.

"You're quite certain?"

"I'm positive."

His expression was disappointed, regretful as he held her gaze and opened the top of the folder. With a flick of his wrist, he sent enlarged color photographs of Kate and Mitchell, locked in passionate embraces, sliding across the shiny surface of the coffee table.

Kate stifled a moan and jerked her gaze from the proof of her intimacy with Mitchell.

Holly leaned forward for a closer look. "*Holy crap,*" she breathed. She picked up one of Mitchell and Kate on the balcony at the Enclave right after they checked in. He was standing in front of her with his hands braced on the wall on either side of her, grinning at her—the moment when she had been laughingly confessing that she thought he hadn't brought any clothes. "I'd love a copy of this one," Holly said into the charged silence. "And this one, too," she added, picking up a photograph of the two of them kissing passionately on the beach—when he had been naming the languages he spoke. His hand was shoved into the hair at her nape holding her mouth to his and his arm was angled down across her back, clamping her hips tightly against his. "I wish it wasn't so grainy." Holly picked up another one taken that night; in this one his right hand was over Kate's breast, and she fanned herself with it. "My God, Kate, I am impressed. I truly mean that."

Oblivious of everything except the explosion of anger inside her, Kate stood up, glaring at Gray Elliott through furious tears. "How dare you!"

"How well do you know Mitchell Wyatt now?" he asked calmly, but he sounded like a prosecutor to her.

"The answer to that is obvious. You didn't need to ask me anything. You have the evidence."

"I'd like an explanation."

Holly leaned around Kate and said mildly, "Go to hell." Then she stood up and looked at Chicago's most eligible bachelor with cool, disappointed hauteur—as if he were a cockroach, but one who should have, could have, been a higher-level insect. "My sister is Laurel Braxton. She'll be representing Kate in this matter should you have some purpose—other than being a voyeur—to question Kate about those pictures again."

"I do have a higher purpose, Miss Braxton."

"*Dr.* Braxton," Holly corrected, and he looked duly chastened and a little surprised.

"Dr. Braxton," he agreed; then he realized he'd been distracted and looked at Kate, who was madly swiping tears off her cheeks. "Kate—that should be Miss Donovan, I assume—since we're unlikely to have a cordial relationship hereafter?"

Kate gave him a glacial stare, and he said with charming chagrin, "I'm glad to see I'm right about something."

Kate wasn't buying his superficial boyish charm; she'd already had all she could stomach of that from Mitchell. "What possible excuse can you have for invading my privacy by taking those photographs and then humiliating me by bringing me here and making me look at them?"

"Your father's death. All I wanted to know was how long you've known Mitchell Wyatt so that I can rule him out—or in—as a possible suspect. The Wyatt family has had two deaths from unnatural causes recently, and your father makes a third instance. It's a little odd for someone to have such a cataclysmic effect on people

surrounding him, but Mitchell Wyatt seems to be one
of those people."

It was strange, inexplicable, but at that moment,
Kate felt a fierce desire to protect the same man she despised for her own reasons from being attacked again
because he was the bastard grandson of the Wyatt family, therefore beneath contempt to people like Evan
and, apparently, Gray Elliott. "I met him in Anguilla a
few days ago for the first time. The rest is in those pictures. He couldn't possibly have had anything to do
with my father's death, and there is no way on earth
that man killed his brother. He was very fond of him!"

"He talked about William with you?"

"Briefly. I pried it out of him. He told me he was
dead— No, that's not right," she amended quickly
when she saw the flare of interest in Elliott's gray eyes.
"I didn't know his brother was William Wyatt, but
when Mitchell talked about him, I assumed the brother
was dead."

"Why?"

"Because when Mitchell told me about him, he said . . ."
Kate had all she could do to keep from weeping as
she repeated the words that had seemed so poignant
at the time. "He said . . . 'My brother's name was
William.' "

"When did he say William was dead?"

"Don't you listen?" Kate said, almost stamping her
foot in frustration. "Mitchell used the word *was,* so I
assumed that meant that William was dead. He never
said William was dead."

"All right, I'm clear on that. Now, will you explain to
me how you know he was fond of William?"

"I could tell by the way he talked about him. It was
obvious that he cared for him."

He nodded, thinking that over. "Okay," he said,
looking convinced. "You made an assumption, based

on Wyatt's tone and expression, that he was fond of William?"

"Yes," Kate said, dying to grab her purse and get out of there.

"Did you also assume, based on Wyatt's behavior, that he was fond of you?"

Kate didn't see the question coming, wasn't prepared for his drawing that parallel. Tipping her head back, she closed her eyes, and swallowed. "You can see that I did," she whispered.

"That's it," Holly said brightly, "we're leaving." She dug her sister's business card out of her purse, thrust it at him, and headed for the door with Kate right behind her.

Elliott turned and watched them. "Miss Donovan?" he said.

Kate turned and glared at him.

"I'm sorry," he said solemnly. "Looking at those pictures, it was impossible to know that you were emotionally as well as physically involved with him. I'm sorry you got burned."

Kate refused to let him get off with an apology, let alone such an insincere one, but she kept her dignity and said calmly, "You would have put me through this even if you had known. What makes you think you're any different than he is?"

In the car on the way home, Kate told Holly the whole story, and ended by telling her that Evan expected Kate to handle seeing Mitchell at the Children's Hospital benefit. "I don't know how I'm going to face him after what he did to me."

"I know exactly how you're going to do it," Holly assured her, "and I will coach you. In fact, if Evan has room for me at your table, I'll come along for moral support."

"We'll make room—"

"The first thing you need is a fabulous gown, which calls for a trip to Bancroft's."

"Actually," Kate admitted, "Evan already phoned Bancroft's to arrange for a personal shopper to help me pick out a gown for Saturday."

"Evan can pay the bill, but *I'm* your new personal shopper."

Chapter Thirty-three

STANDING OUTSIDE THE INTERROGATION ROOM AND flanked by Lily Reardon and Jeff Cervantes, Gray Elliott watched MacNeil and his regular partner, Joe Torello, getting ready to begin interviewing Mitchell Wyatt.

"Who are they?" Cervantes asked.

"Pearson and Levinson," Gray replied.

"*The* Pearson and Levinson? Together in the same room?" Lily said, looking reluctantly impressed. "I'm surprised they didn't refer Wyatt to a criminal defense lawyer."

"They will when the time comes."

Lily reported directly to Gray and handled cases that he was particularly interested in; Jeff reported to her and would assist her at Wyatt's trial. "Have we gotten any reports back yet on what the searches turned up?" she asked.

Gray shook his head. "Not yet."

"Who brought Wyatt in this morning?" Cervantes asked.

"He came in on his own. Levinson called me at home last night when Wyatt was still en route. It seems someone tipped Wyatt off about our searches, and he figured out on his own that our alleged confession was bogus, and that he was our actual suspect."

"And he landed at O'Hare anyway?"

"As you see."

"The act of an innocent man?" Lily suggested.

"Or a moderately clever one who wants us to arrive at that conclusion," Jeff stated.

"I think he's more than moderately clever," Gray said. Reaching into his pocket, he pulled out an article he'd found on the Internet and had translated from Greek to English that morning. "Six years ago, a Greek reporter talked Stavros Konstantatos into giving him an interview about the key to his successes and how he managed to squeeze out his competition."

Gray showed them the picture from the article, in which the Greek tycoon was proudly holding up his arms, fists clenched. The translated caption beneath the photograph read, *"I have two fists with which I do battle. With my right fist, I wield the power and might to vanquish those who would oppose me. My left fist is subtle; it uses reason, shrewdness, and restrained force against my enemies. I strike with either fist."*

"What does this have to do with Wyatt?" Lily said, handing the page back to him.

"Mitchell Wyatt was his 'left fist,'" Gray said. "He refers to him as that in the body of the article."

Cervantes peered through the two-way glass. "Interesting, the way he's sitting in there." The table was oblong with two chairs on the long side facing the two-way mirror, and one chair at each end. Wyatt was sitting on the side facing the two-way mirror, but he'd angled his chair away from the table and was sitting with one foot propped on the opposite knee, his back to Pearson. A tablet and pen were on the table near his elbow, along with an untouched cup of coffee provided by MacNeil. "He's turned his back on one lawyer, and he's ignoring the other."

"He doesn't think he needs them," Gray speculated. "I think he intends to handle this entirely by himself."

"His lawyers undoubtedly warned him not to donate

any of his DNA by drinking anything we give him," Cervantes said. "He also knows this is a two-way mirror and that we're probably standing out here."

As if on cue, Wyatt turned his head to the right and looked straight toward them.

"Shit," Lily said. "He's even better looking in person. If there's a heterosexual woman or a gay man on the jury, I'll never get a conviction."

Gray ignored that and tipped his head toward the glass. "Here we go," he said. "MacNeil is going to start off with the photographs to give him the idea that we may have been following him for months."

MacNeil thumbed through the photographs he and Childress had taken, and selected a close-up of Wyatt and Donovan kissing on the balcony at the Enclave. "Let's work backward toward the day of your brother's murder, shall we?"

Wyatt quirked a brow at him and said nothing.

"Can you explain this for me?" MacNeil said, and casually tossed the photograph on the table.

Wyatt leaned slightly forward, looked at it, and then at MacNeil. "Aren't you a little old to need an explanation?"

MacNeil slapped another, similar photograph on the table, but this one was taken the night before at the villa, and Wyatt's hand was on Donovan's breast. "Explain this."

Wyatt barely flicked a glance at it. "What part of it don't you understand?"

"That's interesting," Gray said. "I didn't think it would be this easy to get a reaction out of him."

"He looks completely unperturbed," Lily argued.

"No, he clenched his jaw, but just for an instant there. He's angry, and he's also very adept at hiding it. Remember that at trial."

MacNeil took his time putting the photos back into the

right folder, letting Wyatt see that there were many folders of photographs in the stack of files. "Maybe we should start from the beginning, instead," MacNeil announced. "Where were you on the day William Wyatt disappeared?"

"I don't know what day that was," Wyatt replied calmly. "He was gone for several days before his wife and son realized he wasn't at the farm and reported him missing."

"Have you ever been to the Wyatt farm?"

"No."

"You're sure about that?"

"Positive."

Detective Torello took over. Reaching into an envelope, he removed a clear plastic evidence bag containing a leather button with a pattern and insignia on the front. "Do you recognize this?" Torello asked.

Pearson and Levinson tensed. "You don't have to answer that," Levinson said quickly.

Wyatt ignored the warning. "It looks like the missing button from one of my overcoats."

"Do you know where we found this button, Mr. Wyatt?" When Wyatt didn't reply, Torello said, "We found it wedged under the cover on the well where your brother's body was found. That well is located a few feet from the property line of the Wyatt farm, which you say you've never been near. Do you want to rethink that answer?"

"No, it was right the first time."

"Can you explain, then, how this button from your coat turned up at that farm?"

"I can't explain it."

Torello perched a hip on the corner of the table. "How do you suppose a button that you admit came from a coat of yours got snagged on a well cover on a farm you've never been to?"

"I repeat—" Wyatt said patiently, "I can't explain it."

Lily shot a pleased look at Gray and was surprised to see that he was frowning, his hands shoved into his pockets. "He's not our man," Gray said in answer to her puzzled stare. "And he's sure he can prove it."

"What do you mean? How?"

"I don't know, but I have a hunch he's getting ready to tell us. He's glanced at his watch twice and he's getting fed up."

In the interrogation room, Torello regarded Wyatt steadily, and when he said nothing more, Torello put pressure on him. "Let me tell you how we think your coat button got snagged on that well cover—"

"I'm sure it would be a very entertaining, imaginative story, but I'm a little short of time. Do you have anything else you want to discuss other than this button?" When Torello frowned at him and said nothing, Wyatt said, "I'll take that to mean you don't. In that case, here's what you need to know: William disappeared in November. The coat that button came off of was made for me in London and delivered to me in Chicago at the end of December."

MacNeil stepped forward and said in a conciliatory "good cop" tone, "Where was the coat purchased and can anyone there verify the date it was delivered?"

"I'll give you my London tailor's name. He can also tell you where the buttons came from, and verify that I have no other clothing with identical buttons."

"Where is the coat now?"

"I sent it back to him so that he could order a new button and mend the hole left by the last one. Is there anything else, or are we finished?"

"Not quite," MacNeil said. "When did you first discover that the button was missing from your coat?"

"In mid-January. I took the coat out of the closet and realized that the button was gone. I don't know where I lost it."

Gray Elliott stared through the window. "Either he doesn't know, or he doesn't want to believe it." Without shifting his gaze, he said, "Tell MacNeil to come out here."

Cervantes knocked on the door and poked his head into the interrogation room. "I'm sorry to interrupt. Detective MacNeil, could I have a word with you?"

MacNeil strolled out, closed the door, and looked at Gray. "Are you buying Wyatt's story?"

Gray nodded. "For now, yes. Get Wyatt's passport, and tell him not to leave Chicago until we've checked with the tailor and had a look at that coat ourselves."

Wyatt took one look at MacNeil's face when he walked back into the interrogation room and stood up. Wordlessly, he pulled his passport out of his inside jacket pocket and tossed it onto the table; then he picked up the coffee, took a swallow, and put the cup down. "There's your DNA, voluntarily given. Try not to mix it up with anyone else's while you're finishing your investigation. Anything else?" he clipped, while his attorneys rose to their feet and picked up their briefcases.

"Yes, don't leave Chicago until you hear from us."

"I'll heed that warning," he said shortly. "And now you'd better heed mine: If I ever see any of those photographs anywhere, I will bury Gray Elliott—and you— under a mountain of lawsuits filed against both of you personally, along with the City of Chicago and the State of Illinois. And while I'm at it, I'll make sure the media learns about your voyeuristic 'hobby,' and your expensive trips to Caribbean islands in pursuit of that hobby— all at government expense. In short, I will smear your names all over the press."

"Are you threatening me?" MacNeil said stiffly.

"Didn't I just make that clear?" Wyatt snapped. "Nice tan, by the way," he added. He started for the door, followed by his smirking attorneys; then he turned back and aimed his next threat toward the two-way mirror. "I'll give you the rest of the afternoon to get in touch with Caroline Wyatt and explain that I had nothing to do with William's death. If you fail to convince her, I'll bring her to your office in the morning and you can do it in front of me."

After Wyatt left, Elliott opened the door and walked into the interrogation room. "That's the second time in one day I've been called a voyeur," he remarked idly, gazing at the open door. Transferring his gaze to MacNeil, he said, "Meet me in my office tomorrow at ten and bring all the files with you. I know who murdered William, but we're going to have to go slowly and build our case very carefully."

"I'll be there," MacNeil said. When he glanced up, Elliott was studying MacNeil's thinning hair.

"Your hair looks different."

"Different how?" MacNeil asked, then quickly looked away.

"I don't know exactly. It's . . . fluffy."

"New shampoo," MacNeil mumbled.

Chapter Thirty-four

UNLIKE LARGE FUND-RAISERS, THE CHILDREN'S HOSPItal benefit was an elite annual affair with an invitation list containing only 350 names, each name chosen based on the individual's exceptional charitable-spending habits. An elaborate dinner was served and a silent auction took place during the evening, with items that included fabulous artwork, museum-quality jewelry, and an occasional priceless antique. Opening bids for the least of the auction items began at $50,000, and tables for ten began at $100,000 each.

Each year, a philanthropist was honored during the dinner portion of the evening, with the mayor of Chicago making the presentation. This year, the honoree, for the fifth time, was Cecil Wyatt.

The location chosen for this year's benefit was the Founders Club, which occupied the top two floors of Endicott Tower, a spectacular eighty-story octagon made of stone and glass, located in downtown Chicago.

Membership in the Founders Club was originally limited to wealthy descendants of Chicago's founding families, but since many of those descendants had failed to maintain the wealth of their forebears—or had committed crimes even more horrendous than that—the Founders Club had loosened its membership restrictions. Currently, in order to be considered for membership, the candidate had only to have had "a significant presence in the Chicago area" for the past one hundred years and to be able to afford annual dues of $50,000. However, as a safeguard, membership was "by invitation only from the board of directors," which prevented the "wrong sort of persons" who otherwise qualified for membership from applying and becoming a nuisance when they were rejected.

Once a coveted membership was granted, the new member was entitled to enjoy the club's spectacular views, its sumptuous luncheon and dinner menus, and, of course, bragging rights.

No expense had been spared on the interior decor of the club; it was designed to impress, and it did. To assist in that goal, the private elevator's lobby was on the second floor of the club, and was an eight-sided rotunda with an elaborate wrought-iron railing around it that guided new arrivals toward a sweeping staircase that curved gracefully downward to the first floor. A grand chandelier, one story in height, was suspended from the center of the second-floor ceiling, its many-tiered gold frame dripping with magnificent crystals.

At the front of the room, standing near their table, Matt Farrell watched his wife walking slowly through the crowd on the first floor, and he excused himself to the people around him.

"Looking for someone?" he asked, walking up behind her as she stood gazing up at the second-floor rotunda, where the silent-auction items were displayed.

"Just checking to make sure everything is going well." She was in charge of this year's benefit, and she'd been working on it for months, dealing with the various committees and the endless details, as well as handling her demanding job as Bancroft & Company's CEO.

Matt looked up at the people on the second floor, moving from table to table with glasses of champagne in their hands, writing down bids, talking and laughing, while a string quartet played in the curve of the staircase. On the main floor, the candlelit tables were laid with sparkling crystal and china, and decorated with spectacular sprays of cream-and-red bicolor roses from South America, blooms the size of softballs.

"More than half of the people are upstairs with pens in their hands, and an army of waiters is passing out drinks to make sure they stay loose. You're a guaranteed success. And," he whispered tenderly, "you are also very beautiful."

She sent him a beaming smile, tucked her hand through his arm, gave it a squeeze, and then she nodded toward the head table, where the guest of honor was talking to the mayor.

Matt suppressed a grimace. "Leave it to Cecil Wyatt to check himself out of the hospital so he can walk up to another podium and accept another award." As if to wash away a bad taste, he swallowed the last of the champagne in his glass. A waiter arrived instantly with a tray of refills. "How much," he teased her, "did you budget for liquor?"

"A lot," she admitted. "Look, there's Mitchell," she added a moment later. She watched him smiling politely as group after group of his new "family friends" stopped to say hello to him or introduce themselves for the first time.

When Cecil arrived at Mitchell's elbow and drew him aside a moment later, Meredith shook her head a little as if to clear it. "I still can't get used to seeing Mitchell with Cecil. We've known Mitchell for so long, and he's stayed with us so many times, that I can't believe he waited six months to tell us he was Cecil's grandson. If we hadn't seen him at Cecil's birthday party, I'm not sure we'd know it now."

"How thrilled would you be to find out you're related to a domineering, egocentric old man? Oh, wait . . . you're already related to one of those," Matt teased, and Meredith burst out laughing; then she pressed a kiss to his cheek. "Shhh," she whispered, "my father is right behind you."

"That's not good. Change places with me," he joked. "I don't like having my back turned to him."

He was half serious about the last part, Meredith knew, and for good reason. Her father had destroyed their marriage when they were young, and when Matt strode back into her life ten years later, her father tried to interfere again and almost lost Meredith in the process. For her sake, Matt tolerated her father, but he'd never forgiven him, and he never would.

"I'm indebted to him tonight for persuading the Founders Club to let us use this place for our benefit," she said. "It was a real feather in our cap."

"He didn't do it for you," Matt teased. "He did it to show *me* that he could still do something for you that I can't do. Former steelworkers from Gary, Indiana, can't be members here, no matter how successful they become. Do you know how I know that?"

Meredith's shoulders shook with laughter, because she had a pretty good idea what the answer was. "How do you know that, darling?"

"Your father told me. Fifty times. This week alone."

Meredith smiled, but her attention had reverted to Mitchell. "Oh, look, Olivia Hebert has him by the arm. It's so funny to see him squiring a little old lady, instead of some gorgeous woman with an exotic name, and he does it with such patience and élan."

"Mitchell does everything with élan," Matt replied, drily, "and it's easy for him to be patient tonight, because he knows he's leaving for Europe tomorrow. He told me he can't wait to put an ocean between himself and Chicago."

Meredith's expression clouded. "Something's been bothering him."

"Something other than being accused of murdering his brother, having to surrender his passport, and being forced to remain in the city until Gray Elliott checked out his story, you mean?"

Meredith ignored the irony in his tone and nodded emphatically. "Something besides that. Those problems are over, and since Caroline is with him tonight, she's obviously accepted that he had nothing to do with William's death. Whatever is on his mind isn't related to any of that."

"I haven't noticed anything different about him."

"Men don't notice subtleties about other men," she said with a sigh. "Has it occurred to you that he's never mentioned Kate to us? She was so important to him that he was going to fly back and forth to the Caribbean to see her every night, but he hasn't mentioned her once. I tried to work around to the subject a few days ago by asking him if there was anyone special in his life. He said no."

"Mitchell doesn't talk about the women in his life."

"Mitchell called Zack in Rome to talk about Kate," Meredith argued. "I wonder what happened to her."

"She never went aboard the yacht. When Zack asked him what happened, Mitchell said 'things got complicated,' " Matt reminded her, as a waiter with a tray of canapés stopped at his side.

"I know. Oh, well, I guess that leaves the way clear for Marissa."

Matt paused, his arm outstretched toward the tray. "Our daughter Marissa?"

"When I kissed her good night, she told me she's decided to marry Mitchell when she's old enough."

"I'm not ready for this," he declared, finally selecting a canapé from the tray.

Meredith grinned. "Your future son-in-law appears to be making his way in our direction."

* * *

"Kate," Holly said sympathetically, "we can't spend the night in the ladies' lounge. Drink this and let's go." As she spoke, Holly removed Kate's empty champagne glass from her trembling hand and substituted her own glass for it. "Bottoms up," she coaxed.

"Mitchell is down there," Kate said, her voice shaking with nerves. "I saw him from the balcony."

"I know that. Now, let's make sure he sees you."

"I'm not ready to go out there."

"Yes, you are."

Mindlessly, Kate sipped her glass of champagne, the second one in ten minutes. "How do I look?"

Holly strolled around her for a final inspection. Reminiscent of the slinky, glamorous gowns worn in 1930s movies, Kate's pewter satin gown was bias cut, with a heart-shaped bodice and a narrow halter strap that made a V between her breasts. To complement the gown's retro look, her hair had been styled into smooth waves and swept back on one side, held in place with an antique amethyst-and-diamond comb borrowed from Evan's mother. "I love that Veronica Lake hairstyle on you," Holly decreed. "That antique comb will make everyone think your earrings are real instead of costume jewelry," she added, admiring the mock amethyst-and-diamond earrings dangling from Kate's ears partway to her shoulders.

They both hesitated while two women who'd been using the adjoining bathroom walked through the mirrored lounge area. The women smiled and nodded as they strolled past, then they opened the door to leave and a blast of laughter and music filled the lounge.

Holly waited until the door closed again; then she removed the empty champagne glass from Kate's fingers, and took Kate's hands in hers. "I promised you that I'd coach you and tell you how to get through this," she said, looking solemnly into Kate's wide, overbright green eyes. "And I deliberately waited until now, when the moment is at hand."

Turning Kate toward the mirror, she said, "Look at yourself. You are absolutely stunning. This is your night, Kate. It's your debut as Evan's future wife, and tonight you're going to find that even the biggest snobs here will welcome you as one of their own. They already know you're not a trashy gold digger; you're the daughter of a Chicago restaurateur who was something of a celebrity in his own right. You're his successor. You also have a natural elegance and poise that people notice, and you have a warm heart that makes you infinitely appealing. Are you following me so far?"

Embarrassed by all the flattery, Kate smiled and said, "I'm following that, tonight, you want me to think I'm wonderful."

"You *are* wonderful. Now, this brings us to Mitchell Wyatt. Sometime in the next couple of hours, you're going to come face-to-face with him—" Three women, laughing and talking, walked into the lounge to check their makeup, and Holly and Kate both turned to the mirror, pretending they were doing the same thing.

Kate reached into her purse for her lipstick, but her entire body was in flight mode at the thought of looking into Mitchell's blue eyes and seeing that hard, handsome face again. He'd made her laugh, he'd made her moan with pleasure, and then he'd held her in his arms as if he never wanted to let her go. Worse, much worse, he'd made her care so much that she thought she was in love with him.

And then he'd sent her back to break up with Evan, never intending to be there when she returned.

Viewed with the clarity of hindsight, she realized now that everything Mitchell did from the moment she met him—even sending for an ambulance and doctor to help Max—was done to ensure the accomplishment of his ultimate goal. There was no doubt in her mind now that he'd sent her that Bloody Mary himself and then sauntered into the restaurant to introduce himself. In fact, just thinking about the way he'd made a date with her after she spilled the drink on him made her grind her teeth: *"If I were you, I'd offer to take me to dinner . . ."* Of all the egotistical, cocky, overconfident . . .

He must have been amazed and very pleased when he introduced himself and she didn't recognize his name. Her ignorance made it so much easier for him, and so much more fun, as he seduced Evan Bartlett's witless girlfriend.

"Stop going over everything he did in your mind!" Holly said urgently, the instant the other women departed. "Just for tonight, you have to forget all the awful details and be completely objective, or you won't be able to pull this off! The simple reality is this: Mitchell Wyatt is a man with an ego that's so fragile he needed to seduce you to get even with Evan for knowing his secret.

"If you'd agreed to jump into bed with him after the two of you had dinner at the villa, it would have been over with that night and you wouldn't have gotten emotionally involved. Instead, you insisted on knowing something about him first, so he had to come back to you and tell you about his brother; then he had to start actively seducing you in the garden. Once he realized you weren't going to sleep with him in Evan's hotel room, he had to get a hotel in St. Maarten. In St. Maarten, he warned you not to have any illusions or false expectations about going to bed with him. He told you he didn't want complications or 'magic,' he just wanted an afternoon of good sex with you. Again, you turned down his offer, so he had to come back at you with that 'Let's get complicated—I felt everything you did last night' routine."

"Are you saying that what happened was partly my fault?"

"God, no! I'm trying to make you see that hurting you wasn't his actual goal; his goal was to either coerce Evan's silence or bring Evan down to his level by having a fling with Evan's girlfriend."

Kate shivered at the coldness of his logic and the ruthlessness of his methods.

"I'll tell you something I haven't said before," Holly continued. "I think that, at some point, Wyatt had a better time with you than he expected. Otherwise, he'd have patted you on the butt when he finished having sex with you the first time and sent you back to the villa."

"Why would he do that when I was such an eager, *cooperative* bed partner?" Kate said with bitter self-recrimination.

"That's a good point, but why would he also take you to a casino, and, most revealing of all, why would he sit up in bed with you and watch the sunrise? Guys who only want sex from a woman roll off her afterward and go to sleep."

To Kate's shame, she clutched at that morsel of consolation, not because she believed it, but because she desperately needed something to reduce the humiliation she felt.

"However," Holly continued brightly, "that doesn't change the fact that he's a cold, calculating bastard with a giant ego and that you're entitled to exact whatever petty revenge you can tonight."

"How can I do that?" Kate asked, leaning back against the vanity table and eyeing Holly with fascination.

"You have to treat him as if he was nothing but a completely forgettable flirtation."

"He's not going to buy that. He knew how I felt. I left to go and break up with Evan and promised to hurry back."

"Yes, but he can't be one hundred percent sure you did it! Furthermore, he can't be one hundred percent sure that you weren't just using him as a temporary stud in Evan's absence. In fact, he can't be one hundred percent sure that you didn't know who he was all along and that your goal wasn't to pry some juicy details about his life out of him to share with all your friends!"

"Who would do such a thing?" Kate scoffed.

"The women in your new social circle—which also happens to be the same social circle he's accustomed to," Holly said flatly. "Believe me, I know what they're like. I grew up in their Temple of Brittle Humor and Barren Hearts. Evan understands instinctively how the game needs to be played; that's why he wanted you to be here tonight. He'll make sure Wyatt sees you with him, laughing and talking and holding your head up. In doing that, Evan will be illustrating to Wyatt that he's so insignificant that nothing he does could possibly matter to either of you."

"And to think," Kate said with a rueful smile, "I'm supposed to be the one with the knowledge of psychology."

"They don't write psychology books to cover the mind-set of the elite few. Anyway, you get the picture now, right?"

"Right."

"So, here is the *only* emotion you're allowed to display when you bump into Wyatt tonight. Here is the only emotion that will get you some revenge—"

"I give up," Kate said, smiling at Holly's dramatic pause. "What is it?"

"Amusement! You are going to treat him with *amusement*—as if you know an amusing little secret that he doesn't know."

"What sort of secret knowledge could I possibly have?" Kate asked, frustrated.

"*That* is the very question he'll start asking himself. That is the question that will trouble him for a long time."

Matt and Meredith exchanged smiling glances with Mitchell as he tried to maneuver his aunt in their direction while she clung to his arm, chattering happily and making him stop every few steps so she could introduce him to someone else. He was over a foot taller than she, and in order to hear her, he had to tip his head way down.

Matt walked over to the bar and ordered vodka for Mitchell. By the time Matt returned with the drink, Mitchell was finally arriving with his aunt. Holding the drink out to him, Matt said, "Here's your reward for the successful completion of a long and arduous journey."

"I can use it," Mitchell replied. Lifting the glass to his lips, he glanced up . . .

And he saw Kate.

He froze, staring, his brows drawn together in disbelief that she was here, and that the jean-clad girl with curly red hair who'd kissed him on the balcony in St. Maarten was the glamorous redhead in a sophisticated satin gown strolling casually through the roomful of wealthy socialites, many of whom were drawing her aside to kiss her on the cheek and chat with her.

"That's Kate Donovan," Matt provided, following his gaze. "Her father died recently, and I understand she's going to try to run his restaurant. Have we ever eaten at Donovan's when you were here?"

"No."

"We'll do that when you're here next time." Drily, he added, "I never had much luck getting reservations with less than two weeks' notice when her father was alive. Maybe Kate will give us a break."

Olivia happily made her own contribution to the discussion. "Did you know Kate just got engaged down in the islands?" she asked Meredith and Matt.

"No," Meredith said, watching Mitchell's gaze stray briefly to Kate again.

Olivia nodded emphatically and included Mitchell in the question. "Isn't that a romantic way to get engaged?"

"I wouldn't know," he said smoothly, curtly.

"The announcement was in the *Tribune* on Thursday," she added. Peering forward, she saw Kate leaving the people who'd stopped her to talk, and Olivia called out cheerfully, "Kate, dear, come over here!"

Satisfied when Kate looked up and nodded, Olivia turned to Mitchell and added, "You've met the future bridegroom, Mitchell."

"Have I?"

"Yes. She's engaged to Evan Bartlett."

Mitchell stared at the vodka in his glass. "Really, to Evan Bartlett?" he said with a cold, ironic smile.

Meredith's gaze flew to Matt's and he gave an imperceptible nod of understanding. This was Mitchell's "Kate."

Kate's knees shook and she wished she had more than a few drops of champagne left in her glass to give her courage, but she managed to look calm and composed as she obeyed Olivia's summons and prepared to face the man who had used her and left her. "Hello, my dear," Olivia said. "I hope you and Evan will be very happy," she added, and then pressed a kiss to Kate's cheek.

It was the identical ritual Kate had been through fifty times that night—a greeting, followed by best wishes, followed by a salutatory kiss on the cheek. She'd as-

sumed an hour before that this was some sort of prescribed engagement ritual known to everyone in Evan's
social circle. Mentally she braced herself for Mitchell to
follow the same ritual as Olivia added with quaint formality, "May I present my nephew, Mitchell—"

Somehow, Kate managed to execute her plan flawlessly: She looked at Mitchell's shuttered eyes as if she
knew an amusing little secret. "We've already met," she
replied, leaning slightly forward and turning her cheek
in automatic expectation of his salutatory kiss.

"—and we've already kissed," Mitchell replied
coolly, ignoring her cheek.

Matt stepped swiftly in front of a startled Olivia,
smilingly tucked her hand through his arm, and escorted her toward her table.

Stunned, but utterly determined to appear lighthearted
and calm no matter what he said or did, Kate tipped her
head to the side and gave him a playful smile. "Haven't
you any good wishes for me?" she teased.

"Let me think of the right one." He paused a moment; then he lifted his glass in a mocking toast, and
said, "To your continued success in climbing up the social ladder, Kate."

Mitchell's accusation that she was a social climber
caused Kate's resolve to slip several notches. "Don't
tempt me to throw another drink at you!"

"That would be inexcusably middle class," he said
scathingly, "and you're trying to move up into the big
leagues. In the big leagues, we cheat, we lie, and we
fuck each other's brains out in private, but we do not
indulge in public displays of temper." Mitchell saw the
banked emerald fires leaping dangerously into flames
in her eyes, and he deliberately threw verbal gasoline at
her. "Take some advice and remember the rules the
next time you pick up a stranger in a hotel—"

"Shut up!" Kate pleaded furiously.

"—so that you can cheat on that pompous asshole you're marrying!"

Kate's temper and anxiety exploded simultaneously, and she silenced him with the only means available— she flung what was left of her champagne at his face. There wasn't enough liquid to reach her target, but a few drops hit his chest and splotched his shirtfront, and with a mixture of fright, shame, and satisfaction, she braced for an explosive reaction.

"That gesture lacked the spontaneity it had in Anguilla—" he remarked imperturbably as he began casually flicking droplets off his shirt, "—however, this color is a definite improvement."

Kate gaped at him; then she jerked her head to the left, where a solicitous waiter was already lowering a tray of champagne. Belatedly desperate to appear normal, Kate traded glasses with him and picked up a napkin with shaky fingers; then her attention swerved back to Mitchell as he continued in that same cool, conversational drawl, "Hand me your napkin and paste an apologetic smile on your face—"

Kate automatically handed him the napkin.

He took it and completed his sentence, his gaze on the spots he was dabbing off his shirt. "—or else Bartlett may figure out he's marrying an amoral bitch with an ugly temper."

"I'm warning you—" Kate said frantically, but she had nothing to threaten him with, so she glanced around to see if they were being observed and tightened her grip on the stem of her champagne flute, because it seemed like the only solid reality to cling to in a world gone mad.

When she didn't complete her threat, Mitchell slanted a glance at her and noticed her fingers tightening on her champagne glass. Without taking his eyes off his shirt-front, he said in a silky voice, "If you so much as tilt that glass in my direction, you'll be sprawled on your ass before the first drops hit the floor."

Mistaking her stillness for indecision, he lifted his head and looked at her with eyes like shards of ice. "Test me, Kate—" he invited softly. "Go ahead. Test me."

Kate's stricken paralysis gave way to a trembling realization that repelled her so much it reduced her voice to a shaking whisper when she said it aloud. "My God . . . underneath all your phony charm and slick social polish, you're actually . . . a *monster.*"

Instead of being insulted or angered, he looked at her in baffled amusement, then he chuckled and shook his head. "What were you expecting to find there, sweet-heart—a heartbroken, jilted lover?"

Before Kate could react to that, he touched his glass to the edge of hers in a mockery of a toast and said in a bored voice, "Good-bye, Kate."

He left, and Kate found herself staring straight into Meredith Bancroft's narrowed eyes. Without a word, Meredith turned on her heel and followed him.

Chapter Thirty-five

"T HAT KID GIVES ME THE CREEPS," MACNEIL TOLD GRAY as he stood outside the interrogation room watching a tearful Billy Wyatt give Joe Torello the details surrounding his father's "accidental" death. They'd picked the boy up that morning and brought him in for questioning, accompanied by Caroline. "I can't believe she hasn't called the family lawyer yet."

Folding his arms over his chest, Gray contemplated Caroline's somewhat surprising behavior. "I think she's feared Billy had something to do with his father's death from that day in my office when he called Wyatt for us. She looked shocked and a little sickened by his ad-lib performance. Later, when I told her the button found at the well was the same as the ones on Mitchell Wyatt's coat, she accepted that very quickly. She didn't ask me if we'd made sure, or checked all of his other clothes for identical buttons, or any of the questions you'd expect her to ask. Caroline has been on Chicago's best-dressed list several times; she knows handmade buttons are very unusual."

"I still can't figure out why she hasn't called a lawyer yet."

Gray thought about that for a moment. "She loved William, and she loves Billy. I think she figures her only chance of saving her son is to make him tell the truth and get it off his chest. The family lawyer is Henry Bartlett, and she knows Bartlett will do whatever Cecil tells him to do. Cecil would tell him to shut Billy up and then find a way to get him off."

"I don't know how she can stand to be in the same room with the kid."

"That's easy. She's blaming herself for not realizing how much damage Mitchell Wyatt's presence in the family was doing to her son."

In the interrogation room, Torello handed Billy a pen and a tablet of paper. "Before you write it all down, let's go over everything one more time to make sure we're all clear."

Caroline was standing behind Billy, her hands protectively on his shoulders. "Does he have to go through it all again? Can't he just write it down?"

In response, Torello looked at the kid. "One more time, from the top."

The fourteen-year-old rubbed his eyes with his palms and said shakily, "I went out to the farm with my dad, just like we planned to do that weekend. I thought we might scare up some quail on the Udall place, so I took the shotgun from the house. While we were walking, my dad told me he was going to sell our farm to the developer who'd bought Udall's. We started arguing. I told him he couldn't do that, and then—"

"Why did you think he couldn't do that?"

"Because the farm was supposed to be mine!" Billy said fiercely, his meek attitude vanishing. "My grandpa Edward always said it would be mine someday, but he forgot to leave it to me in his will."

"Okay, and then what happened?"

"My dad and I were arguing, and I was so upset that I wasn't looking where I was going. I tripped and the gun went off." Reaching for a box of tissues on the table, he scrubbed at his eyes. "My dad was only a few feet in front of me when he fell. I tried to give him CPR, but there was a big hole in his chest, and I got blood all over me, and I freaked out. I was scared my mom would never forgive me and I'd go to jail. The old well was just a few feet away, so I pulled the cover off of it, and I . . . I . . . You know the rest."

"Tell me anyway."

"I dragged my dad over to it, and pushed him down the hole; then I threw the shotgun in after him."

Caroline lifted one hand from his shoulder and briefly covered her eyes while a visible tremor shook her entire body.

"What about fingerprints on the shotgun?" Torello prompted. "What did you do about those?"

"Oh, yeah. I wiped them off on my jacket before I threw the gun down the well."

"Then what?"

"I went back to the house, but then I started thinking I'd done the wrong thing. I should have called an ambulance and the police, so I called Grandpa Cecil, and I told him what had happened. I asked him what I should do. He told me to sit still and not call anyone until he got there. It took him a long time, because it had started to snow."

"What did Cecil do when he arrived?"

"He-He told me nothing could help my dad anymore, and that we had to think about saving me and sparing my mom. He said my dad wouldn't want me to go to jail for an accident, and that my mom would never get over it if she knew how my dad died. He said he'd tell the cops I spent the weekend with him instead of going up to the farm with my dad."

"What about your father's vehicle? How did it end up being abandoned twenty-five miles away from the farm?"

Billy paused to wipe his eyes again, but they looked dry to Gray. "Grandpa Cecil said it would be better if the cops thought my dad wasn't at the farm when he disappeared. That way, they wouldn't search as hard up there and maybe find the old well. Grandpa Cecil said I should drive my dad's car and follow him down the highway until he found a good place to leave it."

"You're only fourteen. Do you know how to drive?"

Billy shot him a disdainful look. "I've been driving up at the farm since I was twelve. Driving on the highway when it was snowing wasn't easy, but I did as good as my dad could have done."

On the other side of the two-way glass, MacNeil grimaced and looked at Gray. "That kid is a total sociopath."

"We're almost done, Billy," Torello said encouragingly. "Now, let's skip ahead two months to January. The search for your father has been called off, no one is looking around at the farm for him anymore, but you went to see Mr. Elliott and told him you heard Mitchell Wyatt pretending to your mom that he'd never been at the farm. You knew that would make us suspect him, and it would also renew our interest in searching the farm again. Why did you open up that can of worms when you'd gotten away with everything already?"

"Because the developer who bought the Udall place came to see my mom about buying our farm. While he was there, he said they were starting to break some ground and they were going to put a stone wall up on the property line. I knew they'd find the old well, because it was right there."

"Okay, so you were thinking. You were using your head," Torello said as if that was a compliment. "You figured they'd find your father's body, so you tore a button off Wyatt's coat, drove up there yourself one day, and planted the button under the well cover where it would be found."

Billy nodded, looking flattered by Torello's comments.

"But what made you decide to try to pin everything on Mitchell Wyatt?"

"Because," Billy said, his face contorting with rage, "that fucking bastard was acting like he belonged in our family. He was stepping into my father's place, and my mom was letting him do it. He was staying at our house, looking after my mom, hanging around her. I was supposed to be the man of the family, but she was asking him for advice, not me. He even advised her to sell the farm.

"My grandpa Cecil was acting just like her about Mitchell. I used to be Grandpa's favorite. He always said we were a lot alike, but all he cared about was Mitchell after my dad died. He started ignoring me, and then I heard him tell Mom that he wanted to introduce everyone to Mitchell at his birthday party. He said she had to be there, so that everyone would know she'd accepted him into the family, too."

"Okay, Billy. I'm satisfied that you're telling the whole truth and you've got all your facts straight. There's a tablet and a pen. Go ahead and write everything down just the way you told it to me. You want a Coke or anything?"

"I want a Dr Pepper," Billy announced, reaching for the tablet.

"How about some chili-cheese Fritos to go with that?"

"Yeah, that would be good. How did you know?"

Torello said nothing, but when he turned away, he sent a meaningful glance toward the two-way mirror. In the last two weeks, they'd canvassed every gas station and convenience store between Chicago and the farm, knowing that Cecil would probably have needed to stop at some point. A clerk in a gas station/convenience store recognized Billy's photograph. Cecil had sent Billy in with cash to pay for the gasoline so there'd be no credit card record, but while he was inside, Billy decided to pick up a Dr Pepper and his favorite snack food. When the clerk told him she carried only regular Fritos, he'd called the store "a dump" and her "a bumpkin."

"I can already hear the kind of defense the family is going to stage for this kid," MacNeil said in resigned disgust. "For starters, they'll argue that we have no jurisdiction because the crime occurred outside Cook County. He's fourteen, so he'll be tried as a juvenile, and once the Wyatt lawyers get into the act, they'll persuade the mother to let them claim that little Billy was secretly abused by his daddy. Hell, Cecil is an old man with heart trouble. If he dies before this goes to trial, they'll change their story and it will turn out that Cecil killed William."

"Not if I can get to Cecil and make him see reason," Gray said, turning away and starting down the hall. "I'm going to pay a call on him right now, and I want you along for effect."

Chapter Thirty-six

"M R. WYATT WILL SEE YOU IN A FEW MINUTES," CECIL'S butler told Gray. It was sleeting, and a fine sheen of icy droplets clung to Gray's cashmere coat as the butler helped him off with it and carried it toward the hall closet.

Cecil received him in his study, seated behind a baronial desk and surrounded by portraits of his illustrious ancestors. "How are your parents, Gray?"

"They're fine, thank you."

The old man studied his features as Gray sat down in front of his desk. "I take it this isn't a social call?" he concluded.

"I'm afraid not."

He nodded, turned his head toward the departing butler, and said, "Get Henry Bartlett on the phone immediately."

"There's a detective waiting in front to take you down to the station house. Henry can meet you there."

"Am I being arrested?"

"That depends on how cooperative you are in the next few minutes. Billy has just given us a statement regarding William's death."

"What did he tell you?"

Gray saw no reason not to answer, since he knew Henry Bartlett would be able to obtain Billy's statement within a matter of hours. He gave Cecil the high points of Billy's confession, and when he was finished, Cecil said coolly, "And you believe the boy's story that I was involved?"

"Absolutely. It has bothered me all along that you kept Mitchell's existence a secret until January. You met him for the first time in August, and the following month, Edward supposedly fell off his balcony to his death. In November, William vanished. And yet, Cecil, you were unconcerned with the fact that your newfound grandson's return to the family fold coincided with both these occurrences. In fact, you kept his existence a secret from the police who were investigating both instances. Do you know what that told me?"

"That I was a sentimental, trusting old man who was blinded by guilt for denying Mitchell his heritage in the past?" Cecil suggested sarcastically.

"No, that you were a devious, arrogant, manipulative old man who had a need for a new heir apparent you could depend on, but you did not want the police or anyone else to know where he'd been for the last thirty-four years."

"Thank you," he said stiffly, but sincerely, "you are quite right. You have always been a rather bright young man."

"Since we both know you aren't sentimental or trusting, there's only one reason left for you not to have suspected that Mitchell was responsible for Edward's death or William's disappearance."

"And that reason would be?"

"That you already *knew* what happened to both men, and that Mitchell hadn't been involved. With that suspicion in mind, I had already reopened the investigation into William's disappearance—with you as a target of the investigation—when Billy suddenly came to my office."

"And told you what?"

"He told me he'd heard Mitchell tell Caroline that

he'd never been to the farm, which Billy said was a lie. That focused us on Mitchell. Now you tell me something, Cecil: When did you find out what Billy had done? When did you discover that he'd planted a button from Mitchell's coat at the well?"

"Caroline came here right after you had Billy call Mitchell down in St. Maarten. She told me what was going on. She was beside herself thinking that she and I were harboring a murderer in our midst. I told her I felt sure there was some mistake."

"You knew Billy had planted the button?"

"Are we talking off the record?"

Gray hesitated; then he nodded. "Off the record."

"I realized at once that it had to be Billy. Who else would have done such a thing? Besides that, he was sitting right in front of me when Caroline told me about the button you'd found, and your suspicions about Mitchell, and the phone call you had Billy make. I could tell from Billy's face that he was responsible for everything. He smiled at me. He was quite proud of his cunning, actually."

Gray nodded, thinking things over, surprised that Cecil was so forthcoming, even off the record. "If Mitchell's coat had been delivered to him any time *before* William's disappearance, we would have arrested him and tried him for William's murder. Were you going to let him be convicted, just to save Billy's hide?"

Leaning forward, Cecil folded his hands on his desk, and said proudly and emphatically, "Mitchell would never have let that happen. He is a survivor, like me, and like them—" Lifting his chin, he indicated the ancestral portraits on the wall across from him.

Rather than pointlessly debate Cecil's logic, Gray got down to the real purpose for his visit. "In helping Billy, you've committed a variety of crimes yourself—"

"We don't need to discuss that today, and you aren't

going to arrest me, either. Henry and Evan Bartlett have already assured me you have no jurisdiction in this case. Furthermore, Billy's confession is worthless because he wasn't represented by an attorney. You had no right to question him without the presence of the family's attorneys."

"His mother was present, and she gave her consent."

"Caroline is in no mental condition to make sound judgments for herself, let alone for Billy in this situation. You're wasting your time by—"

"I have one more minute to waste," Gray said icily, looking meaningfully at the walnut clock on Cecil's desk. "You'd be wise to let me waste it and to listen to me very carefully, because I can and will have you hauled out of here in handcuffs."

Cecil leaned back in his chair, brows drawn together in cold affront, but he was listening.

"Henry Bartlett is telling you what you want to hear. I am taking the position that when Billy left home with his father that weekend, he fully intended to kill him at the farm, which means the crime originated in Cook County. Henry can tie this case up for a year or more with motions for a change of venue and motions to have Billy's confession thrown out, but in the end I'll win, and you will stand trial with Billy as his accomplice. During that time, the media will have a feeding frenzy, digging up every skeleton this family has buried and hidden for the past one hundred years."

Cecil's face was expressionless, but his thin fingers were clenching and unclenching on the desk.

"If you do Henry a favor by dying before the case finally goes to trial, Henry can—and probably would—advise Billy to change his story and claim that *you* murdered William and persuaded that poor young boy to take the rap for it. After all, you'd be dead, and Billy would be paying Henry's fees, so why would Henry want to protect your reputation any longer?" Finished, he waited for Cecil to react, watching the little pendulum on the antique desk clock swing back and forth.

"What are you suggesting as an alternative?"

"I won't charge you as an accomplice, and you will let the Cook County justice system deal fairly with Billy. He's a juvenile, so he's already going to get off lighter than he should."

"I will not let him stand trial without the best defense we can provide."

"I'm not asking you to forgo that. I'm asking you to let him face up to what he's done, now, not two years from now."

Cecil hesitated again, and then he finally nodded.

"One more thing," Gray said as he stood up. "How did Edward die? He called you an hour before he went off the balcony. You said you talked about a meeting that you were both supposed to attend the next morning. But that's not what happened, or you'd have wondered if Mitchell 'helped' him over the railing."

Standing up, Cecil put an end to the unpleasant confrontation. "He was drunk, as usual, and he told me he wanted to say good-bye, that he couldn't bear his life another day. I told him what I always said when he called me like that. I told him to get a grip on himself. I didn't know he was serious this time. I'd been listening to his disgusting whining for so long I'd ceased paying attention to it."

Chapter Thirty-seven

K ATE PUT TWO MUGS OF STEAMING HOT CHOCOLATE ON
a tray beside a huge bowl of liberally buttered popcorn—the traditional fare for the winter movie nights
she and Holly enjoyed a couple of times each month.

Carrying the tray, Kate sidled around Max, who was
lying on the living room floor in front of the coffee
table. Holly looked up from the cabinet next to the television, where she was flipping through the selection of
chick flicks that were the staple of their movie nights.
Holding up her favorite movie, she said brightly, "How
about *An Affair to Remember*?"

"No thanks. I just had one of those, and I'm trying to
forget."

Holly grinned at the quip and turned back to the
movies in the cabinet. "I still can't believe what a total
bastard Wyatt was at that benefit."

Kate couldn't believe it either. That night it had been
obvious that Mitchell thoroughly despised her, which
could only mean he'd despised her all along, even when
he was making love to her in St. Maarten.

"He's sick," Holly said, putting Kate's thoughts into
words.

"Either that," Kate replied, trying to make light of it,
"or he's a little testy about being treated with amusement." Changing the subject to the movie for the
evening, she said, "How about *The Wedding Date*?"

"Not unless you promise not to keep rewinding it

when we get to that dancing scene where Michael Bublé sings 'Sway.'"

"Okay, that's a deal."

Holly started the movie and joined Kate on the sofa. They sat in silence for a minute, afghans over their legs, their feet clad in thick socks and propped side by side on the coffee table. "I'm going to miss our movie nights," Holly said, helping herself to a handful of popcorn from the bowl between them.

"What do you mean?" Kate replied, reaching for the mug of hot chocolate on the lamp table beside her.

"I mean that I can't picture myself sitting between you and Evan on movie night, holding the popcorn. Have you set a date yet?"

Kate shook her head. "We're not even sleeping together yet."

"Why not? You've been back for three weeks."

"We both agreed it was going to take us some time to get over what I did in St. Maarten and make a fresh start."

Holly looked at her in disbelief. "Are you telling me he hasn't wanted to mark his territory since then?"

"You're making me sound like a fire hydrant," Kate said, rolling her eyes. She took a sip of hot chocolate, swallowed, and put the mug down.

"Are you sure he isn't punishing you a little by staying away from you?"

"No, he isn't. In fact, last night he took me out to dinner, and he told me he wanted to come back here afterward and spend the night with me. But—"

"But?"

"But partway through dinner, I started feeling really nauseated. In fact, I'm feeling sort of queasy now. I've been feeling that way for days, and I'm exhausted all the time. All I want to do is sleep."

"Stress can really weaken your immune system and

screw up your body. By the way, how are things going at the restaurant?"

"The staff is patronizing me, which is not surprising, as the only one younger than me is a busboy. Other than that, it's too soon to tell. Let's watch our movie."

Chapter Thirty-eight

"KATE, DR. COOPER HAS YOUR TEST RESULTS."
Kate looked up and smiled at Bonnie Cooper's receptionist. Bonnie was a friend of Holly's and she'd been Kate's gynecologist for years. After examining Kate, Bonnie had ordered a few tests to be done in the office, and she'd asked Kate to wait in the waiting room.

"That was quick," Kate told Bonnie, sitting down on the opposite side of her desk.

Bonnie Cooper opened Kate's file. "I don't have the results of all your tests, but there's no need to wait for them. This test tells me exactly why you're feeling queasy and sleepy."

"What's the answer?"

"You're pregnant."

Kate half rose out of her chair; then she relaxed and smiled. "There's a mistake, Bonnie. You must have mixed my tests up with another patient's. I haven't missed taking a single birth control pill in months."

"The pill isn't one hundred percent effective for everyone."

"It's been one hundred percent effective for me. Evan—my fiancé—and I have been together for almost four years, and I've never gotten pregnant."

"Have you taken any antibiotics in the last two months? Some of them can interfere with the birth control pill's effectiveness."

"I know that, but I haven't taken any antibiotics. I haven't taken anything except some migraine medicine a doctor prescribed for me in St. Maarten."

Bonnie reached for a book lying on the corner of her desk. "I don't know of any migraine medicine that interferes with the pill. What was the name of it? I'll look it up."

"I can't remember," Kate said, frowning, "but it's on the tip of my tongue . . ."

"While you're trying to remember, tell me if you had sexual intercourse with anyone other than your fiancé in the last four years."

Kate hesitated, resenting the fact that she had to acknowledge Mitchell Wyatt's existence. "Yes, last month. But what difference does that make?"

"There's always the possibility that you're one of the tiny percentage of women the pill doesn't protect, and the reason you haven't gotten pregnant before last month is that your fiancé's sperm isn't viable."

Kate suddenly remembered the first part of the migraine medicine's name. "It was butal-something. That's the name of the prescription the doctor in St. Maarten gave me."

Bonnie frowned. "It wasn't butalbital, was it?"

"Yes, that's it."

"Didn't he ask you if you were taking birth control pills?"

"He asked me if I was trying to have children, and I said no. Actually, the doctor only spoke French, but the cabdriver spoke some English, so he translated for both of us. The doctor told the cabdriver to tell me I was probably having migraines."

"Why didn't you go to a hospital instead of to a local doctor?"

"And spend hours waiting for someone to see me? Bonnie, my head was exploding. I'd been throwing up from the pain on the way down to St. Maarten. I just wanted someone to give me something to stop the pain. I didn't *care* what language they spoke. Besides, he wasn't a witch doctor. His office was in his home, but it was very nice and he had well-dressed patients waiting to see him."

"Well, something got lost in the cabdriver's translation, then. He must have asked the cabdriver to find out if you were trying *not* to have children."

"What difference does all this make?" Kate said defensively, but she already knew. God help her, she already knew . . .

"Butalbital is very effective at treating, and preventing, severe headaches. However, it also interferes with the effectiveness of oral contraceptives. When a woman taking birth control pills uses butalbital, she needs to add another form of birth control to protect herself while she's taking it."

The room started to spin and Kate bent forward, her arms crossed over her stomach, trying to steady herself.

"Do you know for certain who the father is?"

Kate looked up at Bonnie. In the three weeks following her father's death she hadn't wanted to make love; that was part of the reason Evan had been so insistent about taking her away for a Caribbean holiday.

She was pregnant with Mitchell Wyatt's baby.

A wave of hysteria welled up inside her, combining with dizziness and nausea, and Kate clutched the edge of Bonnie's desk. "Oh, yes," she said bitterly. "I know who the father is."

Chapter Thirty-nine

"KATE, IT'S ME!" HOLLY CALLED, LETTING HERSELF IN THE front door of Kate's house with the key she'd used to look after the cats while Kate was in the islands. Max ran up to greet her, tail wagging.

"A fine watchdog you are," she teased, absently patting his big head, but she was worried. Kate's car was in the driveway, the windows covered in a half inch of snow, which meant she'd been home awhile that evening, but she wasn't answering her phone and the house was dark. Yesterday, she'd found out she was pregnant, and she'd decided to tell Evan about it earlier today, rather than waiting a few days to think things through as Holly had advised. Kate had, however, planned to take Holly's suggestion about going to Evan's office and telling him there, where he couldn't make a scene.

"Kate?"

"In the living room," Kate called. She turned on a lamp and hastily shoved aside the pillow she'd been clutching to her while she stared numbly into the dark. "I fell asleep," she lied. "Do you want some coffee?"

"Sure," Holly said.

"What time is it?" Kate asked

"A little after six."

Swinging her legs off the sofa, Kate got up and headed for the kitchen with Holly trailing behind. "I have to change clothes and go to work. I should have been at the restaurant two hours ago."

As she started spooning coffee into the coffeemaker, Holly walked over to the cupboard and took out two mugs. "Did it go okay with Evan today?"

In answer, Kate held out her left hand, which was now devoid of an engagement ring. "I didn't really expect it to go well," she said in a carefully expressionless voice as she filled the coffee carafe with water. "After all, I went there to tell him his fiancée was pregnant by another man who he happens to despise. But—"

"But what?" Holly persisted.

Bracing her hands on the sink, Kate let her head fall forward while she watched the water level rise in the carafe. "But I never imagined it could go as *badly* as it did. He turned pale when I first told him, but then he recovered and even put his arm around me and told me it wasn't my fault, that Mitchell had made a victim out of both of us. He said we could undo the damage and go on with our lives like it never happened."

"What went wrong?"

"I told him I wasn't sure I could go through with an abortion."

"Then what happened?"

"He completely lost it," Kate said tonelessly. Belatedly realizing the carafe was overflowing, she turned the water tap off and filled the coffeemaker with fresh water; then she flipped the switch on. "Did you ever wonder how a calm, even-tempered man like Evan could possibly intimidate anyone in court?"

"I've wondered why everyone thinks he's such a good attorney. Turn around and talk to me," Holly said, putting her hands on Kate's shoulders and forcing her to turn.

"Well, you don't have to wonder anymore," Kate said, swallowing audibly. "This afternoon, I got a dose of what it must be like to be cross-examined by him. He started out making quick, deep cuts with a scalpel about little things I've done over the years that he put up with, and then he got out the hacksaw. By the time he was done, he was calling me names and shouting at me so loud that everyone on that floor must have heard him. Finally, he told me to get out and never come back."

"That hypocrite! Don't think for a minute he's been faithful to you for the past four years. There have been plenty of rumors about him."

Turning away, Kate reached for the sugar bowl and two spoons. "Those were just rumors. I'm the one who's guilty and dirty, not him."

"Am I right that he would have been willing to continue 'putting up with you' if you'd agreed to have an abortion?"

"Yep. Definitely," Kate replied, trying to be flippant and sounding haunted instead. "In fact, at times I had the feeling he actually thought an abortion would be a suitable form of payback—Mitchell's baby in return for the insult to Evan's and my pride."

"He doesn't care about your pride. This is about the Bartlett pride. I'll bet he'd have been a lot less affronted if you'd gotten knocked up by someone he regarded as his social equal."

Kate almost, but not quite, smiled at that.

"I've told you for years that Evan has two sides—"

"Don't," Kate said, turning back to the counter. "I despise the way he treated me, and I wouldn't go back to him after today if he begged me to, but he was crushed. I wounded him in Anguilla when I told him what I'd done, but today I devastated him."

In silence, they sat at the kitchen table, waiting for the coffee to finish brewing. Kate gave Holly a mug of it and handed her the sugar bowl; then she picked up her own mug and started for the bedroom. "I hate to leave you here, but I have to get dressed and go to work."

"No, you don't. You've been working until midnight every night since you got back from Anguilla."

"I was off two nights ago for our movie night."

"That was Sunday, and the restaurant was closed. The restaurant can run itself for one night."

Kate turned, looked at the coffee mug she was holding, then she looked at Holly and said in angry misery, "I'm so sleepy because I'm pregnant that I can hardly stand up, and I'm pregnant because I actually thought I was in love with a man who turned out to be a ruthless, depraved monster. If there is a God, I will miscarry!" Kate said, and then the dam broke, and she wept in Holly's arms. "Even if I wanted to have a baby right now, I'd be terrified of the kind of genes this baby could have inherited from its father. He's a m-monster!"

"I know," Holly said, smiling a little and patting Kate's back. "Now, let's go in the living room. You can call the restaurant, and I'll pick out a movie and we'll have a sleepover."

Holly decided on *Pretty Woman*, because it was lighthearted and frivolous. "I cannot have this baby!" Kate whispered from the sofa behind her. She was asleep by the time Holly started the movie and looked around.

"Come on, Max," Holly whispered. "I don't know about you, but I could definitely use something stronger than coffee. Let's raid the wine rack."

With that in mind, Holly started back toward the kitchen; then she jumped in nervous shock when someone knocked at the front door just as she walked past it. Hoping it would be Evan, preferably on his knees, Holly opened the door; then she stepped back in nervous surprise. Standing on the porch was an unsmiling gray-haired man in his early sixties wearing full clerical regalia of black suit and white collar. "My God!" she said to the priest, her shock turning to annoyance. "What is with you right-to-life people, anyway? Are you plugged into every OB in the city? Go away! She can make up her own mind."

"You must be Holly," the priest said, smiling slightly.

"Please don't creep me out. Just leave your literature on the porch, and I'll see that she gets it," Holly said, starting to close the door.

He put his hand on the door to stop her. "I'm Father Donovan, Kate's uncle. Kate came by the rectory late this afternoon when I was out. My housekeeper said she seemed upset. She hasn't answered my phone calls. Now, may I come in?"

Embarrassed but resolute, Holly stepped back, opened the door, and whispered, "She's sleeping right now, and she's upset. I don't want her to wake up. You can come into the kitchen if you want to wait around for a while."

Holly closed the kitchen's swinging door behind them and kept her voice low. "Would you like some coffee?"

"No, thank you. I take it that Kate's pregnant?"

Holly's background had left her with little respect for organized religion and even less for clerics. "You'll have to discuss that with her, Father Donovan," she said, refusing to be intimidated by his collar. The wine rack was in the corner on the counter, and she pulled out a bottle of red wine and began uncorking it, trying to remember whether it was Baptists or Catholics who disapproved of drinking alcohol. "I'm going to drown my sorrows for Kate in a large glass of wine," she warned him. "I hope you don't object," she added in a tone that conveyed that she didn't care whether he objected or not.

"Are you planning to drink the whole bottle yourself?"

"I might. Why?"

When he didn't answer, she turned around and found herself looking straight into eyes as green as Kate's, eyes that were filled with amused curiosity. "If you aren't planning to drink the whole bottle yourself," he said, "I thought perhaps we could sit here and enjoy a glass together while we wait for Kate to wake up."

"Yes, of course," Holly said, feeling confused and rude. "But I'm not going to tell you about Kate's—little problem. If she wants to confess it to a priest, that's up to her."

"I'm not here as her confessor," he remarked. "I'm here as her uncle."

"You're a priest. You're going to tell her she has to have that—that *bastard's* baby."

As she poured wine into two glasses, Holly waited for him to deny it. "That's what you're going to do, isn't it?" she challenged bitterly as she handed him a glass of wine and sat down across the table from him.

"Assuming Kate came to see me today to tell me she's pregnant, then the answer to your question is that Kate already knew what I was going to tell her. Which, in turn, makes me think that's what she wanted to hear. What surprises me is that she's been involved with a man you think is a bastard. She's usually an excellent judge of people."

Holly took a sip of her wine, considering that. "Not this time."

Father Donovan took a sip of his wine. "He must have had some quality that appealed to her?"

"He's a heartless pig," Holly declared angrily, and took another sip of wine. "But a heartless pig with a lot of looks and charm."

"I see. Poor Kate. She's gone with the same young man for four years. I take it the heartless pig we're talking about isn't him?"

"No, that heartless pig broke their engagement today and dumped her. She met the heartless pig who got her pregnant in Anguilla a few weeks ago. Don't ask me to tell you anything more."

"I won't."

Holly drank more of her wine, her thoughts on Kate; then she lifted her gaze to the man with Kate's eyes and said in a wretched voice, "I can't believe the things he did to her, and all to get even with Evan . . ."

"Evan is the heartless pig who dumped her today?"

"Yes. Mitchell Wyatt is the one who used her and broke her heart. I'm the one who coached her about how to treat him when she saw him the last time, and he broke her heart all over again."

"You meant well. It's not your fault."

Holly drank a little more wine and bit her lip. "It's partly my fault that she had anything to do with him in the first place. Evan took her down to Anguilla and left her there alone, and I told her she should have a fling, and that's what she did."

Father Donovan took another sip of wine. "I'm sure Kate made that choice on her own."

"Oh, no, she didn't!" Holly said angrily. "She met Mitchell Wyatt in a restaurant one afternoon when she accidentally spilled a Bloody Mary on his shirt. He knew she was Evan's girlfriend, but he pretended not to . . ."

". . . What a heartbreaking story," Father Donovan declared sincerely an hour later, after Holly finished apprising him of every minute detail, culminating in Kate's confrontation with Wyatt at the Children's Hospital benefit.

A second bottle of wine was on the table between them, along with a tissue box from which Holly had periodically removed a tissue to dab at her eyes. "I could kill him with my bare hands," she said ferociously.

"So could I," Father Donovan declared.

Holly looked at him with new respect. "Really?"

"That was a figure of speech."

"What are we going to do now?" she asked, spreading her hands on the table, palms up. "She has that huge restaurant to run, and she doesn't have anyone who cares about her anymore."

Father Donovan looked at her in surprise. "She has you, Holly," he said with a smile, "and you're loyal and brave and strong. And she has me. We'll get her through this. And when it's all said and done, she'll have a baby to love and to love her back, and we'll share him with her."

In the doorway, Kate paused and looked from Holly to her uncle. "Hi, Uncle Jamie."

Standing up, he opened his arms to her and said tenderly, "Hello, Mary Kate."

Kate fled into his familiar embrace.

Chapter Forty

ON A BALMY JUNE MORNING, WHEN SHE WAS ALMOST four months pregnant, Kate hurried beneath the decorative burgundy awnings of the front windows of Donovan's on her way into work, and she caught sight of her reflection in the glass. With a sense of grim fascination, she kept walking and studying her unfamiliar outline in the glass. Her head was bent; her shoulders were hunched forward as if she had to plow her way through the lunchtime crowd in order to keep moving; her hair was a mass of untamed curls pulled up into a ponytail because that was easiest; and her pregnancy was showing. Mitchell Wyatt's son was making his presence known.

And if that weren't bad enough, the window glass was noticeably grimy.

She pushed through the heavy brass-trimmed oak door, looked around for the maître d', took in the general condition of things, and worriedly glanced at her watch. It was 11:15; fifteen minutes before Donovan's opened for lunch. By now, all the tables should have been covered with snowy-white linen tablecloths and decked out with sparkling crystal, gleaming china chargers with a gold *D* in the center, and ornamental brass lanterns. As she walked toward the lounge, Kate counted ten tables that weren't set, and she noticed that the patterned burgundy carpet didn't look freshly vacuumed.

The lounge was separated from the dining rooms by a richly carved mahogany wall with stained-glass panels. The room occupied the entire right-hand corner of the building, its shuttered windows looking out onto the street at the front and along the side. During the day, the shutters were left open so people who were eating and drinking at the tables could enjoy the street scene. At dark, the shutters were closed, and the atmosphere inside became a candlelit, upscale "hideaway" with a jazz quartet providing music next to a small dance floor.

The remaining two walls were taken up by the bar itself, an L-shaped mahogany replica of an old-world bar, with dark green marble counters, brass foot rails, and a carved wood canopy above burgundy leather barstools. The beveled mirror on the two back walls was all but obscured by tiers of crystal glasses and Donovan's famous selection of spirits from all over the world.

The entire original Irish pub of Kate's youth had occupied about half the area of the current lounge. Normally, being in the lounge evoked nostalgia in Kate. Today, however, she felt a rush of frustrated annoyance when she took a look inside and saw Frank O'Halloran rushing back and forth from one end of the bar to the other, setting out bowls of imported nuts and pulling out trays of fruit from the refrigerators under the bar.

Two bartenders normally manned the bar for weekday lunches, with the number increasing to three on Monday through Wednesday nights, and then to four for the Thursday-, Friday-, and Saturday-night crowds.

"Hi, Frank," Kate said to the balding bartender, who'd worked for Donovan's for twenty years. "Who's supposed to be on duty with you today?"

"Jimmy," he replied, flicking her a noncommittal look.

"I thought Jimmy was working the evening shift."

"He switched with Pete Fellows."

"Where's Jimmy, then?"

"Dunno, Mary Kate."

Scheduling the staff was Louis Kellard's job as the restaurant manager. "I guess Louis is taking care of getting you some help," Kate said, turning to leave.

"Mary Kate, I need to tell you somethin'."

She turned back, suddenly uneasy about his tone. "Yes?" she said, walking over to him. He had a sheen of perspiration on his forehead, presumably from trying to rush.

"I'm gonna have to quit."

Kate's eyes widened in alarm at the thought of another familiar face disappearing from her life. "Are you sick, Frank?"

Lifting his head, he looked her straight in the eye. "Yeah, I am. I'm sick of watchin' this place slide downhill. I've always been real proud of workin' at Donovan's. There's not a customer who comes in here more than a few times that I don't make it a point to remember his name and what he likes. Your dad, God rest his soul, was the same way about the dining room customers."

"I know that—" Kate said, cringing inwardly from the indirect criticism of her stewardship.

"Donovan's has always been special. Even when your dad decided to make this place real classy, he kept it real personal, too. He gave it his special touch, and that's what's made Donovan's the popular place that it is. I'm gonna be honest with you, Mary Kate, and tell you what all of us think who've worked here for a few years: You don't have your dad's touch. We thought you might, but you don't."

Kate put up a valiant struggle against a sudden rush of tears. "I spend as much time here as my father did," she argued.

"Your heart isn't in it," he countered. "Your father wouldn't have seen me alone in here and shrugged and said, 'I guess Louis is taking care of getting you some help.' He'd have made damned sure I had help, and then he'd have made damned sure he knew why Louis hadn't *already* taken care of it."

Heated tears were burning the backs of Kate's eyes now, threatening to spill over, and she turned, starting toward the doorway into the dining room. "Tell Marjorie to give you an extra two months' pay in your final check," she said, referring to the trusted bookkeeper who'd worked for her father for more than a decade.

To her shock, the Irishman called angrily after her, "*You* tell Marjorie to do it, Mary Kate Donovan! That's your job—you're the boss, not me, and not Marjorie."

Kate nodded, trying to breathe steadily and slowly so she wouldn't have to run for the bathroom to either throw up or cry.

"And another thing—" Frank shouted after her. "Why are you lettin' me get away with talkin' to you like that? I wouldn't have gotten away with talkin' to your dad that way!"

"Go to hell," Kate whispered.

"And one more thing besides," he called.

Fists clenched, Kate turned and saw him leaning over the bar, his face red with anger. "What's wrong with your eyes that you didn't notice that the lemons and limes I'm puttin' out are old? Why aren't you storming outta here on your way to the kitchen to see who the hell is letting that produce company get away with giving us this crap?"

Kate refused to reply, but she did notice that the maître d', Kevin Sandovski, still wasn't at his post at 11:25, when she walked by his desk at the entrance. In the kitchen, she found him, Louis Kellard, and several waiters who should have been busy with last-minute details in the dining room, standing around joking with the kitchen staff. "What's going on in here?" she asked in what she hoped was an authoritative, disapproving voice.

Sandovski levered himself up from a stool, but she thought he rolled his eyes at the waiters. Louis Kellard looked at the bulge in her abdomen, smiled sympathetically, and said, "Kate, I've been through two pregnancies with my wife, and I know how hard it is on a woman emotionally and physically to deal with that, along with the stress of holding down a job. Try not to upset yourself."

"I'm not upsetting myself," Kate said, unsure whether he was genuinely trying to help her or patronizing her. "Frank O'Halloran said we're getting inferior produce. Is that true?"

"Of course it isn't," Louis said, shaking his head in affront. "We're just not using as many lemons and limes as we used to in the lounge, so they stand around a little longer."

"Why aren't we using as many as we used to?"

"Ask Marjorie," Louis said. "She has all the figures on how much business we're doing. We're down a little from what we used to do, but not by much."

Kate nodded and backed out of the kitchen. "I'll be in the office if you need me."

Her father's office—her office now—had been relocated years before to an area off the main dining room, separated from it by a paneled hallway with doors opening into the bookkeeper's office and the manager's office as well. The staircase leading up from the old pub to the apartment above had been closed off and a new staircase created that was located next to her father's office. The apartment itself was still there, but her father had used it only rarely, either when the weather was too bad to drive home or when he'd worked unusually late.

Marjorie was sitting at her desk, her fingers racing over a calculator keyboard, her ledger books spread out over nearly every available surface. "Frank O'Halloran is going to quit," Kate said. "Will you please give him two months' extra pay in his final check?"

The gray-haired bookkeeper looked up. "Are you going to let Frank quit?"

"How am I supposed to stop him?" Kate demanded, her fingernails biting into her palms.

"I don't know. I guess I thought maybe you'd have an idea."

"I do have one idea," Kate shot back.

"What's that, Kate?"

"We ought to be using a computerized cash-flow system. Those ledger books are as antiquated as—"

"As me?" Marjorie suggested ironically.

"I didn't mean it that way, Marjorie."

"We are computerized," Marjorie said, taking pity on her. "Food orders, reservations, everything. Haven't you noticed that before?"

"Of course I have!" Kate said, already feeling drained after being there less than half an hour. "I was talking about the ledgers you're using right now. Why isn't that information on computer?"

"It is, actually. Your father liked the consistency of tracking everything using the same method we've always used, so I transfer certain information into the ledgers off the computer." She waited expectantly for Kate to say something, and when Kate didn't she dropped her gaze to her calculator and began inputting figures. "Kate," she said without looking up, "you're not really invested in running this business. You need to think about selling it."

Wounded to the core now, Kate said nothing and backed out of yet another room, retreating again, because she'd lost complete faith in herself. A few months ago—before Mitchell Wyatt—she would have had enough faith in her own judgment to take a firm stand in the kitchen with Louis, and with Frank, and with Marjorie. But not now. Now she'd lost faith in herself, and on top of that, everyone else was losing faith in her, too.

Because of Mitchell, and because of her pregnancy with his child, she'd been reduced to an exhausted mass of raw emotions and uncertainties. Worse yet, she couldn't think of the child she was carrying without immediately thinking of what a gullible fool she'd been about his father. For weeks, she'd been waiting to feel some sort of maternal bond with her baby, but it wasn't happening, and she was starting to fear that her feelings about Mitchell were going to prevent her from loving her baby.

Kate sat down behind her father's desk and faced the fact that things were likely to get much worse, not better, unless she could find some sort of resolution, and peace, about what Mitchell had done to her. She had to be able to forgive him, and then forgive herself for falling for him. Once she did that, she'd be able to put all the bad feelings behind her and look forward to the future.

In order to forgive and forget, she first needed to understand how he thought and what had happened to him to make him so heartless and vengeful.

Propping her chin on the palm of her hand, Kate considered how to find the answers she needed. . . .

Neither Caroline nor Cecil Wyatt would be willing to talk about him behind his back. Matthew Farrell and Meredith Bancroft knew him, but Meredith had witnessed her confrontation with Mitchell at the Children's Hospital benefit, and afterward, she'd looked at Kate as if she didn't exist anymore. In Anguilla, Evan had told her enough about Mitchell's childhood to make her feel horrified, but Evan certainly wouldn't fill in any details for Kate now. . . .

In her mind, Kate suddenly saw Gray Elliott taking some files off a thick stack on his desk and bringing them over to the coffee table where Holly and she were sitting. Those particular files had contained photographs, but there had been a lot more files in a pile on his desk.

Feeling more resolute and optimistic than she had in months, she got a phone book out of her desk drawer.

After a fairly long delay, Gray Elliott picked up the telephone. "Miss Donovan?" he said, sounding brisk but curious. "My secretary said you needed to talk to me about an urgent matter."

"I do," Kate said emphatically, "but it has to be in person."

"I'm booked up for several—"

"It will take only a few minutes, and it is urgent—and very important."

He hesitated, and Kate could almost see him looking at his calendar. "Could you make it at twelve-fifteen tomorrow? I'll see you before I go to lunch."

"I'll be there," Kate said. "Thank you."

Chapter Forty-one

"MR. ELLIOTT WILL SEE YOU NOW, MISS DONOVAN," THE secretary said.

Kate stood up and followed her into his office. Yesterday, Kate had looked like a wreck, but today she'd paid careful attention to her appearance, striving for a feminine, summery look she desperately hoped would help offset her last, unpleasant standoff with the state's attorney. Her sleeveless empire-waisted turquoise jumper concealed her pregnancy and was enlivened by the geometric print, in bright turquoise, lavender, and white, of her linen tote. The jumper was just short enough to be very stylish without revealing too much skin above the knee, and her high-heeled sandals showed off her legs.

To go with the mod sixties look of the jumper, she'd straightened her hair and pulled it back at the sides, holding it in place at the crown with a tortoiseshell clip.

Gray Elliott stood up when she walked into his office, and his brief, startled smile made her feel that she definitely looked better than at their last encounter, and that small success was enough to buoy up spirits that had been at a low ebb for so many months.

"Why don't we sit over there, Miss Donovan," he said, coming around his desk and gesturing toward the sofa and chairs where she and Holly had sat before.

Kate gave him her best rueful smile and said, "Please call me Kate."

"All right—Kate," he said, but his brows drew together in mild suspicion.

Since he was already suspicious, Kate decided to try to outflank him and catch him off guard by firing a round of honesty at him. "I'm hoping that if we're on a first-name basis," she admitted with what she hoped was a charming smile, "you'll be more inclined to agree to the favor I've come to ask you for. It's terribly important, Mr. Elliott."

"Please call me Gray," he said courteously—and because he had little choice if she was going to allow him to call her Kate.

When they reached the coffee table, Kate deliberately sat down on a chair at the end of it rather than on the sofa in front of it, since the soft sofa cushions would have sunk beneath her weight and put her at a height disadvantage. Evidently, Gray Elliott was equally conscious of these subtleties, because instead of sitting on the sofa as she'd hoped he would, he walked around the coffee table and sat down in the opposite chair, facing her.

"Would you like something to drink?" he offered.

"No, thank you," Kate said, crossing her legs. Watching him from beneath her lashes, she leaned to the right to put her tote bag on the sofa. His gaze went briefly to her crossed legs and quickly withdrew. He hadn't meant to look, but he was definitely a leg man, she thought wryly; then a sudden memory of Mitchell, standing on the balcony in St. Maarten, slashed across her heart and vanquished her brief spurt of confident optimism.

Are you smiling because I look surprisingly nice, or because there's something wrong with my dress? she'd asked.

I'm smiling because I just realized you have gorgeous legs, and I never saw them before.

I was wearing both of them earlier. In fact, I distinctly remember that they were attached to me when we were in bed.

Unaware that her hand was still on her tote and her gaze was locked on the back of the sofa, she started when Gray Elliott said, "Kate? Are you feeling all right?"

"Oh, yes, perfectly all right," Kate lied hastily.

He nodded acceptance of her answer and got down to business. "What can I do for you?"

Wetting her lips, Kate drew a long breath and said, "When I was here the last time, you had a stack of files on one corner of your desk. The ones you took off the top had pictures in them of Mitchell Wyatt and me. Am I right that the files you left on your desk involved your actual investigation of him?"

He hesitated, mobile brows narrowing slightly over wary gray eyes. "Why do you ask?"

"Did you investigate him?" Kate said calmly but obstinately, then she answered for him. "Well, of course, you must have. I mean, surely you didn't waste a small fortune of taxpayers' money sending detectives to the Caribbean just to take licentious photographs of him seducing me—and whoever else he seduced," she added as an afterthought.

"If that's what you're trying to find out by coming here today, the answer is that you were the only woman he showed any interest in while he was down there."

"How lucky for me," Kate said, then she shook her head to stop herself from betraying, or feeling, any bitterness. "Actually, he wasn't interested in me at all—" she said, starting to explain the truth, but Gray Elliott's incredulous smile stopped her in midsentence.

"He certainly looks interested in those photographs. I would even have said absorbed," Gray replied.

"That's what he needed me to think. Never mind,

that doesn't matter. I'm getting sidetracked," Kate said, and decided to abandon her carefully thought-out plan and go straight to what did matter. "I need to ask you something, but before I do, is there the slightest chance you'd be willing to give me your word that what I say here won't leave this room?"

"That depends on whether what you're going to say involves the commission of a crime," he said half-seriously.

That struck Kate as funny and almost endearing, and she smiled at him—a natural, warm smile this time. "Unless bad timing and gullibility are crimes, there's no problem. If they are crimes, get out your handcuffs."

He returned her smile and leaned back in his chair, ready to listen. "You have my word that our conversation won't leave this room."

"Thank you. What I need is information about Mitchell Wyatt from your files, but I'm not interested in him as your murder suspect."

"What is it that you're curious about?"

"I'm not curious," Kate said simply. "I'm pregnant."

The words dropped like a bomb, sending shock waves rippling across the room. Finally, he said, "You could probably locate him yourself with some intense snooping on the Internet. However, I'll give you his addresses."

"I don't want to locate him," Kate said, and for the second time Gray Elliott was silent with shock.

"Why not? He has a right to know about this baby, and he also has financial obligations to you and to it."

"Believe me, he would not want to exercise his rights to this baby. He made his first wife divorce him when she wanted to have a child. And as far as I'm concerned, he has no obligations to this baby. I'm the one who inadvertently had unprotected sex with him, and I'm the one who chose not to terminate this pregnancy.

The responsibilities for the baby are all mine, and that's fine with me."

He studied her closely for several moments, as if unable to comprehend her willingness to accept total responsibility for her pregnancy and her baby. "What do you think you'll discover in our files?" he asked finally.

"Evan told me a little bit about the way Mitchell grew up and what the Wyatts did to him. Do you know anything about that?"

"Yes, as a matter of fact, I know all about it."

"Are you also aware that Evan's father orchestrated and supervised everything concerning it?"

To her surprise, Gray nodded.

"Then you should be able to believe this: Mitchell staged that whole seduction effort to get himself a little revenge against the Bartletts. I was just a gullible tool. When I met him in Anguilla, I had no idea he'd ever been to Chicago, let alone that he knew Henry and Evan. He knew who I was from the very beginning, though, and when he realized Evan wasn't with me, he pulled out all the stops to get me into bed."

She waited for all that to sink in, then she said with a sad laugh, "Mitchell got much more revenge than he hoped for: Evan and I aren't together anymore, and I'm pregnant with Mitchell's child."

"How will looking through our files help you?"

"I need to learn about him so that I can understand why he did the things he did. Once I understand why, I'm hoping I'll be able to forgive him, and then I'll be able to love my baby. As it stands now, I can't think of this baby without hating his father and hating myself for being such a fool over him."

Tipping his head back, Gray Elliott contemplated the ceiling, and Kate held her breath. Finally, he looked directly at her and said, "William Wyatt spent a fortune on private investigators because he wanted to find out everything he possibly could about the little brother who'd been sent away to make his own way in the world. Caroline Wyatt gave us that file, thinking it might assist us in our own investigation."

He got up, walked over to a built-in wooden file cabinet, and removed a fat file from it. "Technically," he said, as he walked over to the conference table and laid the file on it, "this file of Caroline's is separate from our own investigatory files, so I'm under no real burden of confidentiality. I don't see why you couldn't sit over here and look through it while I'm out to lunch."

Any emotion, even relief, brought tears to her eyes these days, and she had to brush them away as she smiled at him and got up to walk over to the conference table. "Thank you very much," she said achingly.

He stared at her face for a moment, then he returned to the file cabinet, took out an armload of additional files, and carried those to the conference table, too. "These files are strictly confidential," he said with a meaningful smile. "I'll be back in an hour."

"Miss Donovan is still in your office," Gray's secretary told him.

Gray nodded, opened his office door, and walked inside. Kate Donovan was so engrossed in what she was reading that she didn't even notice that he'd returned. When he sat down at his desk, his leather chair made a noise, and she glanced up, completely startled. "In twenty minutes, I have a meeting scheduled here," Gray said, "but you're welcome to stay until then."

"Thank you," she said, and immediately lost herself in the file again.

Reaching for a tablet and pen, Gray started making notes for his meeting, but his gaze kept straying in her direction, and after ten minutes, he finally gave up and put his pen down to watch her. She was still working her way toward the bottom of William's dark blue file, which, as he recalled, covered the first nineteen or twenty years of Mitchell's life. There was nothing significant in that one; it contained mostly school transcripts, some letters and statements from those teachers who remembered him and were still employed at the boarding schools he'd attended, and copies of any pages from school periodicals or yearbooks that mentioned him.

And yet she was clearly finding items of import there, because at times she'd smile softly or frown, and a minute before, he'd distinctly seen her touch her fingertip almost tenderly to a newspaper photograph of him.

She was to his left, facing in his general direction, her head bent, her shining red hair spilling over her shoulders. She looked very young and very vulnerable, he thought, and very, very pretty, with her fair skin, long russet eyelashes, and the tiny cleft in her chin. Idly, he wondered why he hadn't noticed how truly lovely she was before. She'd always seemed striking with her dark red hair, but he'd never really looked at her face. Now that he'd had a good long look at that face and that red hair, he realized the combination was stunning. And when he added in her emerald eyes and those legs of hers, she was downright fantastic looking.

Unfortunately for her, Mitchell Wyatt hadn't overlooked her attributes and neither had that manipulative, two-faced schmuck Evan Bartlett. Bartlett had made sure everybody in their social circle knew that he'd dumped her and broken their engagement, but he'd neglected to mention that she'd cheated on him first. That would have made him look like less of a stud.

Getting up out of his chair, Gray perched a hip on the corner of his desk closest to the conference table and said, "Are you finding anything that's helpful in all that stuff?"

She lifted jewel-bright eyes to his, nodded, and gave him a winsome smile. "He was an amazing athlete. He excelled at everything he tried, didn't he?"

Surprised that athletic prowess would matter to her, Gray considered her question. "I guess he did. I remember there were a lot of school newspaper and yearbook photographs of him playing sports and getting trophies."

"Did you notice anything else about those photographs?"

"No," Gray said. "What was there to notice?"

Her voice caught. "He was always alone." As proof, she flipped back a few pages in the file and took out the first photograph she came to. Gray shoved off the desk and walked the few steps to the conference table to see what she meant. In the photograph, Wyatt looked to be about sixteen, and he was getting a soccer trophy for breaking the school record for most goals in one season. "He isn't alone," Gray pointed out. "Two of his teammates who also won trophies are standing on either side of him."

"Yes, they are," Kate said softly. "But those two teammates' parents are standing next to their sons. It's the same theme in every photograph."

She flipped slowly backward in the file—and in the chronological order of his life—to a photograph taken of him when he was about six during a cricket match. His bat looked way too big for him, and he was concentrating so hard he was scowling. "That is a kid who is focused on the ball," Gray joked.

She nodded, started to say something, then shook her head and changed her mind. "Did you read this interview with the custodian of the grounds at his boarding school in France?"

"That sort of thing wasn't of interest to me," Gray admitted. "What does it tell you?"

"Mr. Brickley said Mitchell spent several Christmases with his wife and himself, rather than spending them with the headmaster's family. He said Mitchell later wrote to them from the next boarding school he attended, but Mr. Brickley's wife died and he stopped answering Mitchell's letters." Tears clogged her voice as she said, "Do you know why Mitchell was writing letters to a disinterested groundskeeper from his next boarding school?"

"I haven't the faintest idea."

"He was writing to him because it was mandatory at all these boarding schools for boys to write to a family member every two weeks. He didn't have anyone else to write to."

Leaning back in her chair, she said with a choked laugh, "I don't blame him for despising the Bartletts and wanting revenge. In fact, I feel better knowing that—although I was badly used—it was actually for a *very* worthy cause."

Gray grinned at her joke. "You missed the good stuff. His later years were filled with triumphs. In one of those files there's a magazine article about Stavros Konstantatos. He called Wyatt 'my left fist.'"

"His what?"

Leaning across her, Gray sorted through the top files, slid one out, and removed the article he'd shown to Jeff Cervantes and Lily Reardon. Kate read it, her smile faded, and she handed it back. "It's a little easier for me to see him as a boy and young man than as a dynamic businessman. It's harder for me to forgive a successful, intelligent man than it is to overlook the heartlessness of a boy who grew up with rich kids while he thought he himself was a charity case without a relative in the world."

With a vague notion of trying to persuade Gray to let her have a copy of a picture of Mitchell to show her son someday, Kate reached for a file that obviously contained photographs.

The top photograph was a picture of Mitchell standing alone at the wharf in Philipsburg with the sun setting in the background. According to the date and time stamp in the lower right-hand corner, the photograph was taken at 5:45 PM.

It was taken on the date she was supposed to meet him there at four o'clock.

Her hand shook as she picked it up and looked at the date and time again, unable to believe her eyes.

"Oh, my God!" she whispered, looking from the photograph to the one that had been beneath it. That one was taken at 5:15 on the same day in the same place. "Oh, my God!" she said again.

"Why are you upset about that shot? You're not in it."

"I was supposed to be there," Kate said, swiftly sliding the next photograph aside and then the ones beneath it. They were in chronological order. The first shot taken of Mitchell at the wharf that day was time-stamped 3:30 PM.

Not caring that Gray Elliott would think her demented, she touched Mitchell's picture as if she could smooth back a loose black lock near his temple. "You were there," she whispered achingly. "You were waiting there for me . . ." There was no mistaking that date—she'd gotten pregnant in the predawn hours of that day.

Gray straightened, taking in her flushed cheeks and overbright eyes. "Can I get you a glass of water or something?"

Kate started to laugh and ended up weeping.

"You're scaring me, Kate."

She went from weeping to joyous laughter and stood up, wrapping him in a quick, fierce hug with one arm, while she held the picture in her free hand. "You have nothing to be scared about—unless you try to pry this photograph out of my hand," she warned him, with a beaming smile.

"I can't—"

"Yes, you can. No one will ever know. It's for his son to see someday."

When he looked prepared to wrestle her to the ground for it, Kate sketched in the details of why it meant so much to her. When she was finished, he was a beaten man, and she knew it. "Phone me when you'd like to have dinner," she said, "and I will see that you and your guests have a meal fit for a king."

"That sounds like a bribe."

She was so deliriously happy that she patted the arm of a man she barely knew and smilingly said, "Not a bribe, a *payoff*." She picked up her tote bag and headed for the door, then she stopped in the middle of his office and turned back. "Just out of curiosity, where did he go when he left the wharf?"

"He went directly to the airport and flew back here. His brother's body had been found that day, and his nephew phoned him and pleaded with him to come straight home."

"The same nephew who later confessed to killing William?"

Gray nodded, his expression turning grim. "The very same crazy little bastard who duped the most lenient judge in the juvenile court system and got off with a year in a psychiatric facility, followed by outpatient therapy, and three years probation."

Outside on the sidewalk, Kate had to restrain the urge to throw her arms out wide and turn in slow, delighted circles. Mitchell had been waiting for her at the wharf. She wasn't as naïve now as she'd been then, so she didn't deceive herself into thinking he'd been in love with her and waiting there to carry her away with him.

The fact that he was there at the wharf didn't negate the pretenses and secrets he'd built their brief relationship on. He'd pretended he knew nothing about Chicago, he'd pretended he knew nothing about Zack Benedict, and he'd sent her back to the villa to break up with Evan without ever admitting he knew who Evan was.

But he had *not* intended for her to trot back to the Enclave like an eager puppy only to find out that her master had checked out and vanished. He had not been going to let that happen. Maybe he had been waiting at the wharf just to say, "I'm sorry I've used you and hurt you—the Bartletts were my real target."

It didn't matter *why* he'd been waiting there for her. It only mattered that he'd been there. Holly might have been right after all—while he was executing his plan for revenge, he'd started to care for Kate a little, maybe enough to want to watch the sunrise with her. His behavior at the Children's Hospital benefit rather negated that last thought, so Kate decided never to think about that awful night again.

In her heart a little voice pleaded with her to find Mitchell and see if she could make whatever feeling he'd had for her grow deeper and stronger. But then logic pointed out the futility of that. She was pregnant with his child, and Mitchell did not want anything to do with fatherhood. No doubt he felt that looking at his own child would bring back all the helplessness and pain of his own childhood. Kate felt an impulse to do real violence to Henry and Evan Bartlett and Cecil Wyatt, and everyone else who had put a beautiful, black-haired, blue-eyed little boy through a life of senseless misery.

Kate hailed a cab, slid into the backseat, and asked

the driver to take her to Donovan's restaurant. When she started to give him the address, he waved his hand and said, "Everybody in Chicago knows where it is."

That was an exaggeration, but Kate didn't argue. Sliding her hand protectively over her stomach, she whispered to the baby she'd been unable to accept until an hour ago. "Daniel Patrick Donovan," she said, "you and I have a restaurant to run!"

Walking straight and quickly, Kate pushed the heavy door open and walked into Donovan's; then she paused a moment and decided that Daniel Mitchell Donovan was the perfect name.

Chapter Forty-two

KATE PULLED HER CAR TO A STOP AT THE VALET PARKING sign ten minutes before Donovan's regular opening time, but none of Donovan's valet attendants were waiting under the awning as they normally were by 11:20 in the morning.

She'd had a dentist appointment, and now she wanted to see Danny before Molly put him to bed for a nap after his daily outing at the park.

He was twenty-two months old, full of energy and exuberance, and he loved the swings and slides and teeter-totter. Last Sunday, on a beautiful September afternoon, Kate had taken him to a larger park they visited on weekends and she'd gotten some wonderful photographs of him sailing his boat in the big fountain with sunlit trees in the background.

Twice that day, people had stopped to remark on how beautiful he was, which was a normal occurrence for any outing with Danny. He was the image of his father, with Mitchell's thick black hair and dark-lashed, cobalt eyes; he even had his slow smile and effortless charm. He was also showing signs of having inherited Mitchell's magnetism with females. With one of his quick, flashing grins, Danny could conquer the hearts of women—from old ladies to teenagers to an adorable two-year-old girl from the South whose name was Caperton Beirne.

The only genetic contribution from her that Kate

could see was that Danny's hair was slightly curly, although not as curly as hers.

He was tall for his age, surprisingly well-coordinated, and growing up so fast that, at times, Kate wished she could reach out and stop the clock from ticking away the minutes and days of his childhood. He was extremely bright, and—not surprisingly—he was also starting to pick up and repeat words and phrases from the several languages he heard being spoken by Donovan's culturally diverse employees. His most recently acquired phrase—a colorful Polish curse—had Kate thinking he needed to stay upstairs with Molly, in the apartment she'd expanded and renovated so she could keep him near her all the time. Although she could well afford a place of their own now, she'd decided to wait until he was old enough to start kindergarten. Then she would buy a place for them in the best school district around and cut back on her evening hours at the restaurant.

Wondering where the valet attendants were, Kate debated about driving around the corner and putting her car in the lot there, then she decided to risk getting a ticket by leaving it where it was until she could find a valet to move it. She was halfway across the sidewalk when she heard Hank at the corner newsstand shout, "Congratulations, Miss Donovan!"

Puzzled, Kate waved to him and kept walking.

She unlocked the heavy front door, walked inside, and saw—absolutely no one. The dining rooms were set up for lunch, everything looked perfect, except no one was there—not the maître d', not a single waiter or busboy or valet attendant. Puzzled and vaguely uneasy, Kate quickened her pace toward the kitchen, rushed through the swinging doors, and stopped short as a smiling army of loyal employees burst into cheers and applause. At the front of the crowd, Molly was holding Danny, and he was clapping and grinning.

Next to him was a big sign on a floor stand where the specials of the day were usually posted by the chefs for the benefit of the kitchen staff and waiters. Today it said, "Kate Donovan, Restaurateur of the Year."

Kate scooped Danny out of Molly's arms and looked around at the sea of smiling faces. "What's all this about?" she asked.

Frank O'Halloran grinned at Marjorie and then at the rest of the staff. "She hasn't seen it yet," he said, and everyone burst out laughing.

"Seen what?" Kate said.

Drew Garetti, the manager she'd replaced Louis Kellard with a little over two years before, held out the morning's edition of the *Chicago Tribune*. It was opened to a full-page article with a headline that read, KATE DONOVAN, CHICAGO'S RESTAURATEUR OF THE YEAR. According to the article, Kate had been chosen for the honor partly because of the overall excellence of the dining experience at Donovan's and partly because of a program she'd instituted whereby Donovan's chef and sous-chef exchanged places four times a year with their counterparts at equally famous restaurants throughout the country. This gave Donovan's customers a chance to enjoy the fare from other fabulous restaurants, as it did the customers of the other restaurants.

Included in the article were several pictures used in prior stories about Donovan's, including one of Kate with the governor of Illinois and one of Kate meeting with her kitchen staff, with Danny beside her in his high chair.

The caption below that one read, "Kate Donovan runs her restaurant while son Daniel looks on and learns the ropes from his high chair."

Kate scanned the article, then she looked around at her staff and told them exactly who she felt deserved the credit for her award. "I can't thank all of you enough for this," she said simply.

Drew glanced at his watch, then at everyone else. "We're opening in two minutes," he warned them, and patted Kate's shoulder as he walked out. "You're the best," he said.

Kate gave Danny a hug. "Did you hear that, Danny? Drew says we're the best."

In response, Danny planted a kiss on her cheek and said, "Molly and me go to the park, Mommy." Kate let him slide to the floor, and he took Molly's hand. He adored Molly, who'd come to work for Kate when Danny was born, and the middle-aged Irish woman positively doted on him.

"No flirting with Caperton," Kate teased, looking from the little boy to his devoted nanny.

"Billy Wyatt is waiting out in the reception room," Evan's secretary said as he stalked by her desk, carrying his briefcase and a folded newspaper. "He's been here since ten o'clock, and he insists on seeing you."

"Bring me a glass of water, send someone for a Dr Pepper, and then have him come in," Evan said curtly. In his office, he slapped the newspaper on his desk and unloaded the files that he'd worked on the night before from his briefcase.

His secretary arrived with a glass of chilled bottled water, and he sat down behind his desk; then he picked up the *Tribune* and reread the latest story about another of Kate's successes. She was like a splinter in his foot that he couldn't get completely out. Everyone knew they'd been engaged, and every time people started to forget, Kate reemerged as the star in another damned local newspaper or magazine article.

According to the article before this one, the state's attorney and the mayor were two of her regular customers. For weeks after that article appeared, Evan couldn't show his face in the courthouse or anywhere lawyers gathered without being ribbed for failing to recognize what a political advantage he'd sacrificed by not marrying her.

Today's article raved about her, as all the other stories had done, but today's article also included a nice big color photograph of Wyatt's little bastard and her in the kitchen at Donovan's. It was the second time he'd seen that picture, the second time he'd had to look at it. The little son of a bitch looked so much like his father that it was uncanny, and that infuriated him even more.

"Hi, Evan. Thanks for making time for me."

Tossing the paper down in disgust, Evan stood up and shook Billy's hand. At seventeen, Billy was a good-looking kid, a little stocky, as his father had been, but not as pleasant to be around.

The psychiatrists and the court had both agreed—with a little help from the excellent defense lawyers that Evan's law firm had selected—that his ADHD medication had caused Billy's psychotic break the day he shot his father. That didn't require a big stretch of imagination, since there'd been mounting evidence that the medication could cause psychotic episodes in some people. A year of confinement in a psychiatric hospital, plus ongoing therapy during his three-year probation period, had supposedly helped him resolve conflicts and learn impulse control.

"How's your new girlfriend?" Evan asked, trying to remember what Billy had said her name was during his last visit.

"Rebecca's fine."

"Where did you meet her?"

"In group therapy. You probably know her parents— the Crowells?"

Evan didn't know them, so he shook his head and ended the small talk. "What can I do for you?" Evan asked, but he already had a good idea why Billy was there. Cecil had died recently, and he'd left one-third of his estate to charity and one-third to Billy, which was to be held in trust until he was thirty, with the stipulation that he forfeited it if he was convicted of any felony in the meantime. The remaining one-third had been left to Mitchell Wyatt, who had already directed the executors to use his share to create the William Wyatt Foundation for Victims of Violence.

"I want to hire you to break my grandpa Cecil's will. Mitchell is going to start a fucking foundation with *my* money, and I want you to stop him before it's too late. My father is dead, my grandfather and great-grandfather are dead, and everything was supposed to be mine. If my dad hadn't brought Mitchell into the family, Grandpa wouldn't have given him my money, and I'd be rich. Instead, I'm supposed to wait around until I'm thirty to get a little bit of what I should have had, and I'm not going to do it. I get off probation in another year and a half, and I want my money, and I want my own life!"

"Billy, we've already had this conversation. As I told you, Cecil's will was drawn up by the best probate law firm in Chicago. I've looked it over, and there's no way you can get your money back from Mitchell. I know it's not fair, but you're going to have to learn to live with it—"

"You don't understand! I hate that son of a bitch. I hate him so much I can't stand it."

"Believe me, I know how you feel."

Billy looked contemptuous of that possibility, so Evan reached out and shoved the *Tribune* in front of him. "Do you see that picture? That was my girlfriend. Mitchell Wyatt got her pregnant. See that kid—that's his kid."

Billy studied the boy in the photograph, and then he said in a chilling voice, "So—this makes him what—my cousin?"

Chapter Forty-three

THE CLOSEST PARK TO DONOVAN'S TOOK UP AN ENTIRE city block, with paths through the trees leading to all four bordering streets. It was too far away for Danny to walk on his own, but he always insisted on trying anyway and ended up walking beside his stroller part of the way and riding in it the rest. "Look who I see," Molly told him as they neared the park. "There's our friend Reba, with a balloon. I wonder who it's for?"

"For me!" he said excitedly, clapping his hands in his stroller. He scrambled out of the stroller as soon as they reached the bench by the swings, and he ran to Reba, who was sitting there, reading a book. She'd told Molly two weeks ago, when she first started coming to the park, that she was eighteen and taking some time off before starting college.

"Hi, Danny," Reba said, and pretended she didn't know a red balloon was floating by a string from her hand.

"Mine?" Danny asked, pointing to the balloon. "Please?" he added with a lopsided grin that never failed to get an answering smile—and usually whatever he wanted, as well.

Smiling, Reba stood up, still holding the balloon, and gave Molly a wink. "Follow the balloon, Danny, and I'll show you a surprise."

"A turtle!" Danny predicted joyously, following her

toward one of the paths, with Molly holding his hand and pushing the empty stroller.

"Follow the balloon," Reba chanted over her shoulder as she started down the path.

"The balloon is the same color as your shirt," Molly told Danny. "What color is it?"

"Red!" Danny replied gleefully.

A thrashing sound in the brush on her left and slightly behind her made Molly turn to look, but all she saw was a baseball bat an instant before it crashed into her skull. She didn't see the bat being raised again for a second blow or hear Reba say fiercely, "No, don't, Billy! No one is supposed to get hurt!" She didn't hear Danny start to cry or call, "Molly, Molly!" She didn't feel a sheet of paper being shoved down the front of her dress.

In the park near the swings, two mothers looked up and saw a bright red balloon floating upward from the trees. They didn't think anything about it until fifteen minutes later, when a woman staggered from the path with blood streaming from her head.

A block away, on the opposite side of the park, an old man was sitting on a bench tossing peanuts to a squirrel. A young couple emerged from the park, pushing a dark green stroller with a child who was trying to climb out. The young mother laughed and pressed him back down. The old man on the bench didn't think anything about that until twenty minutes later, when police cars, with sirens screaming and light bars flashing, descended on the park from every direction.

On the fifth floor of the Richard J. Daley Center, Gray Elliott was in his office, eating lunch at his desk and writing an outline for a speech he was scheduled to give before the Illinois Anti-Crime Commission the following week. With a sandwich in one hand, he picked up his telephone with the other and answered a phone call from police captain Russell Harvey.

"Gray," the captain said, "I just got a phone call from a lieutenant downtown who knows that you and I have dinner at Donovan's once in a while. Kate Donovan's son was kidnapped from a park near the restaurant an hour ago. I thought you'd want to know."

Gray dropped his sandwich on the desk and stood up. "Who caught the case?"

"A couple of pretty good detectives. They're on their way to tell Kate right now."

"Can you assign MacNeil and Childress instead and put them in charge? They've been partners for a couple of years now, and from everything I hear, they've racked up one of the best arrest records in the department."

"I already did that. Are you going to go to the restaurant to see Kate? If not, I think I'll drop by there and assure her that she has our unconditional support."

"I'm on my way," Gray said, already shrugging into his suit jacket. "I'll give her your message."

Chapter Forty-four

"MISS DONOVAN, I'M DETECTIVE MACNEIL AND THIS IS Detective Childress."

Seated behind the desk that had been her father's, Kate took one look at the detectives' grave faces and an awakening terror, unlike anything she had ever known, sent her slowly to her feet. "Danny?" she said, automatically naming the most terrifying reason of all for their visit. "Where's Danny? What's happened? Where's Molly?"

"Danny was kidnapped from the park about an hour ago—"

"Oh, my God. No. Please!" she cried. "Not Danny. Please, not Danny!"

Across the hall, Marjorie bolted from her chair at the sound of Kate's anguished cry, and she bumped into Drew Garetti, who'd rushed down the hall from the other direction.

"Where's Molly?" Kate asked in tones of rising hysteria. "Is she with Danny? He won't be as scared if—"

"Mrs. Miles was knocked unconscious in the park by the kidnappers," Detective MacNeil said, "but she regained consciousness and managed to attract notice and get help. She was taken by ambulance to Parkston General with a suspected skull fracture. However, she was able to give us a pretty detailed description of a young woman who we think was part of the plot."

In her mind, Kate was screaming in tormented fear,

but all she could do was stand there with her knees knocking together and her body trembling so violently that she wrapped her arms around herself, trying to hold herself still. Detective MacNeil continued in a calm, reassuring voice. "We stand an excellent chance of getting Danny back safely, but we need to move very quickly now, and we need your help."

Kate nodded jerkily, her teeth chattering. "What?" she asked. "What do you need?"

"We're going to issue an amber alert right away. For that, we need a recent picture of Danny, a description of his clothing, his age, weight, and height."

Kate picked up a framed picture of Danny from her desk, started to hand it to Detective MacNeil, then pulled it back, clutching it to her heart and wrapping her arms around it. "My baby," she whispered brokenly. "My baby!"

"I'll get his pictures from upstairs," Marjorie volunteered, already on the way at a run.

"Please try to stay calm for the next few minutes so we can get the alert out," MacNeil said. "We need Danny's height and weight."

Kate made a valiant effort to do what he said and turned to her computer to locate Danny's pediatrician's phone number in her electronic address book. "Danny just went to the pediatrician's for his checkup," she babbled. "He'll know Danny's height and weight exactly."

"What was he wearing?" Detective Childress asked from behind her, his notebook and pencil poised.

Kate glanced over her shoulder. Childress was younger than MacNeil, Kate noted, and not quite as good at pretending everything was going to be fine. "Danny was w-wearing a red shirt and blue denim overalls. . . ." An image of Danny grinning at her in his red shirt and overalls just a little while ago broke down her fragile barrier of control, and she began weeping while she tried to find the pediatrician's number. "I can't—"

"I'll get it for you, Kate," Drew volunteered, squeezing past the detectives and coming around her desk. "What name am I looking for?"

When Kate told him, he found the phone number, made the call for her, and explained the situation to the receptionist who answered. Two minutes later, he hung up and gave the detectives the details.

MacNeil's cell phone rang, and Gray Elliott strode past the detectives while Childress was writing down the information Drew gave him.

"Kate, stay calm," Gray said, putting his arm around her shaking shoulders. "This is going to be okay. You've got the best detectives in Cook County in charge, and a task force is already being organized. Is there somewhere else we can go with more room?"

"Upstairs," Kate said, and led the way up the steps and into the spacious living room where Danny and Molly and she played or watched television whenever Kate could get up there during working hours.

MacNeil paused in the doorway, talking on his phone. When he hung up, he looked at Gray and said with what sounded like relief, "There's a ransom note. The paramedics found it stuffed down the front of Molly Miles's dress. The kidnappers said they'll make contact here at eight o'clock tonight with instructions for the drop."

Kate sank onto a sofa, letting the conversation swirl around her, dimly aware that word had spread downstairs and the doorway was filling up with worried faces.

"Excellent," Gray said.

"Excellent?" Kate repeated numbly, but hopefully, trying to understand.

"Kidnapping for ransom has a much better outcome than other types of child abduction," Gray told her, and looked back at MacNeil. "Anything significant about the ransom note?"

"Nothing that's apparent, but I'm sending a uniform out there to get it and rush it to forensics. All I know right now is that it's printed from a computer on white paper." He looked at Childress and said, "Go ahead and get the wheels in motion for an amber alert." To Marjorie, he said, "Please give the most recent photograph to Detective Childress."

Marjorie handed it over, rubbed her hands on the sides of her skirt, and whirled on her heel, heading for the apartment's kitchen. "I'll make some coffee for everyone."

"Good idea," Gray said, then he exchanged a speaking glance with MacNeil, who followed her and stopped her near the kitchen entrance.

Sitting on the sofa, Kate watched Marjorie nod in reply to whatever MacNeil said, then she asked him a question, and his answer made her cover her mouth as if she was stifling a cry. "What's wrong?" Kate cried, half rising from the sofa as Marjorie headed for Danny's bedroom.

Gray put his hand on her arm and drew her back down. "We need to get a sample of Danny's DNA from his hairbrush or toothbrush."

"Why?" Kate demanded, unable to think as clearly as Marjorie had.

"After the amber alert goes out, we'll start getting calls from all over the country that children matching Danny's description have turned up. We can avoid false alarms if we have Danny's DNA to send to the local authorities for a match."

In her heart, Kate knew there was some other reason, other than healthy children turning up and needing to be ruled out, for the police to want a sample of Danny's DNA, but her brain refused to follow that terrifying path. Gray's next words distracted her from all of that.

"The ransom demand is for ten million dollars, ready to be handed over at nine o'clock tonight."

Gaping at him in disbelief, Kate said, "Ten million dollars? But I don't have that kind of money. I could raise two million dollars if they'll give me a little time to arrange for loans and—"

"The kidnappers aren't going to give you that time."

Nausea welled up in Kate's throat, and she got up to make a dash for the bathroom.

Gray watched her walk back to the sofa a few minutes later, her face the color of chalk, her arms wrapped around her stomach again. In the middle of the room, she paused and looked around. "I keep expecting Danny to dash out of the kitchen or his bedroom," she whispered, looking at Gray, her green eyes swimming with tears. "I want my baby. I want to see him smile at me. You have to p-promise me you'll get him b-back. Please, promise me you will."

"Let's talk about the ransom money—"

"I don't have it!" she cried. "Weren't you listening to me? I can't raise ten million dollars. I'm not sure I can raise two million dollars, but I'll start trying." Suddenly she launched into feverish haste, heading for a telephone on the table beside the sofa. "I'll call our banker—"

"No, you won't," Gray said shortly. "You'll call Danny's father."

She wrinkled her forehead as if she didn't know what he was talking about.

"Are you certain Mitchell Wyatt is Danny's father?"

"Am I certain—" Her mouth dropped open, and she glared at him through her tears. "Of course I'm certain!"

"Then get him on the phone."

Kate felt as if her heart were breaking and her mind were splintering. "Do you think for one minute that if I knew how to reach him—and if he actually took my phone call—that he would believe me or come up with the money?"

"Do you have any other choices?"

"That's not a choice. That's not even a long shot."

"I repeat, do you have any other hope of raising the ransom money?"

Kate stared at him, frozen in a trance of stark terror, anguish, and helplessness. Slowly, the realization began to penetrate that she could take action now, and that any action—no matter how futile—was a way of doing something to help keep Danny safe. In the space of seconds, her realization became resolve, and she threw herself into desperate action. Crossing swiftly to the sofa, she picked up the phone, then she stopped and looked at Gray. "I have no idea how to reach him. Do you?"

"I have various addresses and phone numbers for him, but it could take hours to track him down. He has close friends here in Chicago—Matt Farrell and Meredith Bancroft. Matt Farrell heads Intercorp. He may be able to point us in the right direction."

Kate bit her lip as she dialed information for the phone number of Intercorp. Leaning forward, she jotted it on a pad, then she handed the phone to Gray. "I'll talk to him, but you'll need to get him to take my call first."

He nodded, dialed the number, and shot her a quizzical look.

"The last time I saw Mitchell," Kate explained in answer to his unspoken question, "Meredith was with him and she heard the things he accused me of being. When she walked away, she looked at me as if I'd just become invisible. Believe me, she told her husband all about it, and Matt Farrell won't want to give me the time of day."

"I'll get him to take your call. There's one more thing," he added after he asked Intercorp's operator to connect him to Matt Farrell's office. "Wyatt is going to want some form of proof that Danny is his before he forks over ten million dollars. I have Wyatt's DNA on record, and we'll have Danny's DNA in a few hours. If you will guarantee me that there is no way Danny is anyone else's child, I'll vouch for a DNA match now, on this phone call. If it turns out you're wrong, I'll retract my statement before Wyatt hands over the money and tell him there was a mistake."

"There's no mistake!"

He nodded, then spoke into the phone. "This is Gray Elliott," he told Matt Farrell's secretary. "Is Matt in? This is an emergency."

Kate unconsciously held her breath while the seconds ticked by, and she thought of Danny out there somewhere with strangers.

"Matt," Gray said suddenly into the phone. "I'm with Kate Donovan. Her little boy was kidnapped this morning. You'll hear an amber alert any minute now if you turn on a radio or television set. Kate needs to talk to you. Before she does that, I want you to know that the DNA evidence will back up what she's going to tell you. Here's Kate—" he finished.

Kate stood up as she took the phone from him. "Mr. Farrell," she said formally and firmly, "Mitchell Wyatt is Danny's father." Kate paused, waiting for some reaction, and when there was none, she forged ahead. "The kidnappers are demanding ten million dollars by nine o'clock tonight. I can't even come close to paying that much money." Again Kate paused, and again there was no reaction, so she drew an unsteady breath and said shakily, "Would you please ask Mitchell to call me? I'll give you my phone number. Tell him . . . tell him I'll sign over the restaurant to him in return, and I'll find some way to pay him back the rest." Tears constricted her throat, and Kate grasped the telephone harder. "Please, you have to find Mitchell and tell him. Danny isn't even two yet and he's out there somewhere with—" She broke off, swallowed, and got herself under control. "Tell Mitchell that Gray Elliott will show him proof that Danny's DNA matches the DNA in Mitchell's file at the state's attorney's office. Here's my phone number at the restaurant. Danny and I live in an apartment above it," Kate added quickly so that Matt Farrell wouldn't think she was working as usual while her son was missing.

Finally, the silent man on the other end of the phone spoke. "I will call him," he said, "and I'll give him your message."

"Thank you," Kate said weakly. She'd started to take the phone from her ear when he added, "I'm very sorry about your son."

That snapped Kate from pleading to ire. "Danny isn't just my son; he is also Mitchell's son."

"I'll remind Mitchell of that," he said to her surprise.

Chapter Forty-five

CLAIRE DILLARD FINISHED READING THE CONFIDEN-
tiality agreement that she was required to sign before she could work for Mitchell Wyatt, and added her
signature. She passed it across the desk to his personal assistant, who slid it into a folder containing the rest of the
employment documents Claire had been filling out since
reporting that morning to the Manhattan high-rise for her
first day of work. "What's next?" Claire asked.

"That's all there is," Sophie Putnam replied with a
warm smile, and closed the file. "You're now an official
member of the crew. Welcome aboard," she said as she
reached across her desk and held out her hand. Claire
shook it, returning her smile.

They were both in their late thirties and happily married, with pleasant, professional attitudes, dark hair,
and an obvious preference for well-tailored business
suits and trendy shoes. "I think we're going to get on
very well together," Sophie said, putting Claire's
thoughts into words. She settled back into her chair,
glanced at her watch, and nodded toward a closed door
on her right. "Mr. Wyatt's conference should be over
any minute now. In the meantime, do you have any
questions or concerns about being Mr. Wyatt's secretary
that I haven't addressed?"

"I do have one concern," Claire admitted half seriously. "How long does it take before you stop noticing
how incredibly handsome he is?"

Sophie laughed at her candor. "When you realize he does not play around with his employees, ever, you'll relax and forget his looks—in two or three years," she joked.

"Does he have a lot of girlfriends?"

Since Claire would be involved in facets of his personal life, such as arranging for theater tickets, making dinner reservations, and dealing with everything pertaining to his penthouse apartment on the Upper East Side, Sophie felt that question was well within reason. In a carefully noncommittal tone, she replied, "The lady du jour is Kira Dunhill."

Claire's eyes widened at the mention of the acclaimed Hollywood actress who was costarring on Broadway with Leigh Valente in a new play scheduled to open that night. "What's Kira Dunhill really like?"

"She's a little on the haughty side, but she's so gorgeous and so talented, who can blame her?"

"Was that a tactful way of saying she's a conceited snob?"

"Was I that obvious?"

"No," Claire said with a quick, emphatic shake of her head. "I made an educated guess, based on the fact that she's not only a movie star, but also from a wealthy, privileged background."

"She's only been up here twice," Sophie replied as she picked up Claire's folder and slipped it into her desk drawer. "The first time was a month and a half ago, right after they started going out, and when Mr. Wyatt introduced me to her, she barely bothered to give me a nod. The second time was last week, when she dropped by on the pretense of wanting to give him a book she'd bought for him, even though she knew he wasn't going to be in the office that day. She hung around for a half hour, chatting with me and pretending she wanted us to be best girlfriends."

"What did she really want?"

"Information about Mr. Wyatt—any little tidbits she could get about his friends, his business, his likes and dislikes, his background, his family, and the other women who've been involved with him. When she first started talking, she acted as if they're practically engaged, but based on the kind of questions she asked, I think Mr. Wyatt must be keeping their relationship on a very superficial level, at least at this point. I'm telling you this as a warning, because she may try the same thing on you as soon as she realizes you're his new secretary. Oh, one more thing before we change the subject. You asked whether he has a lot of girlfriends, and I gave you a flippant answer about Kira Dunhill being the 'lady du jour.' The actual answer to your question is that he works a lot harder than he plays."

"What, specifically, does Mr. Wyatt do?"

"I'm sorry," Sophie said, startled. "I automatically assumed you knew, since your former boss had several meetings with him recently."

"I was one of the few people who knew Mr. Kenworth wanted to sell the company, and I knew his meetings with Mr. Wyatt were related to that, but he was very secretive about the meetings themselves. They always took place after everyone had gone home, and although Mr. Kenworth had me stay until the meetings were over, the only thing I did was bring files into the conference room occasionally and arrange for their dinners. I have no specific idea what Mr. Kenworth wanted Mr. Wyatt to do for him. I only know I was thrilled—and amazed—when you phoned me last month to say that Mr. Wyatt's secretary was retiring and you invited me to apply for her job."

Sophie grinned. "Mr. Wyatt was more impressed with your professionalism and your 'people skills' than he was with your boss's managerial skills and personal habits."

"Mr. Kenworth tended to be abrupt with people, but he was always under a great deal of pressure from . . . various directions," Claire said.

Her diplomatic reply made Sophie's grin widen. "Yes, well, that's inevitable when a man has a new French wife who is barely out of her teens, two ex-wives who aren't getting their alimony checks on time, and a floundering corporation with an angry sales force that didn't get their commission checks on time. Evidently, Mr. Kenworth felt it was your job to run interference for him on the telephone with all those people. By the way, Mr. Wyatt was amused and impressed by your tactful forbearance with the tearful child-bride's telephone tantrum. He overheard the conversation when he was leaving."

Claire was horrified. "I lowered my voice almost to a whisper and spoke to her in French, to make certain he wouldn't know what was going on."

"Unfortunately, he has excellent hearing, and he's fluent in French. Evidently, so are you, which was another reason he decided to consider you for this job—Several of our clients are French, and many of our other European clients are more comfortable with French than English. That brings me back around to the original question you asked concerning what goes on here." Folding her arms on the desk, she said, "To put it as simply as possible, Mr. Wyatt arranges mergers and buyouts of privately owned companies for our client companies around the globe. Sometimes, our clients already have a specific company—a 'target company'—in mind that they want to acquire. In that case, Mr. Wyatt initiates the deal and negotiates it for our clients. Sometimes, our clients simply tell him what they want to achieve and they ask him to choose a target company. Unfortunately, not all of these target companies *want* to be acquired at first, and even when they decide it's a good idea, there's always a battle about the money involved. In return for successfully completing the deal, Mr. Wyatt charges an extremely large fee and also receives a block of shares in the company."

She paused a moment to let that sink in, and then she told Claire with quiet pride, "Your new boss is renowned in his field for his global contacts, his judgment, and his negotiating skills. I'm not exaggerating when I tell you that he's absolutely *brilliant* at what he does."

Very pleased with that information, Claire restrained the impulse to confess that she'd failed to question Mitchell Wyatt about the specifics of his work during her brief interview with him because she'd been frustratingly disconcerted by his handsome face and dark blue eyes. Rather than bring up an issue she was determined to somehow ignore in the future, Claire picked up a pen and pad of paper lying on Sophie's desk so that she could make notes. "How many clients does Mr. Wyatt have?"

"Actually, he only agreed to meet with your boss as a courtesy to a mutual acquaintance of theirs. He stopped taking on new clients a long time ago, but the clients he does represent have become very prosperous and very *acquisitive*—thanks to his expertise. I described what he does for his clients, but there are many instances where Mr. Wyatt discovers two or three good companies that aren't doing well, but that he thinks could thrive if they were merged and put under proper management."

"When that happens," Claire speculated, "I assume he contacts one of his clients and recommends that the client let him proceed with the buyout and merger on their behalf?"

"Sometimes he does that, but more often, Mr. Wyatt proceeds on his own. He buys up the companies, merges them, and creates a new management team out of the best members of the old teams. When the newly formed company shows a respectable profit, he sells it, but he continues to receive a share of the profits thereafter, as a condition of the sale."

"He never keeps the companies he creates, no matter how successful he thinks they're going to become?"

"No. He says that in order for a privately owned company to continue to thrive and grow, the owner needs to have a physical presence there, at least periodically."

"And he's not willing to do that?"

Sophie shook her head, remembering the night almost three years ago when she asked him about this issue. He'd just returned from his brother's funeral in Chicago and was preparing for a two A.M. teleconference with a Swiss client who was trying to buy a company that Mitchell had created by purchasing and merging three small, financially embattled French manufacturing companies. He'd shored them up with his own money, restructured them, and handpicked the new management team, several members of which he came to like especially well. When the newly formed company began reporting sizable profits in a very short time, he'd been particularly proud, and since he flew to France frequently, Sophie had asked him why he didn't keep the company for himself, instead of selling it to the Swiss client.

In a rare, unguarded moment undoubtedly caused by fatigue and the convoluted nightmare of his brother's murder, his brief smile and nonchalant tone failed to disguise an underlying emotion that darkened his eyes and hardened his jaw. *"I'm a nomad at heart,"* he said. The following week he accepted an offer from a wealthy tourist who'd seen his partially completed house in Anguilla and had been trying to buy it. *"I have apartments in four cities,"* he told Sophie when she expressed her amazement at his decision. *"I've decided that owning a house is a tether I don't want."*

Rather than revealing that very personal discussion, Sophie said simply and truthfully, "He likes to maintain as much flexibility as possible in his work and in his living style, so be prepared for sudden, last-minute changes in his plans." Deftly switching the conversation back to business, she continued, "I mentioned that when Mr. Wyatt sells a company he's created, he's contractually entitled to a share of the future profits made by that company. To make certain those profits are accurately calculated by the new owners of the companies, we employ two full-time auditors who travel from company to company, examining their books." To help Claire understand the necessity of that, Sophie said, "Occasionally, the new owners decide to try to reduce their profit figures—and therefore, reduce the amount they owe Mr. Wyatt—by disguising personal expenses as business expenses and using company money to pay for them."

"You mean personal expenses like a family vacation?"

Sophie laughed. "No, I mean personal expenses like a country estate near St. Petersburg and a Rolls-Royce!"

Claire started to smile, but a sudden eruption of infuriated, foreign voices from inside the conference room made her turn and glance uneasily in that direction.

"Don't worry, both those men are thousands of miles away," Sophie said with amused resignation. As she spoke, the men's voices suddenly dropped below hearing level, and she added, "Mr. Wyatt just turned the volume down on the speaker system."

"Oh, you mean they're having a conference call?" Claire said with evident relief.

"They're having a three-way teleconference," Sophie

clarified. To stop Claire from thinking that belligerence and shouting were a normal occurrence in the way Mr. Wyatt conducted business, Sophie added, "The voices you just heard belong to Stavros Konstantatos in Greece, and Alexi Radkov in Moscow, and the *only* reason Mr. Wyatt is involved in what's going on in there is because Stavros asked him to act as a . . . well . . . facilitator."

"Facilitator, or referee?" Claire asked wryly.

"You're very astute," Sophie said with a chuckle. "Alexi owns a large Russian trucking company, which he offered to sell Stavros. The two men agreed on the price and terms, and the preliminary documents were signed, but Alexi has started stalling, and Stavros is furious. Mr. Wyatt knew nothing about the deal until yesterday, but he's superb at making things work out for Stavros when Stavros's temper gets in the way of his reason. Stavros and Mr. Wyatt have been friends for a very long time," Sophie added.

Claire, who'd heard of the reclusive Greek tycoon, had jotted down his name on her pad, and in shorthand she wrote next to it, "bad temper—close friend of MW." She jotted down the Russian's name and a notation that he owned a trucking company.

Sophie waited until she finished writing; then she pushed back her chair and stood up. "While we're waiting for Mr. Wyatt to finish up in there, I'll show you around the office, although there isn't much you haven't seen already."

Claire got up and followed her out of her office and across the reception area, a large room furnished with a modernistic sofa upholstered in soft beige leather and two pairs of matching chairs, all of which faced the windows. Behind the sofa, against the back wall of the room, was a large chrome-and-glass desk with a phone and chair for the use of busy visitors. A thick beige carpet with occasional random swirls of dark honey covered most of the reception area's unpolished travertine marble floor, and a framed, impressionist landscape in shades of green hung on the wall above the desk. A few large ferns on travertine pedestals provided the only other decorative touches. The furnishings were sleek and expensive-looking, and the overall effect was intentionally minimalist, so that nothing competed with the dramatic view of Manhattan through the floor-to-ceiling windows.

"These are the auditors' offices," Sophie said, pausing at a pair of doors that opened off a short hallway just behind the desk in the reception room. "As I explained, John and Andrew are rarely here." Claire peeked inside both offices, each of which contained a wall of built-in file cabinets, a desk, and a pair of chairs that matched those in the reception area. From there, Sophie led her to the next, and last, door in the hallway. She swung it open to reveal a small but well-equipped kitchen with stainless steel appliances, a table, and four chairs. "Feel free to use this anytime you like," she said.

As they walked back through the reception area, Sophie glanced at her watch. "Mr. Wyatt was supposed to be done with that teleconference fifteen minutes ago. He'll be running out of patience any minute now," she predicted with cheerful certainty. "In the meantime, let's go into his office and see if there's anything on his desk that I can give you to get started on. I know he has a file full of work somewhere that he's saved to go over with you."

A wide squared-off archway with travertine columns separated the reception area from Sophie's and Claire's offices, which faced each other across a pathway leading to Mitchell Wyatt's office and the conference room. His office door was closed, but Sophie opened it and walked across the room to his desk. Claire had already seen his office when he interviewed her for the position two weeks before, and had been a little surprised that it wasn't fancier. The room itself was just large enough to be spacious, and it was furnished in the same understated, minimalist style as the reception area. His office, however, occupied the corner of the building, which gave him an uninterrupted, breathtaking view of Manhattan in two directions, and she surmised that, to him, the view was always paramount.

His desk was clear except for a large crystal "fist" on a short pedestal at one corner and a sheaf of papers lying in the middle of the desk. Sophie picked up the papers, leafed through them, and laid them back down; then she turned to the credenza behind it, where a laptop computer was open, its bright screen lit up with the same Outlook program that Claire had used for her boss's e-mails, business contacts, and calendar. Next to the computer was a wooden tray with more documents in it, which Sophie flipped through and then put back. "There's nothing here to give you," she said wryly. "Let's go back to my desk, and I'll tell you the names of the people who call him most frequently and I'll give you a little background, so you'll know who you're talking to when they call."

Claire nodded and followed her out, but halfway across his office, the cell phone lying on his desk began to ring. "Should I answer that for him?" Claire asked.

"No," Sophie said. "He handles calls that he receives on his cell phone." When Sophie closed the office door on the ringing phone, Claire said, "Does he prefer to keep his door closed at all times?"

"No. As a rule, I close it if he had it closed before, and I leave it open if it was open before." As she walked back into her office with Claire behind her, the telephone on her desk gave out a low, distinctive double ring. "That's Mr. Wyatt's private line. He answers it himself if he's in his office, but if he isn't, we always answer it," she explained as picked up the receiver and pressed a flashing white button at the end of a row.

"Mr. Wyatt's office," she said; then she listened a moment and replied in a friendly tone, "Yes, he's here, Mr. Farrell, but he's in the midst of a three-way teleconference. He should be finished very soon though, and—" The man on the phone evidently interrupted her, because she stopped talking, listened for a second, and then she said, "Yes, of course. I'll bring him a note right now." She put the call on hold, picked up her pen, and Claire watched her jot two sentences on a small pad that read, "Matt Farrell is on the phone—It's *urgent.* He needs to talk to you *now.*" She underlined the words "urgent" and "now" twice; then she straightened, and with an unperturbed smile, she gestured for Claire to follow her. "You might as well have a glimpse of the faces that belong to the shouting voices you heard earlier."

She swung open the conference room door, Claire took one step into the room—and halted in stunned awe. Unlike the restrained décor and moderate proportions of the other rooms, the vast conference room was paneled in dark wood, gorgeously furnished, and completely equipped with a dazzling array of state-of-the-art audiovisual and teleconferencing equipment. Stretching almost the entire length of the room was a conference table inlaid with parquet wood and surrounded by at least eighteen overstuffed chrome swivel chairs upholstered in butterscotch leather. At the top of the long wall to the right of the conference table was a row of identical clocks indicating the time in different cities, and below the clocks were four giant, built-in television screens. At the moment, two of the screens were dark, but each of the other two was lit up with the image of a different man. Both men had gray hair and angry faces, and they were both shouting, apparently in their two different languages, at the same time—or at least they looked as if they were shouting. The sound system in the conference room had been turned down to a pleasant level, so Claire wasn't certain if they were actually shouting, nor did she know whether the two belligerent men were addressing each other or Mitchell Wyatt. The draperies were drawn over the windows, and the spotlights in the ceiling were dimmed, giving the room a mellow glow, but providing ample light for Claire to see Mitchell Wyatt, who was seated at the center of the conference table, leaning back in his chair, looking at the screens and listening to the angry men with an expression of strained forbearance.

From the corner of his eye, Mitchell saw Sophie walking toward him, carrying a note, and he decided it was time to put an end to his ordeal. Reaching toward a panel of buttons and switches near his elbow, he flipped Stavros's audio connection off; then he angled his chair slightly so that the Russian would see that he'd turned his shoulder to Stavros and was speaking only to him. "I've turned off Stavros's audio connection, so that you and I can speak privately," Mitchell said in a companionable tone. "I've known Stavros for many years, and when he is this angry, he stops listening to explanations and begins concentrating on retaliation, Alexi. He is not going to let you change the terms of your agreement. However, if you want to back out of the agreement entirely, I'm quite certain I can persuade Stavros to let you do it—"

The Russian's face betrayed alarm, not relief, and his distress visibly intensified as Mitchell finished: "There are two other Russian trucking companies that he was thinking of buying when you contacted him and offered to sell him yours. I'll talk to him tomorrow after he's had a night's sleep, and point out the obvious merits of buying one or both of your competitors—"

"—And after he takes them over, he will lower his shipping prices until he's put me out of business," the Russian said furiously. "My business will be worthless then. I will end up with nothing!"

Since Stavros had a reputation for doing exactly that from time to time, Mitchell didn't reply. "If you've decided you want to keep your business, and that's why you want to back out of your agreement to sell it to him, he will understand and overlook that when he calms down. If, however, you've decided to sell it to someone else instead, then you will be making a powerful enemy."

"He should worry about making an enemy out of me!"

"He probably should," Mitchell agreed with some amusement, "but he won't. However, let us not end our own discussion with threats. You and Stavros can threaten each other later."

"Can you persuade him to pay me more?"

"No. Stavros never goes back on his word, and he never lets anyone else go back on theirs. I can't persuade him to let you change the terms of your agreement with him, but I think I can persuade him to let you void your agreement entirely."

"But—"

"Sleep on it," Mitchell interrupted politely. Reaching for the console, he flipped a switch to break the satellite connection with the Russian, and the left-hand screen went blank. He flipped another switch and Stavros's voice became audible. "We're alone," Mitchell said, diverting his gaze to the words Sophie had written on the note.

Stavros's voice exploded in furious, heavily accented English, "Did you tell that whoreson what I said—did you tell him that if he tries to break our agreement, I'll have his genitals hacked off and served to his mother on a saucer?"

"A saucer?" Mitchell repeated with amusement, returning his attention to the screen. "Based on his behavior so far, you're going to need a platter."

"He's found another buyer for his company—"

"No, he hasn't, but that's what he wants you to think. He's simply trying to raise his price. If you stop threatening him and instead break off all communications with him for a couple days, he'll come around. He's a minnow who knows he's being pursued by a shark, but instead of frightening him, it's increasing his sense of self-importance. He wants to sell and you made him a very fair offer. Swim away and he'll realize he's just a minnow," Mitchell finished as he shoved back his chair. Curious, but not alarmed by Matt's message, Mitchell told Stavros why he wanted to end their discussion now: "Sophie just gave me a note that Matt Farrell's on the phone and needs to talk to me."

"Ah, yes, I see her there near the doorway. Good morning, Sophia," Stavros said courteously.

"Good morning, Mr. Konstantatos," she replied.

"Mitchell," Stavros added as Mitchell reached out to terminate the connection, "give Matt my warmest regards."

"I will," Mitchell said. With Sophie's note in his hand, he strode out of the conference room and into his office via a private door between the two.

Sophie used the outer door of the conference room and led Claire back into her office, where they sat down at Sophie's desk. "As soon as he's off the phone with Matt Farrell, he'll want to see you," Sophie said. "The way things have gone this morning, he has probably forgotten that today's your first day here." As she spoke, she glanced at the glowing light on her phone that indicated that he was still talking to Matt Farrell; then she smiled apologetically at Claire and said,

"While we're waiting for him to finish his call, let's get started on your 'who's who' list."

Claire nodded, picked up the pen and paper she had used earlier, and jotted down names and facts as Sophie mentioned them. "Earlier, I said that Mr. Wyatt frequently buys up companies on his own, merges them, and then sells them. However, he doesn't always act alone. Depending upon the amount of money and the risk involved, he occasionally partners up with Stavros Konstantatos, Matt Farrell, or Zack Benedict."

Claire lost control of the pen in her hand and looked up in surprise. "Zack Benedict—_the_ Zack Benedict? The movie star Zack Benedict?"

"That's the one," Sophie said lightly. "Matt Farrell and Zack Benedict are Mr. Wyatt's close friends as well as occasional business partners. Whenever they call, he is always available, which is why I interrupted him when Matt Farrell asked me to." Claire was understandably dazzled by the Zack Benedict connection, and Sophie added mischievously, "Mr. Wyatt is having dinner tonight with Zack Benedict and his wife, Julie, after they all attend Kira Dunhill's opening night." She waited a moment for Claire to write down the names, and she added, "Stavros's son, Alex, is also a close friend of Mr. Wyatt's, and he calls here occasionally. Oh—and you'll hear the name 'Calli' mentioned very soon. Calli is Mr. Wyatt's driver, but he's also a childhood friend of his. His real name is Giovanni Callioroso, and he's more 'family' than 'employee.' He is also a bit of a flirt at times, but it doesn't mean anything. Oh—and he understands English perfectly—so don't let him fool you. The first week I worked here, he deliberately put me through all sorts of antics while I tried to help him understand what I was saying—as a joke. Mr. Wyatt has an elderly aunt, Olivia Hebert," Sophie continued, glancing again at the light on the telephone, which was still lit up. "He always takes her calls no matter how busy he is." She gave Claire a few more names and decided that was enough boring detail to heap on a new employee.

"What about Mr. Wyatt's likes and dislikes?" Claire prompted. "Is there anything I should avoid doing because it makes him angry?"

"You have nothing to worry about," Sophie assured her. "He will expect your best, and in return, he will treat you with respect. Furthermore, he won't forget your birthday or patronize you or send you out to buy gifts for his girlfriends. He is one of the most even-tempered men alive. He doesn't even curse. Oh, good—" she added, glancing at her telephone again, "he just hung up. Come with me and we'll let him welcome you properly."

Barely able to say good-bye to Matt, Mitchell slammed the phone into its cradle. "Son of a bitch!" he said savagely. "SON OF A BITCH!" Picking up the Steuben crystal fist that Stavros had commissioned as a gift for him, Mitchell squeezed it in his hand hard enough to pulverize it, had it been made of mere stone. He was so furious that his mind refused to grasp everything he'd just been told, and he had to keep repeating it to himself. . . . *Kate Donovan had a son who'd been kidnapped, and Gray Elliott had DNA proof that Mitchell was the little boy's father . . . Mitchell was the father of Kate Donovan's son, and she'd never had the decency to let him know he had a child . . . She'd intended to raise his son exactly as Mitchell himself had been raised—without any knowledge of his biological father . . . Kidnappers had grabbed Mitchell's son that morning in a public park and were holding him for ransom!*

As that last piece of knowledge fully sank in, his

seething anger escalated to rage, and he hurled the Steuben fist across the room with all the force of his fury behind it, at exactly the same moment Sophie swung the door open and started into his office with Claire. Claire ducked and stifled a scream, but Sophie froze in astonishment as the ten-pound crystal missile streaked past her, struck the wall, crashed onto the slate floor, and exploded in a loud blast of shattering glass.

Claire hastily retreated several steps into the safety of Sophie's adjoining office, but after a moment of horrified paralysis, Sophie got her expression under control and started forward toward his desk. Outwardly composed, she began picking her way gingerly across the crystalline fallout strewn over the stone floor, but she was inwardly shaken by his inexplicable display of violent wrath and helplessly unnerved by the sound of glass crunching beneath her feet. She was dying to ask what had caused him to make this mess, but his forbidding expression made her fear that any pointed reference to the situation might easily cause another eruption of temper from him. Trying to be calm, tactful, and helpful, Sophie inquired cautiously, "Is something wrong, Mr. Wyatt?"

"Do I look like something is *right*?" he retorted as he surged to his feet, yanked his briefcase off the credenza behind him, and began shoving papers from the top of his desk into it.

Embarrassed by her idiotic choice of words, Sophie refrained from comment and instead bent down to pick up a dismembered crystal thumb lying at the edge of the thick wool carpet that his desk sat on.

Intending to rattle off a list of instructions, Mitchell glanced in her direction, saw what she was doing, and paused just long enough to say with curt courtesy, "Don't touch that, you'll cut yourself. Call maintenance later and have them clean up the glass. I'm leaving for Chicago," he continued, switching swiftly to the matters at hand. "Call Calli and tell him to pick me up downstairs, and then call my pilots and tell them to have the plane fueled up and ready to taxi as soon as I get to the hangar. Next, call Pearson and Levinson's office in Chicago and tell them to have Bill Pearson or Dave Levinson phone me within twenty minutes, no matter where they are or what they're doing."

He paused for a breath, and Sophie interjected quickly, "Your plane's having maintenance work done. It can't fly until tomorrow at the earliest."

"Then get me two tickets on the next flight to Chicago."

"If I can't get first class, is coach all right?"

"Get whatever you can; just get me on the next flight," Mitchell said shortly. "If that isn't possible, try to charter a plane. When you've handled all that, call my housekeeper and tell her to pack suitcases for Calli and me, and then make sure they're put on a plane to Chicago later today. Have a courier pick them up at the airport and deliver them to us."

"Do you want to stay at—"

Mitchell yanked open the bottom drawer of his desk to pull out more files, and interrupted her in mid-question, but he managed to temper his tone. "First, take care of the phone calls I just asked you to make, and then call me in the car with any other questions you need answered."

As she nodded and hurried away, he put the remaining files into his briefcase; then he opened the center desk drawer and pulled out the slim folding case containing his PDA, his passport, and the other items he automatically took with him on trips. He tossed that case on top of the files, slammed the briefcase closed, and turned to the computer on the credenza behind

him. With his right hand, he typed in the name of the
president of The Bank of New York; with his left, he
reached for the telephone.

The president's secretary answered his private line
and explained that he was in a board meeting, but she
agreed to interrupt him when Mitchell advised her that
it was "a matter of extreme urgency."

Sophie was at her desk on her telephone, and Claire
was at her elbow, when Mitchell strode through Sophie's office and paused there for an update. Sophie understood what he wanted and put her palm over the
phone's mouthpiece. "Our travel agent is checking
flights and availability while I wait," she explained
quickly. "Pearson and Levinson are both in court and
can't be reached by phone, but Pearson's secretary is
having a message delivered to him in the courtroom.
There are flights leaving for Chicago from LaGuardia,
Newark, and JFK today, but the nonstop flights will get
you to O'Hare the earliest. Calli is bringing the car
around—"

She broke off as the travel agent came back on the line,
and since Mitchell already had the information he
needed, he turned on his heel and started to leave. Sophie,
however, had an additional worrisome matter to mention
to him before he left, and since she needed to listen to the
travel agent and make decisions, she shoved a desk calendar toward Claire, tapped her finger imperatively on
Mitchell's schedule for that evening, and then nodded urgently toward Mitchell's departing back.

Her meaning was clear, and Claire rose bravely to the
task. Relying on Sophie's explanation that Mr. Wyatt's
behavior in his office was an aberration, and that Sophie's earlier, glowing description of him was completely accurate in every detail, Claire picked up the
desk calendar and raised her voice. "Mr. Wyatt—" she
called after him.

Halfway across the room, he turned in surprise at the sound of her voice, his expression impatient but nonviolent, so Claire forged ahead. Reading from Sophie's notes, she said in a quick, professional voice. "According to your calendar, at eight-thirty tonight, you're supposed to be at the theater for the opening night of *Three Days of Rain*. Afterward, you're supposed to have dinner with Kira Dunhill, Leigh and Michael Valente, and Zack and Julie Benedict."

"Call everyone and tell them an emergency has come up and I can't be there," he said as he turned and headed away.

"Mr. Wyatt?"

He glanced over his shoulder at her, but kept walking, and in an effort to fulfill her professional responsibilities to the fullest extent of her considerable capabilities, Claire hurried after him so that she could warn him of a detail he might be overlooking and would later regret. "This is Miss Dunhill's first opening night on Broadway, and you're not going to be in the audience. There's a note here that Sophie's already ordered flowers sent to Miss Dunhill's dressing room. Since you're going to be absent tonight, do you think you should try to make up for that by—"

"Yes," he interrupted, catching her meaning. "Send her a lot of extra flowers," he instructed without slowing his pace.

"Extra flowers? For missing her opening night?" Claire said, rushing along in his wake as he crossed the reception area. "Are you certain she'll feel that flowers are atonement enough for being stood up by you at the last minute?"

"No, that probably calls for a jewelry," he conceded. "Pick out something and have it delivered to her at the theater before she goes on stage." Without slowing down, he shoved the main office door open, and headed down the hallway. Stunned and a little flattered that he'd evidently decided to entrust her with a task that—according to Sophie—he'd never entrusted to any employee before, Claire halted in her tracks, and then she realized that in order to accomplish that task, she needed to ask him a vitally important, and rather delicate, question. She raced to the door and saw that he was already so far down the hall that she couldn't possibly catch up with him. Left with no other way to find out what she desperately needed to know, Claire raised her voice enough to cover the lengthening distance, and called out, "How much should I spend on her gift, Mr. Wyatt?"

The polished marble floors and marble-trimmed walls acted as an echo chamber, amplifying her voice to the level of a loud, demanding shout that reverberated up and down the hall exactly as if she'd yelled through a megaphone at him while standing in a canyon. Claire winced in dismay, but he seemed not to hear her at all. Instead, he turned into an intersecting hallway that led to the elevators, and disappeared.

Chapter Forty-six

WITH HIS CELL PHONE PRESSED TO HIS EAR AND HIS AT-
tention on the information Sophie was giving
him, Mitchell stepped into the street and jerked the car
door open while Calli was still maneuvering it toward
the curb. "We've got to get to LaGuardia fast," he told
Calli as he slid into the backseat.

"It's going to be tight," Calli replied. "Traffic is
heavy, and if there's a long line at airport security, we're
in trouble."

"Then make sure we're there in time to get through
security," Mitchell said sharply—but not completely
unreasonably. Behind a steering wheel, Calli possessed
the superb reflexes and daring courage of a test pilot,
and—when necessary—the aggressive stealth of an as-
sassin. At that moment, he was already barging at an
angle across four lanes of traffic, aiming for the front of
the line of vehicles waiting at the corner to make a left
turn. Satisfied that Calli would do whatever needed to
be done, Mitchell resumed his conversation with Sophie. "How long is the flight?"

"Two and a half hours. It lands at O'Hare at three-
thirty, Chicago time." When Mitchell didn't comment
on that, she moved efficiently to the next unresolved
issue. "Do you want me to have a car and driver waiting for you when you land?"

"No. Matt Farrell is sending his chauffeur to get us.

You'll need to call him and give him our flight information."

"I'll take care of it. What about hotel accommodations—do you want to stay at your usual hotel?"

"No. Ask Matt Farrell to recommend a hotel that's close to Kate Donovan's restaurant, and get me reservations at whatever hotel he suggests. I'll call you later to find out where it is," he added; then he ended the call and frowned at his watch, waiting impatiently for his attorneys to phone him. He was still frowning when Calli's amused inquiry made him lift his head. "Who is Kate Donovan?" he demanded impertinently, "and why are you busting your ass to get to her restaurant? What is she—a goddess? Or just one *hell* of a cook?"

Normally, anyone who tried to pry too deeply into Mitchell's personal life ended up with a severe case of frostbite—not information. Giovanni Callioroso was one of the few who could pry with relative impunity. Two years older than Mitchell and half a foot shorter, Calli was the youngest of the five Callioroso children Mitchell had believed were his actual brothers and sisters until he was suddenly sent away from them to his first boarding school. Until then, Calli had been Mitchell's hero and his self-appointed protector, the "big brother" who let Mitchell tag along with him everywhere while threatening the older boys with dire physical retribution should they dare give Mitchell any trouble. Unfortunately for Calli, who loved to fight, most of the local children in that picturesque little village in northern Italy were almost as placid as their families. That pretty much eliminated the need for Calli to fight on Mitchell's behalf, as did the fact that by the time Mitchell was three and a half, he was nearly as tall as Calli and becoming almost as cocky. As a result, on Mitchell's fourth birthday, Calli announced his decision to "promote" Mitchell from the rank of "little kid" to the lofty rank of "sparring partner." It was a promotion of which Mitchell was extraordinarily proud, and he applied himself diligently to learning every martial arts move that Calli taught him—most of which Calli was either inventing or learning himself.

When Mitchell left for boarding school, his focus switched to sports and studies, but Calli pursued his own goal with single-minded dedication, eventually fighting his way around the globe, winning championship after championship, moving up the ranks until he was universally regarded as a world-class martial arts contender. He chased women and squandered his winnings with the same success and determination until he took a particularly bad battering during a fight that he nearly lost and decided it was time for him to do something else. He had very little money saved, and no job skills that weren't physical, so he contacted Mitchell and suggested that Mitchell hire him as a driver-bodyguard. At Calli's request, Mitchell sent him for a special training course where sophisticated evasive maneuvers were taught to drivers of high-profile people who were subject to attack on the road or kidnapping. Calli emerged as one of the finest drivers ever taught at the school. Mitchell had Calli's lifelong loyalty; he would have walked in front of a truck for him, Mitchell knew.

For those reasons, Mitchell met Calli's gaze in the rearview mirror and forced himself to state aloud that which he could barely accept himself. "Kate Donovan's little boy was kidnapped this morning."

"Oh, Jesus—" Calli said, sounding sickened and outraged. He had inherited his family's love of children, and although he had none of his own, he carried photographs of all his nieces and nephews and frequently sent them gifts. "How old is he?"

Mitchell paused, calculating the total number of months

that had passed since he'd seen Kate Donovan in St. Maarten, subtracting from that a full nine-month pregnancy. "Twenty-two months."

"I've never heard you mention the mother's name before, so I guess she's an old friend of yours—from before I started working for you?"

"She's no friend of mine."

The scathing distaste in Mitchell's voice registered on Calli, and he glanced in surprise in the rearview mirror again. "Then, I guess the boy's father is a friend of yours?"

"*I'm* the boy's father," Mitchell said, his tone terse with submerged emotions he was struggling to suppress so that he could focus on what needed to be done.

"What!" In his shock, Calli hit the brake; then he slammed down on the accelerator to recover lost speed and glared accusingly over his shoulder at Mitchell. "You've got a son you've never bothered to tell me about—not me, not Mama, or Papa, either?"

"I didn't know he existed until a half hour ago, when Matt Farrell phoned to tell me he'd been kidnapped."

"Do you mean Farrell has known all along that you have a son, but he didn't tell you until this morning?" Calli said, his outrage expressed by his contemptuous use of Matt Farrell's last name alone.

"No one knew anything about the boy until this morning, when his mother phoned Matt and gave him the facts," Mitchell said, staring fixedly out the side window, his patience at the breaking point as the moments ticked by without a phone call from either of the attorneys. "Right now, all I know is that he's being held for a ten-million-dollar ransom—"

In a well-meaning but transparent effort to soothe Mitchell, Calli said, "Maybe she's lying about you being the father because she needs someone rich to give her the money, so she can get her boy back."

"She's not lying about it."

"How can you be so sure?"

"When the Chicago police were investigating my brother's death, I gave them a sample of my DNA. This morning, the state's attorney assured Matt Farrell that he can provide DNA proof that I'm the father."

As he spoke, he stared at the silent cell phone, his jaw clenched with impatience, and abruptly decided he'd waited long enough for his attorneys to return his call. He snapped the phone open just as the screen lit up with an incoming call, and David Levinson's name appeared.

"Mitchell, what's going on?" Levinson asked, managing to sound concerned, rushed, conciliating, and thoroughly competent—all at the same time. "Bill and I are in the middle of arguing an important motion in front of an judge with a bad cold and a surly temper. I managed to wangle a five-minute recess out of him after my secretary had a note brought in to me saying that you have some sort emergency, but—"

"You're going to need a postponement, not a recess," Mitchell interrupted curtly, and then he told him exactly what the emergency was.

Levinson listened in appalled silence to the scanty bits of information Mitchell was able to provide about his unknown son and the kidnapping itself. "That's all you know?" he uttered.

"Yes, and that's all I'm going to know until I hear back from you," Mitchell reminded him pointedly. "However, keeping me informed isn't your first priority. This is—" Mitchell said, and he then outlined the financial arrangements that he'd already put into play during his conversation with his New York banker, James Philson. "Philson is coordinating everything with the Chicago banks," he finished, "but I need you to stay in touch with Philson while I'm on the plane.

He's going to tell you what banks are providing the cash and where to meet the couriers who'll be carrying the money. Find out where Donovan's restaurant is and pick somewhere very close by to make the exchange. The place will undoubtedly be crawling with cops, so your safety shouldn't be a worry, but try not to attract any attention during the exchange or when you arrive at the restaurant."

"Don't worry about that." Levinson expelled his breath in a nervous rush, but he sounded resolute even while he questioned Mitchell's methods. "Why don't you let the couriers deliver the money to the restaurant? Or better yet, why not let the banks send it all in an armored truck?"

Mitchell forced the explanation out. "Last year, in Rome, kidnappers saw their ransom money arrive in an armored truck, and they decided there was no need to keep the victim alive any longer."

After a moment of silence, Levinson said, "Do you want anyone at the restaurant to know you're on your way?"

"No, I want you to get information, not give it out. I don't want to be greeted with rehearsed answers and explanations from the cops or anyone else."

Mitchell hung up after that, but his conversation with Levinson, particularly the last part of it, had brought a sharp, agonizing reality to a situation that had seemed only a painful nightmare before.

Calli had heard the entire conversation and he began firing questions at Mitchell in a transparent effort to prevent him from dwelling on the deadly outcome of that Rome kidnapping. "When I meet my new nephew, what should I call him?"

"What?"

"What's your son's name?"

Mitchell's thoughts were in such upheaval that he

couldn't remember if Matt Farrell had mentioned his son's name during their phone call that morning, and even when he tried to recall the conversation, he could remember only the beginning of it with any clarity because Matt hadn't yet dropped his "bomb." *"Kate Donovan has a little boy who was kidnapped this morning in a city park . . . his nanny was left unconscious . . . police have issued an amber alert . . . kidnappers are demanding a ten-million-dollar ransom, or else they're going to kill him. They're going to phone with instructions at eight o'clock tonight. Kate called me a few minutes ago, Gray Elliott was with her . . . I talked to him.* And then, the bomb dropped: *He's your son, Mitchell."*

Matt had said more after that, but Mitchell's brain and his emotions had been going into overload, and although he'd listened, he couldn't remember now what he'd heard.

"I don't know his name," Mitchell replied to Calli's question. "I don't think Matt Farrell told me what it is."

"What about his mother—how did you meet her?" Calli persisted. "Where was it? Obviously, you two hit it off. What's she like?"

"We barely knew each other," Mitchell said in a cold, sharp tone that warned Calli *not* to question him further on that subject. "She's just someone I met when I was down in the islands. We had a meaningless fling for a day or two, and then my brother's body was discovered. I flew back to Chicago and forgot about the whole encounter."

That last sentence wasn't entirely accurate, Mitchell knew. The embarrassing truth was that he'd missed her terribly, from the time she'd left him standing on the dock in St. Maarten until the night he ran into her at a fund-raiser and discovered what a shallow, manipulative fraud she was. In the brief interval between, he endured all the humbling doubts and the regrets, the painful longing and bewilderment, of a man who has lost something he desperately wanted and had arrogantly believed was already his.

Intellectually, he accepted that when Kate chose to leave St. Maarten with her boyfriend, instead of meeting Mitchell at the dock, she had simply been making what she believed was the right choice for her. He understood that, and yet his besotted brain couldn't understand why she hadn't realized that *he* was the right choice.

He knew the only sensible way to deal with the situation was to put it behind him, and that the only way to put it behind him was to stop thinking about her. Forgetting her was the only solution, and yet he persistently subjected himself to the sweet torture of remembering. He, who was extremely adept at compartmentalizing troublesome emotions and barricading truly painful ones, could not—no, would not—put Kate Donovan out of his conscious awareness, where he knew she needed to be.

Kate had chosen to be with her boyfriend instead of Mitchell. He'd lost her to another man, and it hurt like hell. He laid awake at night, trying to figure out why he'd lost her, thinking of ways he might have prevented it. He did that, even after he realized he was acting like a heartbroken, jilted lover—a cliché he'd never imagined could apply to him.

All that came to an abrupt end the night he discovered that she was Evan Bartlett's fiancée and he watched her saunter up to him with that coy smile on her face. She was a total fake, and he had fallen for her. At the villa in Anguilla, he'd wanted her so badly after less than three hours that he'd let her wheedle information about William out of him, and then he'd gallantly offered to wait until the next day because of "delicate" sensibilities about sleeping with him in her boyfriend's suite.

But worse than that—much, much worse—was the fact that the next day at the hotel in St. Maarten, he'd actually let her con him into admitting that he felt "magic" with her. And worst of all—he'd believed it when he said it.

In two short days, Kate Donovan had managed to discover a weakness in him that he'd never suspected existed—an eager, naïve, sentimental gullibility that filled him with self-disgust whenever he thought of his time with her. Shame and self-disgust were the only emotions he still felt in connection with her, and so he chose to avoid any thought of her or mention of her name. Once he realized what she really was, she became easy to get over and eminently forgettable—but what he couldn't forget or get over was the fact that he had been a malleable dupe in her hands.

In the almost three years since that night, he'd been to Chicago several times, but he'd heard her name mentioned only twice: the day after the fund-raiser, Matt had casually inquired about the confrontation between Kate and Mitchell, and Mitchell had told him brusquely that the subject of Kate Donovan was closed. Forever.

A couple of months after that, Mitchell had flown back to Chicago to see his ailing grandfather, and during that trip, his aunt Olivia insisted he accompany her to dinner at Glenmoor Country Club, where the Wyatts were founding members—and where she could hold court in the dining room while simultaneously showing Mitchell off. As Mitchell had already discovered, Olivia Hebert was much more than a font of social gossip; she was universally regarded as the undisputed authority on all things pertaining to the ancestry, connections, and activities of five generations of Chicago's true "aristocracy." In truth, she was a human encyclopedia of minutiae that encompassed five generations of her social peers, from long-dead ancestors to modern-day teenagers. As a widow without a husband or children of her own to fill her life or occupy her active mind, she'd obviously invested herself in the lives of everyone she knew, but what amazed Mitchell was how apparently accurately she was able to chronicle everything she knew. No matter how long ago something had occurred, she could remember the dates, people, and conversations involved—and with so much accuracy and detail that when Mitchell was with her, people who knew her frequently stopped to ask her a question or verify a fact. Others stopped by to impart or receive tidbits of gossip, and she was happy to participate in either transaction, but woe to anyone who attempted to tell her anything she knew to be slightly inaccurate. Among Chicago's socialites, Olivia was the equivalent of a Hedda Hopper or Liz Smith, but unlike those women, who specialized in "insider" gossip, Olivia Hebert disdained rumor or exaggeration. As much as she loved gossip, she prided herself on accuracy.

Often, she attempted to share her knowledge with Mitchell, who always concealed his detached boredom behind an amused grin, but when she brought up Kate Donovan during their dinner at Glenmoor—and also attempted to extract information *from* him—his reaction was anything but amused and bored. She broached that particular topic after dinner, while finishing her dessert of crème brûlée, but she did it with such feigned nonchalance that Mitchell instantly realized she somehow suspected she was treading on dangerous territory with him. Looking at her lap, she reached for her napkin and daintily dabbed at her lips as she said with false innocence, "The last time you were here, I introduced you to Kate Donovan—Evan Bartlett's fiancée—during the Children's Hospital benefit. Do you remember her, dear?"

Instead of nodding, Mitchell leaned back in his chair and stared silently at her.

"Well, they aren't engaged anymore," she said, meeting his narrowed gaze, then hastily dabbing with her napkin again. "The engagement was called off a few weeks later. According to gossip, Evan and Henry both decided she wasn't really fit to be a Bartlett, and Evan tossed her over. He's been going out with several other women, but he's also said some very ungentlemanly things about Kate. I couldn't help noticing a bit of a strained atmosphere the night of the Children's Hospital benefit when I introduced you to Kate—rather as if you and she already knew each other, and had some sort of falling out. Is that right?"

Instead of replying, Mitchell signaled to the waiter for their check.

Her face fell. "I was hoping to enjoy a glass of sherry with you the way we always do when we dine together. Is dinner over?"

"Is this conversation permanently over?" Mitchell countered as the waiter promptly arrived at their table.

She gazed at him in wary understanding, nodded meekly, folded her hands on the table, and looked down at them; then she drew a shaky breath and blinked rapidly. Aware that she was crushed, Mitchell asked the waiter for two glasses of sherry instead of the check, but that wasn't enough to assuage the guilt he now felt for having hammered his point home about Kate Donovan with absurd—and needless—force on an elderly aunt who normally beamed with pleasure whenever she was with him.

As he contemplated his aunt's bent head and the wide, black velvet ribbon that held her thick white hair in a neat bun, he considered the best way to neutralize the situation. Despite her advanced years, his aunt was astute, curious, and a hopeless romantic. Because she was those things, Mitchell realized that his extremely negative reaction a few minutes ago might cause her to imagine that he harbored some sort of secret, unrequited feelings for Kate Donovan. Since he couldn't and wouldn't go into that subject with his aunt, Mitchell covered her hand with his own and asked her to dance.

She had never mentioned Kate to him again, nor had anyone else, and in the ensuing months, he forgave himself for his blind infatuation with Kate because he realized it was probably the timing of his encounter with her that had caused his total lapse in reason and judgment, rather than a streak of idiocy and sloppy sentimentality that he'd originally blamed. After all, a few short months before his trip to Anguilla, William had traced him to England and turned all of Mitchell's concepts about himself and his life inside out. William had begun by presenting Mitchell with the facts about his birth, and then he'd presented Mitchell with a ready-made family, including an elderly great-aunt who tugged at Mitchell's heartstrings and an aging, autocratic grandfather who awakened all sorts of conflicting reactions in Mitchell. Within a matter of weeks—and somewhat against his will—Mitchell found himself thinking of William's beautiful, gentle wife, Caroline, as "my sister-in-law" and young Billy as "my nephew." And then there was William . . . if Mitchell had ever been asked to describe his vision of an ideal brother, and a magnificent man, he would have described William without knowing him. Long before Mitchell allowed himself to regard any of the others as his relatives, William was already "my brother" in his thoughts. And then William disappeared. As quickly and suddenly as he'd strolled into Mitchell's life, he was wrenched from it.

In view of all the upheaval Mitchell had experienced in his life shortly before meeting Kate, it was logical—and excusable—that his guard had been down and his judgment severely diminished when they met. The truth was, he never thought of her except on those extremely rare occasions when someone, or something, reminded him of her. When that happened, she flickered briefly across his mind like a pale light from a feeble candle, and then she simply . . . went out.

That situation had been the comfortable norm for almost three years, but Matt Farrell's phone call had changed all that. It had changed everything except one thing: Just as in the long-ago past with Kate, Mitchell now found himself, once again, in the position of being her uninformed dupe. Only this time his son was an innocent pawn in her heartless game.

Chapter Forty-seven

KATE PACED SLOWLY BACK AND FORTH ACROSS THE LIVing room, watching the clock on the wall tick off the seconds of each tormenting minute that passed without a return call from Mitchell. Nearly three hours had elapsed since she'd spoken to Matt Farrell, and there hadn't been a word from the heartless man she had once thought she loved.

Her uncle James had rushed over right after Marjorie had called him, and now, seated on one of the sofas, the priest waited helplessly for the phone to ring. His head was bent, his hands clasped loosely in front of him. He was praying Mitchell would call.

Gray Elliott was sitting on a stool at the island counter that divided the kitchen area from the living room. He was Danny's new best friend, intent on doing everything to ensure his safe return. If the darkening scowl on Gray's face was any indication, he was fantasizing about yanking Mitchell from wherever he was, charging him with a gross lack of humanity, and throwing him in jail for life.

MacNeil was standing at the window overlooking the street in front of the restaurant, where police cars with flashing lights were jammed together at crazy angles. The sidewalk was packed with reporters, concerned citizens, and curiosity seekers, who were hoping for firsthand information. Kate wasn't sure what MacNeil was thinking, but he kept glancing at his cell phone as if willing it to ring. He was probably hoping for a tip, Kate thought, a lead that would send all those police cars racing away with sirens wailing to rescue Danny.

Holly had left Maui in the middle of a veterinarians' conference and was on her way back to Chicago. A task force had been set up in the main dining room downstairs, and calls resulting from the amber alert were starting to come in on the newly installed phone lines. Kate had ordered the restaurant closed within minutes of learning Danny was gone, but most of the staff were still down there, keeping a silent vigil for the little blue-eyed boy with the bright grin who had long ago captured their hearts.

Childress was somewhere on the premises, Kate knew, and she supposed he was downstairs working with the task force.

MacNeil's cell phone gave out a sharp chirp, and he snapped it to his ear so swiftly that the motion was blurred. A moment later, he turned around and looked from Kate to Gray. "Two lawyers are downstairs— David Levinson and William Pearson. They represent Mitchell Wyatt."

Gray Elliott had straightened sharply at the sound of the lawyers' names. "Tell the officers at the front door to let them in and bring them up here," he replied. "Hopefully they aren't here to threaten Kate with a lawsuit for claiming Wyatt is Danny's father."

David Levinson announced the actual reason for their appearance as he strode swiftly into the living room, carrying a black suitcase identical to the one in Pearson's hand.

"Mr. Wyatt has instructed us to deliver ten million dollars in cash and to remain here awaiting further developments."

Kate's arms dropped to her sides and she stared at them, overwhelmed with shock and relief, her eyes flooding with tears. If Mitchell had been there, she would have fallen to her knees in front of him and wept with inexpressible gratitude. Instead, she turned away and covered her face with her hands, weeping help-lessly, alternately thanking Mitchell and God over and over again.

"I'll have you at Donovan's restaurant in a few more minutes," Joe O'Hara promised as he hammered on the limousine's horn, ran a red light, and turned down a side street packed with rush-hour traffic.

Too tense to reply, Mitchell glanced at his watch. It was already five P.M. As soon as his flight landed at O'Hare, he'd phoned Levinson, who was waiting at the restaurant with Pearson, the ransom money with them. Levinson had no new information to report about the kidnapping. All he could add was that he'd seen the ac-tual DNA report confirming that Mitchell was the fa-ther of Kate's little boy, and that Mitchell's son's name was Daniel—Daniel *Donovan*, not Daniel Wyatt, a fact that further antagonized Mitchell.

He added that issue to the others he intended to hand over to his attorneys in the morning, when his son was safely home. Not once, not even for a second, did Mitchell allow himself to consider any other outcome of the kidnapping. That would have given fear an opening, and that he could not, dared not, allow.

Beyond that, all he'd learned from Levinson was that Kate had apparently been raising Daniel on her own. Until Levinson said that, Mitchell had been braced for the unpardonable likelihood that she was married and had been raising Mitchell's son as if he were another man's child!

Mitchell looked again at his watch, and then he reached toward the lighted panel of buttons on the car's ceiling and began tuning the radio from one station to the next, hoping to find a local station that was broadcasting information about the kidnapping. He found what he'd been searching for, but the announcer's words sent a chill crawling up his spine:

"This morning, the twenty-two-month-old son of restaurateur Kate Donovan was kidnapped from Danbury Park after his nanny, Molly Miles, was struck in the head and left unconscious. The police department has issued an amber alert."

Mitchell's frayed control began unraveling. The limo was in the left-hand lane, inching along at a crawl toward a red light. "I can walk faster than this," he said, reaching for the door handle. "Tell me where the restaurant is."

"Stay put," O'Hara urged as the red light turned into a green arrow and their lane began surging forward. "It's a mile away and there's a break in traffic up ahead." As he spoke, he handed a slip of paper over his shoulder to Calli, who was sitting directly behind him, facing Mitchell. "This is the phone number in the car," he told Mitchell. "I'll wait for you as close to Donovan's as I can get, but if you don't see me when you come out, call me at this number. I'll be nearby."

"Don't bother to wait," Mitchell said, his attention on the traffic, which was moving more steadily now. "I'll take a cab to the hotel when I'm finished."

"Matt gave me strict orders to wait for you," O'Hara said emphatically, "and he also told your secretary to have your suitcases delivered to him at home. Matt and Meredith are expecting you to stay with them, no matter how late it is when you get there tonight. They're your friends, Mitchell, and you gotta let them be with you at a time like this. Don't bother trying to shut them out, because they're not going to let you do it."

"Fine," Mitchell replied absently, scanning the streets ahead. "Where in the hell is this restaurant?" he demanded after what seemed like at least a mile.

"It's just around the next corner, a block and a half up the street."

Mitchell reached for his briefcase on the floor as O'Hara flipped on the turn signal, made a left, and then swore under his breath at what he saw ahead. "It's a zoo," he said lamely.

In grim silence, Mitchell took in the chaotic scene—a barricaded intersection with cops redirecting vehicles away from it, and beyond the barricades, a street packed with police cars, television vans, and crowds of pedestrians who couldn't find standing room on the sidewalk.

And in the middle of it all, was the canopied entrance to an elegant restaurant that took up most of a city block, and that Kate had once described as "a little Irish pub."

Mitchell flung the car door open and got out with Calli close behind, vigilant, watchful. "There's a television camera aiming at you from the top of that white van," Calli said as they skirted around the barricade and began wending their way around the mass of vehicles and humanity. "Maybe they're just curious because we got out of a limo."

"Reporters have long memories," Mitchell said flatly. During the media uproar surrounding Billy's trial, Mitchell had acted as the Wyatt family spokesman, and he knew there was little chance of getting all the way to the front door without being identified and having microphones shoved in his face. "Ignore them and keep walking." He turned sideways in order to squeeze between the bumpers of two police cars, and added, "No more English when you're inside the restaurant. I want to know what's going on, and people will talk more freely in front of someone they think can't understand what they say."

From his post at a front window in Kate Donovan's apartment above the restaurant, Detective MacNeil watched a very tall man and a shorter man get out of a limousine together. Both men looked lean and athletically built, both had dark hair, and both were wearing suits, but the taller one was carrying a briefcase, and he moved with the long strides and squared shoulders of a man who was supremely confident of himself. MacNeil didn't need to see his face; he identified Mitchell Wyatt by his height, his walk, the width and set of his broad shoulders, and his casual indifference to the crowds on the sidewalk and the reporters and photographers rushing toward him.

In contrast with Wyatt's aloofness, the man with him was sharply alert and subtly aggressive in his movements. Had he been carrying a briefcase, it would have looked out of place. He looked as if he ought to be carrying something else . . . like a handgun? Which meant he was probably . . . a bodyguard?

MacNeil watched both men a moment longer; then he looked over his shoulder and announced his conclusion to Gray Elliott, who was sitting on a stool at the kitchen counter staring grimly into space with the apartment's cordless telephone an inch from his fingers. Father Donovan was sitting next to him, his elbows on the counter and his forehead resting on his clasped hands in a posture of exhausted prayer. Kate Donovan had gone into her son's bedroom a while ago to wait there until it was time for the ransom call, and since MacNeil had no idea if Wyatt's arrival was going to be regarded as a good event or a bad one, he kept his voice low so that only the two men would hear him. "Wyatt is here," he said.

Father Donovan lifted his head and said fervently, "Thank God! Make sure he gets up here right away."

Gray looked sharply at Father Donovan. "It might be better if you went downstairs and persuaded him to wait there with his attorneys. If he wants a more active role, we could ask him to help answer the hotlines."

"He wouldn't settle for that, nor should he be asked to do so. Based on what Kate told me long ago about his prior behavior, I didn't think that man was capable of doing 'the right thing,' but today he's done it twice, and he's done it magnificently. First he arranged for the ransom money immediately, and without protest. Now he's come here to wait with Kate for news of their son, which is exactly the right and proper thing for him to have done."

"I wholeheartedly agree, but—" Gray began; then he paused long enough to look at MacNeil and say, "Call down to the uniforms at the front door and tell them to get Wyatt through the crowd as quickly as possible and without calling unnecessary attention to him. If the media recognize him, his arrival tonight will start an uproar of conjecture, and I don't want anything distracting public attention from Danny's kidnapping."

MacNeil nodded, and Gray turned back to Father Donovan to explain his concerns about Wyatt's arrival. "I agree that he's acted admirably today—more than admirably, in fact—but Kate is in an emotionally charged, treacherous situation right now, and when Wyatt gets up here, he's probably going to be feeling—" the phrase *royally pissed off* lodged itself in Gray's mind, and he stared at the priest, completely unable to think of an adequate substitute, so he uttered the first lame one that occurred to him. "He's no saint."

"Believe me when I tell you this—" Father Donovan replied somewhat grimly, "I am not under the slightest delusion that there's anything remotely 'saintly' about

Mitchell Wyatt. However," he finished in a more normal tone, "that doesn't change the fact that he has a legal, moral, and ethical right—and responsibility—to be up here with us, and to be granted all the consideration he's due as Danny's father."

Chapter Forty-eight

*T*WO COPS WERE STATIONED UNDER THE DARK GREEN awning at the front door, and another one was standing on the sidewalk near the curb, apparently waiting for Mitchell, who by then was completely under siege from a battalion of reporters who had recognized him and were trying to get a statement. The cop at the curb shouldered his way through them to Mitchell. "Come with me, Mr. Wyatt, and don't talk to anyone," he said; then he turned and began plowing a path toward the front door.

Mitchell followed in his wake, his expression carefully neutral, while cameras tracked his progress and a barrage of shouted questions assailed him from every angle. . . .

"Mr. Wyatt, why are you here?"

"Is your nephew Billy involved in this?"

Another reporter scored a direct hit: "Are you Danny's father?"

Mitchell ground his teeth against the urge to say, "*Yes!*" He'd grown up wondering who his own father was and overhearing adults speculating about his origins behind his back. Because of Kate, his son was in the same humiliating position now, and the entire city of Chicago was doing the speculating. The only thing that kept him from telling the reporters that he was Danny's father was fear that it might somehow put his son in more jeopardy.

One of the cops guarding the entrance reached for the ornate brass handle on the heavy wooden door and shoved it open just enough for Mitchell, Calli, and the cop escorting them to squeeze past. It closed behind them, shutting out the uproar outside. In comparison to that, the interior of the large restaurant seemed almost tomblike, but it was far from deserted.

Two long rows of tables had been set up on the far left of the main dining room, and at least two dozen people were seated there, answering ringing phones that were obviously newly installed, their cords strung haphazardly across the floor. A few restaurant employees were keeping coffee cups filled and passing out sandwiches to the task force on the telephones, while other employees looked on in watchful silence, clearly hoping for some indication that one of the people on the phones was getting a good tip.

Pearson and Levinson were sitting at a nearby table with two black suitcases between them, openly eavesdropping on the people manning the telephones.

"Come this way," the cop told Mitchell, and both attorneys looked around sharply to check out the new arrival. Mitchell nodded at them but continued following the cop, who seemed to be leading him toward a pair of large doors at the rear of the restaurant that opened into a kitchen, where more employees were gathered. At the kitchen, the cop turned to the right, however, and headed down a long paneled hallway lined with offices. At the end of the hallway, a staircase led up to a landing with an open door. The cop gestured toward it, stopped, and stepped aside for Mitchell to pass. "The apartment is up there," he said.

Mitchell glanced at Calli, told him in Italian to stay downstairs, and continued walking. The back hallway with its staircase leading up to an apartment were the only identifiable characteristics that this restaurant shared with the one Kate had invented and used as a backdrop for her charming stories about her childhood escapades, Mitchell realized.

However, he had no difficulty recognizing the first two men he saw when he strode into the spacious apartment's comfortable living room. The same detectives who'd questioned Mitchell when he was a suspect in William's death and who'd photographed him in the islands with Kate were standing in the kitchen area now, watching him. Gray Elliott walked forward, held out his hand, and said with a grim smile, "I'm sorry we're once again meeting under very difficult circumstances—"

Mitchell ignored his outstretched hand along with his implied sympathy. "Have you heard anything?"

When he said that he hadn't, Mitchell turned around expecting to see Kate somewhere in the living room, and instead found his view blocked by a stocky man with sandy hair, green eyes, and a Roman collar. "I'm Kate's uncle, James Donovan," the priest said, holding out his hand and studying Mitchell's face. "You're Mitchell, of course."

"Of course," Mitchell agreed sardonically. He shook the priest's hand and then he terminated the social niceties. "Where is she?" he asked bluntly.

Unfazed by Mitchell's rudeness and lack of respect, the priest turned and gestured toward a hallway at the far end of the living room. "Danny's bedroom is the first door on the right," he said calmly. "Kate is in there."

The last thing Mitchell had expected to feel when he walked into Danny's room and saw Kate Donovan was a surge of pity, but pity was exactly what he felt. She was sitting in a rocking chair next to Danny's bed with her eyes closed and her head tipped back, clutching a big gray flop-eared rabbit to her chest. One bare foot was curled beneath her, the other foot on the floor, gently pushing the rocker back and forth. Other stuffed animals, all of them in seemingly perfect condition, were neatly lined up on the floor behind her, but the faded, scruffy rabbit in her arms looked as if it had been dragged behind a car . . . or dragged behind a little boy who'd taken it everywhere with him.

The bedroom itself had been designed to delight a child and inspire his imagination, Mitchell noticed as he looked around. Bright jungle murals covered the walls, with whimsical animals and colorful birds peeking out from tall grass and frolicking in the branches of lush trees that stretched up to and partway across the ceiling.

On the wall to his right, two rows of long shelves were mounted within child's reach and filled with toy trucks. On the wall to his left was a small bed with a mock picket fence for a headboard, with carved parrots, macaws, canaries, and parakeets roosting atop the white slats—all of them fast asleep.

Trying to adjust to the reality of being in a bedroom that belonged to a two-year-old son he'd never known existed, Mitchell gazed at the woman who'd conceived his son during an unforgettable night of lovemaking. Clad in jeans and a yellow turtleneck sweater, with her red hair loose around her shoulders and her russet eyelashes lying like curly fans on her unnaturally pale cheeks, she looked painfully forlorn, totally defenseless, and very young . . .

But then, Kate Donovan's looks had always been deceptive, Mitchell reminded himself. The proof of her true nature, of her boundless arrogance and audacity, was all around him in the form of a bedroom that belonged to a son he didn't know, and who did not know him; a son she'd intended to deprive of all contact with his father—just the way Mitchell had been raised. Those thoughts demolished Mitchell's pity and toughened his tone as he announced his presence with two curt words: "Hello, Kate."

Her entire body lurched in shock, her eyes snapped open, and she stared at him in utter disbelief; then she gave him a trembling smile and gazed at him with unabashed warmth, her wide emerald eyes shimmering with tears of gratitude and suppressed anguish. "Thank you," she whispered.

For one of the few times in his adult life, Mitchell's ability to remain coolly objective and logical deserted him, and he stared at her in distracted uncertainty. With her wounded green eyes lifted to his and her curly red hair lying like a mantle around her shoulders, Kate Donovan reminded him of a heartbroken Irish Madonna who was bravely trying to smile through her tears. . . .

The same "Madonna," Mitchell reminded himself cynically, who'd entertained herself in St. Maarten by taking him for a mental and physical roller-coaster ride, and then left him standing on a dock waiting for her like an idiotic, lovesick schoolboy while she flew back to Chicago with Evan Bartlett.

Abruptly, Mitchell disengaged himself emotionally from her and from their past history, and focused solely on the present situation. "What are you thanking me for?" he asked shortly.

Until that moment, Kate had been content to remain in the rocking chair, letting what she thought was a dream unfold in front of her, but Mitchell's curt tone hit her like a warning slap, jarring her into the reality of his presence and doing so with nerve-wracking suddenness.

Still clutching the rabbit, she stood up in order to more properly convey her respect and gratitude, and she answered his question by saying with earnest formality, "Thank you for lending me the ransom money. I've already given your lawyers an IOU and asked them to draw up a formal loan agreement. I told them I'll put my restaurant up as collateral and pay you back over a twenty-year period—"

She broke off when she realized that the undeniably lenient repayment terms she was suggesting were making him so furious that his eyes were turning to shards of ice and a muscle was beginning to tic in his jaw. It hit her then that he could still change his mind about lending her the money, and she decided the sooner he left, the better, so long as he left his $10 million behind. "I'll pay you back in fifteen years, maybe even less than that, and naturally I'll pay you interest, too," she added frantically. "I'm solvent and my restaurant is thriving; I'll agree to whatever terms you want. Just tell your lawyers what terms you want, and I'll sign the loan papers." In a last desperate effort to keep matters cordial and to show him gratitude and consideration while simultaneously persuading him to leave, Kate said carefully, "There was no reason for you to come here personally—although," she lied, "I'm very glad you did. However, there's no reason for you to stay. You can't do anything more than you already have—"

Incensed because she had the gall to stand there and treat him as if his kidnapped son's welfare were none of his business, and that he had no right to be present or involved in anything except "loaning" the ransom money to her, Mitchell gave her a brief, frigid warning. "Don't thank me and don't dismiss me. You and I are going to have a very long, very unpleasant, meeting with attorneys present, just as soon as the boy is safely back here."

"Don't call him *'the boy'*," Kate retorted fiercely. "His—"

"Why not?" Mitchell snapped. "You've made damned sure I couldn't call him my son. Until today, I didn't even know he existed."

"I took you off my birth-announcement list when you called me an amoral bitch the last time we saw each other!" Kate flung back with blazing sarcasm. "Furthermore, you *divorced* the last woman who wanted to have your child—" Her brief spurt of fortifying fury dissolved in the realization that while she was standing there arguing, Danny was in the hands of brutal strangers. She glared at Mitchell through a haze of hot tears. "*Go away!*" she whispered fiercely, and turned her back on him. "Get out of here and leave me alone!"

Stunned by her indignant attempt to justify an inexcusable, grievous injustice with two feeble excuses for it, Mitchell watched her collapse into the rocking chair and double over, face buried in the rabbit, her shoulders jerking violently. "My baby is gone," she sobbed. "He's gone. Oh, God, he's gone . . ."

Despite his desire to be completely impervious and to see her only as a shallow, manipulative liar, he found himself standing there, trying to remember the two conversations she'd brought up. In the years since then, he'd eradicated her so successfully and so completely from his consciousness that he had to concentrate in order to recall what he'd said.

Their confrontation at the charity fund-raiser came back to him with surprising clarity, but his only reaction now to the way he'd spoken to her there was the same one he'd had moments after he walked away from her: disgust at his unprecedented loss of control over his temper and at the fact that Kate Donovan had gotten under his skin enough to cause him to do that. The words he'd said to her were the ugly truth, and the fact that she'd denied Mitchell his right to know that he had a son was further proof of it, rather than justification for her action.

However, the realization that he'd also told Kate that he'd insisted on a divorce when his wife wanted to have a baby was difficult for him to overlook. It made it a little less easy to thoroughly despise her for her arrogant treachery, as he'd done since Matt's phone call. That, combined with the sound of her agonized weeping, was making it impossible for him to continue thinking of her as completely heartless and unprincipled, and it also made it very difficult for him to continue regarding himself as a thoroughly righteous victim of her duplicity. And so he turned his back on her and walked out of the room, exactly as she'd wanted him to do.

He could still hear her shattered weeping as he walked down the hall, but unlike Kate, Mitchell refused to consider the possibility that his son would come to any harm or that he wouldn't be safely returned tonight, when the ransom was paid. Not once, since that morning, had the thought that he might never see his son alive slipped past his barriers. The possibility was there, though, sinister and hideous—an evil specter crouching in the darkness at the edges of his mind. Despite all his money, power, and influential contacts, he couldn't do one thing to help ensure the safety or the return of a little boy. His own son.

His jaw clenched with the effort it took to drive out the insidious thoughts and to shake free of the terrible dread trying to wrap its tentacles around his mind. He wasn't helpless. He had money and power, and knew how to use them. He also had a plan; a simple, effective plan. Last but not least, he was an expert at persuading people to go along with his way of thinking, particularly greedy, desperate businessmen, who were the easiest kind of adversaries he dealt with. Kidnappers were greedy and desperate. And so, when the kidnappers made their ransom call, Mitchell was going to calmly take that call, and instead of agreeing to pay their $10 million ransom, he was going to offer them a much better deal: $20 million. One half would be paid at the first drop-off site they named; the second half would be taken to a second drop-off site of their choosing and handed over *simultaneously* while someone verified to him that his son was in sight and alive.

With his thoughts on that, Mitchell walked back into the living room, noticed that the priest was openly scrutinizing him, and decided he'd be better off waiting downstairs until the time for the ransom call approached. "I'm going to wait downstairs," he advised the priest as he started in the direction of the apartment's door.

"That would be a mistake."

Surprise made Mitchell pause and turn toward him. "Why?"

"Because despite whatever Kate said to you just now, you're Danny's father. As his father, you have a right—and a responsibility—to be here and support his mother in this terrible time."

Mitchell hesitated, walked over to a chair, and sat down.

"While it's on my mind," the priest added, "how is it that a man and woman who only knew each other three days could end up being so agonizingly disappointed in each other that neither of them can get over it even now, after three years?"

"I have no idea," Mitchell said shortly.

"I have a very clear idea," the priest said implacably, but he didn't offer an explanation, and Mitchell didn't ask for one.

Chapter Forty-nine

FROM HIS VANTAGE POINT IN A CHAIR FACING THE doorway, Mitchell contemplated the apartment Kate had talked about in Anguilla. It was nothing like the small, dark space he'd envisioned, but it was evident that the whole dwelling had recently undergone expansion and renovation. Everything was fresh and bright, including the woodwork and mullioned windows that marched along three sides of the apartment and were partially concealed by airy draperies that were pulled back at the sides and held in place with ties.

The floor plan was a large rectangle that occupied one entire end of the building from front to back. A modern kitchen with the latest appliances and granite countertops was separated from the living space by a large island counter with four stools. The living room was spacious enough for a pair of leather sofas, which faced each other across a coffee table and were positioned at right angles to the big easy chair in which Mitchell was sitting. Beyond the living space was a large play area with a table and chairs at a child's height, a chalkboard, and what Mitchell assumed were long toy boxes disguised as window seats. A hallway that was parallel to the stairs led from the play area to what Mitchell knew were bedrooms.

Mitchell picked up a copy of *Gourmet* magazine from the end table beside his chair and leafed through it, partly to avoid giving the priest an opportunity to bring up scriptures, morality, and other topics of interest to the clergy, and partly to stop himself from looking at the kitchen and trying to imagine an old wooden table there with a seven-year-old girl draped across it, as she pretended it was a piano.

The room lapsed into silence, and Mitchell struggled against a sudden impulse to get up and go over to the play space to look at his son's things. A minute later, all that changed. MacNeil came trotting up the staircase, looking tense but excited.

He went directly to Gray Elliott for a whispered conference, then nodded and hurried out of the apartment. Elliott got up and walked over to Mitchell, and to Mitchell's initial surprise, he directed his remarks to him rather than Kate's uncle. "I think we have very good news. The parents of a young woman who is in group counseling with Billy Wyatt saw the amber alert tonight. Their daughter has been in their guesthouse today babysitting a little boy as a favor to a friend. They went to have a closer look at the little boy, and they're sure it's Danny. We have cars on the way there right now, and we'll know for certain if it's him in ten minutes or less. Until we do, I don't think we should risk raising Kate's hopes. She's very fragile right now. We have two hours before we're supposed to receive the ransom call. I'd like to sit tight for a few minutes with no unusual activity in here. If we're wrong about Billy's involvement, then for all we know the real kidnappers are watching us now through the windows from another building."

Father Donovan nodded, but Elliott waited for Mitchell's response. Mitchell hesitated, hating to subject Kate to ten more minutes of the agony he'd witnessed in Danny's bedroom, but in the end, he deferred to Gray Elliott. "That's probably the best plan," he said. The moment Gray Elliott had mentioned the connection between Billy Wyatt and the emotionally troubled babysitter in the guesthouse, Mitchell knew in his gut that the little boy with her was Danny, and his relief that Danny was probably safe was so immense, so overwhelming, that he could ignore for now the fact that his maniacal nephew was likely the kidnapper. Later, he would deal with that, but right now, he wanted nothing to intrude on his forthcoming meeting with his son. Then, because he couldn't resist the temptation anymore, he walked over to Danny's play area.

He studied the scribbles on the chalkboard and concluded that his son was probably not an artistic prodigy. Since no one seemed to be paying any attention to Mitchell, he leaned over and opened one of the window seats. It contained an assortment of toy trucks and cars. From that, Mitchell concluded that Danny's future might be in the transportation industry. He didn't realize he was hoping his son might share his love of airplanes until he looked inside the second box: there were at least half a dozen toy planes.

Mitchell straightened and looked at his watch, wondering why it was taking so long to get confirmation that the boy in the guesthouse was Danny. Fifteen minutes later there was a commotion on the stairs, and Elliott got off his stool, striding swiftly to the door. "Why in the hell didn't you call us?" he said, but underneath the reprimand he sounded excited, and Mitchell automatically tensed.

When Elliott walked back into the room, he was carrying a little boy and grinning from ear to ear. Kate's uncle walked a few steps toward the bedroom hallway and called, "Kate, come out here right away. There's someone who wants to see you."

Elliott lowered the child to the floor as Kate rounded the corner from the hallway. People began crowding into the room from the stairwell, and the scene ex-

ploded with joy and motion. "Danny?" Kate cried, and
the child laughed out loud at the same time his mother
burst into tears and dropped to her knees in front of
him. "Danny!" she whispered, running her hands over
his face and chest, then dragging him into a crushing
embrace, weeping while she chanted his name like a
prayer. "Danny, Danny, *Danny.*"

It was an exhibition of maternal love beyond anything Mitchell had ever imagined. It imprinted itself on
his mind and touched something deeper as he came to
terms with the reality that the weeping, joyous mother
who was holding her son in a fierce embrace was the
same woman he had held in an even fiercer embrace in
bed in St. Maarten.

She swept her son up and carried him to the doorway
to show him to the crowd gathered there, and it
dawned on Mitchell that the people in the doorway
were mostly dressed in white, like kitchen staff, or in
black suits, like waiters.

"Kate?" Father Donovan whispered. "I'm going to
leave now. I'll handle the press downstairs and make a
public statement on your behalf, thanking everyone for
their prayers."

"I should do that myself," Kate said, clutching
Danny more tightly, and stepping forward. "While I'm
doing it, will you call Holly and leave a message on her
cell phone that Danny is back? I want her to know he's
okay as soon as her plane lands. And I need to phone
Molly at the hospital right away, too."

"I'll take care of all the phone calls, and I'll tell the reporters that you'll make a personal statement outside in
a little while," her uncle said firmly. "Right now,
Mitchell has a right to some private time with Danny
and you."

Kate stared at him blankly and slowly emerged from
her mindless euphoria. "I forgot," she said aloud, her

voice filled with disbelief that she could actually have forgotten Mitchell was there. Or that he'd dispatched lawyers with $10 million to pay Danny's ransom within two hours of her phone call to Matt Farrell. Or that she'd told him to get out of Danny's bedroom.

Filled with shame, she searched the faces in the doorway and stairwell, looking for a hard, unsmiling face, but he wasn't there. She turned around with Danny in her arms and saw Mitchell standing motionless at the far end of the room, his hands thrust in his pockets, watching for a clearer glimpse of Danny . . . waiting there to meet his son. Danny's safe return was unquestionably the happiest moment in Kate's life. Oddly, this moment felt very much like the second-happiest one. She'd never allowed herself to hope that she'd ever see Mitchell again or that he'd want anything to do with Danny, but he was here, and he did.

With her mind on Mitchell, Kate thanked everyone in the stairwell for their prayers and waited while her uncle followed them out. Gray Elliott and Detective MacNeil were the last to leave. Gray reached out to ruffle Danny's curls, and grinned when Danny intercepted the gesture and gave him a "high five" instead. He continued smiling at Danny as he chose his words carefully and addressed Kate and Mitchell in a deceptively lighthearted tone. "Danny spent the day with Rebecca Crowell, watching cartoons and having fun in the guesthouse on the Crowell estate. She made popcorn for Danny and they had lots of strawberry ice cream after dinner tonight. Rebecca is Billy Wyatt's girlfriend and he convinced her that Danny was his biological offspring, so she agreed to help him this morning. Rebecca is a very softhearted girl, whose emotional problems have nothing to do with violence—just the opposite, in fact."

Instead of cloaking his next topic in innuendo, he

transferred his gaze directly to Kate, but he kept his tone mild. "I'll keep police officers at all the entrances downstairs tonight, but as soon as you reopen for business, this place will become a security nightmare. You're either going to have to keep the restaurant closed so we can protect him until Billy Wyatt is apprehended, or else you're going to have to stay somewhere else, ideally someplace with limited access and good security of its own in addition to what we'll provide."

"I'll figure something out," Kate promised, but her mind was on Mitchell, and she was desperately anxious to put an end to his wait to meet his son. She conveyed that to Gray Elliott by giving him a quick hug and a kiss on the cheek; then she turned to Detective MacNeil, bestowed a kiss on his cheek, too, and ushered them both out into the hall. She closed the door behind them, and lowered Danny to the floor.

He looked sleepy and rumpled, so she deliberately kept him out of Mitchell's sight for a few more moments while she crouched down to tuck his red shirt into his coveralls and tug the cuffs into place over his shoes. "Before I introduce you to your son," Kate said as she combed her fingers through Danny's tousled curls, "I want to tell you two things." Behind her she heard Mitchell move forward, and she stole a glance over her shoulder, actually looking at the handsome face she'd barely seen through her tears in the bedroom.

"What are they?" he asked, and her heart swelled a little at the sound of his well-remembered deep voice, devoid now of anger.

"First, I am very sorry for the way I treated you in the bedroom. I was hurting so badly that I couldn't think or see or hear. I was in such a horrible daze that I actually forgot you were here until a moment ago."

"What you said in there was true," he replied unemotionally.

"The second thing I want to tell you," Kate said as she stood up, still blocking Danny from his view, "is that you're in for a bit of a shock."

"Why is that?"

Danny was trying to peer around her legs to see who she was talking to, but Kate managed to keep him behind her while she turned toward Mitchell. "Mitchell, this is Daniel," she said with a smile. "I think you'd recognize him even without an introduction," she added, and then she stepped aside so that Mitchell could see what she meant.

The tableau that followed was so poignant that Kate felt her throat constrict. With an expression resembling awed disbelief, Mitchell gazed down at a miniature version of himself, while Danny tipped his head way back and stared up at Mitchell with much the same expression until Mitchell's intense blue stare suddenly unnerved him. His chin began to tremble and he looked worriedly at Kate. Mitchell looked worriedly at her, too.

"It's okay," Kate assured Danny lightly. "How about shaking hands?"

To her amusement, Mitchell thought she was reassuring him, and he nodded gratefully, stepped forward, and held out his large hand to Danny. Danny solemnly laid his small hand in Mitchell's large palm, and Mitchell's fingers tightened and relaxed reflexively as if he was having trouble controlling his grip. Another awkward lull ensued, but before Kate needed to intervene with a new suggestion, Mitchell suddenly crouched down as if inspired and gave Danny a grin. "I have an airplane," he confided.

"Me, too!" Danny replied, giving Mitchell back his own grin.

"I like jets," he said.

"Me, too," his son replied in a tone of wonder.

Mitchell's voice dropped to a hoarse whisper. "How many jets do you have?"

In order to answer, Danny pulled his hand free, spread his fingers wide apart, and held them up in front of Mitchell. "I got this many," he proudly proclaimed. When Mitchell seemed incapable of speech, Danny prompted, "How many jets do you got?"

In reply, Mitchell held up his own hand and lifted his forefinger. "This many," he said tenderly, and Kate turned aside to keep her face from betraying her emotions.

Danny showed Mitchell his airplanes, and Mitchell admired each one, but it was obvious to Kate that Danny was getting very sleepy and needed to go to bed. "Would you like to read Danny his bedtime story after I give him his bath and put him to bed?" she asked.

"Yes," Mitchell replied simply. "Thank you," he added, grateful for the moment that she was allowing him—no, *helping* him—to step into the very role she'd deliberately denied him for nearly two years.

"While you're doing that," Kate said, "I'll take a shower and change clothes."

She reached for Danny's hand, but the mention of his bedtime routine suddenly reminded him of Molly, and he twisted around in sudden panic. "Where's Molly?" he cried. "Molly fell down—" His face crumpled at the memory, and Kate scooped him into her arms, hugging him close.

"Molly is fine," she soothed. "We'll call her on the phone right now, and you can talk to her. In a few days, she'll be back here, sleeping in her bedroom, just like always." When Danny still looked dubious and worried, Kate started down the hallway toward the phone in her bedroom, pausing just long enough to explain to Mitchell, "Molly is Danny's nanny. She's been with us since Danny was born."

Chapter Fifty

SEATED IN THE ROCKING CHAIR BESIDE DANNY'S BED, Mitchell stole another glance at his son as he turned to the third page of the little book Kate had given him to read aloud. Danny was lying on his side, his arms wrapped around the gray rabbit, his gaze riveted on Mitchell.

Despite Danny's intent expression, Mitchell sensed that his mind was on something else, and he attributed that worrisome situation to his own inadequacy and lack of experience as a bedtime-story teller. Determined to redeem himself in Danny's eyes and regain his attention before he lost it completely, Mitchell tried harder to sound convincing while he read his son an amazingly ludicrous story about a train engine named Thomas who was not only capable of human thoughts and emotions, but also immune to all the laws of physics and chemistry, particularly those involving weight, fuel, and self-propulsion.

Danny's apprehensive voice stopped him before he finished the first sentence on the page. "A bad man took me away—"

Mitchell made a Herculean effort to keep his expression from betraying the rage he felt, and laid the book down on his lap. "I know he did, but he will never come near you again."

"Why?"

Completely taken aback by the question, Mitchell settled for the only explanation he could think of that would be simple enough for a child to accept. "Because he's afraid of me."

"Why?"

Because I'm going to make certain he can't get near you, and if he tries, I'll kill him myself. "Because I know who he is, and I'm going to make sure he spends the rest of his life in—" He broke off that vengeful sentence because he didn't want his son to start fearing him; then he choked on a laugh when Danny helped him finish it.

"Time-out?"

"Yes," Mitchell said.

"Why else?"

"Why else is he afraid of me?" Mitchell thought hard for a reassuring but nonthreatening answer to give and said, "Because I'm a lot bigger than he is."

"Why else?" Danny prodded.

It dawned on Mitchell that he'd been lured into a conversational loop by a two-year-old who was prepared to continue the game all night. Mitchell smoothly switched roles with him. "Why do *you* think he's afraid of me?"

Danny regarded him in surprise for a moment, as if the answer should have been obvious all along. "You're my daddy."

Mitchell's heart slammed into his ribs and he had to swallow before he could breathe.

Danny mistook his silence for uncertainty. "Mommy said so," he added emphatically, as if that alone should be enough to remove any doubt Mitchell could have.

"Your mommy is right," Mitchell said tenderly. Reaching out, he smoothed the cover around Danny's shoulder. "What else did she say?"

"Mommy said—you came my house. You told peo-

ple—'Find Danny!' You said—'Bring Danny right
straight home!' And so—and so—they did!" The words
tumbled out in an excited, halting rush; then he seemed
to run out of words altogether, and his brows drew together as if that baffled him. Mitchell watched him, his
own brows drawing together in bafflement because
Kate had obviously convinced his son that Mitchell had
raced to his rescue today and was solely responsible for
his safe return. She apparently wanted Danny to see
Mitchell in a heroic light, and yet, Mitchell would have
expected just the opposite of her.

Danny's next words pulled Mitchell back to the present and made his throat tighten again. "You see me
soon?" he asked, and wagged his head in the affirmative, urging Mitchell to say yes.

"Yes," Mitchell whispered, smiling. "I'll see you tomorrow."

"And the next day?" He wagged his head again.

His son, Mitchell realized with amused pride, had obviously inherited Mitchell's knack for knowing when,
and how, to press an advantage—a clear indication that
he could have a stellar career in the world of mergers
and acquisitions. In answer to his question, Mitchell
said, "Yes, the next day, too," and then he decided to
broach another, very important subject. "I brought a
special friend along with me. His name is Calli and he's
downstairs right now. He's going to sleep up here, and
whenever you go somewhere, he's going to go with
you."

"Is he big as you?"

Absurdly pleased that his son apparently regarded
him as a giant among men, Mitchell said, "No, but he's
very, very strong."

Danny nodded and closed his eyes. Moments later, he
was asleep, and Mitchell gazed down at the sweet face
of his son, a cherub with sooty curls, dusky lashes, soft

cheeks, and a small, square chin. Mitchell's chin—he realized with a jolt. He recognized that chin; he stared at a larger version of it in the mirror every day while he shaved. The small hand lying against the rabbit's head was Mitchell's hand in miniature. Leaning forward, Mitchell carefully lifted the little hand from its resting place and pressed it to his lips.

In the room across the hall, the shower stopped running, and he stood up; then he turned and looked around at his son's things, but it was the three photograph albums atop the chest of drawers that ultimately captured his attention. Two of the albums had labels on the spine indicating the time frame of the pictures inside them. Mitchell took one off the dresser, opened it, and saw pictures of his son in a high chair, surrounded by balloons, with a chocolate cake in front of him that had one candle on it. His son's first birthday had come and gone without Mitchell knowing it. The anger he would have felt at that was softened by everything he'd seen Kate do and say, and by the fact that she'd not only told Danny right away that Mitchell was his father, but had also succeeded in making him a hero in Danny's eyes, rather than a frightening stranger.

He flipped to the front of the album and saw Kate, very pregnant, standing in Danny's bedroom, hanging some sort of toy above his crib.

A long-buried memory suddenly re-surfaced with vibrant clarity, the memory of a sexual experience so powerful, and an orgasm so intense, that it had seeemed profoundly spiritual. Afterward, he'd held Kate in his arms, sensing somehow that they'd just conceived a baby, and so he'd held her tighter because he didn't mind if it was true. . . . No, because he'd *wanted it to be true.*

The third album was shorter and fancier, with an embossed title on the spine that said *My Baby's First Book.*

Mitchell picked up all three albums, took them into the living room, and laid them on the coffee table; then he glanced at his watch, and reached for his phone. He'd already gone downstairs and dismissed his attorneys while Kate was bathing Danny, and he'd phoned Matt Farrell to tell him that Danny was safely back. However, he'd left Calli down there with the two suitcases because he didn't want Danny present when he explained to Kate what Calli's role was going to be.

When Calli answered his call, Mitchell told him to call Joe O'Hara in the limo and transfer the suitcases into the trunk, and then he explained to Calli that he wanted him to act as bodyguard for Danny for the time being. His last call was to Caroline Wyatt, Billy's mother. Her fiancé, a prominent banker named Gordon Nather whom Mitchell liked very much, answered her private line. "Gray Elliott is with her now," Nather explained, "but I know she wants desperately to talk to you. We saw you going into Donovan's tonight on the six o'clock news, and Caroline started trying to reach you then. We didn't know Billy was involved until Gray got here. It's all over the news now, however. There's a full-blown manhunt under way."

He paused and then said awkwardly, "I wouldn't ask you what I'm about to ask, but if Danny Donovan is your son, then what Billy did is going to be even harder for Caroline to bear. I just want to be prepared so—"

"He's my son," Mitchell interrupted. "Tell Caroline that no harm was done to Danny, so she needn't feel badly on my account."

"It's amazingly kind of you to dismiss the whole thing," Nather said, sounding more astonished than grateful.

"I'm not dismissing anything," Mitchell retorted. "I am going to do everything in my power to make sure Billy spends the rest of his life behind bars, and if he comes near my son or his mother again, I will hunt him down myself—and I won't bother with the police when I find him."

"In your position, I would feel exactly as you do."

"Then I hope you'll be able to make Caroline understand how I feel."

"She will understand," Nather said with sad certainty. "She cares very much for you."

Mitchell promised to call her in a few days and hung up.

Calli arrived a few minutes afterward, and by the time Kate walked into the living room, he was sitting at the kitchen island, already on duty.

Chapter Fifty-one

MITCHELL WAS STANDING IN THE LIVING ROOM WITH HIS shoulder turned to her, looking through a photograph album, and Kate paused in the doorway, her emotions in a turmoil of uncertainty, guilt, relief, and happiness.

The shower she'd taken had revived her and cleared her head, and when that happened there was no escaping the truth: she should have told Mitchell she was pregnant. Everything Mitchell had done in the hours since he'd learned of Danny's existence was proof of that. And the most indisputable, poignant proof of all was the tenderness on Mitchell's face when he looked at his son.

She'd wronged Mitchell, and she'd wronged Danny, by depriving them of each other. She had no doubt Mitchell intended to make her understand that now, and whatever means he used to do it were going to be deservedly unpleasant.

In an effort to assuage a little of her guilt, she reminded herself of how deceitful he'd been in the islands, and how badly he'd treated her the last time she saw him. Unfortunately, that was little comfort, and it was no buffer against the visual jolt of seeing him standing there, looking exactly as she remembered him—tall, wide-shouldered, immaculately groomed, and wickedly handsome. Every detail about him was as sharply, poignantly familiar as if she'd seen him yesterday—the shape of his hard jaw, the curve of his cheek, the sensual mouth.

She realized she was wringing her hands, dropped them to her sides, and stepped forward, prepared to face the outrage he'd been holding back until Danny was asleep. "I'm sorry I took so long," she said, and then added a lame explanation. "I stayed in the hall outside Danny's bedroom for a few minutes in case you needed a little help." He put the photograph album down abruptly and turned toward her, his dark brows drawing into a frown. Kate braced herself for an angry salvo.

"I don't think I did a very good job reading to him," he said. "I lost his attention right away."

Kate's emotions veered from anxiety to amusement. "When you read to him next time, try to sound less incredulous."

He nodded, but his gaze shifted to the floor, where Kate's cats were making their decorous entrance into the living room.

"Lucy and Ethel," Kate explained, and she could have sworn he almost smiled.

"What happened to Max?"

"My head chef volunteered to take him home today. He kept growling at Detective MacNeil."

The small talk that had been Kate's reprieve came to an end. He gestured toward the photograph albums on the table and said in a businesslike voice, "I'd like to borrow these."

"You don't need to do that. Leave them here and I'll have a set made for you."

"I have two years of my son's life to catch up on. I'd like to start on that tonight."

The television set was on and turned down very low, but it pulled their attention to it because the station was running a tape of Father Donovan's statement to the press earlier, and at the end, several reporters were calling out the same question: "Is Mitchell Wyatt Danny's father?" Kate's uncle simply ignored the question and thanked everyone again for their prayers for Danny.

"I want that taken care of tonight," Mitchell said flatly, his blue eyes shifting to Kate in a cool challenge. "We can confirm it to the press together, or I can do it myself when I leave. Either way, I want the conjecture about my son's parentage ended immediately."

"Why don't you speak for both of us? You could say something like 'Kate and I want to thank everyone for their prayers for our son's safe return.' That has a nice ring to it."

It had a very nice ring to it, but Mitchell was more interested in her reasoning. "Why don't you want to go out there with me?"

"I don't know," she joked half seriously. "Could it be because I'm the niece of a Catholic priest who has been dealing with the press all day, and I just can't work up any enthusiasm about publicly announcing to all his parishioners—and the entire Archdiocese of Chicago—that Father Donovan's niece had an illicit fling and got knocked up? I know I'll regret passing up this opportunity someday, but—"

"I'll handle it when I leave," he said, but this time Kate was almost certain she saw amusement flicker in his eyes. There was none in his voice, however, when he said, "You and I need to talk. What are my chances of getting a sandwich while I'm here?"

Mitchell understood why the press announcement was going to be embarrassing for her. He also realized that her pregnancy was probably what put an end to her hope of marrying Bartlett. Mitchell had been furious with her the last time he saw her, but ultimately she had paid an extremely high price for their time in St. Maarten.

Instead of blaming Danny for the sacrifice she'd had to make, she had obviously lavished him with her love. Whatever bitterness she harbored toward Mitchell for his role in ruining her life, she hadn't taken it out on his son. In fact, she hadn't taken it out on Mitchell either. At least not yet. However, the time for a showdown was at hand, as long as it was out of Danny's earshot.

"This is a restaurant," Kate pointed out with a hesitant smile. "Tell me what you'd like to have and I'll bring it up here."

"I'd rather eat downstairs."

"I can't leave Danny alone."

"He won't be alone." In explanation, Mitchell nodded toward Calli, who immediately got off the stool and walked into living room. "This is Giovanni Callioroso," Mitchell explained. "Calli is a bodyguard. Until Billy Wyatt is arrested, Calli is going to be with Danny wherever Danny is."

Kate's initial reaction was shock at the discovery that there was someone else in the room; it was followed by uneasiness over his profession, followed by uncertainty over whether she wanted a stranger in constant proximity to Danny, followed by . . . a vague memory.

"You're a bodyguard?" she said idiotically, and then the memory snapped into focus. Callioroso! That was the name of the family Mitchell had lived with in Italy when he was a child; she remembered seeing it in the file on Mitchell that she'd pored over in Gray Elliott's office. Her doubts about having him with Danny dissipated. Smiling, she held out her hand and said sincerely, "I'll feel much better knowing you're with Danny. Thank you."

Instead of shaking her hand, Calli took it between both of his, grinned at Mitchell, and said in Italian, "Her smile is warm enough to bake bread. She has eyes like green jewels, hair the color of flame, and skin like cream. If you took this woman to bed and then forgot about it, like you said, you need to see a doctor about your memory."

Kate smiled uncertainly at Mitchell, hoping for a translation; but he shot Calli a quelling look, then he looked at Kate and said firmly, "You and I have some things to discuss. Let's go." He walked over to the coffee table and picked up his briefcase along with the photograph albums.

Nervous anxiety set in, and Kate glanced briefly toward Calli, unaware that her emotions were written all over her face. "Will you ask Calli what he'd like to eat so I can have it brought up?"

Mitchell opened the door and stepped aside for Kate to precede him. "Calli ate downstairs."

Behind him, Calli issued a warning. "She is your son's mother, and she is very nervous. She watched you from the living room doorway wringing her hands. No matter what she has done, do not forget that she is the mother of your son. She is entitled to—"

Mitchell closed the door on the end of Calli's sentence.

Chapter Fifty-two

"Y̶OU'RE IN LUCK," KATE SAID. "THE LIGHTS ARE STILL on in the kitchen."

"Why is that lucky?" Mitchell asked, following her down the wide, oak-paneled hallway, lined with offices, at the bottom of the staircase.

"Because it means that someone else may be preparing our meals, which means they'll be edible," she said with a laughing glance over her shoulder.

As she spoke, she shoved open a pair of wide stainless-steel doors concealed behind an antique oak screen inlaid with ebony parquet, and Mitchell saw a small group of men and women who, he surmised, were still celebrating Danny's return. Rather than going in there with Kate, he retraced his steps to the hallway so that he could look at the assortment of framed photographs, plaques, and magazine and newspaper articles he'd noticed moments before.

It was a very impressive display, he realized as he looked at the many awards Donovan's had received and the articles written about it. The items were arranged in chronological order, so he didn't come to Kate's accolades until he neared the far end of the hallway. Based on what he saw of those, not only had she managed to maintain the restaurant's reputation, she'd enhanced it. When he came to the last, most-recent item, he felt an inappropriate twinge of pride—which he immediately reclassified as mere admiration—that Kate had just been named Chicago's Restaurateur of the Year.

She returned from the kitchen while he was still reading the *Tribune* article. After her shower she'd changed into tan-colored jeans and a soft cashmere sweater that was the same green as her eyes, with an open cowl-neck that threatened to bare one shoulder. With her long red hair falling in wavy curls around her shoulders and her hips swaying gently as she walked, she looked feminine, poised, and sexy at the same time.

Mitchell tipped his head toward the *Tribune* article and said, "I remember when you were terrified you wouldn't be able to keep this place open, but look what you've accomplished."

"I made a mess of everything the first few months, and I would have given up back then if it hadn't been for Danny. I needed to make a success of the business for his sake."

As she spoke, she led him to the front of the restaurant, walking past the maître d's desk and through a doorway. She flipped on a light switch, and mellow lights illuminated a stylish lounge with an ornate bar lining two walls; despite its size, the room was cozy and inviting. "I asked Tony to bring our meals to us in here," she explained, walking toward the bar.

Mitchell suddenly remembered the way she'd looked presiding over a candlelit table in a villa by the sea. Now as he watched her, he understood why she'd seemed so sure of herself and self-possessed that night.

From beneath her lashes Kate watched him studying the room. This day had begun as the worst of her life, and it was ending as one of the very best, because no matter what he said to her now, it couldn't offset the fact that he was going to be a part of Danny's life. He took off his jacket and tie, draped them over the back of barstool, and loosened the top buttons of his white shirt. The minute he put his jacket over the chair, her mind flashed to the night in the villa in Anguilla when he'd left his jacket over a chair and forgotten it there when he left abruptly. Her stomach knotted at the memory, and painful questions popped into her mind, questions she didn't want to ask, with answers she didn't need to hear and probably wouldn't believe if she did. Obviously, the best thing to do, for both their sakes, was to scrupulously avoid any discussion, any reminders, and any recriminations about the past. She was prepared to let him vent his anger at her for not telling him about Danny, but everything else was off limits. At least for the immediate future.

Kate resolved to stick to that decision tonight, and to make Mitchell stick to it. And if that wasn't possible, then she would make light of their past and persuade him to follow suit.

Anticipating that his answer to her next question would be yes, Kate stepped behind the bar. "Would you like a drink?"

"Yes," Mitchell said, watching her in the mirror.

He drank vodka, Kate remembered, and automatically reached for the best bottle on the shelf; then she jerked her hand down and in a belated attempt to stick to her own decision, she glanced over her shoulder at him, and politely inquired, "What would you like?"

His gaze pinned her. "You know the answer to that."

Kate turned back to the shelves of liquor. "Apparently, you still prefer vodka," she concluded wryly.

"And you're still very beautiful."

Kate's hand froze on the vodka bottle; then she took it carefully down and reached for a glass. "I wasn't aware that you thought I was beautiful."

"The hell you weren't."

Kate knew she wasn't beautiful; at best, her coloring might qualify her looks as striking. And except for an indirect reference to her legs the night they went to the casino, Mitchell had never commented on her appearance. No, that wasn't true at all, she remembered. In bed, he'd lavished her with whispered praise while he stroked and touched—

Kate mentally put her foot down, pushed all those thoughts away, and added ice to his glass. She finished making his drink and poured a glass of red wine for herself; then she turned around, glasses in hand. "Let's talk about Danny," she said with an overbright smile. Walking out from behind the bar, she nodded toward a nearby pair of small burgundy upholstered sofas facing each other across an oval cocktail table, and Mitchell followed her there. She put his glass and a cocktail napkin in front of one of the sofas; then she walked around to the sofa on the opposite side and curled up on it, her legs tucked beneath her, her wineglass in hand. Across from her, Mitchell reached for his glass, propped his ankle on the opposite knee, and took a swallow of his drink. "What would you like to know about Danny?" she said as soon as he started to lower his glass.

Mitchell already had his own conversational agenda firmly in mind, and he had no intention of letting her divert him from it; however, there was one thing he did want to ask her about Danny before he started. "In the bedroom tonight, he was talking, and then he stopped and looked at me as if he couldn't say a word, but he was trying to."

"And tomorrow," Kate explained, "he may lapse completely into baby talk and not say two words you understand. If he's extremely upset or agitated, he'll look at you in mute, heartbreaking misery. If that happens when he's with you, say quietly to him, 'Use your words.'"

"Does that help?"

"Often it does."

"If there's a problem with his speech—"

"Danny's verbal skills are remarkable," Kate assured

him. "So much so that, right now, they're outpacing his brain's ability to simultaneously process his thoughts and words. He's also extremely well-coordinated. In addition to inheriting all of your features," she finished with a smile, "he also inherited your gift for language and your physical coordination."

In response, Mitchell stretched his left arm across the back of the sofa and casually inquired, "Whose temper did he inherit?"

"Yours," Kate said without thinking.

"What a relief. I won't be afraid to put a glass in his hand."

His deliberate reference to their confrontation at the fund-raiser doused Kate's smile. "Please don't go there," she warned. "That's very deep water, and—"

"Our history is all deep water. Because of Danny, we can't avoid going, so let's discuss it now, but try to tread water instead of trying to drown each other."

"What exactly are you suggesting?"

"Honesty and restraint."

Kate stared at him in wary silence.

"Shall I start?" Mitchell volunteered, and when she nodded slightly, he said, "All right. You gave me two reasons for not telling me you were pregnant: my refusal to have children with my ex-wife and my treatment of you the last time we met. As to my behavior at the hospital benefit, I apologize for that. It was inexcusable, and there will never be a repetition."

Kate looked at him over the rim of her glass and decided to test the depth of his commitment to honesty and restraint. Very politely, she said, "I'd rather have an explanation than an apology."

"Fair enough. If you'd sauntered up to me with that same coy expression on your face and told me you'd just gotten engaged to anyone except Evan Bartlett, I would have courteously and insincerely offered you my very best wishes and that's all. If I'd have known about your engagement to Bartlett longer than twenty seconds before you were standing in front of me with that same playful expression on your face, I wouldn't have given you the satisfaction of evoking any reaction from me whatsoever. Unfortunately, things didn't happen that way." He reached for the cocktail napkin on the table, knowing she'd find it easier to lie if he wasn't looking at her. "I have an unpleasant history with the Bartletts. Did Evan tell you about that?"

"Yes," she admitted. "He told me how you feel about them and why."

Pleased with her reply, Mitchell transferred his gaze to hers and rewarded her honesty with a forthright explanation about the second issue: "I refused to have a child with Anastasia because I knew she wouldn't sacrifice her freedom or change her lifestyle if we had one. She was doing recreational drugs, and it was getting out of hand. She went on tangents. She came home from Paris with two Yorkshire terrier puppies that she dressed up in clothes from doggie boutiques, played with constantly, and took everywhere she went. They were the center of her life for a few months, and then she lost interest and ignored them. When they still tried to follow her around, they became an annoyance, so she gave them away. She decided she wanted horses instead and she bought two Thoroughbreds that she never went near. Then she wanted a baby."

"Babies are different; they capture your heart. Just because she lost interest in puppies and horses doesn't necessarily mean she'd have been an indifferent mother."

"Maybe not, but in those days, I had additional reasons to feel that fathering children was a pointless risk for me: I knew nothing about being a father, and I had no idea what sort of genes I carried. Based on what Bartlett told you happened to me as a child, you should be able to guess why I felt that way."

Overwhelmed that he was willing to admit so much to her now and saddened by the needless fears he'd endured, Kate looked down at her lap and decided he'd been right to insist on this conversation. Lifting her eyes to his, she said with soft candor, "I don't have to fill in any blanks. I know everything about you. Evan only knew how the Wyatts disposed of you when you were a baby. I know everything about your life afterward."

"Such as?"

"Let's see . . ." she said with a sudden smile, eyeing him from beneath her lashes, "I know that you broke sports records at all your schools starting when you were eight. I know you excelled at all your studies except art. I know that you had nowhere to go when school closed, so you stayed with a faculty member or a custodian during the holidays, and that during the summers you went to camps. I know that students were required to write home twice a month, and so you wrote letters to a custodian at your previous school. I also know you were fascinated with religion, but no one religion in particular. You changed your religion at each new school." Tipping her head to the side, she asked, "Were you interested in theology, by any chance?"

"No, I was interested in spending the least possible amount of time in church. Since church attendance was mandatory at all my boarding schools, I 'reoriented' my beliefs according to whatever church service was shortest at the current school. "

"Judaism takes up a lot of time."

"Not when there's no rabbi in the vicinity."

She burst out laughing, and an answering smile tugged at Mitchell's lips—until he realized that after three years, he was still helplessly captivated by those russet-lashed, glowing green eyes smiling into his. He doused his smile and took a quick swallow of his drink. Despite her claim that she knew everything about him, it was obvious that she knew only what was in his school records. He was wondering how she got her hands on those when she sobered and said something that made him stare at her over the rim of his glass.

"I know who Calli is, Mitchell. I wouldn't have agreed to leave Danny upstairs with him otherwise. The Calliorosos were the closest thing you had to a family."

"Where did you get all this information?"

"Your brother's investigators put together a file on you."

"He told me he had a file. How did you get it?"

"The day after I got back from St. Maarten, Gray Elliott 'invited me' to his office for a chat. He had a huge file on you, including pictures of us in St. Maarten, and he told me you were a suspect in your brother's murder."

"What the hell did he expect to find out from you?"

"He wanted to know how long we'd known each other, and what you'd told me about your brother." Kate paused, momentarily diverted by the scowl on Mitchell's handsome face because he suddenly looked like a formidable version of Danny when he scowled. "Anyway, four months after that, I was in the terrifying position of carrying a baby inside me whose father was a dark mystery to me. I remembered those files in Gray Elliott's office, and so I went to see him and asked if I could look through them. Ethically, he couldn't let me see anything the police had accumulated about you. But since your brother's file didn't fall into that category, he let me look through it at his office."

"He had no business letting anyone see that file."

"Be glad he did," Kate said forcefully. "Before that day, I didn't know how I was going to be able to love my baby. But once I read that file, I understood you. I understood why you needed to get even with the Bartletts and why you would have seized the chance to do it by seducing me."

Shock and disbelief annihilated every other emotion in Mitchell's body. Outwardly relaxed and inwardly tensed, he studied her, assessing her face, her inflections—even her logic—for indications that she was lying. But as she continued, what Mitchell heard was truth, and it was so painful to endure that he found himself almost wishing she were lying to him while at the same time he wanted everything she said to be true.

"To be fair to you," she went on, oblivious to the havoc she was wreaking in Mitchell, "you were very straightforward the first night at the villa in Anguilla. You made it clear that you didn't want to share anything with me except a bed—not even meaningless information, like your brother's name and how many languages you speak. You told me straight out in St. Maarten that you didn't want complications, and that if I went to bed with you, nothing would come of it.

"I had to have magic, though, or I wouldn't go along, and when you realized I meant it, you reversed your attitude in a matter of seconds and told me we had magic. And then you took me to bed and made sure I believed it. I thought I loved you, and I think you knew that. Even so, you let me go to meet Evan in Anguilla, knowing exactly what was going to happen and what Evan was going to tell me. That was despicable, by the way."

Kate paused, waiting for him to react, but all he did was nod, wordlessly accepting her condemnation and urging her to go on. So Kate went on. "I couldn't find a way to forgive you for that—or the baby in my womb either—until I read your file. Once I did that," she said, looking at him without rancor, "I realized that you meant me no real harm, but I was a once-in-a-lifetime opportunity for revenge that you simply couldn't pass up. Actually," she said, flashing Mitchell a wayward smile, "after I read your file, I actually felt a little bit of satisfaction that I was the tool you used to retaliate."

Desperate for her to continue, Mitchell drew a steady-ing breath and said quietly, "You have a very loyal, for-giving nature, Kate."

Kate's hand shook at the soft caress she imagined in his voice when he said her name, and she stared hard at him, but his handsome face was composed, attentive, and nothing more. "Actually," she said briskly, in case he'd noticed her momentary loss of concentration when he said her name, "it was a picture of you, taken at the dock in St. Maarten, the day I left with Evan, that changed everything for me."

"How did it do that?"

"It was a police photograph with the date and time stamped on it. It was five forty-five and you were waiting for me. Until I saw it, I never imagined that you went to the dock at all that day."

Mitchell's expression didn't change, but he had just registered the first flaw in her logic, a large flaw that called her other claims into question.

Across from him, she finished the wine in her glass and said drily, "You have a gift for diabolical revenge. Evan's reaction at the villa was all you could have hoped for."

Mitchell lifted his brows inquiringly. "Really? Do you mind telling me what happened?"

His complete imperturbability suddenly rubbed Kate the wrong way. "Yes, I think I do mind," she said.

"I'm sorry. I shouldn't have asked. That's completely between Evan and you."

Kate gaped at him. His last sentence absolved him from any part or responsibility for what took place at the villa, which was completely, outrageously arrogant and unfair. Without an inkling that his remark was verbal bait being dangled in front of her nose by an expert, Kate swallowed the hook, and decided she deserved the op-portunity to tell him *exactly* how brutal he'd been. Un-fortunately, she couldn't do that without feeling a little humiliated, so she stared at the empty wineglass, twisting the stem in her fingers. "The day I left you at the Enclave in St. Maarten, I went straight to the villa and packed my suitcases like a good little idiot; then I waited for Evan. When he arrived, I told him I'd met you and that I thought we had something special—"

Mitchell interrupted with a quietly spoken instruction. "Look at me."

Kate automatically obeyed because she assumed he wanted her looking at him while he told her something important. Instead, he nodded and said, "Go on."

It was the first inkling she had that his relaxed pose and pleasant, dispassionate expression were feigned, and that he was weighing everything she said. It was not a pleasant realization, and her voice sharpened a little.

"Without trying to list the revelations in the order of their heartbreaking effect, Evan told me that he'd met you at Cecil Wyatt's party, that he'd told you my name and that I was going to be staying at the Island Club with him. He also told me about your childhood and the reasons you hate his father and him. Then he asked me if I knew you were staying on Zack Benedict's yacht, building a house on Anguilla, and living in Chicago with Caroline Wyatt." She waited for Mitchell to respond, and when he didn't, she shook her head at her own stupidity. "I was so insane about you that none of that mattered, except for the one thing that I couldn't invent an excuse for."

"What was that?" he asked quietly, but his brows had narrowed imperceptibly.

"The one thing I couldn't ignore was that you'd let me talk about Chicago while you acted as if you'd never been here. You even asked me how long it takes to fly from Chicago to St. Maarten. As far as I know, there are only two reasons a man hides from a woman the fact that he lives in the same city she does: either he's married or he has no intention of seeing her again when they're both back in that city. I wanted to believe that you might have a third reason, so do you know what I did?"

"No," he said.

"I called you at the Enclave to ask you why you hadn't told me those things. The operator at the Enclave told me you'd checked out. Naturally, I thought that had to be a mistake, because I remembered the way you stood on the balcony and told me to 'Hurry back.'" Trying unsuccessfully to keep her voice steady, Kate went on, "So there I was, with my suitcases all packed, standing in the villa, facing the ugly truth: you seduced me to get even with Evan; then you sent me back to the villa to break up with him, reminding me to hurry back to you. And then you checked out of the hotel."

Drawing a shaky breath, Kate said, "I cried my heart out on Evan's shoulder. I cried until I was so exhausted I fell asleep."

Instead of sounding remorseful or argumentative, Mitchell sounded vaguely puzzled. "You thought you were in love with me, and yet, only a few days later, you walked up to me at a party wearing Bartlett's engagement ring, looking very smug, and offered me your cheek to kiss?"

His impression of her feelings that night was so wrong that Kate went from being on the verge of tears to the verge of laughter, and she stood up quickly, trying to steady her disintegrating composure. "I practiced that scene for hours with my friend Holly because we knew you were going to be there, but 'smug' definitely wasn't what I was supposed to convey," she said with a quick smile as she reached for his glass. "Let me fix you another drink and then I'll check on dinner."

He moved the glass out of her reach, and rolled to his feet, trapping her between the cocktail table and his body. "What were you trying to convey?" he persisted so calmly and courteously that Kate assumed he didn't realize she couldn't step around him.

"Playful," Kate replied, trying to sound offhanded when the collar of her green sweater was an inch from the front of his shirt and she had to tip her head way back to meet his thoughtful gaze. "You'd used me as a pawn in your game, so I pretended you hadn't mattered to me any more than I'd mattered to you."

"And your engagement to Bartlett—that was, what?"

"Evan brought the ring to Anguilla," Kate explained quickly. "He put it on my finger after I cried myself to sleep. At the time, marrying Evan seemed like reparation and salvation to me. My reprieve from reality lasted for a few weeks until I found out I was pregnant. Evan and I hadn't been intimate after my father died, and although we got engaged the same day I slept with you, we both agreed that we needed to wait awhile before we slept with each other. There was no possibility that you weren't the father."

"I assume he broke off the engagement as soon as you told him you were pregnant?"

"One thing hasn't changed—" Kate said, feeling suddenly angry, "I always end up doing all the talking and you don't reveal anything."

"I'll start talking as soon as you answer two questions for me—beginning with the last one."

"He did not want to break the engagement; he wanted me to have an abortion."

"But you wouldn't?"

"No."

"And when you were four months pregnant, you saw a picture of me waiting for you at the wharf, and you thought you'd been in love with me, and yet you never thought to contact me and tell *me* you were pregnant?"

"Of course I thought about it, and you're out of questions. Excuse me—" she added, putting her left hand against his chest in an agitated effort to get him to step back. To her shock, instead of stepping back, he captured both her upper arms and held her firmly in front of him, but his tone was puzzled, not threatening. "Why didn't you take a chance and come to me and tell me you were pregnant?"

"Because I knew that even if you had cared very much for me in St. Maarten—even if you still cared for me when I told you I was pregnant—you would probably want me to get an abortion."

"And it wasn't worth your trouble to come to me and find out for sure?"

Kate snapped her head back, intending to glare at him, but he was staring at her intensely, no longer looking as if he were an impartial investigator. "I couldn't take the risk."

The minute she said "risk" an expression of dawning horror tightened his jaw. "You took that risk with Bartlett. Why couldn't you take it with me?"

"Because," she said brokenly, "I was afraid that if you tried hard enough, you'd be able to talk me into doing it!"

Mitchell's hands tightened, pulling her roughly against his chest in a fierce, protective embrace. Now he understood the real reason she'd not told him she was pregnant, and he believed her. He believed everything she'd told him in the last few minutes—every heartbreaking thing—and Bartlett was responsible for it all.

He laid his jaw against the top of her head, his hand drifting soothingly up and down her spine while long-suppressed memories of their time together in the islands spun through his mind, each one sweeter and more poignant than the one before.

A waiter shouldering a tray laden with dishes walked through the doorway, saw Kate in Mitchell's arms, hesitated, and then backed out of the room.

"Mitchell—" she said quietly.

Her voice pulled him out of his trance, and he realized her hands were flattened against his chest, gently pushing him away. Refusing to let her go yet, he touched his lips to the top her head and whispered tenderly, "Thank you for our son."

The tension went out of her body, and she nodded, her cheek rubbing against his chest, her body relaxing against his, the fingers of her right hand spreading over his heart. Mitchell's heart missed a beat and his thighs tightened. Startled by his body's reaction, he lifted his chin and frowned at her shiny red hair—and then he remembered how easily she'd aroused him three years ago. His frown turned into an amused grin. Surprise turned into hope.

He loosened his arms, and she stepped back out of his reach, which disappointed him until he realized that she couldn't possibly read his mind, no matter how tightly he held her. "Kate," he said solemnly, "everything Evan told you at the villa was a lie. When I met him at Cecil's party, he didn't tell me your name, or that he was bringing anyone here. Even if he had, why would I bother to exact revenge on him? He's a supercilious asshole with a sadistic streak he shares with his father. At least, that's all he was to me until tonight." Mitchell waited, fully expecting that what he'd said would be enough to remove all her doubts.

Kate shoved her hands into her back pockets, a little embarrassed by the comfort she'd felt in Mitchell's arms, but accepting it as inevitable, under the circumstances. She was happy he was there, but she was not willing to let him shift the blame for what happened three years ago onto Evan. In a calm, reasonable voice, she said, "Did Evan lie when he pointed out that you'd been living in Chicago right up until I met you?"

"No—"

"Did he lie when he said you'd been staying on Zack Benedict's boat?"

"No."

"Did you pretend you knew nothing about Chicago? Did you go so far as to ask me how long it took to fly from Chicago to St. Maarten?"

"Yes, and I had reasons for both. I have my own plane. I've never flown on a commercial jet from Chicago to St. Maarten, so I had no idea how many stops they make." At the end of his explanation, she arched her graceful brows at him, and Mitchell almost smiled because she looked like a pretty schoolteacher waiting for the recalcitrant student in front of her to trap himself in his own lie. "It's a little harder to explain why I didn't admit I knew anything about Chicago. When I was in school, my classmates' parents often asked me if I was related to the 'Chicago Wyatts,' because they were trying to assess my social connections—ergo, my worthiness to associate with their sons. I had to say no. A few weeks before we met, Cecil publicly acknowledged me and all of a sudden, I was a celebrated Chicago Wyatt. I didn't like it," he said bluntly. "In fact, I rather resented it."

"You'd made it on your own, without them," Kate speculated.

"That's close enough. When I met you, you were staying at an exclusive hotel frequented by the very wealthy, and when you said you were from Chicago, I avoided the possibility that you'd either be 'dazzled' with my social connections or else want to start figuring out who we both know."

She nodded, but Mitchell had no idea whether she believed that was the true reason for his withholding information from her.

"And the day we passed Zack Benedict's boat? When I went on and on about what a huge fan of his I am, you let me do it without mentioning that he's not only a close friend of yours, but that you were staying on his boat."

"I plead guilty to that one," Mitchell said with an absent smile, because it was finally sinking in that the delightful, irate redhead who was confronting him now was the same Irish girl who'd spilled a Bloody Mary down his shirt, drugged his senses, and stolen his heart. And borne his child. From the very beginning, they'd been meant for each other. They still were. It was so obvious that he had simultaneous impulses to laugh and to pull her into his arms so he could start proving it to her. He wisely decided against doing either when he realized she now looked extremely unhappy with him.

"It doesn't really matter that you can't explain about Zack Benedict," she said, twisting around and trying to pick up his glass from the table.

"I can explain," Mitchell said quickly, touching her arm. She hesitated and then straightened. "As I recall, I experienced a twinge of something that made me not want to tell you right then, but I intended to take you aboard the *Julie* the next day."

"'A twinge of something'?" she repeated, her eyes lighting up with reluctant laughter.

"I think it was jealousy. It felt like jealousy."

Her lips trembled with laughter, and Mitchell grinned. "I hadn't felt it since I was a grown man, but I remembered it." Since she was smiling at him and relaxed now, Mitchell tried to make her understand what had really happened the day they were supposed to meet at the wharf, but the more he told her, the more she seemed to recoil. "Right after you left for the Island Club, my nephew called me and told me my brother's body had been found. I checked out of the hotel, because I had to leave for Chicago, but I made arrangements with Zack for you to cruise the islands on his yacht during the day. I intended to fly back and forth every night to wherever the yacht was docked so we could spend the nights to-gether. I waited for you at the wharf in Philipsburg until it got dark; then I called the vet and he told me that you and another man had picked Max up hours before. I couldn't believe you'd left me waiting there. When I saw you at the fund-raiser, I felt exactly like the heartbroken, jealous lover I announced to you that I *wasn't*. How do you think that description happened to come out of my mouth?"

"Mitchell, it doesn't matter anymore really—"

"You don't believe me, do you?"

"Let's just say that I find it much easier to forgive you than believe you. And let's leave it at that."

Mitchell was dumbstruck, but not angry. "Would you rather believe that Evan told you the truth than believe what I'm telling you?"

Kate turned her face away, unable to look at him. The picture he'd painted of what happened that day was too unbearable to fathom. The possibility that he'd actually planned to fly back and forth every night to join her on that boat made her stomach ache; the possibility that he'd loved her as much as she'd loved him while he waited for her at the wharf made her cringe inside; the thought of how he would have felt at that fund-raiser when she showed off her engagement ring to him was unendurable.

Her overburdened emotions sent her reeling precari-ously close to hysteria. In the last twelve hours, she'd al-ready endured the torment of Danny's kidnapping and the turmoil of Mitchell's reentry into her life. The idea that, by trusting Evan, she had been the cause of all the misery and missed opportunities for Mitchell and her was just too much bear.

Mitchell watched the color drain from her cheeks, saw the tears sparkling on her lashes, and realized exactly why she was reacting that way.

He tipped her chin up and said with a grin, "You're exhausted; so let's just step back from this conundrum and then move around it."

"What did you just say after 'you're exhausted'?"

"I'm suggesting that you get some sleep and we deal with the other things tomorrow. In the meantime, we need to arrange for you and Danny to stay somewhere with limited access."

Dealing with mundane details was a welcome reprieve from other thoughts, and Kate rose to the occasion. "My friend Holly lives in a high-rise that has a guard at a security desk in the lobby."

That was not the solution Mitchell had in mind, so he threw in as many complications as he could think of. "Does she have room for Calli and Danny's nanny, too? You may need to stay there for weeks until Billy is captured."

"She only has one spare bedroom."

"Good," Mitchell said before he could catch himself. "I'll make all the arrangements. All you have to do is pack what you need and be ready to leave with Calli by ten in the morning."

"All right," she said with a weary, grateful smile.

"Let's find something to write on," he continued, taking her arm and pointing her toward the bar. He wrote down his cell phone number and the Farrells' home number on a cocktail napkin for her, and then he wrote down the numbers she gave him.

"What about your meal?" Kate said, her brain snapping into focus now that she understood that he was about to leave. "I can't imagine what happened. Let me go see—"

"The waiter brought it and left when he saw us. I'll get something to eat at the Farrells'."

"I feel really badly about this—your food, I mean."

"Don't worry about it," Mitchell said as he picked up

his jacket and shrugged it on. She followed him, watching, her expression anxious because he hadn't eaten.

"Will you give Danny a good-night kiss for me?" he asked, turning around and smiling into her eyes.

She nodded unhesitatingly.

"Good," he said. Curving his hands around her shoulders, he pressed a light kiss to her smooth cheek. "That one's for Danny . . . " His arms slid around her, drawing her against his full length, and Kate braced herself for what was coming next. "This one . . . " he whispered, holding her gaze and very slowly bending his head, "is for . . . *me.*"

Kate had expected him to say the kiss was for her, and she giggled an instant before his lips touched hers. His warm mouth brushed over hers softly and slowly, and then possessively, and Kate yielded to the sweetness of the moment, sliding her arms around him and holding him close. He ended the kiss rather abruptly, gazing down at her with heavy-lidded eyes and a warm, thoughtful smile. "Why don't I take you upstairs and tell you a bedtime story?"

Kate smiled helplessly but shook her head. "No thank you."

"I'll tell you the story of my life," he joked.

"I already know the story of your life."

"But you haven't heard it in French. It's much better in French."

He was so sexy and so endearing when he teased her that she leaned up and kissed his hard cheek. "No."

Completely satisfied with the outcome of the evening, Mitchell picked up the scrapbooks and his briefcase, then turned to her. "I'll have a car here to pick you up at ten."

Kate watched him stride out of the room; then she leaned weakly against the back of a chair, filled with happiness and doubt and disbelief.

Chapter Fifty-three

"H E IS HANDSOME AS SIN," HOLLY CONCLUDED IMPAR-
tially, watching a rerun of Mitchell's statement to the
press the night before when he left the restaurant. The
television stations were running that newsclip adjacent to
the police bulletin involving the search for Billy Wyatt, po-
sitioning the two news items adjacent to each other to
make certain that a mere kidnapping was elevated into a
titillating scandal for their viewers. "He also has presence.
And I liked the statement he gave."

"I'll take a little credit for the last part," Kate said,
walking into the living room of her apartment, carrying
a duffel filled with additional articles for Danny and a
few for herself. Holly had arrived at Donovan's a few
minutes after Mitchell had left the night before, and
she'd gone upstairs with Kate to see Danny, but exhaus-
tion overcame Kate before they could talk about
Mitchell. Holly'd returned a few minutes ago, hoping to
have some time to talk, but it was five P.M., and Kate
was anxious to get back to the hotel and find out how
Danny and Mitchell had fared together.

"Would you like to know what worries me about
him?" Holly added quietly.

"I guess so."

"For a start, I can't forget how vicious he was to you
the last time you saw him. I can't forget how despon-
dent you were until you found a photograph of him at
the wharf and were able to fantasize that he cared about

you at least a little. However, right now, there are two things that worry me more than all that. Can I tell you what they are?"

Holly had supported Kate through the awful aftermath of Mitchell three years before, and Kate knew Holly wanted only the best for her. She also knew Holly was intuitive, loyal, and fair. "All right, tell me."

"Not in the order of importance, here are my concerns: I'm worried because he installed himself in the same hotel where you and Danny are staying."

Kate nodded and tucked two of Danny's toys into the duffel. That morning, Mitchell had arranged for a limousine to pick Kate, Danny, and Calli up at the restaurant, and bring them to the Barclay Tower, a luxurious high rise hotel on Lake Shore Drive. The manager greeted them in the lobby and escorted the small entourage to the elevators, with Calli carrying Danny, who was napping on his shoulder. "No one can get up to the penthouse floor without first inserting this key into the elevator panel," he'd assured Kate as he demonstrated how to use the key. "Our staff has been given Billy Wyatt's photograph, and we will be on the lookout, although I'm sure he'd never be able to get past the security personnel that Mr. Wyatt has stationed in the lobby."

He ushered her off the elevator into an elegant foyer with wide hallways leading in four directions, each one terminating with a set of double doors bearing the name of the suite. "If there's anything at all you need," the manager continued as he slid a keycard into the slot on the door of the Lakeview Suite, "our staff is entirely at your service. We're honored that Mr. Wyatt is entrusting us with your comfort and safety during this difficult transitional time."

He swung open the door with a flourish and stepped aside, allowing Kate the full impact of a mammoth living room with a wall of glass that offered a gorgeous view of Lake Michigan and an unnerving view of Mitchell, standing with his back to her, his hands in his pockets, contemplating the waves far below. He turned at the sound of their arrival, and strode forward, looking amused and pleased. "It just occurred to me," he said, lifting Danny out of Calli's arms, "that you and I have spent our entire acquaintance in hotel suites, except for a few hours."

Kate rolled her eyes in exasperation. "Thank you for sharing that tidbit with the hotel manager," she whispered.

"I'm sorry," Mitchell lied, grinning, and lowering his voice very slightly. "I forgot how prim you are when we're in hotels together."

Biting back a helpless laugh, Kate said sternly, "Stop talking about hotel rooms." Another concern struck her then, dislodging and outweighing that one, and she narrowed her eyes at him. "You aren't thinking about staying in this suite with me, are you?"

"I've thought of little else since I walked into it," Mitchell replied meaningfully, and Kate felt her face heat. "However, to put your mind at rest, I'm staying in the Boulevard Suite at the end of the hall."

"Good," Kate said, glancing quickly around just in time to see Calli grinning at his own reflection in a mirror over the sofa. "I have to go to work," she said regretfully, glancing at her watch.

"What time will you be back?"

"Seven o'clock," Kate had replied. "I'm going to let my manager handle the Saturday night crowd, but I need to be sure everything is in order before I leave."

Eager to see Danny and to find out how Mitchell and he had gotten along all day, Kate had decided to leave work early, but now Holly was there, and she owed it to Holly to listen to her fears: "I'm worried that he's going to insinuate himself into your life, and then take it over, before you've had time to keep him at a distance and evaluate what kind of man he really is."

"I'm not going to let that happen."

"Good, because I was worried that you planned to break your date with Doug tonight."

"Oh, my God," Kate said. "I forgot about it."

"He's been trying to take you out for a month, and you've canceled on him three times—all with good reasons," Holly put in before Kate needed to. "He's my partner, and my friend, and if you break your date with him tonight, I'm going to be really embarrassed. I work with him—"

"I know. I understand," Kate said miserably.

"I'll call Doug and tell him to pick you up at the hotel instead of here, so you don't have to bother making the call. Look at you," Holly said gently. "You're over-wrought at the prospect of dating a handsome vet who thinks you are very, very cool. Mitchell Wyatt—"

"Holly, Mitchell didn't spoil dating for me three years ago, if that's what you're getting at. I was pregnant, and then I had a little baby and a restaurant to run, but I've gone out with several men in the last year."

"You've had several first dates," Holly pointed out, heading toward the kitchen counter, where she'd left her purse. "How many second dates have you had?"

"Point taken," Kate said, shoving her hair back off her forehead, feeling thoroughly beleaguered. "I have to leave. Call Doug for me." She zipped the duffel closed, looked around the room to see if she'd forgotten anything, and Holly walked to the door with her.

"Do you know what worries me most of all right now?" Holly said as they started down the stairs with Kate in the lead.

"I don't think I want to know that one," Kate joked with a quick smile over her shoulder.

"You're already glowing as if life is filled with promise." After a moment's thought, Holly added jokingly, "I've just realized there is a cheering possibility that, after spending an entire day taking care of Danny, Mitchell Wyatt will look ten years older and be too exhausted to look at you with bloodshot eyes, and fall back asleep."

Kate knocked on the door to Mitchell's suite, and Calli let her in, smiled, and pointed toward a hallway off the living room. A few steps down the hall, Kate heard Danny's gleeful voice and she followed the sound. "Where is everyone?" she called.

"Mommy!" Danny yelled excitedly.

"We're in here," Mitchell called at almost the same time. Kate crossed the master bedroom to the adjoining bath and stopped dead in the doorway, caught between laughter and poignant tears. Mitchell was standing at the sink with a white bath towel around his waist, a razor in his hand, and shaving cream on his face. Danny was standing *on* the sink beside him, with a small hand towel around his waist, shaving cream on his face, and what Kate assumed was a bladeless razor in his hand. "Hi," Kate said, trying to steady her voice.

"I shaving!" Danny cried.

"I see that," Kate said; then she met Mitchell's gaze in the mirror and lifted her brows for some input from him.

"I exhausted," he announced.

Kate grabbed for the doorframe and laughed so hard her eyes filled with tears.

Mitchell watched her, smiling at the musical sound of her laughter.

"What did you guys do today?" she asked when she could speak.

"Danny and I went to the park that you suggested," Mitchell replied, drying off his face. "Danny has lots of friends there, and their mommies were very happy to see him," he said, carefully communicating to Kate that the scene had been filled with relieved mothers who knew about the kidnapping.

"Did you have a good time?" Kate asked Danny, and he nodded emphatically, rubbing his face in a towel in imitation of what Mitchell had just done.

Kate switched her gaze to Mitchell's, aware of the warmth in his eyes and unable to look away from it. "And did you have a good time?" she asked him in the same tone she'd used to ask Danny that question.

"I had a very good time—" he began, but Danny's protest said otherwise.

"No," he told Mitchell. "You hot!"

"Except for that," Mitchell qualified lightly. "Danny was convinced I should take my shirt off, and he was determined to help me."

"Daddy hot!"

Kate dismissed that as an unsolvable puzzle and asked if he'd seen his friends Caperton and Trent. When he gave an emphatic nod and declared that he had, Kate said, "I'll bet Caperton's mommy and Trent's mommy were extra happy to see you, weren't they?" He nodded, and in an automatic effort to encourage him to speak, Kate said, "What did they say when they saw you?"

"They say, 'Danny! Hi!'" Danny replied, grabbing for the can of shaving cream, "They say—Daddy Hot! Mommies all say—Daddy Hot!"

Mitchell's expression didn't change, but Kate giggled helplessly. "You are so busted," she teased him in the mirror, and then she realized that a flush had crept up his neck. Wordlessly, he leaned over the sink and splashed water on his face; then he picked up a fresh towel. "Assuming I still have the strength to stand up tonight," he said as if Danny's words hadn't been spoken, "we're entertaining tonight."

Kate looked at him in surprised dismay, thinking of the date she'd promised to keep with Doug Ferris that night. "Entertaining? You didn't mention anything about that to me earlier."

He nodded and dried off his face. "I know. I wasn't sure I could get everyone together tonight, but it worked out."

"Who's coming?"

"I invited my aunt, Olivia Hebert, Matt and Meredith Farrell, and another couple over to meet Danny and to get to know you a little better. They won't be here long, because the other couple is on their way to California, and my aunt rarely stays up past nine o'clock."

"What time is this supposed to happen?"

Mitchell finally caught the hesitation in her voice and turned around to face her. "Seven o'clock. Is there a problem?"

Kate wanted more than anything to spend the evening with him, but he should have checked with her first. Holly's words came back to her and so did Danny's words, and she realized that in a world of women who thought he was "hot," Mitchell was probably accustomed to having women fall in with any plan. She felt uneasy, and the insecurity she'd suppressed when Danny reported that all the mothers thought Mitchell was hot surfaced with force.

"I can come to the party, but I have to leave at eight."

He waited for her to explain why, and when she didn't, he turned and began putting away his shaving things. "If you're here for an hour, that will be enough," he said mildly.

"Someone's picking me up," Kate provided lamely. "I can't cancel it. I've already done that several times."

"Is he someone special?" Mitchell asked casually—too casually, Kate realized.

"Yes, he's very special. But not to me."

"Next time," Mitchell suggested mildly, "put the end of that sentence at the beginning."

Kate's brief bout with jealous insecurity disintegrated and she laughed.

"Stay at the party for an hour," he said, his good spirits restored. "That should be long enough."

Standing slightly off to the side of the living room, Mitchell proudly watched Kate mingle with his guests. She was poised, unaffected, and artlessly sophisticated. In a matter of minutes, she'd recovered from the shock of finding out that Zack and Julie Benedict were two of the guests, and if she felt any awe, she kept it hidden. She chatted easily with his aunt, whom she knew, and slightly less easily with the Farrells, who'd witnessed the scene at the benefit. To complete Mitchell's satisfaction with the progression of the evening, the redhead who he loved looked sexy as hell in high heels that showed off her gorgeous legs and a silky green dress that clung to her beautiful figure.

Outside, lightning streaked across the sky and thunder boomed while Mitchell prepared to entice his guests to spontaneously reveal information that would erase all Kate's doubts about his actions and feelings for her while they were in St. Maarten. He could have prompted them, but Kate was intuitive and still mistrustful of him, so he needed the revelations to be completely convincing to her.

In his heart, he expected her to cancel her date tonight when she discovered what Mitchell intended her to learn. That's what he wanted her to do; however, he was prepared for her to leave if that's what she still felt she should do. He was prepared, but not pleased at the prospect. His aunt—who was never awed by any-one she met, including two United States Presidents and countless celebrities—was gazing worshipfully at Zack and sipping a second glass of sherry. Mitchell headed toward the group before the sherry relaxed Olivia so much that she wouldn't feel her usual need to supervise social gossip and speak up when she heard an inaccuracy.

Kate looked up at him with a smile when he walked up behind her and laid his hand lightly on the small of her back. He waited until there was a break in the conversation about Danny, and then he said to Zack and Julie, "Kate and I met in the islands three years ago when I was staying aboard the *Julie*."

"Really?" Zack replied, and Julie smiled.

"I think you were staying at my place in Rome at the time," Mitchell prompted.

Zack remembered what film he'd been making, mentioned it, and said nothing else. That's when it belatedly occurred to Mitchell that discretion would prevent the Benedicts from saying anything for fear of bringing up the "wrong Kate" in front of the current Kate, and so he looked pointedly at Julie who was watching him closely, and said, "I phoned you in Rome, and I think I mentioned Kate to you. I thought she might enjoy a cruise."

Julie looked warily at him, but Zack finally sensed what Mitchell was trying to do, and he rose to the occasion magnificently. "So you're *that* Kate!" he exclaimed. Directing the full force of his movie-star smile at Kate, he confided, "My God, Julie and I were dying to meet you."

"Why is that?" Kate asked.

"Because when Mitchell phoned, he told me he wanted you to be able to cruise on the *Julie* during the day, but your destination islands had to have runways long enough to accommodate his plane. He said he intended to fly back and forth to join you every night, and then fly back to Chicago the next morning. I told him you must be one woman in ten million. He said you were," Zack finished.

Against his hand, Mitchell felt Kate stiffen as if tensing against a blow; then she bent her head briefly. He glanced at his watch, realized that it was fifteen minutes to eight, and steered her over to his aunt.

Kate walked where he guided her, her emotions in turmoil over what Zack Benedict had said. She realized that Mitchell had nudged him to open up, but what Zack Benedict said hadn't sounded rehearsed, or untruthful. On the other hand, he was an actor. She was so upset that she actually found comfort in reminding herself that the yacht was a minor issue. But then she realized that if Zack Benedict had told the truth, then Mitchell had been waiting for her at the wharf for one reason only—he'd cared about her then as much as she'd cared about him.

She tried to look as if she was listening to Mitchell and his aunt's conversation, but her stomach cramped and she winced.

"Is something wrong, dear?" Olivia Hebert asked, tipping her head to the side. She was seated in a chair, her white hair drawn into its customary bun, her pearls around her neck, her eyes bright. She was an icon in the Bartletts' social circle, and Kate had met her at various functions, but when Mitchell spoke to her, she positively beamed, Kate noticed.

"No, I'm fine," Kate assured her.

"I just realized something," Mitchell said, and that was enough to make Olivia beam expectantly at him. "You were standing beside me at Cecil's party when Evan Bartlett mentioned that he and Kate were going down to Anguilla." Not until his aunt looked at him in

wary silence did Mitchell take into account his stern
long-ago warning to her that she was not to discuss
Kate Donovan with him. Evidently, she was prepared to
follow that to the letter now, even though Kate was beside him and Olivia had spent several minutes admiring
Danny. She had to realize that the situation had
changed, Mitchell thought. But on the other hand, she
hadn't known what the situation was before that, because he had refused to discuss it with her, so she *didn't*
necessarily know that it had changed.

Thoughtfully, he reached for a small plate of hors
d'oeuvres on the coffee table and cautiously switched
the focus of his conversation strictly to Evan and Kate,
while withdrawing himself from it.

"Did Evan Bartlett ever buy a plane?" Mitchell inquired. "As I remember, he mentioned that he wanted
to, but then he said he had to leave for Kate's father's
funeral."

"His wake," Olivia corrected. "He said a client had
died and he had to leave for his wake." She looked at
Kate and said, "I remember because I was surprised he
didn't mention your father's name."

Having failed to get her to make a statement about
Kate, Mitchell deliberately imparted incorrect information in the hope that she'd be absolutely unable to resist
correcting his mistake. "Since he'd already told me
Kate's name, there was really no reason for him to tell
me her father's—"

"He didn't mention any names at all, dear. I particularly remember thinking that was very unforthcoming
of him. I assumed that was because he'd sensed the fric-
tion when I introduced you to his father, and Evan decided to be—Kate, dear, you look very pale."

Kate put her drink on the table beside Olivia. "I'm
sorry to be abrupt," she said in a voice that sounded
surprisingly normal given her emotional state. "I'm

orry I can't stay." She turned to Mitchell, her green
eyes dazed and almost accusing. "I—I have to leave.
We'll talk later," she added.

"Kate has a date," Mitchell told his aunt, hiding his
surprised hurt behind a glib explanation.

"A what?" Olivia gasped.

Kate made her excuses to the Benedicts and Farrells,
picked up her purse, and then realized that Mitchell
was politely walking her to the door. "I'll come back as
early as I can," she offered inanely.

Mitchell nodded.

Drink in hand, he stood at the windows staring down
at the street. When she left him in St. Maarten, the day
had been bright blue and he'd seen her get into a cab.
Now rain was lashing the windows, and he could
barely see a foot beyond them. He couldn't believe
she'd left. Her departure, coupled with his remark that
she had a date, put a damper on the party, and when he
turned around, his guests were standing up to leave.

After they left, he phoned room service to have them
clean up the remains of the party, and when they departed a half hour later, he found himself alone in his
suite, waiting for a woman to return who should not
have left in the first place. The rain was coming down
in sheets, and he stood at the windows, watching lightning skewer the sky, reluctantly facing reality:

If Kate really cared about him, then what she'd
learned tonight should have relieved her mind and sent
her straight into his arms. There was no other possibility, but he tried to think of one anyway as he shoved his
hands into his pants pockets and stared at the storm.
An image moved across the glass and he frowned because it was slightly distorted.

"Mitchell—" Kate said behind him, her teeth chattering from the cold, her arms wrapped around herself.

He swung around, and as she gazed at him in mute misery and tortured regret, Mitchell realized why she'd fled earlier. Smiling, he brushed a strand of wet hair off her cheek. "Use your words, darling," he whispered.

Her shoulders shaking with tears and laughter, she collapsed against him, wrapping her arms fiercely around his shoulders, pressing her cheek to his chest. "I'm so sorry. I am so, so sorry."

Mitchell slid his arms around her, pulling her against his full length, and buried his face in her wet hair. "I missed you so much," he whispered. "I missed your magic."

She shivered and lifted her face to his, and he touched his mouth to her parted lips, remembering their softness and texture, while his hands remembered her curves . . . and the location of her zipper.

She leaned into him, kissing him back with desperate fervor as the top of her dress slid down her arms, exposing her breasts. Mitchell intended to prolong this momentous reunion for hours if possible, and he lifted his mouth out of her reach, curved his hands over her breasts and watched the expression on her lovely face as he tightened his fingers on her nipples. She gasped and bit her lip . . . and then demolished his plan to go slowly by remembering the location of his zipper.

The bedroom was far away, the sofa was closer, but the carpet was soft, and she stretched out there beneath him, her body shifting against his. Mitchell closed his eyes, straining for control, poised at the entrance to her body, but instead of entering her, he bent his head to her breasts, determined to give her the pleasure of foreplay. Her hands cradled his face, lifting it from her breasts, and she gazed into his eyes, her own filled with wonder, her long fingers tenderly brushing the hair at his temples. "Mitchell," she whispered, "please."

"No," he whispered hoarsely while she shifted her

...ips slightly, inviting him inside her, and his body hrummed like an aching drum.

She nodded slowly, sure of herself now, and arched ...er back, torturing him.

Trying to smile, Mitchell slid an inch inside her, and ...hen another. His smile vanished as his body began to ...ove against his will, driving slowly, rhythmically into ...er. His hands caught her thighs, clamping them to his, ...nd he drove into her with fierce urgency; her body ...onvulsed and he pushed her harder, forcing her with ...im until she twisted and arched and cried out. He ex-...ploded inside of her with a force that made him gasp ...nd then drop his head in reverent disbelief. Summon-...ng all the strength he had left, Mitchell rolled onto his ...ide and pulled her tightly into his arms, smoothing her ...damp hair off her shoulders. "Witch," he whispered with a smile in his voice.

Chapter Fifty-four

HOLLY REACHED INTO KATE'S REFRIGERATOR, TOOK OUT two bottles of water, and held one toward Calli. "Would you like a bottle of water?" she asked.

Calli looked at her, smiled politely, shook his head no, and said in Italian, "You are very beautiful. I would rather have you."

Understanding only the negative shake of his head, Holly said, "I'll take that to mean no," and put the bottle back in the refrigerator.

She glanced over her shoulder as Kate came out of the bedroom wearing her third possible outfit for dinner with Mitchell that night. The other two choices were draped over the sofa in the living room. He'd taken Danny shopping, and they'd been gone since eleven that morning. "Too dressy?" Kate asked, pirouetting in front of Holly, with Calli looking on from the kitchen island.

"No, but I like the blue wool better."

Frustrated and uncertain, Kate decided to ask the opinion of a man who knew Mitchell's taste. Reaching over to the sofa, she collected the other two dresses and held them up one at a time while she looked questioningly at Calli. "For Mitchell?" she asked.

Calli grinned, pointed confidently at the black sheath and said in Italian, "Mitchell will be in a hurry to get it off you tonight, and the blue one has too many small buttons."

"Okay, the black sheath it is," Kate said. "*Grazie,*" she added with a warm smile, using one of the two Italian words she knew.

Calli nodded and said, "You have a mouth made for kissing, but Mitchell is like a brother to me. Also, he would cut out my heart if he thought I noticed."

"It must take a lot more words to say something in Italian," Holly observed, and then she said very solemnly, "Kate, you're already in love with Mitchell again, aren't you?"

"No, I'm not," Kate replied firmly.

Calli's head swiveled around, his brows drawing together in surprised dismay.

"Yes, you are."

Kate slumped against the back of the sofa, hangers and dresses suspended from both hands, and nodded. "He's completely addictive. If I could pull him over me like a blanket and wrap myself up in him, I'd do it and still want to be closer—body and soul. And what makes it so hard is that I really think he feels the same way."

"You thought that last time."

Kate shoved away from the sofa, and looked at her with a smile. "And I was right. You keep forgetting that he wasn't guilty of anything we thought he was."

"What time is he coming back?"

Glancing at her watch, Kate said, "He called and said Danny and he were running late, but that they'd be here by six. I need to be downstairs at eight tonight to greet the mayor and his party, then Mitchell and I are going somewhere for dinner."

Holly stood up. "It's five-thirty, so I'd better get going. Now that the police know Billy Wyatt's somewhere in Florida, are you still going to stay at the hotel?"

"Yes," Kate said, already heading for her bedroom to

put away the clothes. She'd already put on her makeup
and fixed her hair so she'd look nice when Danny and
Mitchell got back, and now she had time on her hands.
"Mitchell wants us there until the police capture Billy. I
keep the local news on all day, expecting to hear an announcement that he's been taken into custody."

"How's Molly doing?"

"She's doing really well. She wants to come back to
work tomorrow, but I want her to stay home and rest
for a few more days."

"Mommy, look—" Already smiling, Kate hurried
down the hallway from her bedroom to see what
Mitchell and Danny had bought during their outing.
The sight of Danny standing in the middle of the room,
grinning expectantly, almost stopped her heart. Gone
were his long curls and clothes from BabyGap. His
black hair was styled just like Mitchell's; he was wearing a suit, vest, and tie, and shiny black shoes. And to
top it off, he was standing with one hand in his pocket,
and his other hand behind his back, posing.

The sight of him made her heart swell with pride and
contract with helpless longing for the baby he had
seemed to be only hours before. "You've been shopping
at Baby Brooks Brothers!" Kate joked.

"Got you present," Danny said and took his hand
out from behind his back, proudly showing her a
bedraggled daisy, which he delivered to her at a run.

"It's beautiful," Kate said, sending a smiling glance to
Mitchell.

He smiled back and said to Danny, "Give Mommy
her other present."

Grinning Mitchell's grin, Danny dug into his suit
pocket and pulled out an ornate gold locket on a slender chain. Kate's hand shook a little as she looked at the
beautiful heart. She was being drawn deeper and deeper

into fantasies of being a family, of being loved and cherished by the black-haired man who was already teaching his son to bring flowers to his mommy.

She looked up to say thank you to Mitchell, but his attention was suddenly riveted on the television set and he was striding swiftly toward it, turning up the volume.

"At four o'clock this afternoon, Florida authorities apprehended Billy Wyatt, seventeen, who is suspected of kidnapping Daniel Donovan from a local park yesterday. Sources inside the police department say that Wyatt has admitted the kidnapping, but he is blaming Chicago attorney Evan Bartlett for giving him the idea. According to these sources, Wyatt conceived the idea of kidnapping Daniel Donovan after Bartlett showed him a recent newspaper article with a picture of Daniel and his mother, restaurateur Kate Donovan. Bartlett allegedly told Wyatt that Daniel's father is Mitchell Wyatt, on whom Billy has long blamed his misfortunes.

"Our reporter, Sidney Solomon, caught up with Bartlett tonight at Gleneagles Country Club."

Kate turned around, and stepped back in alarm at the sight of Mitchell's clenched jaw and blazing eyes as he watched Evan, with tennis racket in hand, cite attorney-client privilege and stride off to play tennis.

"That son of a bitch!" Mitchell said between his teeth.

"Sonofbitch!" Danny echoed feelingly.

Mitchell made an unsuccessful effort to look calm for Danny's sake; then he kissed Kate goodbye as if he scarcely knew she was there. In the doorway, he turned and said, "I have an errand to run; I'll pick you up at eight."

Chapter Fifty-five

"I'LL GET IT, CALLI," KATE CALLED WHEN THERE WAS A knock at the apartment door shortly after nine o' clock. Calli didn't understand and ignored her, so he got to the door first. Mitchell was an hour late, and when Kate saw Detective MacNeil and Gray Elliott standing in the doorway, she panicked. "Oh, my God, what's happened?" she cried.

"Evan Bartlett is in the hospital with a broken jaw and several cracked ribs," Gray said, peering around her into the apartment. "May we come in?"

"Yes, of course you can," Kate said.

"Where's Wyatt, Kate?"

Kate knew before he finished the question what he was getting at, and her mind went into overdrive, thinking of ways to protect Mitchell. "Is Evan saying Mitchell did it?" she said, trying to sound very scornful.

"Evan didn't see who assaulted him. His assailant was waiting for him in the parking lot at Gleneagles Country Club when he finished playing tennis tonight."

"Evan works out at a gym; he can protect himself," Kate said, stalling for time, trying to think of an alibi for Mitchell when the inevitable question was asked.

"Where is Wyatt?" Gray repeated more firmly.

"I don't understand why you're looking for Mitchell—um—Did you find any evidence that it was him?"

"The assailant was wearing thin rubber gloves—like the kind your kitchen workers use."

"Oh, well, then there's your proof it wasn't Mitchell. He's never been in our kitchen."

"A busboy said he stopped in there at about six o'clock tonight and asked for a glass of water."

Unable to think clearly—or, more accurately, *deviously*—with Gray's eyes boring holes through her, Kate said, "Would you excuse me for just a minute? This is very upsetting."

She turned on her heel and headed for the bedroom hallway, and to her alarm, she heard Gray's footsteps on the carpet, following her far enough to note where she was going. Inside her bedroom, Kate leaned against the closed door, trying to think of a believable alibi.

An idea hit her, and she raced over to her bed and dragged the covers loose; then she pulled a corner of the mattress off the box springs so it was angled to the floor. She studied the effect; then she hurried to the wall behind the headboard and tilted the two paintings there askew. Since she was standing beside the night-stand, she carefully overturned the lamp on it so the shade was hanging over thin air. Finished, she raced into the adjoining bathroom, soaked a washcloth in water, and sauntered back into the living room, dabbing at her face. "I'm so sorry," she said. "I just can't handle any more violence. I got ill. Anyway, it couldn't have been Mitchell, because he was here with me until a few minutes ago."

"Where is he now?"

"He left a minute ago to run an errand."

"Florida police took Billy Wyatt into custody this afternoon."

Kate widened her eyes. "Oh. Really?"

"Really," Gray said drily. "Would you mind if Detective MacNeil had a look inside the rooms down that hallway?"

"Not at all," Kate replied, dabbing at her face in earnest and trailing nervously behind MacNeil. "Don't wake up Danny," she warned. "He's in the bedroom on the right."

Intensely serious about his job as Danny's bodyguard, Calli followed right behind MacNeil, scowling at him from the doorway as the detective quietly explored Danny's closet and bathroom.

"What's this room?" MacNeil said.

"My bedroom."

"May I?" he asked, his hand on the doorknob.

Kate started to say, "Of course!"; then she changed her mind and said, "I really wish you wouldn't." She waited until MacNeil gave her an *I can get a search warrant* look, before she said in feigned embarrassment. "Oh, go ahead, Detective."

MacNeil opened the door, flipped on the lights, and froze. Calli crowded next to him to see what he was looking at and gave a bark of laughter, which enabled Kate to blush furiously and in earnest when she looked at Gray. "What's that look about?" he asked mildly, looking from Kate to MacNeil to Calli, who wasn't even trying to control his grin. Twisting the washcloth in her hands, Kate said, "Mitchell and I—we—um— spent tonight in bed."

"This doesn't have to turn into a big deal," Gray said. "When Mitchell gets back, have him call us."

"And then you'll do what to him?" Kate said, her voice tinged with suspicion, fear, and anger—and a little surprise that he'd referred to Mitchell by his first name.

"We'll have a look at his knuckles. If they aren't bruised or swollen, we'll know he's not the assailant."

"Oh, good. That's easy."

"Yes, but it's also evidence that can't be hidden or disguised."

"Why are you involved in such a little matter, Gray?" she demanded.

He squeezed her arm. "I've started to think of myself as a family friend," he said, and turned to leave, with MacNeil on his heels.

"I'll have Mitchell call you the minute he gets back here," Kate promised as they left. "He may decide to stop on his way to pick up dog food and things."

On the other side of the apartment door, MacNeil and Elliott descended the stairs. "What's the story with the bedroom?" Gray asked.

Biting back a grin, MacNeil said, "From the looks of that bedroom, there's no way Wyatt would have had the strength left to assault Bartlett."

"If I thought I could get away with burying this little episode, I'd do it," Gray said. "In fact, if I thought I could get away with beating the shit out of Bartlett, I might have tried it myself. Unfortunately, among other things, he's a lawyer, and even with his jaw wired, he's screaming for Wyatt's blood."

"What do you want to do next?"

"We have to keep looking for Wyatt and document our efforts," Gray replied with a sigh. "If I don't, Bartlett will turn this into a media event that makes all of us look bad. As much as I'd like to turn a blind eye to what Wyatt did tonight, I can't do that. On the other hand, we don't have to be overly diligent. Bartlett isn't a capital murder case. Wyatt flew here on a commercial airline because his own plane was grounded for repair. We've notified O'Hare to detain him if he tries to goes through security there. That's due diligence on our part, as far as I'm concerned. I'm not going to put up roadblocks because Bartlett is unhappy and uncomfortable."

On the sidewalk outside the restaurant, where Childress was waiting, Gray paused and looked up at the sky. "Beautiful night," he said. "Too bad I have to go back to the office."

"Wyatt is going to turn up," Childress predicted, ever-vigilant.

"Call me if you hear or see anything," Gray said to both of them, and left with a brief wave.

Kate struggled with her heavy mattress, trying to shove it back into place, but her mind was on Mitchell and she was worried. She was worried for him, and worried for herself, too.

In the kitchen, Calli listened to the instructions he was being given. When he hung up, he took several large plastic trash bags into Danny's room and began quietly filling them with clothing and favorite toys. Finished, he stepped into the hallway, made certain that Kate was still in her bedroom, and then he carried the trash bags down the stairs and out a back entrance into the ally behind the restaurant. He left them there, walked around the side of the building to the front entrance and told one of the valet attendants to bring the rental car, which was being delivered momentarily, around to the alley entrance as soon as it arrived, and then to call him on his cell phone.

By ten o'clock, Kate was literally wringing her hands over Mitchell's plight. She couldn't think of any reason for Mitchell to have disappeared without a phone call unless he was Evan's "assailant." Or—and this was a possibility—Mitchell made a habit of dropping out of women's lives when things got too complicated or feelings got involved.

"Mitchell wants to say good-bye to you and Danny. He's at the airport, and he has to leave on an urgent business trip. I'm supposed to bring you out there."

Kate whirled around in shock at the sound of Calli speaking English with only a trace of a charming Italian accent, but her mind was focused on the painful realization that Mitchell was leaving. In the long run, she told herself firmly, it would be easier on her emotionally if he went away and stayed away. Trying to have a relationship with him was clearly impossible. At least this time, he was saying an official good-bye for Danny's sake.

Keeping that firmly in mind, she looked at Calli and said in an offhand voice. "Are you going with him?"

"Yes."

"We'll miss you," she said. "I'll wake Danny up."

"I'll bring the car around in back," Calli said, already heading for the door with his suitcase in hand. "There were a couple reporters hanging around out in front," he lied.

His attention focused on the documents he was reading, Gray Elliott reached out and picked up his telephone. MacNeil's voice was tinged with carefully concealed frustration. "While I was grabbing a cup of coffee a minute ago, Childress got an idea and phoned LaGuardia."

"And?" Gray said irritably.

"And it seems that Wyatt's plane took off an hour ago, and the flight plan the pilots filed was for Indianapolis. A few minutes ago they changed it to Chicago-Midway."

"Shit. Leave it to Childress."

"Yeah, he has great instincts," MacNeil said carefully. "We're on our way out to Midway now."

Gray leaned back in his chair, contemplating the fact that Bartlett had caused Danny Donovan's kidnapping and potential death at the hands of a deranged Billy Wyatt, and he'd also managed to make it public knowledge that Kate was an unwed mother with a child fathered by one of the Chicago Wyatts. Now he wanted to see Mitchell Wyatt put on trial. Lurching forward, Gray made up his mind and said, "I think I'll take care of this on my own. Tell Childress I said good work."

"Sure," MacNeil said, "I'll tell Childress that. He's got a sinus headache and he won't mind keeping an eye on the restaurant while you and I play tag with Wyatt's plane between O'Hare and Midway. It's not a good idea for you to try to handle it yourself without a detective along. Sticking with protocol is important when the victim's a lawyer."

"Thanks, Mac," Gray said, touched.

"I'll pick you up. We're just a few blocks from you. I guess we'll have to take your car."

Chapter Fifty-six

"WHY DID YOU PRETEND YOU DON'T SPEAK ENGLISH, Calli?" Kate asked when she couldn't think of anything else to distract her from the impending good-bye to Mitchell. Danny was fast asleep, his head on her lap, and her fingers kept searching automatically for his curls whenever she laid her hand on his head.

"People talk openly in front of someone who does not speak their language, and Mitchell wanted me to eavesdrop on the police."

They were at Midway, driving past hangars with private planes dotting the tarmac. Calli flipped on the turn indicators and swung the car through open gates; then he turned again and headed toward a large, brightly lit hangar. In front of it a sleek jet with swept-back wings and "1 2 T F" printed in large black letters on the tail was waiting on the tarmac, its boarding steps down and its interior lights on. "I will carry Danny," Calli volunteered, reaching into the backseat and scooping the sleeping boy up as if he were weightless.

Partway up the steps, something interfered with the light spilling over the steps from the doorway, and Kate lifted her head. Mitchell was standing there, his tall broad-shouldered frame filling the opening. *This is good-bye,* she thought, and the knowledge was suddenly so excruciating that she could barely breathe.

He stepped forward and held out his hand to her. "Hi," he said, smiling tenderly into her eyes. "Are you ready for a trip?"

"Where are we going?" she asked, confused.

Instead of answering, he took Danny from Calli's arms and went back inside the plane, where he sat down on a long, gray leather sofa and drew Kate down beside him. Kate forgot that he hadn't answered her question as she watched him carefully place his sleeping son across his lap and gently lay his big hand on Danny's cheek. His big hand . . . with light bruises on the knuckles. He lifted his left arm and put it around Kate's shoulders. "We're going to a little village near Florence, Italy."

Calli said something in Italian, and Mitchell leaned forward, peering out the plane's window opposite him, and picked up a telephone, talking in some language to the pilots, Kate assumed, since the phone had no dial or buttons.

A moment later, she heard an odd loud sound from the rear of the plane; then Calli came walking forward, smiling. He continued past her and settled into a big leather recliner close to the cockpit.

The plane lurched slightly; she glanced out the window and realized it was starting to move. Just beyond the window, a car with a revolving light on the dashboard was racing down the road toward the gate near their hangar. The plane's engines revved up to a whine, then it began to pick up speed. Over the plane's sound system, the copilot's voice provided the answer to her question as he said to an air traffic controller, "Midway Ground, this is Gulfstream One Two Tango Fox requesting expeditious taxi if possible. We will be ready at the runway."

"Roger, One Two Tango Fox," an answering voice said over the intercom. "Taxi via Kilo Yankee to runway 31 center."

Kate had arrangements to make if she was going to Italy, but they could wait until tomorrow. Right now, all that really mattered was that Mitchell wanted Danny and her with him, which meant he'd told her the truth last night about how he felt.

The other thing that mattered was that an unmarked police car appeared to be after them! Kate unconsciously held her breath, watching the car through the plane's window while the plane made a sharp left turn and gained speed, taxiing fast toward the runways ahead.

Finally the police car slowed, dropped back, and stopped, its light still revolving. Over the intercom, a voice said, "Gulfstream One Two Tango Fox, this is Midway Tower. You are cleared for immediate takeoff, runway 31 center."

"Midway Tower," the copilot confirmed, "Gulfstream One Two Tango Fox Rolling—runway 31 center." As he spoke, the plane hurtled forward on a surge of power and speed, and was airborne within seconds.

"Why are we going to this village?"

"Because there's a little church there I want to show you."

He remembered a flight he'd made from St. Maarten to Chicago when he'd thought she was lost to him. "Kate," he said. "I'm in love with you."

In response, Kate lifted his hand and pressed his bruised knuckles to her cheek.

On the road below, near the hangar, Gray and MacNeil stood outside the car, leaning against it, watching the Gulfstream roar down the runway with its landing lights on and then lift off gracefully and begin to climb. The landing lights went off, the landing gear retracted, and the plane began to fade into the night sky.

Referring to Mitchell Wyatt, Gray smiled and said thoughtfully, "That is a man with style."

MacNeil glanced sideways and said quietly, "So are you."

Chapter Fifty-seven

THE DAY AFTER MITCHELL'S PLANE TOOK OFF FROM
Midway Airport, handwritten messages were delivered to certain select people.

In Chicago, Matt and Meredith Farrell received theirs at nine-thirty P.M. Matt read it and grinned.

"What is it?" Meredith asked.

"A wedding invitation from Mitchell," he said, handing it to her. Meredith read it and laughed. "He kidnapped Kate and Danny, flew them to Italy, got them temporary passports, and he's convinced Kate to marry him, but he's afraid to give her time to change her mind. The wedding's in three days. How like Mitchell to ignore all the obstacles and do whatever it takes."

Meredith reached for the phone and called Julie Benedict, who had just received a similar message. "Zack is canceling a shoot right now," Julie said. "Can you and Matt get away?"

Meredith looked at her husband and held up the invitation with a smile. He nodded, and Meredith told Julie, "Of course."

The third message was delivered to the home of Mrs. Olivia Hebert and brought to her by her elderly butler. Mrs. Hebert opened the envelope, read the message, and burst into a jubilant smile. "Mitchell is marrying Kate Donovan in Italy in three days, Granger! You and I will be flown there in his private plane."

"I shall look forward to the trip, madam," Granger assured her.

"Guess who will be flying with us," Olivia said dreamily as she pressed the message to her bosom and sighed.

"I haven't any idea, madam."

"Zack Benedict!" she exclaimed.

The fourth message was delivered the following morning to the rectory of St. Michael's Church in Chicago. Father Mackey, the young assistant pastor, answered the door, accepted the envelope, and then carried it down the hall to Father Donovan's office.

"This envelope is for you, father."

"Just put it on my desk. I'm working on the budget for next month."

"I promised the man who delivered it that I would hand it to you personally and at once."

"Very well," Father Donovan said, laying down his pencil and reaching for the envelope. "Have you made the changes I suggested on your sermon for Sunday?" he inquired of the young priest, who'd been sent to St. Michael's to work under his tutelage.

"Some of them," Father Mackey replied as Father Donovan slipped his thumb beneath the flap and opened the envelope.

His reply made Father Donovan sigh. "You're a dedicated priest, Robert, and you write an excellent sermon, but you have a tendency to take a hard line when you should bend a little bit. Conversely, you bend a little too easily when you ought to take a hard line. I particularly notice that tendency when I listen to you trying to counsel parishioners who come to you for advice with their problems. As time goes by, I suspect you'll learn when to be inflexible and stand up for principles and church doctrine, and when you need to relax and respect the realities of a parishioner's life." As he spoke, Father Donovan extracted and unfolded a single sheet of paper bearing the initials *MW* at the top right-hand corner. He read what it said and half rose out of his chair, his mouth open in indignation.

"Not bad news, I hope?"

"He has lot of a nerve!" Father Donovan said when he recovered his power of coherent speech. Since the newspapers had already broken the story about the identity of the father of Kate's baby and his sudden arrival in Chicago to pay the ransom, Father Donovan had no compunction about telling Father Mackey the contents of the letter in his hand. "Mitchell Wyatt apparently took my niece and her son, Danny, to Italy, and now he is summoning me there to perform their wedding in a little village near Florence the day after tomorrow! That man has b—gall," he corrected himself.

Snatching up the telephone, he dialed the operator. "I need to place a call to Rome, Italy, immediately," he said, and then he read her the telephone number printed on the bottom of Mitchell Wyatt's personal letterhead. "Is this going to be an expensive call?"

"Excellent," he replied when the operator quoted him what seemed an exorbitant per-minute rate. "Make sure it's a *collect* call. Really? . . . A collect call is even more expensive? Excellent!" he replied vengefully.

"What's that?" Mitchell asked Kate as she began unwrapping a package that had just been delivered to her by overnight international mail.

"I don't know, but it's from Gray Elliott," Kate said.

"Be careful, it's probably bugged."

"It's a wedding gift," she said, reading the card.

"We should call the bomb squad."

Ignoring that, Kate lifted the lid off the inner box and folded back the tissue. It was a beautiful antique photograph album. Carefully, Kate lifted the album's cover; then she looked up at Mitchell with shining eyes. Inside the album were enlargements of some of the photographs taken by MacNeil and Childress.

The first one was of Kate and Mitchell on the balcony of the hotel in St. Maarten. They were standing very close, smiling at each other, and a kiss was just a moment away.

"Mr. Wyatt?" Mitchell's secretary said as she walked into the living room of his apartment. Out of deference to Kate, who was sitting beside him on the sofa, she explained in English, "The collect call you've been expecting is on your private line. He sounds . . . upset."

Mitchell took his arm from around Kate's shoulder. "This will be your uncle," he said mildly as he stood up and walked over to a large, comfortable upholstered chair that was positioned in front of the windows overlooking Via Veneto. He sat down in the chair, glanced out the windows at one of his favorite views, and lifted the receiver of the phone next to it. "Good morning, Father Donovan. I assume you've gotten my letter?"

Father Donovan focused his gaze on the young priest he was trying to coach while he launched his opening verbal salvo at Mitchell Wyatt in an angry, no-nonsense voice. "Mitchell, do you honestly think for one moment that I would bind Kate for the rest of her life, with the sacred vows of holy matrimony, to a man who won't allow her to have children?"

"No."

"Then what is the purpose of sending me this—this outrageous 'invitation' to perform the ceremony in Italy?"

"I have promised Kate that she can have as many children as she wants whenever she wants to have them."

Father Donovan nodded encouragingly to Father

Mackey, but in his enthusiasm over his success thus far, he pressed for added assurances instead of accepting what was already a clearly worded assurance from Mitchell. "And you won't oppose her in any way?"

"On the contrary—I will take the greatest pleasure in helping her conceive them."

"If that was intended to be a lewd, provocative remark, I am disappointed but not shocked." At that statement, Father Mackey leaned forward worriedly in his chair, but Father Donovan smiled and dismissed the young priest's concern with a silent wave of his fingers; then he moved on to the next skirmish he faced with the man on the telephone.

"Are you Catholic? . . . Yes, being baptized as one qualifies as being Catholic. . . . Have you been married before in a religious ceremony? . . . Well, if you haven't been in a church, or near a cleric, in fifteen years, then I guess it's safe to assume you haven't been. However, I cannot make assumptions about anything as important as this, so I have to ask you to answer that question with a yes or no."

Father Donovan repeated Mitchell's curt negative answer for Father Mackey's benefit, and then he braced himself for a major skirmish, but first he offered a little reassurance—in order to soften Mitchell up a little. "In that case, Mitchell, I see no insurmountable obstacles to my participating in your wedding to Kate. I gather from your note that you've already made arrangements for the ceremony with the local village priest and that he's rushing the paperwork through proper channels. Is he willing to let me participate?"

Father Donovan nodded at Father Mackey, indicating that Mitchell's answer to the last question was yes. "Well, that's very good," Father Donovan said delightedly; then he smoothly added, "If you haven't been near a priest in fifteen years, then it's been at least that long since you went to confession. Naturally, you'll need to take care of that matter before the ceremony—"

He stopped because Mitchell cut him off with a clipped, annoyed question; then Father Donovan responded in a tone meant to convey understanding and patience—but slightly strained patience: "No, Mitchell, I assure you I was not 'joking.' When you and Kate stand before me in God's house on your wedding day, prepared to take your sacred vows, I want you to have souls as clean and shiny as you had when you were babies. That means you will both have been to confession beforehand. That is not a request, it is a requirement."

After a pause to let that sink in, Father Donovan said much more kindly, "Children frequently dread going to confession because they associate it with guilt and embarrassment, but the sacrament of confession is actually intended to offer forgiveness and understanding, to help us feel truly absolved."

He paused again, waiting for a reaction, but the line was dead silent, so he forged ahead. "If there's a language barrier, or some other reason you don't want to make your confession to the local village priest, then I'll hear your confession myself if you'd like—"

That offer got an instantaneous response from Mitchell, one that made Father Donovan's shoulders shake with laughter. Clamping his palm over the phone's mouthpiece, he whispered to Father Mackey, "He just told me I could take that fantasy with me all the way to hell."

Recovering his composure with an effort, Father Donovan said almost gently, "Mitchell, I'm not going to hell and neither are you. You may confess to any priest you like, so long as you've taken care of the matter before the ceremony. Now, please put Kate on the phone. Your future wife and I need to have a little talk."

In Rome, Mitchell jerked the phone away from his ear and handed it to Kate, who had perched on the arm of his chair. "It's your turn," he said irritably, and got up to fix them both a cocktail. As he listened to Kate's end of the conversation, however, a little of his ire began to transform into amusement, because she apparently wasn't getting off any easier than he had. In fact, whatever her uncle was saying to her caused her to frequently murmur, "Yes, I know," and "Yes, you're right," and "Yes, I will."

It was at least five minutes later when she finally said, "Good-bye, we'll see you in a couple of days," and hung up the phone.

Mitchell handed her the drink he'd fixed her, then sat down beside her and pulled her onto his lap. "Your uncle is a self-righteous, pompous, sanctimonious, petty tyrant—" he announced irritably.

Smiling softly into his eyes, Kate pressed her fingers to his chiseled lips to silence him. "He was giving me a lecture on the need to give you the benefit of the doubt in the future and reminding me about my part in what went wrong with us before. He was telling me that you're a man of tremendous character and personal integrity, a man who is capable of loving Danny and me deeply and forever with gentleness and strength."

"As I was saying a moment ago," Mitchell replied with a grin, "your uncle is a man of surprising perception as well as an excellent judge of character."

Father Mackey was not so confident of that. In fact, he had serious misgivings about the wisdom of Father Donovan's willingness to support Kate's marriage to Mitchell. He stood up, started to leave, then turned back. Father Donovan was leaning against his desk, smiling with satisfaction at the outcome of his phone call, when be he noticed the young priest's worried expression. "You look troubled, Robert. What's wrong?"

"I just don't see how you can feel any confidence about marrying two people who only knew each other a few days and who have the kind of unpleasant history they have."

Folding his arms across his chest, Father Donovan contemplated his reply for a moment, and then he said, "I'm going to answer that with the same question I posed once to Mitchell: How is it possible that two people who knew each other only a few days could end up being so agonizingly disappointed in each other that neither of them was able to forget about it after almost three years?"

"There could be psychological undercurrents, unresolved parental issues; who knows what the answer is?"

"*I* know what the answer is," Father Donovan said with certainty. "The answer is that when they were together during those few days, those two people loved each other so much that neither one of them could come to terms with the suffering they inadvertently inflicted on each other later."

"You could be right, I suppose. But even so, a man and a woman—"

"Please don't quote to me from another book on the sanctity of marriage that you read in the seminary. In fact, I want you to read a book that may actually help you grasp the spiritual reality that can exist between couples who truly love each other. You won't find it on the usual reading lists."

"I'll be happy to read whatever you suggest. What's the title?"

"It's called *The Prophet* by Kahlil Gibran."

Father Mackey looked dubious but willing. He walked over to Father Donovan's desk and wrote down the book's title and the name of the author on a piece of paper. Then he stopped and stared, openmouthed, at

the older priest. "Didn't we excommunicate Gibran a
century ago?"

Father Donovan shrugged. "Yes, and we excommu-
nicated Galileo, too, for daring to claim that God's
earth actually circled the sun and not the reverse. Just
look who's laughing now."

Chapter Fifty-eight

ANY WEDDING WAS A SOURCE OF CURIOSITY AND A REASON for celebration in the village near Florence where Mitchell had lived with the Callioroso family. Mitchell had chosen this village to be married in because he said it was the place of his innocence, his childhood.

On the day of Mitchell and Kate's wedding, the back of the small church was occupied by several local people who simply enjoyed weddings. These individuals did not recognize Matthew Farrell and his wife, or Stavros and Alex Konstantatos, but they had an unexpected thrill when they saw the famous American film star who escorted his wife, Julie, up the aisle. They had a second thrill when he walked past them again on his way to escort a tiny, elderly woman who smiled proudly on her way to her seat at the front of the church.

The front of the church, where the invited guests were seated, was occupied by people who were very special to Mitchell and Kate, including Holly and the Callioroso family. It was exactly the kind of small, intimate wedding that Kate and Mitchell both wanted.

The day before, Mitchell had dutifully gone for confession to Father Lorenzo. He emerged from the church with a bemused expression on his face and joined Kate, who was waiting for him on a bench in the village's square. "How did it go?" she'd teased him, linking her arm through his.

"Actually," Mitchell replied, "I had the feeling Father

Lorenzo may have been a little disappointed in my lack of imagination. Although, considering how many Our Fathers and Hail Marys I have to say as penance, I think he may have been impressed with my tenacity."

"How many Our Fathers and Hail Marys did he give you as penance?"

"If I start praying right away, there's a chance I may be on time for our wedding."

Kate had burst out laughing.

Now, as she stood in front of the altar, with Father Lorenzo and her uncle both officiating and Mitchell smiling into her eyes, she felt truly blessed. She said her vows clearly and proudly. Mitchell said his vows the same way, answering in Italian for the benefit of the Callioroso family, while Father Donovan looked on approvingly. His expression faltered, however, near the end of the ceremony when Mitchell was asked if he promised to love, honor, and cherish Kate.

Instead of replying *"Lo giuro,"* Mitchell replied, *"Con ogni respiro che prendo."*

For a brief moment, Father Donovan wondered if Mitchell's answer had been perhaps a little indefinite, but Father Lorenzo looked very gratified, which allayed Father Donovan's concerns.

At the reception after the ceremony, however, Father Donovan sought out Father Lorenzo, who was bilingual and who was chatting with the American guests. "Father Lorenzo," Father Donovan said, "what did Mitchell say when you asked him if he promised to love, honor, and cherish Kate?"

The Americans were obviously as curious as he was, because they turned attentively to hear Father Lorenzo's reply.

"When I asked Mitchell if he promised to love. honor, and cherish Kate, Mitchell did not merely say ' do.' Instead, he replied, 'With every breath I take.'"

Like all the women in the group, Kate found her eyes misted with tears when Father Lorenzo said that, but Kate had already known at the altar what Mitchell was saying. It was the same phrase he'd had inscribed inside her wedding band.

Can't Take My Eyes Off of You
Judith McNaught's
next spellbinding novel
of breathless suspense and
breathtaking romance—
read on for a preview.

The wedding of Mitchell Wyatt and Kate Donovan took place in a little village near Florence, Italy, where the wealthy American bridegroom spent the first five years of his life, being raised by the Calliorosos, a simple family who knew as little about his true origins as Mitchell did. The bride was a Chicago Irish girl who owned a successful restaurant—and the bridegroom's heart.

The entire Callioroso family was at the church, where the groom spoke his vows in Italian for their benefit. Two priests officiated at the wedding: Father Lorenzo, the local padre, and Father James Donovan, the bride's uncle. When the groom was asked if he promised to love, honor, and cherish his bride, he answered solemnly in Italian, "With every breath I take."

Father Lorenzo accepted Mitchell's unusual vow with a grave nod and smiling eyes, while the other Italians in the church exchanged teary smiles and grabbed for handkerchiefs. The other guests spoke no Italian, so they had to wait until later to ask Father Lorenzo what the groom had said.

Among those guests were an American industrialist and his wife; an American film star and his wife; two Greek tycoons; an elderly lady who was a scion of Chicago society; and a young woman named Holly Braxton—the maid of honor and daughter of one of the wealthiest families in New York.

I was there, too, standing by the altar near my brother, Father James, watching my little Kate be wed to the man who fate meant her to have. No one saw me there, but Kate suddenly sensed my presence. I know exactly when she did, because she looked up a little and then she smiled at me, and in her shining green eyes there was a hug.

My name is Daniel Patrick Donovan. I am the proud father of the bride, and the fact that I've been deceased for three years doesn't change a thing. She's still my Mary Kate, and I've been watching over her since I drew my last earthly breath. I was there the day she sang "Danny Boy" at my wake, and I was there, three days later, when she sang it in the rain for me one last time, and made all my mourners weep. My Mary Kate has a fine voice, by the way.

I was also there the day she met Mitchell Wyatt. In fact, I brought them together, and when my headstrong girl let Mitchell get away, I brought them back together. In life, I was a successful restaurateur, and a better father than I thought—Mary Kate is proof of that. She'll have Mitchell to look after her now, though, and you're probably thinking my work is done. I was feeling that way, too, as I watched Mitchell slip a wedding band on Kate's finger—but just then, Kate's maid of honor looked away from them and straight at me while she brushed tears off her lashes.

I saw something in her eyes, too. It wasn't a hug. It was longing.

She is Holly Braxton, formerly a rich young aristo-crat, and now a dedicated veterinarian.

I am Daniel Donovan, former restaurateur, and now—matchmaker extraordinaire!

It isn't necessary for you to remember my other cre-dentials. From now on, you may think of me simply as . . . Fate.